The Alchemist's Secret

Scott Mariani

W F HOWES LTD

This large print edition published in 2010 by
W F Howes Ltd
Unit 4, Rearsby Business Park, Gaddesby Lane,
Rearsby, Leicester LE7 4YH

1 3 5 7 9 10 8 6 4 2

First published in the United Kingdom in 2007
by Robert Hale Ltd

A CIP catalogue record for this book is available
from the British Library

ISBN 978 1 40745 941 7

Typeset by Palimpsest Book Production Limited,
Falkirk, Stirlingshire

Printed and bound by CPI Group (UK) Ltd,
Croydon, CR0 4YY

'Seek, my Brother, without becoming discouraged; the task is hard, I know, but to conquer without danger is to triumph without glory.'

The Alchemist Fulcanelli

To Marco, Miriam and Luca

CHAPTER 1

France, October 2001

Father Pascal Cambriel pulled his hat down tight and his coat collar up around his neck to protect against the lashing rain. The storm had ripped open the door to his henhouse and the birds were running amok in a panic. The sixty-four-year-old priest herded them back in with his stick, counting them as they went. What a night!

A flash of lightning illuminated the yard about him and the whole of the ancient stone village. Behind the wall of his cottage garden lay the tenth-century church of Saint-Jean with its simple cemetery, the crumbling headstones and ivy. The roofs of the houses and the rugged landscape beyond were brightly lit by the lightning flash that split the sky, then plunged back into darkness as the crash of the thunder followed a second later. Streaming with rainwater, Father Pascal pushed home the bolt of the hen-house door, locking the squawking birds safely in.

Another bright flash, and something else caught

1

the priest's eye as he turned to dash back to the cottage. He stopped dead with a gasp.

Visible for just an instant, a tall, thin, ragged figure stood watching him from across the low wall. Then it was gone.

Father Pascal rubbed his eyes with his wet hands. Had he imagined it? The lightning flashed again, and in the instant of flickering white light he saw the strange man running away across the edge of the village and into the woods.

The priest's natural instinct after all these years as pastor to his community was to try immediately to help any soul in need. 'Wait!' he shouted over the wind. He ran out of his gate, limping slightly on his bad leg, and up the narrow lane between the houses, towards where the man had disappeared into the shadows of the trees.

Father Pascal soon found the stranger collapsed face down among the brambles and leaves at the edge of the woods. He was shaking violently and clutching at his skinny sides. In the wet darkness the priest could see that the man's clothes were hanging in tatters. 'Lord,' he groaned in sympathy, instinctively taking off his coat to wrap around the stranger. 'My friend, are you all right? What's the matter? Please, let me help you.'

The stranger was talking to himself in a low voice, a garbled mutter mixed with sobbing, his shoulders heaving. Father Pascal laid the coat across the man's back, feeling his own shirt instantly soaked with the pouring rain. 'We must go inside,' he said in a soft voice. 'I have a fire, food and a bed. I will call Doctor Bachelard. Are you able to walk?' He tried gently to turn the man over, to take his hands and help him up.

And recoiled at what he saw in the next lightning flash. The man's tattered shirt soaked in blood. The long, deep gashes that had been cut into his emaciated body. Cuts on cuts. Wounds that had healed and been slashed open again.

Pascal stared, hardly believing what he was seeing. These weren't random slashes, but patterns, shapes, symbols, crusted in blood.

'Who did this to you, my son?' The priest studied the stranger's face. It was wizened, gaunt almost to the point of ghoulishness. How far had he wandered in this state?

In a cracked voice the man muttered something: '*Omnis qui bibit hanc aquam . . .*'

Father Pascal realized with amazement that the man was speaking to him in Latin. 'Water?' he asked. 'You want some water?'

The man went on mumbling, staring at him with wild eyes, clawing at his sleeve. '. . . *si fidem addit, salvus erit.*'

Pascal frowned. Something about faith, salvation? He's talking nonsense, he thought. The poor soul was deranged. Then the lightning flashed again, almost directly overhead, and as the thunder roared an instant later he saw with a start that the man's bloody fingers were wrapped tightly around the hilt of a knife.

3

It was a knife like no other he'd ever seen, a cruciform dagger with an ornate gold hilt set with glittering jewels. The long, slim blade was dripping with blood.

It was then that the priest understood what the stranger had done to himself. He'd carved these wounds into his own flesh.

'What have you done?' Father Pascal's mind swam with horror. The stranger watched him, rising to his knees, his bloody mud-streaked face suddenly lit up by another flash of lightning. His eyes were empty, lost, as though his mind was in some other place. He fingered the ornate weapon.

For a few moments Pascal Cambriel was quite convinced that this man was going to kill him. So here it was at last. Death. What would it bring? Some kind of continued existence, he was sure about that, even though its exact nature was unclear to him.

He'd often wondered how he would face death when the time came. He'd hoped that his deep religious faith would prepare him to meet whatever end God intended for him with serenity and composure. Now, though, the prospect of that cold steel sinking into his flesh turned his legs to water.

In that moment, when there was no longer any doubt in his mind that he was going to die, he thought about how he'd be remembered. Had he been a good man? Had his been a worthy life?

Lord, give me strength.

The madman stared in rapt fascination at the dagger in his hand, and back at the helpless priest, and he began to laugh – a low gurgling cackle that rose up to a hysterical shriek. '*Igne natura renovatur integra!*' He screamed the words over and over again, and Pascal Cambriel watched in terror as he started feverishly slicing the blade into his own neck.

CHAPTER 2

Somewhere near Cadiz, Southern Spain
September 2007

Ben Hope dropped from the wall and landed silently on his feet inside the courtyard. He stood crouched for a moment in the dark. All he could hear was the rasping chirp of crickets, the call of some night bird disturbed by his approach through the woods, and the controlled beat of his heart. He peeled back the tight black sleeve of his combat jacket. 4.34 am.

He did a last press-check of the 9mm Browning, making sure there was a round in the chamber and that the pistol was ready for action. He quietly clicked the safety on and holstered it. Took the black ski mask from his pocket and pulled it over his head.

The semi-derelict house was in darkness. Following the plan given to him by his informant, Ben skirted the wall, half-expecting a sudden blaze of security lights that never came. He reached the rear entrance. Everything was as he'd been told. The lock on the door put up little resistance, and after a few seconds he crept inside.

He followed a darkened corridor, went through a room and then another, the thin light-beam from his pistol-mounted compact LED torch picking out mouldy walls and rotten floorboards, heaps of garbage on the floor. He came to the door that was shut from the outside with a padlock and hasp. When he shone his light on the lock he saw it was an amateur job. The hasp was only screwed to the worm-eaten wood. In under a minute, working in silence, he had the lock off the door and went inside, slowly and cautiously so as not to alarm the sleeping boy.

The eleven-year-old Julián Sanchez stirred and groaned as Ben crouched down by the side of the makeshift bunk. '*Tranquilo, soy un amigo*,' he whispered in the boy's ear. He flashed the Browning's light in Julián's eyes. Virtually no pupil reflex – he'd been drugged.

The room stank of damp and filth. A rat, which had been up on the little table at the foot of the bed eating the remains of a frugal meal in a tin dish, jumped down and scampered away across the floor. Ben gently turned the boy over on the filthy sheets. His hands were tied with a plastic cable tie that had bitten into his flesh.

Julián groaned again as Ben carefully slipped a slim knife through the cable ties and cut his arms free. The boy's left hand was bound with a rag, encrusted with filth and dried blood. Ben hoped that it was just the one finger that had been removed. He had seen a lot worse.

7

The ransom demand had been for two million Euros in used notes. As a token of their sincerity the kidnappers had sent a severed finger in the mail. One foolish move, such as calling the police, had said the voice on the phone, and the next parcel would contain more bits. Maybe another finger, maybe his balls. Maybe his head.

Emilio and Maria Sanchez had taken the threats the right way – seriously. Raising the two million wasn't an issue for the wealthy Malaga couple, but they knew perfectly well that paying the ransom would in no way guarantee that their boy wasn't coming home in a bodybag. The terms of their kidnap insurance stipulated that the negotiations must at all times go through official channels. That meant police involvement – and it would be signing Julián's death warrant to bring the cops in on this. They'd needed to find a viable alternative to even the odds in favour of Julián's safe return.

That was where Ben Hope entered the equation, if you knew the right number to call.

Ben rolled the groggy child out of the bunk and hefted his limp body over his left shoulder. A dog had started barking from somewhere behind the house. He heard stirrings, a door opening somewhere. Holding the silenced Browning out ahead of him as a torch, he carried Julián back through the shadowy corridors.

Three men, his informant had told him. One was passed out drunk most of the time but he'd have to watch out for the other two. Ben believed the informant, as he usually believed a man with a gun to his head.

A door opened ahead of him and a voice shouted in the darkness. Ben's light settled on the figure of a man, unshaven, his body rippling with fat, dressed in shorts and a ragged T-shirt. His face was contorted with the bright beam shining in his eyes. In his hands was a sawn-off shotgun, the fat twin muzzles slung down low and pointing at Ben's stomach.

The Browning instantly coughed twice through its long sound suppressor and the thin LED beam followed the arc of the man's body as it slumped dead to the floor. The man lay still with two neat holes in the centre of the T-shirt, blood already spreading out beneath him. Without thinking about it, Ben did what he'd been trained to do in these circumstances, stand over the body and finish the job with a precautionary head shot.

The second man, alerted by the sound, came running down a flight of stairs, a bobbing torch in front of him. Ben fired at the light. There was a short scream and the man crashed headlong down the stairs before he'd had a chance to fire his revolver. The gun slid along the floor. Ben strode over to him and made sure he wasn't getting up again. Then he paused for thirty seconds, waiting for a sound.

The third man never appeared. He hadn't woken up.

He wasn't going to.

With Julián unconscious over his shoulder, Ben walked through the house to a sordid kitchen. His pistol-light flashed on a running cockroach, followed its scuttling path across the room and settled on an old cooker that was connected to a tall steel gas bottle. He gently rested Julián in a chair. Kneeling down in the darkness beside the cooker he cut the rubber pipe from the back of the appliance with his knife, and used an old beer crate to jam the end of the pipe against the side of the cold cylinder. He opened the wheel-valve on top of the cylinder a quarter-turn, flipped his lighter and the trickle of hissing gas ignited in a small yellow flame. Then he opened the valve full on. The flickering flame became a roaring jet of fierce blue fire that licked and curled aggressively up the side of the cylinder, blackening the steel.

Three muted rounds from the Browning and the twisted padlock fell from the front gates. Ben was counting the seconds as he carried the boy away from the house towards the trees.

They were on the edge of the woods by the time the house went up. The sudden flash and a massive unfolding orange fireball lit up the trees and Ben's face as he turned to see the kidnappers' hideout blown to pieces. Flaming bits of wreckage dropped all around. A thick column of blood-red incandescent smoke rose up into the starry sky.

The car was hidden just the other side of the trees. 'You're going home,' he told Julián.

CHAPTER 3

The western Irish coast, four days later

Ben woke up with a start. For a few moments he lay there, disorientated and confused as reality slowly pieced itself together. Next to him, on the bedside table, his phone was shrilling. He reached out his arm for the handset. Clumsy from his long sleep, his groping hand knocked over the empty glass and the whisky bottle that stood by the phone. The glass smashed across the wooden floor. The bottle hit the boards with a heavy clunk and rolled away into a heap of discarded clothes.

He cursed, sitting up in the rumpled bed. His head was throbbing and his throat was dry. The taste of stale whisky was still in his mouth.

He picked up the phone. 'Hello?' he said, or tried to say. His hoarse croak gave way to a fit of coughing. He closed his eyes, and felt that unpleasantly familiar feeling of being sucked spinning backwards down a long, dark tunnel, making his head feel light and his stomach queasy.

'I'm sorry,' said the voice on the other end of

the line. A man's voice, clipped English accent. 'Have I got the right number? I'm looking for a Mr Benjamin Hope.' The voice had a note of disapproval that irked Ben immediately despite his fuzzy head.

He coughed again, wiped his face with the back of his hand and tried to unglue his eyes. 'Benedict,' he muttered, then cleared his throat and spoke more clearly. 'That's *Benedict* Hope. Speaking . . . What time do you call *this*?' he added irritably.

The voice sounded even more displeased, as though its impression of Ben had just been confirmed. 'Well, ten-thirty actually.'

Ben sank his head into his hand. He looked at his watch. Sunlight was shining through the gap in the curtains. He began to focus. 'OK. Sorry. I had a busy night.'

'Evidently.'

'Can I help you?' Ben said sharply.

'Mr Hope, my name is Alexander Villiers. I'm calling on behalf of my employer Mr Sebastian Fairfax. I've been instructed to tell you that Mr Fairfax would like to retain your services.' A pause. '*Apparently* you're one of the very best private detectives.'

'Then you've been misinformed. I'm not a detective. I find lost people.'

The voice went on. 'Mr Fairfax would like to see you. Can we arrange an appointment? Naturally, we'll collect you and pay you for your trouble.'

Ben sat up straight against the oak headboard

and reached for his Gauloises and Zippo. He trapped the pack between his knees and plucked a cigarette out. He thumbed the wheel of the lighter and lit up. 'Sorry, I'm not available. I've just finished an assignment and I'm taking a break.'

'I understand,' said Villiers. 'I'm also instructed to inform you that Mr Fairfax is willing to offer a generous fee.'

'It's not the money.'

'Then perhaps I should tell you that this is a matter of life or death. We've been told you may be our only chance. Won't you at least come and meet Mr Fairfax? When you hear what he has to say, you may change your mind.'

Ben hesitated.

'Thank you for agreeing,' said Villiers after a pause. 'Please expect to be picked up in the next few hours. Goodbye.'

'Hold on. Where?'

'We know where you are, Mr Hope.'

Ben went for his daily run along the deserted beach, with just the water and a few circling, screeching seabirds for company. The whispering ocean was calm, and the sun was cooler now that autumn was on its way.

After his mile or so up and down the smooth sand, his hangover just a faint echo, he picked a path down to the rocky cove that was his favourite part of the beach. Nobody ever came here except him. He was a man who liked solitude, even though his job was seeking to reunite people with those they'd lost. This was where he liked to come sometimes when he wasn't away working. It was a place where he could forget everything, where the world and all its troubles could slip out of his mind for a few precious moments. Even the house was out of sight, hidden behind the steep bank of clay and boulders and tufty grass. He cared little for the six-bedroomed house – it was far too large for just him and Winnie, his elderly housekeeper – and he had only bought it because it came complete with this quarter mile stretch of private beach, his sanctuary.

He sat on the same big, flat, barnacled rock as he always did, and idly flung a handful of pebbles one by one into the sea as the tide lapped and hissed at the shingle around him. With his blue eyes narrowed against the sun he watched the curving drop of a stone against the sky, and the little white splash it made as it disappeared into the roll of an incoming wave. *Nice going, Hope,* he thought to himself. *It took that stone a thousand years to reach the shore, and now you've thrown it back.* He lit another cigarette and gazed out to sea, the gentle salt breeze stirring his blond hair.

After a while he reluctantly got up, jumped down off his rock and made his way back up towards the house. He found Winnie pottering about in the huge kitchen, making him some lunch. 'I'm going to be leaving in a couple of hours, Win. Don't fix me anything special.'

15

Winnie turned and looked at him. 'But you only got back yesterday. Where are you off to this time?'

'I've no idea.'

'How long will you be away?'

'I don't know that either.'

'Well you'd better eat something,' she said firmly. 'Running about all the time, never in one place long enough to draw a breath.' She sighed and shook her head.

Winnie had been a faithful and stalwart companion to the Hope family for many years. For a long time now, Ben had been the only one left. After his father had died, he'd sold the family home and moved out here to the west coast of Ireland. Winnie had followed. More than just a housekeeper, she felt like a mother to him – an anxious, often exasperated, but always patient and devoted mother.

She abandoned the cooked lunch she'd started making for him and quickly prepared a pile of ham sandwiches. Ben sat at the kitchen table and munched a couple of them, far away in his thoughts.

Winnie left him and carried on her other chores around the house. There wasn't much for her to do. Ben was hardly ever there, and when he did come home she would barely notice his presence. He never talked about his work, but she knew enough about it to know that it was dangerous. That worried her. She worried about the drinking, too, and the cases of whisky that arrived a little too regularly by van. She'd never spoken of it openly to him, but she fretted that, one way or another, he was going to put himself in an early grave. Only the good Lord knew which one would get him first, whisky or a bullet. Her greatest fear was, she didn't think it mattered to him either way.

If he could just find something to care for, she thought. *Someone* to care for. He kept his private life a closely guarded secret, but she knew that the few times a woman had tried to get close to him, to make him love her, he'd cut her off and let her drift away. He'd never brought anyone back to the house, and many phone calls had gone unanswered. They always stopped phoning in the end. He was afraid to love anyone. It was as though he'd killed that part of himself, hollowed himself out emotionally, made himself empty inside.

She could still remember him as a youngster full of bright optimism and dreams, with something to believe in, something to give him strength that didn't come out of a bottle. That had been a long, long time ago. Before *it* happened. She sighed at the memory of those terrible times. Had they ever really ended? She was the only person, other than Ben himself, who understood what it was that secretly drove him. Knew the pain that was in his heart.

CHAPTER 4

The private jet carried him over the Irish Sea and southwards towards the Sussex coast. It touched down at an airfield, where they were met by a sleek black Bentley Arnage limousine. Ben was ushered into the back of the car by the same anonymous men in grey suits who'd collected him from his home that afternoon and sat with him on the plane, grim-faced and taciturn. The two men climbed into a black Jaguar Sovereign that sat on the tarmac with its engine purring, waiting for the Bentley to move off.

Settling into the plush cream leather interior of the Bentley, Ben ignored the on-board cocktail cabinet, took out his battered steel hip-flask and swallowed down a mouthful of whisky. As he slipped the flask back in his pocket, he noticed that the eyes of the uniformed driver had been watching him in the mirror.

They drove for about forty minutes. The Jaguar followed all the way. Ben watched the road-signs and took note of the route, orientating himself. After a few miles of dual carriageway the Bentley headed cross-country, speeding at a smooth whisper through empty country roads. A village flashed past. Eventually the car turned off a quiet country lane and drew up at an archway in a high stone wall. The Jag pulled up behind. Automatic gates, black and gilt, swung open to let the cars through. The Bentley rolled down a winding private road, past a terrace of estate cottages. Ben turned to watch as some fine-looking horses galloped by in a white-fenced paddock. When he looked back at the rear window, the Jaguar had vanished.

The road continued, with neat formal gardens on either side. Down an alley of stately cypress trees the house appeared before them, a Georgian mansion fronted by a sweep of stone steps and classical columns.

Ben wondered what his prospective client did for a living. The house looked as though it must be worth at least seven or eight million. This would probably turn out to be another K&R job, as was the case with the vast majority of his wealthier clients. Kidnap and ransom had become one of the world's fastest expanding businesses these days. In some countries, the K&R industry had even overtaken heroin.

The Bentley passed a large ornamental fountain and drew up at the foot of the steps. Ben didn't wait for the driver to open the door for him. A man came down the steps to greet him. 'I'm Alexander Villiers, Mr Fairfax's PA. We spoke on the phone.'

Ben only nodded, and studied Villiers. He looked to be in his mid-forties or thereabouts. His hair was slick and greying at the temples. He was wearing a crisp navy blazer and a tie with what looked like a college or public school emblem.

'So glad you came,' Villiers said. 'Mr Fairfax is waiting for you upstairs.'

Ben was led through a large marble-floored entrance hall that was wide enough to accommodate a medium-sized aircraft, and up a wide curving staircase to a wood-panelled corridor lined with paintings and glass display cabinets. Villiers guided him wordlessly down the long corridor and stopped at a doorway. He knocked, and a resonant voice inside called 'Come in'.

Villiers showed Ben into a study. Sunlight streamed brightly in through a leaded bow window that was flanked by heavy velvet drapes. The smell of leather and furniture polish hung in the air.

The man sitting at the broad desk stood up as Ben entered the study. He was tall and slender in a dark suit, a mane of white hair swept back from his high forehead. Ben put his age at around seventy-five, though he looked fit and upright.

'Mr Hope, sir,' said Villiers, and departed, closing the heavy doors behind him. The tall man approached Ben from behind the desk, extending his hand. His grey eyes were quick and penetrating. 'Mr Hope, I am Sebastian Fairfax,' he said warmly.

'Thank you so much for having agreed to come all this way, and at such short notice.'

They shook hands. 'Please, take a seat,' said Fairfax. 'May I offer you a drink?' He approached a cabinet to his left, and took up a cut-crystal decanter. Ben reached into his jacket pocket and brought out his old flask, unscrewing the top. 'I see you've brought your own,' said Fairfax. 'A resourceful man.'

Ben drank, aware that Fairfax was watching him keenly. He knew what the old man was thinking. 'It doesn't affect my work,' he said, screwing the top back on.

'I'm sure,' said Fairfax. He sat down behind the desk. 'Now, shall we get straight to business?'

'That would be fine.'

Fairfax leaned back in his chair, pursing his lips. 'You're a man who finds people.'

'I try,' Ben replied.

Fairfax pursed his lips and continued. 'I have someone I want you to find. It's an assignment for a specialist. Your background is highly impressive.'

'Go on.'

'I'm looking for a man by the name of Fulcanelli. It's an extremely important matter and I need a professional of your talents to locate him.'

'Fulcanelli. Does he have a first name?' Ben asked.

'Fulcanelli is a pseudonym. Nobody knows his true identity.'

'That's a help. So I take it that this man isn't an especially close friend of yours, a missing family member or anything like that?' Ben smiled coldly. 'My clients normally know the people they want me to find.'

'That's correct, he isn't.'

'So, what's the connection? What do you want him for? Has he stolen something from you? That's a matter for the police, not me.'

'No, nothing like that,' said Fairfax with a dismissive gesture. 'I have no ill will towards Fulcanelli. On the contrary, he means a great deal to me.'

'OK. Can you tell me when this person was last seen, and where?'

'Fulcanelli was last sighted in Paris, as far as I've been able to trace,' Fairfax said. 'As to *when* he was last seen . . .' He paused. 'It was some time ago.'

'That always makes things harder. What are we talking about, more than, say, two years?'

'A little longer than that.'

'Five? Ten?'

'Mr Hope, the last known sighting of Fulcanelli was in 1926.'

Ben stared at him. He did a quick calculation. 'That was more than eighty years ago. Are we talking about some child abduction case?'

'He wasn't an infant,' stated Fairfax with a calm smile. 'Fulcanelli was a man of some eighty years at the time of his sudden disappearance.'

Ben narrowed his eyes. 'Is this some kind of joke? I've come a long way, and frankly–'

22

'I assure you I'm perfectly serious,' replied Fairfax. 'I'm not a humorous man. I repeat, I would like you to find Fulcanelli for me.'

'I look for people who are living,' Ben said. 'I'm not interested in searching for departed spirits. If you want that, you need to call the parapsychology institute and they could send one of their ghost-busters out to you.'

Fairfax smiled. 'I appreciate your scepticism. However, there *is* reason to believe that Fulcanelli is alive. But perhaps we need to narrow the focus here. My main interest isn't so much the man himself, but certain knowledge of which he is, or was, in possession. Information of a crucially important nature, which I and my agents have so far failed to locate.'

'Information of what sort?' Ben asked.

'The information is contained within a document, a precious manuscript to be precise. I want you to locate and bring me back the Fulcanelli manuscript.'

Ben pursed his lips. 'Has there been some mis-understanding here? Your man Villiers told me this was a matter of life and death.'

'It is,' Fairfax replied.

'I don't follow you. What information are we talking about?'

Fairfax smiled sadly. 'I'll explain. Mr Hope, I have a granddaughter. Her name is Ruth.'

Ben hoped his reaction to the name didn't show. 'Ruth is nine years old, Mr Hope,' Fairfax

23

continued, 'and I fear she will never see her tenth birthday. She suffers from a rare type of cancer. Her mother, my daughter, despairs of her recovery. So do the top private medical experts, who, despite all the funds I have at my disposal, have been unable to reverse the course of this terrible illness.' Fairfax reached out a slender hand. On his desk facing him was a photograph in a gold frame. He turned it around to show Ben. The photograph showed a little blonde girl, all smiles and happiness, sitting astride a pony.

'Needless to say,' Fairfax went on, 'this picture was taken some time ago, before the disease was detected. She doesn't look like that any more. They've sent her home to die.'

'I'm sorry to hear that,' Ben said. 'But I don't understand what this has to do with –'

'With the Fulcanelli manuscript? It has everything to do with it. I believe that the Fulcanelli manuscript holds vital information, ancient knowledge that could save the life of my beloved Ruth. Could bring her back to us and restore her to what she was in that picture.'

'Ancient knowledge? What kind of ancient knowledge?'

Fairfax gave a grim smile. 'Mr Hope, Fulcanelli was – and still is, as I believe – an alchemist.'

There was a heavy silence. Fairfax studied Ben's face intently.

Ben looked down at his hands for a few moments.

He sighed. 'What are you saying, that this manuscript will show you how to make some kind of . . . some kind of life-saving potion?'

'An alchemical elixir,' Fairfax said. 'Fulcanelli knew its secret.'

'Look, Mr Fairfax. I understand how painful your situation is,' Ben said, measuring his words. 'I can sympathize with you. It's easy to want to believe that some secret remedy could work miracles. But a man of your intellect . . . don't you think perhaps you're deluding yourself? I mean, *alchemy*? Wouldn't it be better to look for more expert medical advice? Perhaps some new form of treatment, some modern technology . . .'

Fairfax shook his head. 'I've told you, everything that can be done, according to modern science, has been done. I've looked at every possibility. Believe me, I've researched this subject in extreme depth and am not taking the matter lightly . . . there is more in the book of science than present-day experts would have us believe.' He paused. 'Mr Hope, I'm a proud man. I have been extraordinarily successful in my life and I wield a very considerable amount of influence. Yet you see me here as a sad old grandfather. I would get down on my knees to beg you to help me – to help Ruth – if I thought that could persuade you. You may think my quest is a folly, but for the love of God and the sake of that dear sweet child, won't you indulge an old man and

25

accept my offer? What have you got to lose? We're the ones who stand to lose a great deal, if our Ruth doesn't survive.'

Ben hesitated.

'I know you have no family or children of your own, Mr Hope,' Fairfax went on. 'Perhaps only a father, or a grandfather, can really understand what it means to see one's dear offspring suffer or die. No parent should have to endure that torture.' He looked Ben in the eye with an un-wavering gaze. 'Find the Fulcanelli manuscript, Mr Hope. I believe you can. I'll pay you a fee of one million pounds sterling, one quarter of that sum in advance, and the balance on safe delivery of the manuscript.' He opened a drawer of the desk, took out a slip of paper and slid it across the polished wood surface. Ben picked it up. The cheque was for £250,000 and made out in his name.

'It only requires my signature,' Fairfax said quietly. 'And the money's yours.'

Ben stood up, still holding the cheque. Fairfax watched him intently as he walked to the window and looked out across the sweeping estate at the gently swaying trees. He was quiet for a minute, and then he breathed out audibly through his nose and turned slowly to Fairfax. 'This isn't what I do. I locate missing people.'

'I'm asking you to save the life of a child. Does it matter how that's accomplished?'

'You're asking me to go on a wild goose chase

that you *believe* can save her.' He tossed the cheque back across Fairfax's desk. 'But I don't see how it can. I'm sorry, Mr Fairfax. Thanks for your offer, but I'm not interested. Now, I'd like your driver to take me back to the airfield.'

CHAPTER 5

In a large open field full of wild flowers and gently swaying lush grass, a teenage boy and a little girl were running, laughing, hand in hand. Their blond hair was golden in the sunshine. The boy let go of the little girl's hand and dropped to his knees to pick a flower. Giggling, she ran on ahead, looking back at him with her nose crinkled in mischief and freckled cheeks rosy. The boy held out the flower to her, and suddenly she was standing far away. Beside her was a gateway, leading to a high-walled maze.

'Ruth!' he called to her. 'Come back!' The little girl cupped her hands around her mouth, shouted 'Come and find me!' and disappeared, grinning, through the gate.

The boy ran after her, but something was wrong. The distance between him and the maze kept stretching further and further. He shouted 'Don't go, Ruth, don't leave me behind!' He ran and ran, but now the ground under his feet wasn't grass any more but sand, deep soft sand into which he sank and stumbled.

Then a tall man in flowing white robes was

blocking his way. The boy's head only reached as high as the man's waist, and he felt small and powerless. He got around the man and made it to the entrance of the maze just in time to see Ruth flitting away into the distance. She wasn't laughing any more, but crying out in fear as she vanished around a corner. Their eyes met a last time. Then she was gone.

Now there were other tall men in white robes, with black beards. They crowded round him and towered over him, blocking his way and his sight, jabbering at him in a language he couldn't understand, eyes round and white in mahogany faces that loomed close up to him, grinning with gaps in their teeth. And then they grabbed hold of his arms and shoulders with powerful hands and held him back and he was shouting and yelling and struggling but there were more and more of them and he was pinned and couldn't move . . .

He gripped the glass tightly in his hand and felt the burn of the whisky against his tongue. In the distance, beyond the heaving dark grey waves that crashed against the rocks of the bay, the arc of the horizon was slowly lightening to red with the dawn.

He turned away from the window as he heard the door open behind him. 'Morning, Win,' he said, managing a smile. 'What are you doing up so early?'

She looked at him with concern, her eye flickering to the glass in his hand and the empty bottle on the table behind him. 'Thought I heard voices. Everything all right, Ben?'

'I couldn't get back to sleep.'

'Bad dreams again?' she asked knowingly.

He nodded. Winnie sighed. Picked up the worn old photograph that he'd been looking at earlier and had left lying on the table next to the whisky bottle. 'Wasn't she beautiful?' the old lady whispered, shaking her head and biting her lip.

'I miss her so badly, Winnie. After all these years.'

'You think I don't know that?' she replied, looking up at him. 'I miss them all.' She laid the picture down carefully on the table.

He raised the glass again, and drained it quickly. Winnie frowned. 'Ben, this drinking–'

'Don't lecture me, Win.'

'I've never said a word to you before,' she replied firmly. 'But you're just getting worse. What's wrong, Ben? Since you came back from seeing that man you've been acting restless, not eating. You've hardly slept the last three nights. I'm worried about you. Look at you – you're pale. And I know you only opened that bottle last night.'

He smiled a little, leaned across and kissed her forehead. 'I'm sorry if I snapped. I don't mean to worry you, Win. I know I'm hard to live with.'

'What did he want from you, anyway?'

'Fairfax?' Ben turned towards the window and looked back out to sea, watching as the rising sun touched the undersides of the clouds with gold.

'He wanted me . . . he wanted me to save Ruth,' he said, and wished that his glass weren't empty.

He waited until just before nine, then he picked up the phone.

'You're reconsidering my offer?' Fairfax said.

'You haven't found anyone else?'

'No.'

'In that case, I'll take the job.'

CHAPTER 6

Oxford

Ben arrived early for his rendezvous at the Oxford Union Society. Like many old students of the university he was a life member of the venerable institution that nestles off the Cornmarket and has served for centuries as a meeting-place, debating hall and members-only club. As he'd done in his student days, he avoided the grand entrance and went in the back way, down a narrow alley next to Cornmarket's McDonald's restaurant. He flashed his tatty old membership card at the desk and walked through the hallowed corridors for the first time in nearly twenty years.

It seemed strange to be back here. He'd never thought he would set foot in this place again, or even in this city again, with all the dark memories it held for him – memories of a life once planned, and of the life that fortune had made for him instead.

Professor Rose hadn't yet arrived as Ben entered the Union's old library. Nothing had changed. He

32

gazed around him at the dark wood panelling, reading tables and high galleries of leather-bound books. Up above, the frescoed ceiling with its small rose windows and priceless Arthurian legend murals dominated the magnificent room.

'Benedict!' called a voice from behind him. He turned to see Jonathan Rose, stouter, greyer and balder but instantly recognizable as the history don he'd known so long ago, striding happily across the burnished floorboards to shake his hand. 'How are you, Professor? It's been a long time.'

They settled in a pair of the library's worn leather armchairs, and exchanged small-talk for a few minutes. Little had changed for the professor – Oxford academic life went on much as it had always done. 'I was a little surprised to hear from you after all these years, Benedict. To what do I owe this pleasure?'

Ben explained his purpose in asking to meet him. 'And then I remembered that I knew one of the country's top ancient history scholars.'

'Just don't call me an *ancient historian*, as most of my students do.' Rose smiled. 'So, you're interested in alchemy, are you?' He raised his eyebrows and peered at Ben over his glasses. 'Didn't think that sort of stuff was your cup of tea. You haven't become one of those New Age types, I hope?'

Ben laughed. 'I'm a writer these days. I'm just doing some research.'

'Writer? Good, good. What did you say this fellow's name was – Fracasini?'

'Fulcanelli.'

Rose shook his head. 'Can't say I've ever heard of him. I'm not really the man to help you there. Bit of a far out subject for most of us fuddy-duddy academics – even in this post-Harry Potter age.'

Ben felt a pang of disappointment. He hadn't entertained high hopes that Jon Rose would have much to offer him on Fulcanelli, let alone on a Fulcanelli manuscript, but with so little to go on it was a shame to lose any potential source of dependable information. 'Is there anything you can tell me generally about alchemy?' he asked.

'As I say, it's not my field,' Rose replied. 'Like most people, I'd be inclined to dismiss it all as complete hocus pocus.' He smiled. 'Though it has to be said that few esoteric cults have endured so well over the centuries. All the way from ancient Egypt and China, right through the Dark Ages and medieval times and onwards into the Renaissance – it's a sub-current that keeps resurfacing all throughout history.' The professor stretched back in the worn leather chair as he spoke, adopting the tutor pose that was second nature to him. 'Though heaven knows what they were up to, or *thought* they were up to – turning lead into gold, creating magical potions, elixirs of life, and all the rest of it.'

'I take it you don't believe in the possibility of an alchemical elixir that could cure the sick?'

Rose frowned, noticing Ben's deadpan expression

34

and wondering where he was going with this. 'I think that if they'd developed a magic remedy for plague, pox, cholera, typhus, and all the other diseases that have ravaged us through history, we'd have known about it.' He shrugged. 'The problem is it's all so speculative. Nobody really knows what the alchemists might have discovered. Alchemy's famous for its inscrutability – all that cloak-and-dagger stuff, secret brotherhoods, riddles and codes and supposed hidden knowledge. Personally I don't think there was much substance to any of it.'

'Why all the obscurity?' Ben asked, thinking of the reading he'd been doing over the last couple of days, running Internet searches on terms like 'ancient knowledge' and 'secrets of alchemy' and wading through one esoteric website after another. He'd turned up a wide variety of alchemical writings, ranging from the present day back to the fourteenth century. They all shared the same baffling and grandiose language, the same dark air of secrecy. He hadn't been able to decide how much of it was genuine and how much was just esoteric posturing for the benefit of the credulous devotees they'd been attracting over the centuries.

'If I wanted to be cynical I'd say it was because they didn't actually *have* anything worth revealing,' Rose grinned. 'But you've also got to remember that alchemists had powerful enemies, and perhaps some of their obsession with secrecy was a way of protecting themselves.'

'Against what?'

'Well, at one end of the scale there were the sharks and speculators who preyed on them,' Rose said. 'Once in a while some hapless alchemist who'd bragged too loudly about gold-making would be kidnapped and made to tell how it was done. When they failed to come up with the goods, which of course they probably always did, they'd end up hanging from a tree.' The professor paused. 'But their real enemy was the Church, especially in Europe, where they were forever burning them as heretics and witches. Look what the Catholic Inquisition did to the Cathars in medieval France, on the direct orders of Pope Innocent III. They called the liquidation of an entire people God's work. Nowadays we call it genocide.'

'I've heard of the Cathars,' Ben said. 'Can you tell me more?'

Rose took off his glasses and polished them with the end of his tie. 'It's a terrible story,' he said. 'They were a fairly widespread medieval religious movement that mainly occupied the part of southern France now known as the Languedoc. They took their name from the Greek word *Catharos*, meaning "pure". Their religious beliefs were a little radical in that they regarded God as a kind of cosmic principle of love. They didn't attribute much importance to Christ, and may not even have believed he existed. Their idea was that, even if he had existed, he certainly couldn't have been the son of God. They believed that all matter was fundamentally crude and corrupt, including human beings. For them, religious worship was all about spiritualizing, perfecting and transforming that base matter to attain union with the Divine.'

Ben smiled. 'I can see how those views might have upset the orthodoxy a little.'

'Absolutely,' Rose said. 'The Cathars had essentially created a free state that the Church couldn't control. Worse, they were openly preaching ideas that could seriously undermine its credibility and authority.'

'Were the Cathars alchemists?' Ben asked. 'The part about transforming base matter sounds very like the ideas of alchemy.'

'I don't think anyone knows that for certain,' Rose said. 'As a historian, I wouldn't stick my neck out on that one. But you're quite right. The alchemical concept of purifying base matter into something more perfect and incorruptible is certainly well in tune with Cathar beliefs. We'll never know for sure, because the Cathars never lived long enough to tell the tale.'

'What happened to them?'

'In a nutshell, mass extermination,' Rose said. 'When Pope Innocent III came to power in 1198, the alleged heresies of the Cathars gave him a magnificent excuse to extend and reinforce the Church's powers. Ten years later he put together a formidable army of knights, the biggest ever seen in Europe at that time. These were hardened soldiers, many of who had seen service fighting in the Holy Land. Under the command of former crusader Simon de Monfort, who was also the Duke of Leicester, this huge military force invaded the Languedoc and one by one they massacred every fortress, town and village with even the remotest Cathar connection. De Monfort became known as the "glaive de l'eglise".'

'The sword of the Church,' Ben translated.

Rose nodded. 'And he meant business. Reports at the time spoke of a hundred thousand men, women and children slaughtered at Béziers alone. Over the next few years the Pope's army swept over the entire region, destroying everything in its path and burning alive anyone who didn't die under the sword. At Lavaur in 1211 they threw four hundred Cathar heretics on the pyre.'

'Nice,' Ben said.

'It was a vile affair,' Rose continued. 'And it was during this time that the Catholic Church formed its Inquisition, a new wing of Church officialdom to lend greater authority to the atrocities performed by the army. They oversaw duties of interrogation, torture and execution. They were answerable only to the Pope personally. Their power was absolute. At one point in 1242, the Inquisitors were acting so bloodthirstily that a detachment of disgusted knights broke away from their station and slaughtered a whole bunch of them at a place called Avignonet. Of course, the rebel knights were quickly suppressed. Then, finally in 1243, after the Cathar resistance had held out much longer than anyone had anticipated, the Pope decided it was time to finish them off once and for all. Eight thousand knights laid siege to the last Cathar stronghold, the mountaintop castle of Montségur, firing enormous rocks at its ramparts from their catapults for ten solid months until the Cathars were finally betrayed and forced to surrender. Two hundred of the poor souls were brought down the mountain and roasted alive by the Inquisitors. And that was more or less the end of them. The end of one of the most scandalous holocausts of all time.'

'I can see alchemical heresy might have been a risky thing to get into,' Ben said.

'Still is, in some ways,' Rose replied playfully.

Ben was taken aback. 'What?'

The professor threw his head back and laughed. 'I don't mean they're still executing heretics in the public square. I was thinking of the danger for people like myself, academics or scientists. The reason nobody wants to touch this subject with a bargepole is the reputation you'd get for being a crank. Every so often someone takes a bite of the forbidden apple and their head rolls. Some poor sod got the sack for just that reason, a while ago.'

'What happened?'

'It was at a Parisian university. American biology lecturer got into hot water over some unauthorized research . . .'

'On alchemy?'

'Something of that sort. Wrote some articles in

the press that rubbed a few people up the wrong way.'

'Who was this American?' Ben asked.

'I'm trying to remember the name,' Rose said. 'A Dr . . . Dr Roper, no, Ryder, that's it. There was a big furore about it in the academic world. It even got mentioned in the French Medieval Society bulletin. Apparently Ryder went to a university tribunal for unfair dismissal. Didn't do any good, though. As I said, once they brand you a crank it's a real witch-hunt.'

'Dr Ryder in Paris,' Ben repeated, noting it down.

'There's a whole article about it in a back issue of *Scientific American* that was lying about in the college common room. When I'm back there later I'll look it out for you and give you a call. There might be a contact number for Ryder.'

'Thanks, I might well check that out.'

'Oh . . .' Rose suddenly remembered. 'Just a thought. If you do find yourself in Paris, another person you might want to contact is a chap called Maurice Loriot. He's a big book publisher, fascinated by all sorts of esoteric subjects, publishes a lot of that sort of stuff. He's a good friend of mine. This is his card . . . if you meet him, tell him I said hello.'

Ben took the card. 'I will. And do let me know that Dr Ryder's number, if you can find it. I'd really like to meet him.'

They parted with a warm handshake. 'Good luck

with your research, Benedict,' said Professor Rose. 'Try not to leave it another twenty years next time.'

Far away, two voices were speaking on the phone.

'His name is Hope,' one of them repeated. 'Benedict Hope.' The man's voice was English and spoke in a hurried, furtive whisper, slightly damped as though he were cupping his hand around the receiver to prevent others from hearing.

'Do not be concerned,' said the second voice. The Italian sounded confident and unruffled. 'We will deal with him as we dealt with the others.'

'That's the problem,' the first voice hissed. 'This one isn't like the others. I think he may cause trouble for us.'

A pause. 'Keep me informed. We will take care of it.'

CHAPTER 7

Rome, Italy

T he big man flipped through the old copy
of *Scientific American* until he reached the
bookmarked page. The article he was
looking for was called *Medieval Quantum Science.*
Its author was Dr Roberta Ryder, an American
biologist working out of Paris. He'd read it before,
but because of the reports he'd been receiving over
the last few days, he was reading it again in a
whole new light.

When he'd first seen Ryder's article he'd been
pleased at the way the magazine editors had attacked
her work. They'd torn her to pieces, devoting an
entire editorial to debunking and ridiculing everything she'd said. They'd even made a fool of her
on the front page. Making such a public example
of her had been an undisguised hatchet job, but
what else could you do with a once-respected, award-
winning young scientist who suddenly started
making wild and unsubstantiated claims about
such a thing as alchemy? The scientific establishment would not, could not tolerate a radical of this

sort who demanded that alchemical research should be taken seriously and given proper funding, asserting that its popular reputation as quackery was undeserved, possibly even a conspiracy, and that it would one day revolutionize physics and biology.

He'd followed her career since then, and been pleased at the way it had plummeted. Ryder had been thoroughly discredited. The science world had turned its back on her, virtually had her excommunicated. She'd even lost her university job. When he'd heard this news at the time, he'd been delighted.

But now he wasn't so happy. In fact, he was furious, and anxious.

This damn woman wouldn't go away. She'd shown an unexpected toughness and determination in the face of adversity. Despite the universal derision of her peers, despite almost running out of money, she continued to persist in her private research. Now the reports from his source were telling him she'd had a breakthrough. Not a major one, necessarily – but big enough for him to worry about it.

Clever, this Ryder woman. Dangerously clever. On a shoestring budget she was getting better results than his whole well-equipped, highly-paid team. She couldn't be allowed to go on like this. What if she discovered too much? She'd have to be stopped.

CHAPTER 8

Paris

I f the choice of items a person went to the
trouble of keeping in a heavily guarded bank
vault said something about their priorities,
then Ben Hope was a man with a very simple view
of life.

His safe deposit box at the Banque Nationale
de Paris was virtually identical to the ones he kept
in London, Milan, Madrid, Berlin and Prague.
They all contained only two things. The first thing
they contained varied only in its currency from
country to country. The amount was always the
same, enough to keep him moving freely for
indeterminate periods of time. Hotels, transport,
information were his biggest expenses. Hard to
say how long this job was going to keep him in
France. As the security guards stood outside the
private viewing-room he loaded about half of
the neat stacks of Euro banknotes into his old
canvas army bag.

The second thing Ben kept locked away in the
heart of those half dozen major European banks

44

never varied at all. He took out the top tier of the box with the remainder of the cash, set it down on the table and reached into the bottom of the box for the pistol.

The Browning Hi-Power GP35 9mm semi-automatic was an old model, mostly superseded nowadays by plasticky new generations of SIG, HK and Glock combat pistols. But it had a long proven record, it was utterly reliable, it was simple and rugged with enough power and penetration to stop any assailant. It carried thirteen rounds plus one in the breech, enough to bring just about any sticky situation to a quick halt. Ben had known the weapon for nearly half his life, and it suited him like an old glove.

The question was, should he leave it in the bank or should he take it with him? There were pros and cons. The pros were, if there was one thing you could predict in his job, it was that it was totally unpredictable. The Browning represented peace of mind, and that was worth a lot. The cons were, there was always going to be some risk in carrying an unregistered firearm around. The concealed weapon meant you had to be extra careful in everything you did. It only took an overzealous cop to decide to search your things, and if you were careless enough to let them find the gun it could land you in a heap of trouble. An eagle-eyed citizen happening to spot the Di Santis hip holster under your jacket could go hysterical and turn you into an instant fugitive. On top of all that, it was almost certain that he'd never need it on this job, which looked as though it was going to turn out a complete wild goose chase.

But hell, it was worth the risk. He put the pistol, the long tubular sound suppressor, the spare magazines, ammunition boxes and holster into his bag along with the money and called the guards in to take the deposit box back to the vault.

He left the bank and walked through the Paris streets. This was a city he'd spent a lot of time in. He felt at home in France and he spoke the language with only a slight trace of an accent.

He took the Métro back to his apartment. The place had been a gift from a rich client whose child he'd rescued. Although it was well located in the centre of Paris, it was tucked away unseen down an alley and hidden among a cluster of crumbling old buildings. The only way in was through the underground parking lot beneath it, up a dingy stairway and through a heavy steel security door. He thought of the hidden apartment as a safe-house. Inside, it was comfortable but Spartan – a utilitarian kitchenette, a simple bedroom, a living room with an armchair, a desk, a TV and his laptop. That was all Ben needed for his doorway to Europe.

The cathedral of Notre Dame loomed above the Parisian skyline under the late afternoon sun. As Ben approached the towering building, a tour guide was addressing a group of camera-toting Americans. *'Founded in eleven sixty-three and taking a hundred and seventy years to build, this splendid jewel in stone came close to being destroyed during the French Revolution, later to be restored to its former glory in the mid-nineteenth century . . .'*

Ben entered through the west front. It was many years since he'd last set foot in a church, or even taken any notice of one. It was a weird feeling to be back. He wasn't sure he liked it much. But even he had to admit to the spectacular grandeur of the place.

Ahead of him the central nave climbed dizzyingly to its vaulted ceiling. The arches and pillars of the cathedral were bathed in the rays of the setting sun that filtered through the magnificent stained-glass rose window in the west façade of the building.

He spent a long time walking up and down, his footsteps echoing off the stone tiles, gazing this way and that at the many statues and carvings. Under his arm was a secondhand copy of a book by the man he was supposed to be looking for – the elusive master alchemist Fulcanelli. The book was a translation of *The Mysteries of the Cathedrals*, written in 1922. When Ben had come across it in the Occult section of an old Paris bookshop he'd been excited, hoping to find something of value. The most useful leads he could have wished for were a photo of the man, some kind of personal information such as an indication of his real name or family details, and any sort of mention of a manuscript.

But there was none of these things. The book was all about the hidden alchemical symbols and cryptograms that Fulcanelli claimed were carved into the décor of the same cathedral walls that Ben now found himself staring at.

The Porch of Judgement was a great Gothic archway covered in intricate stone carvings. Beneath rows of saints were a series of sculpted images depicting different figures and symbols. According to Fulcanelli's book, these sculptures were supposed to have some hidden meaning – a secret code that only the enlightened could read. But Ben was damned if he could figure any of it out. I'm obviously not enlightened, he thought. *As if I needed Fulcanelli to tell me that.*

In the centre of the massive portal, at the feet of a statue of Christ, was a circular image showing a woman seated on a throne. She was clutching two books, one open and the other closed. Fulcanelli claimed that these were symbols of open and hidden knowledge. Ben ran his eye along the other figures on the Porch of Judgement. A woman holding a caduceus, the ancient healing symbol of a snake wrapped around a staff. A salamander. A knight with a sword and a shield bearing a lion. A circular emblem with a raven on it. All, apparently, conveying some veiled message. On the north portal, the 'Portal of the Virgin', Fulcanelli's book guided him to a sculpted sarcophagus on the middle cornice that depicted an episode in the life of Christ. The decorations along the side of the sarcophagus were described in the book as being the alchemical symbols for gold, mercury, lead, and other substances.

But were they really? To Ben, they just looked like flower motifs. Where was the evidence that the medieval sculptors had been consciously inserting esoteric messages into their work? He could appreciate the beauty and the artistry of these sculptures. But did they have anything to teach him? Could they possibly be of any use to help a dying child? The problem with this kind of symbology, he reflected, was that just about any given image could be interpreted pretty much as the interpreter wanted it. A raven might just be a raven, but someone looking for a hidden significance could easily find it, even if it was never intended to be there. It was all too easy to project subjective meanings, beliefs, or wishful thinking onto a centuries-old stone carving whose creator was no longer around to say otherwise. Such was the stuff of conspiracy theories and cults surrounding 'hidden knowledge'. Too many people were desperate for alternative versions of history, as though the real facts of times gone by were insufficiently satisfying or entertaining. Perhaps it was to compensate for the drab truth of human existence, to inject a bit of intrigue into their own dull and unstimulating lives. Whole subcultures grew up around these myths, rewriting the past like a movie script. It seemed to him, from his research into alchemy, that this was just another alternative subculture chasing its tail in search of kicks.

He was getting itchy feet. Not for the first time, he regretted having taken this job. If it hadn't been for the two hundred and fifty grand of Fairfax's money sitting in his bank account, he'd have sworn that someone was playing a joke on him. What he should do was to walk out of here right now, take the first plane to England and give the old fool back his money.

No, he's not an old fool. He's a desperate man with a dying grandkid. Ruth. Ben knew the reason he was standing here.

He sat on a pew and gathered his thoughts for a few minutes among the scattered figures who'd come to pray. He opened Fulcanelli's book again, took a deep breath and ran back in his mind what he'd managed to glean from it so far.

The introduction to *The Mysteries of the Cathedrals* was a later addition to Fulcanelli's text, written by one of his followers. It described how, in 1926, Fulcanelli had entrusted his Parisian apprentice with certain material – nobody seemed to know what exactly – and then promptly disappeared into thin air. Since then, according to the writer, many people had tried to find the master alchemist – including, apparently, an international intelligence agency.

Yeah, right. It was the same with most of the stuff he'd uncovered in his web searches. There were several other versions of the Fulcanelli tale,

50

depending on which far-out website you visited. Some said Fulcanelli had never existed at all. Some said he was a composite figure drawn together out of a number of different people, a front for a secret society or brotherhood dedicated to exploring the occult. Others claimed that he was a real person after all. According to one source, the alchemist had been sighted in New York decades after his mysterious disappearance, when he must have been well over a hundred years old.

Ben didn't buy any of it. None of the claims was substantiated. If there were no known photos of the alchemist, how could any reported sightings be trusted? It was all a mess of confusion. There was only one thing that all these sources of so-called information had in common, and it was that he couldn't find a single mention anywhere of a Fulcanelli manuscript.

He didn't spot anything very illuminating during his tour of Notre Dame. But one thing he did spot, not long after he came in, was the man following him.

The guy wasn't doing an especially good job of it. He was too furtive, too careful to stay out of Ben's way. One minute he was standing in a distant corner glancing over his shoulder, the next he was in the pews trying to hide his plump form behind a prayer book. If he'd smiled and asked Ben for directions he'd have been less conspicuous.

Ben's eyes were on the cathedral décor, his body

language was relaxed and his demeanour was that of Joe Tourist. But from the moment he'd seen him, he was studying his follower closely. Who was he? What was this about?

In such cases, Ben was a big believer in honesty and direct action. If he wanted to find out why someone was following him, he'd just ask them straight out who they were and what they wanted. The two things he needed to do first were to get the man into a quiet spot, and to cut off any chance he had of escaping. Then Ben could squeeze him like an orange. How politely he dealt with the situation depended entirely on the guy's reaction to being cornered and challenged. An amateur like this might well just fold right away with only the gentlest pressure.

Ben moved to the inner corner of the cathedral, near the altar. A spiralling staircase led upwards to the towers, and he started climbing it. Just before he moved out of sight, he saw his man's body language shift nervously. Ben carried unhurriedly on up the stairs until he arrived at the second gallery. He came out onto a narrow stone walkway that emerged outside into the sunlight, high over the Parisian rooftops. He was surrounded by nightmarish gargoyles, stone demons and goblins put there by the medieval stonemasons to ward off evil spirits.

The walkway connected the two high towers of the cathedral, right over the huge rose window in its façade. Only a stone latticework barrier, less than waist high, stood between him and a 200-foot drop to the ground below. Ben moved out of sight and waited for his follower to appear.

The man reached the parapet after a minute or two, looking around for him. Ben waited until he was far from the doorway to the stairs, and then he stepped out from behind a grinning devil statue. 'Hey, there,' he said, bearing down on him. The man looked panicky, his eyes darting this way and that. Ben pressed him into a corner, using his body to cut off his line of escape. 'What's your business following me?'

Ben had seen lots of men reacting under stress, and he knew they all reacted differently. Some folded, some ran, some resisted.

This guy's reaction was instant lethal violence. Ben saw the twitch in his right hand a fraction of a second before it snaked into his jacket and came out with the knife. It was a military-style weapon with a black double-edged blade – a cheap copy of the Fairbairn-Sykes fighting knife that Ben knew from the past.

He dodged the stab, grabbed the man's knife wrist and smashed the arm down over his knee. The blade clattered onto the walkway. Ben kept hold of the wrist, bending it into a lock that he knew from experience was extremely painful. 'Why are you following me?' he repeated quietly. 'I don't really want to hurt you.'

He wasn't prepared for what happened next.

There is no way out of a good wristlock. Unless

the person deliberately lets their wrist be broken. No sane person will do that, but this man did. He twisted against Ben's grip. At first, Ben thought he was just trying to get away, and he tightened his hold. But then he felt the bones give in the man's wrist. With no resistance from the limp hand, he suddenly had no purchase on the man's arm. His follower wriggled away from him, his eyes bulging, sweat beading on his brow, whimpering in agony as his hand dangled like a dishrag out of his sleeve. And before Ben could stop him, he turned, ran for the edge and hurled himself over the low barrier into space.

While the man was still tumbling in mid air, Ben was already heading quickly down the spiralling stone steps. By the time the body had cartwheeled down to a grisly stop on the spikes of the iron railing right next to a party of tourists, Ben was well on his way back into the dark corner of the cathedral. As the first tourists started screaming and people rushed outside to see what had happened, Ben slipped unnoticed through the building and merged with the babbling, pointing crowd.

He was far away before the first gendarme arrived on the scene.

CHAPTER 9

Luc Simon was running late. He'd changed into his smart suit at police headquarters, dashing to the car still tying his tie as his officers wondered where the inspector was dashing off to all dressed up.

He checked his watch as he skidded through the Paris traffic. He'd booked the table at Guy Savoy for eight. It was 8.33 when he got there. A waiter ushered him across the room. The restaurant was full of diners and a buzz of conversation. Soft jazz played in the background. He could see Hélène sitting at the table for two in the corner, her glossy black hair obscuring her face as she flipped tensely through a magazine. He asked the waiter to bring champagne right away, and went to join her.

'Let me guess,' she sighed as he sat down opposite her at the small round table, 'you couldn't get away.'

'I got here as fast as I could. Something came up.'

'As usual. Even on your wedding anniversary, work comes first, doesn't it?'

'Well, this is the thing. Homicidal maniacs don't generally have a lot of respect for people's personal schedules,' he muttered, feeling that familiar barrier of tension rising up fast between them. That was pretty usual, too. 'Ah, here's the champagne,' he said, trying his best to smile.

They sat in silence while the waiter popped the cork, poured out their champagne and placed the bottle in the silver ice bucket. Luc waited until he was gone. 'Well . . . happy anniversary.' He clinked his glass against hers.

She was silent, watching him. This wasn't going too well. 'Here.' He fumbled in his pocket and took out a small packet. He placed it on the table.

'I got you something. Go on, open it.'

Hélène hesitated before unwrapping the gift with her long, slender fingers. She flipped open the jewellery box and looked inside. 'An Omega Constellation?'

'I know you always wanted one,' he said, watching her face for a response.

She stuffed the watch back in its box and tossed it into the middle of the table. 'It's very nice. But it's not for me.'

'What do you mean? Of course it's for you.'

She shook her head sadly. 'Give it to the next woman.'

His face darkened. 'What are you talking about, Hélène?'

She looked down at her hands, avoiding his eye. 'I want out of the marriage, Luc. I've had enough.'

He paused for a long time. Their champagne stood untouched, losing its fizz. 'I know things have been crazy lately,' he said, trying to keep his voice steady. 'But it will get better, Hélène, I promise.'

'It's been four years, Luc. It's not going to happen.'

'But . . . I love you. Doesn't that count for anything?'

'I met someone else.'

'You certainly picked a great time to let me know about this.'

'I'm sorry. I've been trying. But I never see you. We had to have an appointment just so we could sit and talk like this.'

He felt his face go into a spasm. 'So you met someone. Nice. Who is the fucker?'

She didn't reply.

'*I – asked – you – who – the – fucker – is,*' he exploded, banging his fist violently against the table at every word. His glass toppled, rolled, and smashed on the floor. The restaurant went quiet for a few seconds as everyone turned to stare.

'That's right, make a scene.'

A waiter approached, looking sheepish. Simon turned to glare at him.

'Monsieur, I must ask you to respect –'

'Get away from this table,' Simon said quietly through clenched teeth. 'Or I will put you through that fucking window.' The waiter backed off quickly, and went to have a word with the frowning manager.

'See? Always the same. Your response.'

'So perhaps you'd like to tell me who you've

been screwing while I'm out there up to my chin in blood and shit.' He knew that talking like this was only making it worse for both of them. *Calm, stay calm.*

'You don't know him. You only know cops, crooks, murderers and dead people.'

'It's my job, Hélène.'

A tear rolled down her face and he watched it trace out the perfect contour of her cheek. 'Yes, that's your job, and that's your life.' She sniffed. 'It's all you ever think about.'

'You knew what I did when we met. I'm a cop, I do what cops do. What's changed?' He fought to control his voice as he felt his temper rise again.

'*I've* changed. I thought I could get used to it. I thought I could live with the waiting and the worrying that one day my husband's coming home in a coffin. But I can't, Luc. I can't breathe, I need to feel alive again.'

'He makes you feel alive again?'

'He doesn't make me feel like I'm dying inside,' Hélène burst out. She mopped her eyes. 'I only want a normal life.'

He reached out and took her hands. 'What if I gave it up? If I was just an ordinary guy . . . I'll hand in my notice, get a job doing something else.'

'Doing what?'

He paused, realizing that he couldn't think of a single thing in the world that he could be doing instead of police work. 'I don't know,' he conceded.

She shook her head, and snatched her hands

away from his. 'You were born to be a cop, Luc. You'd hate anything else. And you'd hate me, for making you leave the thing you love most.'

He was silent for a few moments, thinking. He knew, deep down, that what she was saying was true. He'd neglected her, and now he was paying for it. 'Then what if I just took some time off, say a month? We could go away somewhere together – wherever you like, how about Vienna? You always talked about going to Vienna. What do you think? You know, the opera, take a ride on a gondola, all that stuff.'

'Gondolas are Venice,' she said dryly.

'Then we'll go to Venice as well.'

'I think we're a little past that, Luc. Even if I said yes, then what? After a month it would all start up again, same as before.'

'Can you give me a chance?' he asked quietly. 'I'll try to change. I know I have the strength to change.'

'It's too late,' she sobbed, looking down into her glass. 'I'm not coming home with you tonight, Luc.'

CHAPTER 10

The place wasn't quite what Ben had expected to find. To him, the term 'laboratory' conjured up images of a modern, spacious, purpose-built and fully equipped facility. His surprise had mounted as he followed the directions the guy on the phone had given him and arrived at the old apartment building in central Paris. There was no lift, and the winding staircase with its tatty wrought-iron banister rail carried him up three creaking floors to a narrow landing with a door on either side. He could smell the musty, ammonia smell of damp.

As he climbed the stairs, he kept thinking about the incident at Notre Dame. It haunted him. He'd been cautious on the way here, stopping frequently, looking in shop windows, taking note of people around him. If there was a tail on him now, he couldn't spot it.

He checked the apartment number and rang the buzzer. After a few moments a thin young man with curly dark hair and a sallow complexion opened the door and showed him into what turned out to be just a pokey little flat.

He knocked at the door marked LAB, paused a beat and went inside.

The lab was no more than a converted bedroom. Work surfaces sagged under the weight of at least a dozen computers. Piles of books and folders everywhere threatened to tip over. At one end was a sink unit and an array of battered scientific equipment, test tubes on a rack, a microscope. There was barely space for the desk, at which sat a young woman in her early thirties, wearing a white labcoat. Her dark red hair was tied up in a bun, giving her an air of seriousness. She was attractive enough to wear no makeup, and her only adornment was a pair of simple pearl earrings.

She looked up and smiled as Ben came in.

'Excuse me. I'm looking for Dr Ryder?' he said in French.

'You found her,' she answered in English. Her accent was American. She stood up. 'Please, call me Roberta.' They shook hands.

She watched him for a reaction, waiting for the inevitable raised eyebrow and mock-surprise *'oh – a woman!'* or *'my, scientists are becoming prettier these days'* kind of comment that virtually every man she met came out with, to her great annoyance. It had almost become her standard test for gauging men she met. It was just the same infuriating knee-jerk response she got when she told guys about her black belt in Shotokan karate: *'oh, I'd better watch my step'*. Assholes.

But as she invited Ben to sit down, she didn't

notice a flicker of anything cross his face. Interesting. He wasn't the typical sort of Englishman she'd come to know – no pink jowls, beer belly, awful taste in clothes or combed-over bald patch here. The man opposite her was tallish, something under six feet, with an easy grace in jeans and a light jacket over a black polo-neck that hung on a slender but muscular frame. He was maybe five, six years older than she was. He had the deep tan of someone who'd been spending time in a hot country, and his thick blond hair was bleached by the sun. He was the kind of man she could go for. But there was a hardness in the set of his jaw, and something in those blue eyes that was cold and detached.

'Thanks for agreeing to see me,' he said.

'My assistant Michel said you were from the *Sunday Times*.'

'That's right. I'm working on a feature for our magazine supplement.'

'Uh-huh? And how can I help you, Mr Hope?'

'Ben.'

'OK, what can I do for you, Ben? Oh, by the way, this is Michel Zardi, my friend and helper.' She waved a hand at Michel, who had come into the lab to look for a file. 'Listen, I was just going to make a coffee,' she said. 'Want one?'

'Coffee would be good,' Ben said. 'Black, no sugar. I need to make a quick call. Do you mind?'

'Sure, go right ahead,' she said. She turned to Michel. 'You want a coffee?' she asked him. Her French was perfect.

'*Non, merci.* I'm going out in a minute to get some fish for Lutin.'

She laughed. 'That damn cat of yours eats better than I do.'

Michel grinned and left the room. Roberta made the coffee while Ben took out his phone. He called the number for Loriot, the book publisher Rose had mentioned. No reply. Ben left him a message and his number.

'Your French is pretty good for an English journalist,' she said.

'I've travelled around. Yours is pretty good too. How long have you lived here?'

'Nearly six years now.' She sipped the hot coffee. 'So let's get down to business, Ben. You want to talk to me about alchemy? How did you hear about me?'

'Professor Jon Rose at Oxford University put me on to you. He'd heard about your work and thought you might be able to help me. Naturally,' he lied, 'you'll be fully credited for any information used in the article.'

'You can leave my name out of it.' She laughed grimly. 'Probably best not to mention me at all. I'm officially the untouchable of the scientific world these days. But if I can help you, I will. What d'you want to know?'

He leaned forward in his seat. 'I'm looking to find out more about the work of alchemists such as . . . Fulcanelli, for instance,' he said, sounding deliberately casual. 'Who they were, what they did, what they might have discovered, that kind of thing.'

'Right. Fulcanelli.' She paused, looking at him levelly. 'How much do you know about alchemy, Ben?'

'Very little,' he said truthfully.

She nodded. 'OK. Well, first off, let me get one thing straight. Alchemy is *not* just about turning base metals into gold, all right?'

'You mind if I take notes here?' He drew a small notepad from his pocket.

'Go ahead. I mean, in theory it's not impossible to create gold. The difference between one chemical element and another is only a question of manipulating tiny energy particles. Strip off an electron here, add one on there, and you can theoretically change any molecule into any other. But for me, that's not what alchemy is really about. I see the base metals into gold thing as more of a metaphor.'

'A metaphor for what?'

'You think about it, Ben. Gold is the most stable and incorruptible metal. It never corrodes, never tarnishes. Objects of pure gold stay perfect for thousands of years. Compare that to something like iron, which rusts away to nothing in no time. Now, imagine if you could find a technology that could stabilize corruptible matter, prevent deterioration?'

'Of what?'

'Of anything, in principle. Everything in our

64

universe is fundamentally made of the same stuff. I think that what the alchemists were ultimately looking for was a universal element within nature that could be extracted, or harnessed, and used to maintain or restore perfection to matter – any kind of matter, not just metals.'

'I get you,' he said, making a note in his pad.

'OK? Now, if you could find a technology like that, and get it to work, its potential would be boundless. It would be like the atomic bomb in reverse – using nature's energy to create instead of destroy. For me personally, as a biologist, I'm interested in the potential effects on living organisms, especially humans. What if we could slow down the deterioration of living tissues, perhaps even restore healthy functioning to diseased ones?'

He didn't have to think about it for long. 'You'd have the ultimate medical technology.'

She nodded. 'You certainly would. It would be incredible.'

'You really think they were on the right track? I mean, is it possible they could have created something like that?'

She smiled. 'I know what you're thinking. It's true, most alchemists probably were nutty, shot-away old guys with a lot of crazy ideas about magic – maybe some even thought of it as witchcraft, just like the Internet or even a telephone would seem like the dark arts to someone teleported here from a couple of centuries ago. But there were also alchemists who were serious scientists.'

'Examples?'

'Isaac Newton? The father of classical physics was also a closet alchemist – some of his major discoveries, that scientists still use today, might have been based on his alchemical research.'

'I didn't know that.'

'Absolutely. And another guy heavily involved in alchemy you might have heard of was Leonardo da Vinci.'

'The artist?'

'Also the brilliant engineer, designer and inventor,' she replied. 'And then there was the mathematician Giordano Bruno – that is, until the Catholic Inquisition burned him at the stake in 1600.' She grimaced. 'Those were the kind of alchemists I'm interested in, the ones who were laying the foundation for a whole new modern science that's going to change everything. That's what I believe, and that's basically what my work is about.' She paused. 'Tell you what, instead of me just talking at you, why don't I show you something? How d'you feel about bugs?'

'Bugs?'

'Insects. Some people are freaked out by them.'

'No, I'm OK.'

Roberta opened a double door leading to what must originally have been a walk-in cupboard or wardrobe. It had been adapted, with fitted wooden shelving, to hold glass tanks. Not full of fish. Full of flies. Thousands of them. Black, hairy swarms massing on the surface of the glass.

'Jesus,' he muttered, recoiling.

'Pretty gross, huh?' Roberta said cheerfully. 'Welcome to my experiment.'

The two tanks were labelled A and B. 'Tank B is the control group,' she explained. 'Meaning that those flies are just ordinary flies, well cared for but untreated. Tank A are the experimental flies.'

'OK . . . so what happens to those?' he asked warily.

'They get treated with a formula.'

'And what *is* the formula?'

'I don't have a name for it. I invented it – or copied it, I ought to say, from old alchemical writings. It's really just water that's been through some special processes.'

'What kind of processes?'

She smiled slyly. 'Special ones.'

'And what happens to the flies that are treated with it?'

'Ah, now that's the interesting part. The lifespan of a normal adult housefly, well fed, is six weeks. That's more or less how long my B flies are living. But the flies in tank A, which receive tiny amounts of the formula in their food, are consistently living thirty to thirty-five per cent longer, around eight weeks.'

Ben narrowed his eyes. 'You're sure about that?'

She nodded. 'We're into our third generation, and the results are holding.'

'This is just a recent breakthrough, then?'

'Yeah, we're really at the first stage. I still don't

know why it's working, how to explain the effect. I know I can get better results, and I will . . . And when I do, it's going to fire a chilli pepper up the asses of the scientific community.'

He was about to reply when his phone rang. 'Shit. Sorry about this.' He'd forgotten to turn it off for the interview. He took the phone out of his pocket.

'Well? Aren't you going to answer it?' she asked, raising one eyebrow.

He pressed REPLY and said, 'Hello?'

'*Loriot here. I received your message.*'

'Thanks for calling back, Monsieur Loriot,' Ben said, glancing apologetically at Roberta and raising a finger as if to say 'this'll just take a minute'. She shrugged and took a sip of her coffee, then snatched a piece of paper from her desk and started reading it.

'*I would be interested in meeting you. Would you like to come out to my home this evening for a drink and a talk?*'

'That would be great. Where do you live, Monsieur Loriot?'

Roberta threw down the sheet, sighed and exaggeratedly checked her watch.

'*My home is the Villa Margaux, near the village of Brignancourt, on the other side of Pontoise. It is not far from Paris.*'

Ben noted down the details. 'Brignancourt,' he repeated quickly, trying to get the conversation over without being impolite to Loriot. The man might be an important contact. *But if you're going to play the journalist, at least try to do it with a bit of professional fucking style,* he thought, irritated with himself.

'*I will send my car to pick you up,*' said Loriot.

'OK,' Ben said, writing on his pad. 'Eight forty-five tonight . . . Yes . . . Looking forward to that . . . Well, thanks again for calling back . . . Goodbye.' He switched off the phone and dropped it back in his pocket. 'Sorry about that,' he said to Roberta. 'It's off now.'

'Oh, don't worry about it.' She let him hear the edge of sarcasm in her voice. 'Not like I have a job to go to, is it?'

He cleared his throat. 'Anyway, this formula of yours . . .'

'Yup?'

'Have you tried it out on other species? What about humans?'

She shook her head. 'Not yet. That'd really be something, wouldn't it? If the results matched the fly experiment, the life expectancy of a healthy human could increase from, say, eighty years to about a hundred and eight years. And I think we could do even better.'

'If one of your flies was sick or dying, would this thing have the power to cure whatever was wrong with it, keep it alive?' he asked tentatively.

'You mean, does it have medicinal properties?' she replied. She clicked her tongue and sighed. 'I wish I could say yes. We've tried giving it to dying flies in group B to see what would happen, but they still died. So far it only seems to work preventatively.' She shrugged. 'But who knows? We're only getting started here. With time, we might be able to develop something that won't just extend life in healthy specimens, but will cure illnesses in sick ones, maybe even stop one from dying indefinitely. If we could replicate that effect in humans, ultimately . . .'

'Sounds like you might have discovered some kind of elixir of life?'

'Well, let's not pop the cork just yet,' she said with a chuckle. 'But I think I'm onto something, yeah. Problem is lack of funding. To really get it out there and verified you'd have to launch some serious clinical trials. Those can take years.'

'Why can't you get funding from medical companies?'

She laughed. 'Boy, you are really naïve. This is *alchemy* we're talking about. Witchcraft, voodoo, hokum. Why do you think I'm running this operation out of a spare bedroom? Nobody takes me seriously since I wrote about this stuff.'

'I heard you'd had some trouble over it.'

'Trouble?' She snorted. 'Yeah, you might say that. First I was plastered all over the cover of *Scientific American* – some wiseguy editor put a witch's hat on me and a sign round my neck saying "Unscientific American". Next thing, those assholes at the university gave me the boot, left me hanging out to dry. Hasn't exactly helped my career. They even fired poor old Michel from his lab-tech post. Said he was wasting university time and money on my hocus-pocus project. He's the only one who's stood by me through all this. I pay him what I can, but it's been tough for both of us.' She sighed and shook her head. 'Bastards. But I'll show them.'

'Have you got any of your formula here?' he asked. 'I'd be keen to see it.'

'No, I haven't,' she said firmly. 'I ran out, need to make some more up.'

He watched her eyes for signs of a lie. Hard to tell. He paused for a moment. 'So, do you think there's any chance you might let me have a copy of your research notes?' he asked, hoping the request didn't come over as too bold. He toyed with the idea of offering her money for them, but that would have made her instantly suspicious of him.

She wagged her finger. 'Ha ha. No way, pal. Anyway, you think I'd be dumb enough to write down the formula?' She tapped her head. 'It's all in here. This is my baby, and nobody's getting their hands on it.'

He grinned ruefully. 'OK, forget I mentioned it.'

There were a few seconds of silence between them. Roberta looked at him expectantly, then placed her hands flat on her knees as though to signal the end of the interview. 'Anything else I can help you with, Ben?'

'I won't take up any more of your time,' he said,

71

worrying that he'd blown it by asking to see her notes. 'But if you get any major breakthroughs, will you give me a call?' He handed her a card.

She took it, and smiled. 'If you want, but don't get too excited. It's a slow process. Call me again in, say, three years' time.'

'It's a date,' he said.

CHAPTER 11

Roberta Ryder suddenly looked much less the austere scientist, with her wavy dark red hair let down past her shoulders and the labcoat switched for a denim jacket. 'Michel, I'm going out. You can take the rest of the day off, OK?' She got her sports holdall from the bedroom, grabbed her car keys and headed off for her weekly session at the martial arts centre across town in Montparnasse.

As she drove she was thinking about her interview with the journalist Ben Hope. She always had to come over like the ballsy, tough, defiant maverick scientist who was going to show 'em all one day . . . it was the image she clung to. Nobody knew about the fragile reality of her situation. They didn't know about the fears she had, the worries that kept her awake at night. The day she'd been fired from the university, she could so easily have packed a bag and jumped on the next flight home to the States. But she hadn't. She'd stayed to tough it out. Now she was wondering at the wisdom of that decision. Had all the sacrifices she'd made been worth it? Was she just chasing rainbows, kidding herself that the stand she'd taken was ever going to make a difference? Soon her money would be all gone, and she'd have to try to find some supplementary income from somewhere – maybe private science tuition for schoolkids. Even that might not even bring in enough to scrape by on, pay Michel's meagre wages and fund her research. The next two or three months would tell whether she could go on, or whether she'd have to give it all up.

She got back to her apartment at around 5.30. Her legs felt heavy as she climbed the spiralling, echoing stairs to the third floor. It had been a tiring session that day, and she was hot from the rush-hour traffic.

When she reached her landing and took out her keys, she found the door unlocked. Had Michel come back for something? He was the only other person with a key, apart from the concierge. But it wasn't like him to leave the door open.

She went inside, peering into the lab room through the slightly-open door. 'Michel? You there?' There was no reply, no sign of him. She went into the lab.

'Oh, *Jesus*.'

It had been turned over. Files spilled all over the floor, drawers up-ended, everything gone through. But that wasn't what she was standing gaping at. It was the big man in the black hood who was rushing towards her.

A gloved hand shot out towards her throat.

Without thinking about it, she blocked the move by throwing her hands up and outwards to deflect his arms aside. The surprised attacker hesitated for half a second, long enough for her to follow up her move with a low stamping kick to his knee. If it had landed it would have ended the fight there and then. But he skipped backwards just in time and her foot only grazed his shin. He moved back with a grunt of pain, stumbled and fell heavily.

She turned and ran. But he threw out a big arm and tripped her, sending her sprawling to the ground. Her head whacked the wall and she saw stars. By the time she was on her feet he was just two metres away with a knife in his hand. He came at her, lifting the knife high to stab down at her.

This was something Roberta knew a little about. A trained knife fighter keeps the weapon close to his body and stabs outwards, using the rotation of his back muscles to deliver lethal force to the blow. Very little can be done to block the move or take the knife off them. But the downwards stab, holding the knife in an underhand grip, was a different matter. Theoretically, she knew she could block this. *Theoretically*. At the karate club they'd only ever practised this move with a soft rubber blade, and then never at full speed.

The very real blade flashed down hard and fast. Roberta was faster. She caught his wrist and levered it down sideways while with her other hand she wrenched his elbow the other way with all her strength. At the same time she launched herself into him with a hard knee to the groin.

The move worked. She felt a terrible cracking as his arm broke. Heard his scream in her ear. His face contorted in agony behind the mask. The knife fell, and his twisting body fell on top of it. He hit the floor, landed writhing on his belly, and screamed again.

She stood poised over him, staring in horror, as he contorted and rolled onto his back. The knife was buried deep in his solar plexus. He'd landed on it, driven the blade in with his own weight and momentum. He clawed desperately at the handle, trying to pull it out. After a few seconds his movements slowed, the convulsions slackened, and then he lay still. Blood spread slowly outwards in a slick stream across the tiles.

She screwed her eyes shut, knees quaking violently. Maybe when she opened them, there wouldn't be a dead guy lying there in a pool of blood. But no, there he was all right, staring up at her glassily, mouth half open like a fish on a slab.

Every nerve in her body was screaming at her to run, but she fought the impulse away. Slowly, her heart in her mouth, she crouched down next to the body. She reached out a trembling hand and slipped it into the front of the dead man's black jacket. Inside she found a small diary, half-soaked in blood. She turned the dripping pages, shuddering in revulsion at the blood on her fingers and looking for a name, a number, a clue.

The diary was almost completely blank. Then on the last page she found two addresses, scribbled in pencil. One was hers. The other was Michel's.

Had they got to him? She dug out her phone, feverishly scrolled down her address book entries as far as 'M.Z', and hit the dial button. 'Come on, come on,' she muttered, waiting.

No reply, just his answering machine.

She wondered whether she should call the police. No time for that now, she decided – it would take an age to get through the receptionists and she had to get over to his place right away. She stepped over the corpse and opened the front door a crack.

All clear. She locked the door behind her and bounded down the stairs.

The car screeched to a halt at a crazy angle outside Michel's apartment building, and she ran to the doorway. She buzzed the button next to his name on the intercom panel several times, kicking her heels, tension mounting.

After two or three minutes a laughing couple came out of the building and she slipped inside. She found herself in a dark, stone corridor leading to the stairway, past the concierge's door and into the central courtyard. Michel's apartment was on the ground floor. She thumped on his door. No response. She ran back through the foyer and into the courtyard. Michel's bathroom window was slightly open. She scrambled up to the window ledge. It was a tight squeeze, but she was slim enough to wriggle through.

Once into the apartment, she crept furtively from room to room. There was no sign of life. But a near-empty cup of coffee on the table, next to the remains of a meal, was still warm to the touch and the laptop on his desk was running. He must have just gone out, she thought. And if that was the case, it had to mean he was all right. She felt relief unstiffen her muscles. Maybe he wouldn't be long.

The phone suddenly rang, making her jump. After two rings the answering machine came on automatically. Michel's familiar mumbled recording came over the speaker, followed by a beep, and then the caller left their message.

She listened to the deep, gravelly French voice. *'This is Saul. Your report has been received. The plan has been carried out. BH will be taken care of tonight.'*

What was going on here? What report? What had Michel been sending, and to whom? Was this guy, her friend and assistant, someone she trusted – mixed up in this too? *The plan has been carried out.* She shivered. Did that mean what she thought it meant?

She walked over to the desk and flipped up the lid of Michel's computer. The machine was on standby, and whirred quickly into life. She double-clicked on the email icon on the desktop. Her head

78

swam as she scrolled down through the SENT ITEMS list. It didn't take her long to discover the whole column of sent messages marked REPORT. They were numbered in consecutive order and dated from a few months ago to the present. Running down the list she saw that they'd been sent at regular intervals of about two weeks.

She clicked on a recent one, number 14. It flashed up on the screen and she scanned through it. Her heart picked up a beat. She sat on his desk chair and read it again, more slowly, hardly believing what she was seeing.

It was a report on her latest scientific findings, her breakthrough with the lifespans of the group A flies. It was all there, down to the last tiny detail. Her heart beat faster.

She opened the most recently sent post. It was dated that day, sent just an hour or so ago. It had an attachment with it. She read the accompanying message first: *Today, 20 September, meeting with English journalist Ben Hope.* Shaking her head in bewilderment, she clicked on the paper-clip logo in the corner of the message. As the attachment opened up she saw that it contained a series of JPEG files, digital photos. She clicked on each one in turn, and her frown deepened with every click.

They were shots of her and Ben Hope in her lab. They'd been taken just that morning, and there was only one person who could have done it. Michel, using his phone while he'd been pretending to fetch a file.

BH will be taken care of tonight, the phone message had said. And now she knew who BH was.

She stiffened and looked up from the screen. She'd heard something. Someone was approaching the front door. She recognized the familiar tune that Michel often used to whistle to himself at the lab. Keys jangled at the lock, and the door creaked open. Footsteps came down the hall. Roberta dived behind a couch and crouched there, hardly daring to breathe.

Michel came into the room. He was carrying a shopping bag, and as he whistled his little tune he started unloading groceries. He reached out and played back his phone message. Roberta peeked over the top of the couch and watched his face as he listened to Saul's voice. There was no emotion, just a nod.

Her mind was racing, dizzy at the thought that this was the same Michel she knew. She ought to challenge him, have it out with him right here. But it was becoming clear that she didn't know him as well as she thought. What if he had a weapon? Maybe confrontation wasn't a good idea.

He deleted the phone message. 'Christ, it's warm in here,' he muttered to himself. He opened a window across the other side of the room. Then he grabbed a chocolate bar and a bottle of beer from the grocery bag, flopped down in a chair and switched on the TV with the remote. He sat chortling at a cartoon and sipping his beer.

This was her chance. She ducked back down and

started crawling out from behind the couch, keeping low. She was going to crawl right across the room and make it out through that open window while he was distracted by the television.

She was half out from behind the couch when he shouted, 'Hey! What are *you* doing there?'

He rose from his chair.

She didn't dare to look up. *Shit, I'm caught.*

'You come down from there, now,' he was saying in a gentler voice. She looked up, startled and confused.

He was across the other side of the room, by the desk. 'Come on, my baby, you shouldn't do that.' A fluffy white cat had jumped up on the desk and was licking out the plate that he'd left sitting there from his earlier meal. He picked it up in his arms, stroking it lovingly. It meowed in protest and wriggled free of his grip, jumped down on the floor and ran out of the room. He ran after it, nursing a scratched finger. 'Lutin! Come back!' He disappeared out of sight and Roberta heard him shouting at the cat. 'Lutin – come out from under there, you little turd!'

Seeing her chance, she leapt to her feet and dashed up the short passageway to the front door, silently turned the latch and slipped out.

CHAPTER 12

When Michel Zardi had first been contacted a few months earlier by the man he knew only as 'Saul', he'd no idea who was approaching him, or what they really wanted. He only knew he was being asked to observe Roberta Ryder's work and send back reports on the progress of her research.

Michel wasn't an idiot. He'd been with her project from the start, and he had a pretty good idea of its potential value if she could convince anyone to take it seriously. Now it looked like someone was, although it wasn't the kind of attention that Roberta would have wanted. Michel was smart enough not to ask too many questions. What they wanted him to do was simple enough, and the money was good.

Good enough to make him start thinking that maybe he didn't *want* to spend the rest of his life bumming around as a low-paid lab tech, especially now that Roberta had been forced to relocate her operation to her own apartment. The project wasn't going anywhere, they both knew that. He also knew her well enough to know that she'd never accept the reality. Her stubborn pride was what kept her going, but it was also going to drag them both down.

For a long time, Michel had toyed with the idea of leaving and getting better work elsewhere. Just when he'd been on the brink of telling her it was over for him, Saul had turned up out of nowhere. Suddenly, everything had looked different. The promise of a more stable and interesting future working for Saul and his people, whoever they were, meant that he had prospects. And it had helped to harden his attitude towards the American scientist he'd once thought of as his friend. Every couple of weeks or so he'd send in his report, and at the end of each month the cash-stuffed envelope would appear in his mailbox. Life was good.

It was a pyramid of power, broad at the bottom, small at the top. At the bottom, it was made up of lots of ignorant, insignificant men like Michel Zardi – little men whose loyalty could be bought cheaply. The top of the pyramid was occupied by just one man and a select group of his close associates. They were the only ones who knew the true nature, purpose and identity of the organization that so carefully kept its activities hidden from prying eyes.

The two men at the top of this pyramid were now sitting together in a room talking. It was no ordinary room, situated in the domed tower at the centre of an elegant Renaissance villa outside Rome.

The big authoritative man standing by the window was called Massimiliano Usberti. Fabrizio Severini was his private secretary and the only man Usberti trusted completely and spoke openly with.

'In five years we will have evolved into a far more powerful force than we are now, my friend,' Usberti was saying.

Severini sipped wine from a crystal glass. 'We are already powerful,' he said with a note of caution in his voice. 'How do you hope to conceal our activities from those around us, if we should grow even more in size and strength?'

'By the time my plans are in place,' Usberti said, 'we will no longer need to worry about conceal-ment. This position we find ourselves in, the need to preserve secrecy, is only a temporary phase in our development.'

Fabrizio Severini was the closest man alive to Massimiliano Usberti. Now both in their late fifties, they had known one another for many years. When they had first met as young men, Massimiliano had been just another priest, though an exceptionally driven one and with the backing of the great wealth of his noble family to achieve his ambitions. But even Severini didn't fully know what Usberti's ultimate objective was, the end goal of these plans he so often alluded to. He didn't push too hard or inquire too openly. Their rela-tionship as friends had evolved over the years as Usberti had grown in power, self-confidence and

84

– he didn't like to use the word, but it was the only one to use – fanaticism. Severini knew that his friend, or indeed his master as he'd slowly become, was a highly ruthless man who would stop at nothing. He feared him, and he knew that Usberti secretly enjoyed the fact that he did.

Usberti came away from the window and rejoined his secretary under the grand dome. On the ornate seventeenth-century gilt wood table sat a laptop computer displaying a slideshow. The photos were of a woman and a man talking. One of them was a familiar face. Dr Roberta Ryder. The soon-to-be *late* Dr Roberta Ryder.

The man in the photos was someone Usberti had hoped never to see. He already knew all about the Englishman from one of his informers, who'd told him that a professional investigator was going to be sniffing around. The informer had warned him that Benedict Hope had a specialist background and that he was a man of certain talents. This seemed to be confirmed when the hired assassin sent after him had failed to return or report back. Nobody had heard from him, and then one of his sources in Paris had called to say it had been on the news that a man had flung himself off the parapet of Notre Dame Cathedral. Their man.

Usberti hadn't expected Hope to get this far. But it didn't worry him. He wouldn't get much further.

'Archbishop . . .' Severini began, wringing his hands nervously.

'Yes, my friend?'

'Will God forgive us for what we do?'

Usberti looked sharply up at him. 'Of course He will. We do it to protect His house.'

When Severini was gone, the archbishop went over to the antique gold-bound Bible on his desk.

And I saw Heaven opened, and behold a white horse; and he that sat upon him was called Faithful and True, and in righteousness he doth judge and make war.

And he was clothed with a vesture dipped in blood: and his name is called the Word of God. And the armies which were in Heaven followed him.

And he hath a sharp sword, that with it he should smite the nations: and he should rule them with a rod of iron: and he treadeth the winepress of the fierceness and wrath of Almighty God.

Usberti shut the book. He gazed into space for a moment, a grim, set expression on his face. Then, nodding solemnly to himself, he picked up the phone.

CHAPTER 13

Paris

Roberta made it back to the 2CV, glancing over her shoulder and half expecting Michel Zardi to come tearing out of the doorway of the building after her. Her hands were shaking so badly she could barely get the key in the lock.

As she drove back to her apartment she dialled 17 and was put through to police emergency. 'I want to report an attempted murder. There's a body in my flat.' She gave her details in a breathless rush as she sped back through the traffic, driving with one hand.

An ambulance and two police cars were arriving just as she pulled up outside her building ten minutes later. The uniformed agents were headed by a brisk plainclothes inspector in his mid-thirties. He had thick dark hair brushed back from his brow, and his eyes were an unusually vivid green. 'I'm Inspector Luc Simon,' he said, staring at her intently. 'You reported the incident?'

'Yes.'

'So you are . . . Roberta Ryder? US citizen. Have you identification?'

'Now? OK.' She fished in her bag and took out her passport and work visa. Simon ran his eyes over them and handed them back.

'You have the title *Dr.* A medical doctor?'

'Biologist.'

'I see. Show us to the crime scene.'

They climbed the winding stairs to Roberta's apartment, radios crackling in the stairway. Simon led the way, moving fast, his jaw hard. She trotted along behind him, followed by the half-dozen uniformed cops and a paramedic team headed by a police doctor carrying a case.

She explained the situation to Simon, watching his intense green eyes. 'And then he fell, and came down on the knife,' she said, gesticulating. 'He was a big, heavy guy, must have landed really hard.'

'We'll take a full statement from you presently. Who's up there now?'

'Nobody, just him.'

'Him?'

'*It*, then,' she said with a note of impatience. 'The body.'

'You left the body unattended?' he said, raising his eyebrows. 'Where have *you* been?'

'To visit a friend,' she said, wincing to herself at the way it sounded.

'Really . . . OK, we'll talk about that later,' said Simon impatiently. 'Let's see the body first.'

They arrived at her door, and she opened it. 'Do you mind if I wait outside?' she asked.

'Where's the body?'

'He's right there inside the door, in the hallway.'

The officers and medics went inside, Simon leading the way. A cop stayed outside on the landing with Roberta. She slumped against the wall and closed her eyes.

After a couple of seconds Simon stepped back out onto the landing with a severe yet weary expression. 'Are you sure this is your apartment?' he asked.

'Yeah. Why?'

'Are you on any medication? Do you suffer from memory loss, epilepsy or any other mental disorder? Do you do drugs, alcohol?'

'What are you talking about? Of course not.'

'Explain this to me, then.' Simon grabbed her by the arm and thrust her firmly into the doorway, pointing and looking at her expectantly. Roberta gaped. The detective was pointing at her hall floor.

Empty. Clean. The body was gone.

'You have an explanation?'

'Maybe he crawled away,' she muttered. *What, and cleaned up the blood trail after himself?* She rubbed her eyes, head spinning.

Simon turned to stare hard at her. 'Wasting police time is a serious offence. I could arrest you right now, you realize that?'

'But I tell you there was a body! I didn't imagine it, it was right there!'

'Hmm.' Simon turned to one of his men. 'Go get me a coffee,' he commanded. He faced Roberta with a sardonic look. 'So where's it gone to? The bathroom? Maybe we'll find it sitting on the toilet reading *Le Monde*?'

'I wish I knew,' she replied helplessly. 'But he *was* there . . . I didn't imagine it.'

'Search the place,' Simon ordered his officers. 'Talk to the neighbours, find out if they heard anything.' The men went off to comb through the apartment, one or two of them casting irritable glances at Roberta. Simon turned to her again. 'You say he was a big, powerful man? That he attacked you with a knife?'

'Yes.'

'But you're not injured?'

She tutted with annoyance. 'No.'

'How do you expect me to believe that a woman of your size – about one metre sixty-five? – could kill a large armed attacker with her bare hands, and not have a mark on her?'

'Hold on – I never said I killed him. He *fell* on the knife.'

'What was he doing here?'

'What does a criminal normally do inside somebody's apartment? He was burgling the place. Turned my lab upside down.'

'Your lab?'

'Sure, the whole place has been ransacked. See for yourself.'

She pointed to the lab door, and he pushed it

open. Peering in past his shoulder she saw with a shock that the room had been tidied up – everything neatly in its proper place, files neatly ordered, drawers shut. Was she going crazy?

'Tidy burglar,' Simon commented. 'Wish they were all like that.'

One of the agents looked in the door. 'Sir, the neighbours across the landing were in all afternoon. They say they heard nothing.'

'Huh,' Simon snorted. He looked around the lab, snatched up a piece of paper from her desk. 'What's this? *The Biological Science of Alchemy?*' His eyes flashed up from the page and bored into her.

'I told you, I-I'm a scientist,' she stammered.

'Alchemy is a science now? You can turn lead into gold?'

'Give me a break.'

'Maybe you've invented a way of making things . . . disappear?' he said with an expansive gesture. He tossed the paper down on the desk and strode purposefully across the room. 'And what's in here?'

Before she could stop him he'd opened the doors to the fly tanks. '*Putain!* This is disgusting.'

'It's part of my research.'

'This is a serious health and safety matter, madame. These things carry disease.' The police doctor was standing behind Roberta in the doorway, nodding in agreement and rolling his eyes. The other officers were returning from their search of the small apartment, shaking their heads. She could feel hostile looks coming at her from all directions.

'Your coffee, sir.'

'Ah, thank Christ.' Simon grabbed the paper cup and took a deep gulp. Coffee was the only thing that took away these stress headaches. He needed to rest more. He hadn't slept at all last night.

'I know this looks weird,' Roberta protested. She was gesticulating too much, on the defensive. She didn't like the way her voice was going high. 'But I'm telling you –'

'Are you married? Have you a boyfriend?' Simon asked sharply.

'No – I did have a boyfriend – but not any more . . . but what does that have to do with anything?'

'You're emotionally upset that he has left you,' suggested Simon. 'Perhaps the stress . . .' *That's ironic*, he was thinking, remembering last night's performance with Hélène.

'Oh, so you think I'm having a nervous breakdown? The little woman can't cope without a man?'

He shrugged.

'What the hell are these questions? Who's your superior officer?'

'You should be careful, madame. Remember you've committed a serious offence.'

'Please, listen to me. I think they're planning to kill somebody else. An English guy.'

'Oh really? Who's planning this?'

'I don't know *who*. The same people who tried to kill me.'

'Then I'd suggest that our English friend is in no great danger.' Simon regarded her with an obvious look of contempt. 'And do we know who this Englishman is? Perhaps the friend you went to have tea with while the imaginary corpse was lying in your apartment?'

'My god,' she exclaimed helplessly, almost laughing with frustration. 'Tell me you're not really this dumb.'

'Dr Ryder, if you don't shut up right now I'll take you in. I'll have you locked up while I wrap this place in police tape and have forensics go through it with a fine-tooth comb.' He threw down the empty cup and moved towards her. His face was reddening. She backed away. 'You'll be examined by the police surgeon,' he went on. 'Every inch of you. Not to mention a full psychological appraisal by the psychiatrist. I'll have Interpol go through your bank account. I'll take your fucking life apart shred by shred . . . is that what you want?'

Roberta had her back to the wall. His nose was almost touching hers, his green eyes blazing. 'Because that's what'll happen to you!'

The agents were all staring at Simon. The doctor came up behind him and laid a hand softly on his shoulder, breaking the tension. Simon backed off.

'Do it!' she yelled back at him. 'Take me away! I've got evidence – I know who's involved in it.'

He glowered at her. 'So you can be the star in your own movie? You'd love that, wouldn't you?

But I'm not going to give you that satisfaction. I've seen enough here. Disappearing bodies – tanks full of flies – alchemy – murder plots. Sorry, *Doctor* Ryder, the police service doesn't cater for attention-seeking weirdos.' He pointed a warning finger. 'Consider yourself under caution. Do *not* do this again. Understood?' He motioned to the others and led the way out. They brushed past her, leaving her alone in the hallway.

She stood there paralysed for a moment with shock and surprise, staring at the back of the hall door and listening to the echoing tramp of footsteps from outside as the policemen headed back down the stairs. She couldn't believe it. Now what was she going to do?

BH will be taken care of tonight. Ben Hope. However he was involved with all this, she had to warn him right away. She hardly knew the guy, but if the cops weren't going to take this situation seriously, it was up to her to alert him to whatever the hell was going on.

She'd tossed the business card he'd given her into the waste-paper basket, with no intention of ever calling him – thank Christ, she thought now, that she hadn't put it through the shredder. She upended the bin, spilling crumpled papers, orange peel and a crushed fizzy drink can onto the lab floor. The card was lying underneath, stained with spots of Coke. She grabbed her phone and stabbed the keys, pressed it to her ear and waited for the ringing tone.

94

A voice answered. 'Hello? Ben?' she began urgently. But then she realized what she was hearing.

'*Welcome to the Orange answerphone. I'm sorry, but the person you have called is not available . . .*'

CHAPTER 14

The Opera Quarter, central Paris

The rendezvous point Ben had chosen for that night's meeting was the Madeleine church on the edge of the Opera quarter. It was his habit never to make contact or be picked up too near a place he was staying in. He hadn't liked the way that Fairfax's people knew his location in Ireland and sent for him at home.

He left the apartment at 8.20 and walked briskly to the Richelieu Drouot Métro station. It was only two stops to his destination on the jerking, rumbling train. He threaded through the crowds that filled the underground tunnels and emerged back onto the street at the Place de la Madeleine. At the foot of the towering church, he lit a cigarette and leaned against one of the Corinthian columns, watching the traffic go by.

He didn't have to wait long. At the appointed time, a large Mercedes limousine veered out of the traffic and glided to a halt at the kerbside. The uniformed driver climbed out.

'Monsieur 'Ope?'

Ben nodded. The chauffeur opened the rear door for him and he got in. He watched Paris go by. It was getting dark as they left the outskirts of the city and the long, silent limo made its way outward along increasingly narrow, unlit country lanes. Bushes and trees, the occasional darkened building, and a little roadside bar flashed by in the headlights.

His driver was short on conversation, and Ben lapsed into thought. Loriot was obviously a highly successful publisher, judging by the mode of transport that had been sent out to collect him. It didn't seem likely that the success of his business depended much, if at all, on publishing titles with an esoteric or alchemical theme – a search of the *Editions Loriot* website had flagged up only a handful of them, and nothing that seemed related to what he was looking for. In any case it was hardly a very commercial sector of the book market. But Rose had said Loriot was a real enthusiast. It was probably just a hobby thing for him, perhaps a personal interest in the subject that he'd brought into the business as a sideline, to cater for like-minded alchemy buffs. Maybe he'd be able to point him in the right direction. A wealthy collector might even have rare books, or papers or manuscripts of his own, that could be of interest. Perhaps even . . . no, that was hoping for too much. He'd just have to wait and see where tonight's meeting took him. He glanced at the luminous dial of his watch. They should be there soon. His thoughts meandered.

He felt the Mercedes slow. Had they arrived? He looked out past the driver at the dark road. They weren't in any village, and there didn't seem to be any houses nearby. He saw a large road sign lit up in the headlamps.

DANGER
LEVEL CROSSING

The wooden barriers were raised upwards, allowing the car to pass underneath. The limo eased slowly onto the tracks and halted. The driver reached down to press a button on the console next to him and there was a *clunk* as the central locking was activated. A whirring sound, and a thick glass partition rose up, screening him off from the driver.

'Hey,' he called, rapping on the glass. His voice sounded hollow in the soundproof compartment. 'What's going on?' The driver ignored him. He tried the door, knowing in advance it was going to be locked. 'Why've we stopped? Hey, I'm *talking* to you.'

Without a glance at him or a word in reply, the driver turned off the ignition and the headlights darkened. He swung open the heavy door and the car's internal light came on. Ben noticed that the partition between them was steel reinforced, crisscrossed internally with a grid of stiff wire.

The driver calmly got out of the car. He slammed the door shut and the interior of the car went dark. A bobbing beam of pale torchlight appeared as the man searched ahead of him, walking away up the empty road. The torch beam was sweeping from side to side as though looking for something up ahead. The trembling pool of light settled on a black Audi parked at the roadside, some fifty yards away beyond the level crossing. Its taillights came on and a door was thrown open as the limo driver neared it. He got in.

Ben hammered on the glass partition, then on the tinted window. The Audi's taillights were all he could see in the dark. After a minute or so the car pulled away and disappeared up the road.

He groped about in the back of the Mercedes for a way out. He tried the doors again, knowing it was pointless and fighting a rising tide of anxiety. There would be a way out. There was always a way out of everything. He'd been in worse situations than this.

He heard a sound from outside, the ring of a bell. It was followed by a series of mechanical noises, and the wooden barriers came down. Even though he was blind in the darkness, he could visualize the scene all too clearly. The Mercedes was sitting astride the tracks, caught between the barriers, and now there was a train coming.

'All taken care of, Godard?' asked Berger, the fat guy behind the wheel, glancing over his shoulder as the limo driver climbed into the back of the Audi.

Godard took off his chauffeur's cap. 'No problem.' He grinned.

Berger started the car. 'Let's go for that beer.'

'Shouldn't we hang about for a while?' asked the third man, glancing nervously at his watch. He looked uneasily at the shadow of the Mercedes fifty yards behind them.

'Nah – what the fuck for?' Berger chortled as he put the Audi into gear and drove off, accelerating hard up the road. 'Train'll be here in a couple more minutes. The Brit motherfucker's not going *anywhere*.'

Ben's eyes were fully adjusted to the dark by now. Through the side window of the Mercedes, the horizon was a plunging black V of starry sky flanked by the blacker steep embankments on either side that rose up from the track. As he watched, a dull glow between the embankments grew steadily brighter. It became two distinct lights, still a long way off but swelling alarmingly in size as the train got nearer. Through the roar in his head he could faintly make out the sound of steel wheels on tracks.

He thumped harder on the window. *Keep your cool.* He unholstered his Browning and used it like a hammer, whacking the butt hard several times against the window. The glass wouldn't give.

He flipped the gun round in his hand, shielded his face with his free arm and fired a shot at the inside of the glass. The growing rumble of the train disappeared in a high-pitched whine as his ears sang from the gunshot. The pane distorted into a wild spider's web of cracks but didn't give. Bulletproof glass. He lowered the gun. Not much point trying to take out the door locks. It would take a lot more than a dozen rounds of a flimsy 9mm to chew through the solid steel.

He hesitated, then started banging again. The distant lights were getting bigger and brighter, flooding the valley between the embankments with a haloed white glow.

There was a crash and he recoiled from the window. Another crunching impact and the crumpled pane bulged in towards him.

A voice from outside, muffled but familiar. 'You in there? Ben?' It was a woman's voice, American. Roberta Ryder's voice!

Roberta took another swing at the window with the tyre-iron from her Citroën's emergency kit. The reinforced glass was smashed in but it wouldn't give. The train was fast approaching.

She yelled through the cracked window, 'Ben, hold on tight. There's going to be an impact!'

The howl of the train was getting louder. He barely heard the door of the Citroën slam and the sound of its whiny little engine. The 2CV lurched forward, smashing through the barriers and hurling its feeble weight against the heavy metal of the Mercedes' rear end. Roberta's windscreen was shattered by the wooden pole. Metal screeched against metal. She grabbed the gearstick and crunched brutally into reverse, dumping the clutch and skidding backwards for another hit.

The limo had been shunted forwards a metre, its locked wheels making trenches in the dirt. She rammed the Mercedes a second time, and managed to get the nose of the big, heavy car under the opposite barrier. But it wasn't enough.

Ben was crouched tightly down in the back of the limo. Another impact sent him sprawling. The Mercedes was shunted across the second track, the remaining barrier clattering across its roof.

The train was almost on them, 250 metres and closing fast.

Roberta floored the accelerator viciously one more time. Last chance. The badly buckled 2CV crunched squarely into the back of the Mercedes and she whooped with relief as the limo was knocked clear of the railway lines.

The driver had seen the cars on the tracks. In the wall of noise that was descending on Roberta she could hear the scream of brakes. But nothing could stop it in time. For one terrifying moment the 2CV was locked to the Mercedes and sitting right in the train's path, torn bodywork meshed together, her wheels spinning in reverse.

Then the wreckage disentangled and the car bounced backwards off the tracks to safety just a second before the train howled past with a great slap of wind. Its massive length hurtled by for ten seconds, then it was gone into the night and its little red lights receded away to nothing.

They sat silently for a moment in their separate cars, and waited for their hearts and breathing to settle. Ben tucked the Browning back into its holster and clipped it into place.

Roberta climbed out of the 2CV, looked at it and gave an involuntary groan. Her headlights were smashed to hell, dangling from their stalks amongst the twisted ruin of the car's bonnet and front wings. She stepped over the tracks to the limo, knees shaky. 'Ben? Talk to me!'

'Can you get me out?' said his muffled voice from inside.

She tried the Mercedes' driver door. '*Duh* – smart thinking, Ryder,' she muttered to herself. 'Open the whole time.' At least the keys weren't in the ignition. That would have been *really* stupid. She climbed inside and thumped on the glass partition dividing her from Ben. His face appeared dimly on the other side. She looked around. There must be a button for the glass panel. If she could lower it, he could scramble out that way. She found what looked like the button and pressed it. No reaction. Probably needed the ignition on. *Shit.* She found another button and pressed that, and with a satisfying clunk the rear central locking mechanism opened.

He tumbled out, groaning and rubbing his aching body. He shut his jacket, keeping the holster carefully covered up.

'Jesus, that was close,' she breathed. 'You all right?'

'I'll live.' He pointed at the ruined 2CV. 'Will it still go?'

'*Thank you Roberta,*' she said in a mock-sarcastic tone. '*How lucky you turned up. Thank you for saving my ass.*'

He made no reply. She threw him a look, then gazed back at the wreck of her car. 'I really liked that car, you know. They don't make them any more.'

'I'll get you another,' he said, limping towards it.

'Damn right you'll get me another,' she went on. 'And I think you owe me an explanation as well.'

After a few twists of the key the 2CV engine coughed into life, making a terminal-sounding clanking noise. Roberta turned the car round, its wheels grinding against the buckled wings, and drove away. As they gained speed, the rubbing of tyres on metal rose to a tortured howl, and the wind whistled around them through the broken windscreen. The engine was overheating badly and acrid smoke began to pour from under the mangled bonnet.

'I can't go far in this,' she shouted over the blast of wind, peering out of the shattered glass into the darkness.

'Just get it down the road some way,' he shouted back. 'I think I saw a bar back there.'

CHAPTER 15

The Citroën managed to see them as far as the quiet roadside bar before it finally expired from a pierced radiator. Roberta gave it a last sad look as they left it in a shadowy corner of the car park and walked in, past a couple of motorcycles and a few cars and under the flickering red glow of the neon sign over the doorway.

The bar-room was mostly empty. A couple of long-haired bikers were playing pool and laughing raucously in the back, drinking beer straight from the bottle.

They said little as they took a corner table away from the hard-rock blare of the jukebox. Ben went over to the bar and came back a minute later with a bottle of cheap red wine and two glasses. He poured a glass out for each of them and slid hers across the stained tabletop. She took a gulp and closed her eyes. 'Boy, what a day. So what's *your* story?'

He shrugged. 'I was just waiting for a train.'

'You nearly caught one, too.'

'I noticed. Thanks for stepping in.'

'Don't thank me. Just tell me what's happening and why we've suddenly become so popular.'

'We?'

'Yeah, *we*,' she said hotly, stabbing the table with her finger. 'Since I first had the pleasure of meeting you earlier today, I've had intruders trying to kill me, friends turning out to be enemies, dead men disappearing from my apartment and asshole cops who think I'm a whacko.'

He listened carefully and with growing apprehension as she told him all that had happened during the last few hours. 'And to cap it all,' she finished, 'I almost get mashed by a train rescuing your ass.' She paused. 'I take it you didn't get my message,' she added indignantly.

'What message?'

'Maybe you should keep your phone switched on.'

He gave a sour laugh as he remembered he'd turned it off during their interview earlier on. He pulled the mobile out of his pocket and activated it. 'Message,' he groaned as the little envelope logo flashed up on his screen.

'Nice going, Sherlock,' she said. 'Then it's just as well that when you didn't call back, I decided to come and warn you in person. Though I'm beginning to wonder why I bothered.'

He frowned. 'How did you know where to find me?'

'Remember? I was *there* when you got the call from–'

'Loriot.'

'Whatever. Charming friends you have. Anyway, I remembered you mentioned you were going to

Brignancourt tonight, figured I might catch up with you there if I wasn't too late.' She looked at him hard. 'So are you going to tell me what's going on, Ben? Do *Sunday Times* journalists always live such exciting lives?'

'Sounds like you had a more exciting day than me.'

'Cut the bullshit. You have something to do with all this, don't you?'

He was silent.

'Well? Don't you? Come on. Am I supposed to think it's all a coincidence that you turn up asking questions about my work, and we're being photographed, and someone tries to kill us both on the same day? I don't buy this journalist thing. Who are you, really?'

He refilled both their glasses. His cigarette was finished. He tossed the stub out of the window. Reached for his Zippo and lit another.

She coughed when the smoke drifted across the table towards her. 'Do you *have* to do that?'

'Yes.'

'It's banned.'

'Like I give a shit,' he said.

'So are you going to tell me the truth – or do I just call the cops?'

'You think they'll believe you this time?'

The train driver's heart was still in his mouth as he drove on down the line. By the time his lights had picked out the two cars in his path, it would have been too late to do anything about it. He breathed deeply. *Jesus.* He'd never had anything more than a deer on the line before. He didn't like to think what might have happened if the cars hadn't got out of the way in time.

What kind of idiot would drive under the level-crossing barrier with a train coming? Kids, probably, messing about with stolen cars. The driver let out a long sigh as his heart rate eased back down to normal, and then he reached for his radio handset.

'Oh, fuck.'

'*Told* you we should've hung around.'

The three men sat in the Audi overlooking the railway line where they'd left the Mercedes earlier on. Naudon shot his colleagues a caustic glare and settled back in his seat. While Berger and Godard had been sitting giggling in the bar, he'd been listening to the radio. If there'd been a train crash it would've been mentioned. Nothing – so he'd kept going on about it to the others until they eventually relented, just to shut him up.

And he'd been right. No wreckage, no derailed train, no dead Englishman. The empty Merc was sitting a few metres from the track, and it certainly didn't look like a car that had been hit by a fast-moving train.

Worse, it wasn't alone. Its dark bodywork reflected the spinning blue lights of two police patrol cars parked either side of it.

'This is fucking bad,' Berger breathed, gripping the wheel.

'Thought you said the cops never came out this way,' said Godard. 'That was the whole fucking *point* of this spot, wasn't it?'

'Told you,' Naudon repeated from the back.

'How did –'

'Well, boys, the boss isn't going to be pleased.'

'Better call him.'

'I'm not doing it. *You* do it.'

The police officers combed the scene, torch beams darting this way and that like searchlights while radios popped and fizzled in the background. 'Eh, Jean-Paul,' said one, holding up a cracked Citroën grille badge he'd found lying in the dirt. 'Bits of headlamp glass all over the place here,' he added.

'Train driver mentioned a Citroën 2CV,' replied another.

'Where'd it go?'

'Not far, that's for sure. Coolant everywhere.'

Two more officers were casting pools of torch-light around the inside of the limo. One of them spotted a small shiny object lying in the rear footwell. He took a ballpoint pen out of his pocket and used it to pick up the empty cartridge case. 'Hello, what's this? Nine-mil shell case.' He sniffed at it, getting the scent of cordite. 'Recently fired.'

'Bag that.'

Another cop had found something, a business

card lying on the seat. squinted at it in the glow of his Maglite. 'Some foreign name.'

'What d'you reckon happened here?'

'Who knows?'

Twenty minutes later the police tow-truck arrived. By the swirl of blue and orange lights the battered Mercedes was hitched up and taken away, a police car in front and another bringing up the rear. The railway tracks were left in silent darkness.

CHAPTER 16

Rome

The two men who had come for Giuseppe Ferraro at his home that night and driven him out of the city now escorted him up the grand stairway to the dome of the Renaissance villa. They had barely said a word to him all the way. They hadn't needed to – Ferraro knew what this was about, and why the archbishop had sent for him. His knees were a little weak as he was shown into the dome and the door shut behind him. The enormous room was unlit apart from the starlight and moonbeams that streamed in through the many windows around its circumference.

Massimiliano Usberti was standing at a desk at the far end. He slowly turned to face Ferraro.

'Archbishop, I can explain.' Ferraro had been working on his story ever since the call had come through from Paris earlier that evening. He'd been expecting that Usberti would summon him to the villa – just not this soon. He began blurting out his excuses. He'd hired idiots who had let him down. It wasn't his fault that the Englishman had got away. He was sorry, so sorry, and it wouldn't happen again.

Usberti walked towards him across the room. He raised his hand in a gesture that silenced Ferraro's frantic stream of apologies and excuses. 'Giuseppe, Giuseppe – you do not need to explain,' he said with a smile, putting his arm around the younger man's shoulders. 'We are all human. We all make mistakes. God forgives.'

Ferraro was amazed. This wasn't the reception he'd expected. The archbishop led him over to a moonlit window. 'What a glorious night,' he murmured. 'Do you not think so, my friend?'

'. . . Yes, Archbishop, it is beautiful.'

'Does it not make one feel so happy to be alive?'

'It does, Archbishop.'

'It is a privilege to live on God's earth.'

They stood looking out of the window at the inky-black night sky. The stars were out in their millions, the moon was crystal-sharp and the Milky Way galaxy arched glittering and pearly over the Roman hills.

After a few minutes, Ferraro asked, 'Archbishop, may I have your permission to leave now?'

Usberti patted him on the shoulder. 'Of course. But before you go, I would like to introduce you to a good friend of mine.'

'I am honoured, Archbishop.'

'I called you here so that you could meet him. His name is Franco Bozza.'

Ferraro almost collapsed with shock at the words.

'Bozza! The Inquisitor?' Suddenly his heart was thudding at the base of his throat, his mouth was dry and he felt sick.

'I see you have heard of my friend before,' Usberti said. 'He is going to take care of you now.'

'What? But Archbishop, I . . .' Ferraro fell on his knees. 'I implore you . . .'

'He awaits you downstairs,' Usberti replied, pressing a buzzer on his desk. As Ferraro was dragged away screaming by the two men who had brought him, the archbishop crossed himself and muttered a prayer in Latin for the man's soul. '*In nomine patris et filii et spiritus sancti, ego te absolvo . . .*'

CHAPTER 17

'So where to now?' asked Roberta as the taxi arrived to pick them up from the bar.

'Well, you're going home for a start,' Ben replied.

'Are you kidding? I'm not going back there.'

'What's your assistant's address?'

'What do you want that for?' she asked, getting into the car.

'I want to ask him a few questions.'

'And you think I'm not coming along too? I have a few questions I'd like to ask that son of a bitch.'

'You should stay out of this,' he said to her. He took out his wallet.

'What are you doing?' she asked as he counted out banknotes.

He held out the money, offering it to her. 'There's enough here for you to check in at a decent hotel tonight and fly back to the States in the morning. Take it.'

She looked down at the notes, then shook her head and pushed them away. 'Listen, pal, I'm just as involved in this as you are. I want to find out what the hell's going on. And don't get any ideas

115

about giving me the slip.' Before he could reply she slid forward across the car seat and told the taxi driver an address in the tenth arrondissement of Paris. The driver muttered something under his breath and drove off.

As they arrived at Michel's place, they found the street illuminated with blue flashing lights. An ambulance and a number of police cars were parked outside the apartment building, and crowds were milling about the entrance. Ben asked the taxi driver to wait, and he and Roberta pushed through the crowd.

People from nearby bars had gathered in groups on the pavement, watching, pointing, covering their mouths in shock. A team of paramedics were pushing a stretcher on a trolley from the entrance to Michel's building. They weren't in a hurry. The body on the stretcher was draped from head to foot in a white sheet. Where the sheet lay over the figure's face, a huge bloody stain seeped through the cloth. They loaded the stretcher into the back of the ambulance and shut the doors.

'What happened here?' Ben asked a gendarme.

'Suicide,' the cop replied tersely. 'A neighbour heard the shot.'

'Was it a young guy called Michel Zardi?' Roberta asked. Somehow she just knew.

'You knew him?' said the policeman unemotionally. 'Go through, mademoiselle. The chief might want to speak to you.'

Roberta headed towards the entrance. Ben took her wrist. 'Let's get away from here,' he warned. 'There's nothing you can do.'

She tore her arm out of his grasp. 'I want to know,' she retorted, and she pressed on ahead of him, through the police tape and in the door. He followed, cursing. A crowd of police blocked his way. 'What a mess,' one officer was saying to another. 'Even the guy's own mother wouldn't recognize him. Blew his whole face right off.'

Amongst the uniformed officers, a small fat lieutenant in plain clothes was giving orders. He glared at Roberta as she approached him. 'You from the press? Piss off, nothing to see here.'

'Are you the officer in charge?' she demanded. 'I'm Dr Roberta Ryder, Michel is my–' She checked herself. '*Was* my employee. It was his body they just took out of here, wasn't it?'

'We were just passing by,' Ben cut in, catching up with her. In English he muttered in her ear, 'Let's keep this short and simple, OK?'

'And your name, monsieur?' the plain-clothes policeman asked, swivelling his dour gaze towards him.

Ben hesitated. If he gave a false name, Roberta's reaction would give him away.

'His name's Ben Hope,' she filled in for him, and he winced inwardly. 'Listen,' she went on in a loud, adamant voice, looking the lieutenant in the eye. 'Michel didn't kill himself. He's been murdered.'

'Madame sees murders everywhere,' someone said behind them, and they turned. Roberta's heart sank as she recognized the man coming into the room. It was the young police inspector from earlier that day.

'Inspecteur Luc Simon,' he said, striding towards them. He fixed Roberta with his green eyes. 'I've warned you about this already. Stop wasting our time. This is a simple suicide. We found a note . . . What are you doing here, anyway?'

'What note?' she asked suspiciously.

Simon held up a small clear plastic bag. Inside, curled against the cellophane, was a small sheet of notepaper with a few lines of handwriting on it. Simon gazed at it. 'He says it wasn't worth it any longer. Stress, depression, debts, the usual problems. We see this all the time.'

'*Eh oui,*' said the lieutenant, with a philosophical shake of the head. '*La vie, c'est de la merde.*'

'Shut up, Rigault,' Simon growled at him. 'Madame, I asked you a question. What are you doing here? That's twice today, when I get called out on a false alarm homicide, *you* turn up.'

'Let me see that bullshit note,' she snapped. 'He never wrote that.'

'I'm sorry,' Ben said to Simon, jerking Roberta's arm and cutting in before she said too much. 'My fiancée's upset. We're leaving now.' He pulled her aside, leaving the inspector standing there staring keenly at them as assistants scuttled around him.

'*Your fiancée?*' she hissed at him. 'What's that supposed to mean? And let go of my arm, you're hurting.'

'Shut up. You don't want to spend the next ten hours being grilled by the police, and neither do I.'

'It's not suicide,' she insisted.

'I know,' he nodded. 'Now listen to me. We've only got a few seconds. Is anything in here different, moved, changed in any way?'

'Someone's been through the place.' She motioned towards his desk and tried not to look at the huge vertical splatter of blood on the wall and ceiling. The desk was empty, Michel's computer gone.

'Rigault, get these people out of here! Come on, let's move!' Simon was shouting from across the room, pointing at them.

'We've seen enough,' Ben said. 'Time to go.' He led her towards the door, but Simon intercepted them. 'I hope you're not thinking of leaving town, Dr Ryder? I might want to talk to you again.'

As they left the apartment, Simon watched them with a frown. Rigault gave him a knowing look and tapped his head with his finger. 'Crazy Americans. They see too many of their Hollywood movies.'

Simon nodded pensively. 'Maybe.'

CHAPTER 18

Montpellier, South of France

'Marc, pass me the screwdriver. Marc . . . Marc? Where are you, you dozy little shit?' The electrician got down from his ladder, leaving loose wires hanging, glaring around him. 'That little sod'll never learn anything.' Where had he disappeared off to now?

The kid was a liability. He wished he'd never given him a job. Natalie, his sister-in-law, doted on her son, couldn't see that he was just a loser like his father.

'Uncle Richard, look at this.' The apprentice's excited voice echoed up the narrow concrete corridor. The older man put down his tools, wiped his hands on his overalls and followed the sound. At the end of the shadowy corridor was a dark alcove. A steel door was hanging open. Stone steps led down into a black space. Richard peered down. 'What the hell are you doing in there?'

'You've got to see this,' the kid's voice echoed from inside. 'It's weird.'

Richard sighed and clumped down the steps.

He found himself in a huge, empty cellar. Stone columns held up the floor above. 'So it's a bloody cellar. Come on out, you're not supposed to be in here. Stop wasting time.'

'Yeah, but look.' Marc shone his torch and Richard saw steel bars glinting in the darkness. Cages. Rings bolted to the wall. Metal tables.

'Come on, beat it out of here.'

'So what is it?'

'I dunno. Kennels for dogs – who gives a shit?'

'Nobody keeps dogs in a cellar . . .' Marc's nostrils twitched at the smell of strong disinfectant. He shone his torch around and saw where the smell was coming from, a concrete sluice cut into the floor leading to a wide drain cover.

'Move it, kid,' Richard grumbled. 'I'm going to be late for the next job – you're holding me up.'

'Wait a minute,' Marc said. He stepped over to the glinting thing he'd seen in the shadows and picked it up off the floor. He studied it in the palm of his hand, wondering what it meant.

Richard strode over to the lad, grabbed him by the arm and pulled him towards the steps. 'Look,' he warned. 'I've been in this job since before you were born. One thing I've learned, if you want to stay in work you mind your own business and keep your mouth *shut*. OK?'

'OK,' the boy mumbled. 'But –'

'No buts. Now come and help me with this bloody light.'

CHAPTER 19

Paris

For the last four years, Ben had worked alone. He relished the freedom it gave him, the ability to sleep where he wanted, to move as fast and as far and as light as possible, to slip in and out of places alone and inconspicuous. Most important of all, working alone meant that he was responsible for himself and himself only.

But now he was lumbered with this woman, and he was breaking all his own rules.

He took a convoluted route back to the safehouse. Roberta's puzzled expression deepened as he led her down the cobbled alleyway, through the underground parking lot, and up the back stairway to the armoured door of his hidden apartment.

'You live here?'

'Home sweet home.' He locked the door behind them and punched in the code for the alarm system. He flipped on the lights and she gazed around the apartment. 'What is this, minimalist neo-Spartan?'

'You want a coffee? Bite to eat?'

'Coffee's good.'

Ben went into the kitchenette and lit the gas ring under his little percolator. After a few minutes it bubbled up and he served the coffee with hot milk out of a saucepan. He opened a tin of cassoulet, heated it up and dumped the steaming sausage-and-ham stew onto a couple of plates. He still had half a dozen bottles of red table wine. He grabbed one and pulled the cork.

'You should eat something,' he said as she ignored her plate.

'I'm not hungry.'

'OK.' He finished his own plate, then pulled hers across the table and wolfed down the last of the stew with gulps of wine. As he ate, he could see she was shaking, her head in her hands. He got up and put a blanket around her shoulders. She sat in silence for a few minutes. 'I can't stop thinking about Michel,' she whispered.

'He wasn't your friend,' he reminded her.

'Yeah, I know, but still . . .' She sobbed, wiped her eyes and smiled weakly. 'Pretty stupid.'

'No, not stupid. You have compassion.'

'You say that as though it were a rare thing.'

'It is a rare thing.'

'Do you have any?'

'No.' He poured the last of the wine into his glass. 'I don't.' He looked at his watch. 'It's late. I've got work to do in the morning.' He drained his glass, jumped up from his chair, and grabbed a pile of blankets and an armchair cushion. He chucked them on the floor.

'What're you doing?'

'Making up a bed for you.'

'Call that a bed?'

'Well, you could have had the Ritz if you'd wanted. I did offer, remember?' He saw her look. 'It's only a one-bedroom flat,' he added.

'So you make your guests sleep on the floor?'

'If it's any consolation, you're the first guest I've had up here. Now, can I have your bag, please?'

'What?'

'Give me your bag,' he repeated. He snatched it from her and began rifling through it.

'What the hell are you doing?' She tried to grab it back from him. He pushed her away. 'I'll have this,' he said, pocketing her phone. 'The rest you can keep.'

'Why are you taking my phone off me?'

'Why do you think? I don't want you making any calls from here behind my back.'

'Boy, you really have a *big* problem with trust.'

Roberta couldn't sleep well that night, couldn't shut out the memory of the day's events. What had started out like any other day had turned her whole world upside-down. Maybe she was crazy, hanging on here when she could have taken the money and been on a plane home first thing in the morning.

And what about this Ben Hope? Here she was, locked in a hidden apartment with a guy she'd only met that day and barely knew. Who was he?

He was attractive, and he had that winning smile. But there was that coldness, too, the way he could look at her with those pale blue eyes and she couldn't tell what he was thinking.

There was another thought that wouldn't go away. It was the knowledge that someone was interested in her research. Very interested indeed. Interested enough to kill for it. That meant several things. It meant that someone was threatened by what she'd been discovering. Which meant it had real value. She was on the right track, and even if it was a dangerous position she was in, she couldn't help feeling a tingle of excitement. She had to know more.

She broke off from her thoughts and lifted her head off the cushion, tensed and listening. A voice. She struggled to get her bearings in the dark, unfamiliar room. After a few seconds she orientated herself and it dawned on her that the sound was coming from behind the bedroom door. It was Ben's voice. She couldn't make out what he was saying. His voice grew louder, protesting against something. Was he on the phone? She got up from her makeshift bed and crept to his door in the dim moonlight. She pressed her ear softly to the door, careful not to make a noise, and listened.

He wasn't talking in there, he was *moaning* – and his voice sounded pained, tortured. He muttered something she didn't catch, and then he called out more loudly. She was about to open the door when she realized he was dreaming. No, not a dream. A nightmare.

'Ruth! Don't go! No! No! Don't leave me!' His cries diminished back into a low moan, and then as she stood there in the dark she listened to him for a long time sobbing like a child.

CHAPTER 20

Ever since his impoverished childhood in rural Sardinia, Franco Bozza had enjoyed giving pain. His first victims had been insects and worms, and as a young boy he'd spent many contented hours developing increasingly elaborate ways of slowly dissecting them and watching them writhe and die. Before the age of eight, Franco had progressed to practising his skills on small birds and mammals. Some fledglings in a nest suffered first. Later, local dogs started to disappear. As Franco progressed through his teens he grew into a master torturer and an expert in inflicting agony. He loved it. It was the thing that made him feel most alive.

By the time he'd left school at the age of thirteen he'd become almost equally fascinated with Catholicism. He was entranced by the crueller images of Christian tradition – the crown of thorns, the bleeding stigmata of Christ, the way the nails had been hammered through the hands and feet into the cross. Franco polished the basic literacy skills he'd learned in school just so he could read about the deliciously gruesome history of the Church. One day he came across an old book that described the persecution of heretics by the medieval Inquisition. He read how, after the conquest of a Cathar stronghold in the year 1210, the commander of the Church forces had ordered that a hundred Cathar heretics have their ears, noses and lips cut off, their eyes gouged out, and be paraded before the ramparts of other heretic castles as an example. The boy was deeply inspired by such macabre genius, and he would lie awake at night wishing he could somehow have taken part in it.

Franco fell in love with religious art, and would walk miles to the nearest town to visit the library and drool over historic prints showing grisly images of religious oppression. His favourite painting was *The Hay Wagon* by Hieronymus Bosch in the 1480s, showing horrible tortures at the hands of demons, bodies pierced by spears and blades, and – most exciting of all – a nude woman. It wasn't her nudity in itself that provoked such choking feelings of lust in him. Her arms were tied behind her back, and all that covered her nakedness was a black toad clapped to her genitals. She was a witch. She would be burnt. This was what generated such intense, almost frantic, excitement in him.

Franco learned about the historical backdrop to Bosch's painting, the furious misogyny of the Catholic Church during the fifteenth century when Pope Innocent VIII had issued his Witch

Bull, the document that gave the Vatican's seal of approval to the torture and burning of women suspected, however vaguely, of being in league with the Devil. Franco went on from there to discover the book known as the *Malleus Malificarum*, the 'Witches' Hammer', the official Inquisition manual of torture and sadism for those who served God by drenching themselves in heretic blood. It instilled in young Franco the same violent horror of female sexuality that had permeated medieval Christian faith. A woman who indulged in sex, who enjoyed it, didn't just lie there, *must* be the Devil's bride. Which meant she had to die. In a horrible way. That was the part he liked best.

Franco became an expert on the entire bloody past of the Catholic Inquisition and the Church that had spawned it. While others admired the beautiful artwork by Botticelli and Michelangelo in the Vatican's Sistine Chapel for its own sake, Franco revelled in the fact that while these works of art were being commissioned by the Church, a quarter million women across Europe were being put to the stake with the Pope's blessing. The more he learned, the more he came to appreciate that to subscribe to the Catholic faith and its legacy was, tacitly or otherwise, to espouse centuries of systematic and unrestrained mass murder, war, oppression, torture and corruption. He'd found his spiritual calling, and he rejoiced in it.

Eventually, in 1977, it came time for Franco to marry his intended, the daughter of the local gunsmith. He reluctantly agreed to the marriage to Maria, to please his parents.

On his wedding night, he discovered that he was completely impotent. At the time, this caused him no concern. He'd never cared that he was still a virgin, because he already knew that the only thing that could excite him was when he had his knife and could inflict pain. That was what drew him and made him feel powerful. Female flesh had no allure for him.

But as weeks turned into months and he continued to show no interest in her sexually, Maria started taunting him. One night she pushed him too far. 'I'm going out to find a real man with balls,' she screamed at him. 'And then everyone will know that my husband is nothing but a useless *castrato*.'

Franco was already powerful and muscular at the age of twenty. Enraged, he grabbed her by the hair and dragged her up to the bedroom where he threw her brutally down on the bed, knocked her semi-conscious and took a knife to her flesh.

That had been the night that Franco had made a life-changing discovery, that a woman's body could excite him after all. He didn't touch her – only the steel touched her. He left Maria tied to the bed, mutilated and permanently disfigured.

He fled the village in the middle of the night. Maria's father and brothers came after him, vowing revenge.

Franco had never ventured more than a few miles from his village before, and he was soon lost, penniless and hungry in the verdant Sardinian countryside. It was outside a bar near Cagliari, begging for food, that Maria's elder brother Salvatore found him one night. Salvatore crept up on the unsuspecting Franco from behind and slashed his throat with his knife.

A weaker man would have collapsed and died, let himself be butchered. Franco was half starved and drenched in the blood that spurted from the gash in his neck. But the pain and the smell of the blood gave him new strength, raw energy. He stayed on his feet like a wounded animal. Instead of running, he attacked. If Salvatore had brought a gun that night, it would have been different. But Franco took the knife from him, overpowered him and cut his liver out. Slowly.

It was the first time he'd killed a man, but it wouldn't be the last. He robbed Salvatore's body of money, and fled to the coast where he took the ferry to the Italian mainland. His cut throat healed, but he would speak in a strangled whisper for the rest of his life.

With the ensuing vendetta against him, Franco Bozza was exiled from Sardinia. He travelled around southern Italy, bumming from job to job.

But his lust for inflicting pain was never far away, and before the age of twenty-four his talents were being put to good use by Mafia hoods who employed him to press information out of their captured enemies. Franco Bozza was a natural, and his fearsome reputation soon spread through the criminal underworld as an exceptionally callous and cold-hearted torturer. When it came to prolonging life and maximizing agony, he was the undisputed maestro.

When Bozza – or the Inquisitor, as he now styled himself – wasn't performing his art on some hapless criminal he'd stalk the streets at night and prey on prostitutes, luring them to their death with his whispering voice. Their pitiful remains began to appear in dingy hotel rooms all over southern Italy. Rumours spread of a 'monster', a maniac who feasted on pain and death the way a vampire feasted on blood. But the Inquisitor always covered his tracks. His police record was as virginal as his sexuality.

One day in 1997 Franco Bozza got an unexpected phone call – not from the usual underworld kingpin or Mafia boss, but from a Vatican bishop.

It was through the shadows of the underworld that Massimiliano Usberti had heard of this Inquisitor. The man's notorious religious zeal, his absolute devotion to God and his unflinching will to punish the wicked, were just the qualities Usberti wanted for his new organization. When Bozza heard what his role was to be, he seized the opportunity right away. It was perfect for him.

The organization was called *Gladius Domini*. The Sword of God.

Franco Bozza had just become its blade.

CHAPTER 21

Paris

'Hello – put me through to Monsieur Loriot, please?'

'He is away on business at the moment, sir,' replied the secretary. 'He won't be back until December.'

'But I got a call from him just yesterday.'

'I'm afraid that isn't possible,' the secretary said testily. 'He's been in America for a month.'

'Sorry to bother you,' Ben said. 'Obviously I've been misinformed. Could you tell me if Monsieur Loriot is still living at the Villa Margaux in Brignancourt?'

'Brignancourt? No, Monsieur Loriot lives here in Paris. I think you must have the wrong number. Good day.' The line went dead.

It was clear now. Loriot hadn't called him at all – the train hit had been someone else's idea. Just as he'd thought. It was too improbable.

He sat and smoked, thinking about it. The evidence pointed in a new direction. He'd called Loriot's office from Roberta's place. Michel Zardi had been

134

in the room with him, listened in, taken his number. He'd gone straight out through the door soon afterwards – to buy fish for his cat. *Yeah, and to pass the number on to his cronies, too.* So they'd called him back pretending to be Loriot. It was a risk – what if the real Loriot had called back too? Maybe they'd checked first that he was out of town.

It wasn't a perfect plan, but it had been good enough. Ben had let himself get picked up like an apple off a tree, and only Roberta's chance intervention had saved him from being smeared over a hundred metres of railway line. Without her, they'd still be spooning him out of the cracks in the sleepers.

Was he slipping? This couldn't happen again.

It also meant that the same people who were after Roberta Ryder were after him too. They meant business, and that, like it or not, drew Ben and her together.

He'd been awake since dawn and had been pondering all morning what to do with her. The day before, he'd been thinking that he'd have to ditch her, pay her off, force her to return to the States. But maybe he'd been wrong. She might be able to help him. She wanted to find out what was going on, and so did he. And he sensed that for the moment she wanted to stick by him, partly out of fear, partly out of fierce curiosity. But that wouldn't last if he went on keeping her in the dark, freezing her out, not trusting her.

He sat on his bed and thought about it until he heard her moving about in the next room. He stood up and pushed open the door. She was stretching and yawning, the rumpled bedclothes heaped up on the floor at her feet. Her hair was tousled.

'I'm making coffee, and then I'm getting out of here,' he said. 'The door's open. You're free to go.'

She looked at him, said nothing.

'Time to decide,' he said. 'Are you staying or leaving?'

'If I stay, I have to stay with you.'

He nodded. 'We have a lot of figuring out to do. And we need to do this my way.'

'Are we trusting one another now?'

'I suppose we are,' he said.

'I'm staying.'

He walked along the row of used cars, casting his eye over each one in turn. Something quick and practical. Not too ostentatious, not too distinctive. 'What about this one?' he asked, pointing.

The mechanic wiped his hands on his overall, leaving parallel oil smears down the blue cloth. 'She is one year old, perfect condition. How you paying?'

Ben patted his pocket. 'Cash all right?'

Ten minutes later Ben was gunning the silver Peugeot 206 Sport along Avenue de Gravelle towards the main Paris ring-road.

'Well, for a journalist you sure seem to throw a

lot of money around, Ben,' Roberta said next to him.

'OK, time for the truth. I'm not a journalist,' he confessed, slowing down for the heavy traffic on the approach to the Périphérique.

'Ha. Knew it.' She clapped her hands. 'Am I allowed to know what you *do* do, Mr Benedict Hope? That your real name, by the way?'

'It's my real name.'

'It's a nice name.'

'Too nice for a guy like me?'

She smiled. 'I didn't say that.'

'As for what I do,' he said, 'I suppose you could say I'm a seeker.' He filtered through the traffic, waited for a gap, and the acceleration of the sporty little car pressed them back in their seats as its fruity engine note rose to a pleasing pitch.

'A seeker of what? Trouble?'

'Well, yes, sometimes I'm a seeker of trouble,' he said, allowing a dry smile. 'But I wasn't expecting as much trouble this time.'

'So what are you seeking? And why come to me?'

'You really want to know?'

'I really want to know.'

'I'm trying to find the alchemist Fulcanelli.'

She arched an eyebrow. '*Riiight* . . . Uh-huh. Go on.'

'Well, what I'm really looking for is a manuscript he was supposed to have had, or written – I don't know much about it.'

'The Fulcanelli manuscript – *that* old myth.'

'You've heard of it?'

'Sure, I've *heard* of it. But you hear a lot of things in this business.'

'You don't think it exists.'

She shrugged. 'Who knows? It's like the holy grail of alchemy. Some say it does, some say it doesn't, nobody knows what it is or what's in it, or even if it really exists. What do you want with it, anyway? You don't seem to me like the sort who goes for all this stuff.'

'What sort's that?'

She snorted. 'You know what one of the biggest problems with alchemy is? The people who are drawn to it. I never met one yet who wasn't some kind of fruitcake.'

'That's the first compliment you've paid me.'

'Don't take it to heart. Anyway, you didn't answer the question.'

He paused. 'It's not for me. I'm working for a client.'

'And this client believes the manuscript can help with some kind of illness, right? That's why you were so interested in my research. You're looking for some kind of medicinal cure for someone. The client's sick?'

'Let's just say he's pretty desperate for it.'

'Boy, he must be.'

'I was wondering if your fly elixir could be of any use to him.'

'I've told you. It's not ready yet. And I wouldn't

even try it on a human being. It would be totally unethical. Not to mention practising medicine without a licence. I'm in enough shit as it is, apparently.'

He shrugged.

'So, Ben, are you going to tell me where we're going in this fancy new toy of yours?'

'Does the name Jacques Clément mean anything to you?' he asked.

She nodded. 'He was Fulcanelli's apprentice back in the twenties.' She shot him a questioning look. 'Why?'

'The story goes, Fulcanelli passed on certain documents to Clément before he disappeared,' he filled in. She was waiting for more, so he went on. 'Anyhow, that was back in 1926. Clément's dead now, died a long time ago. But I want to know more about whatever it was that Fulcanelli gave him.'

'How can you find out?'

'One of the first things I did when I got to Paris three days ago was to check out any surviving family. I thought they might be able to help.'

'And?'

'I traced his son, André. Rich banker, retired. He wasn't very forthcoming. As a matter of fact, as soon as I mentioned Fulcanelli he and his wife basically told me to piss off.'

'That's what happens when you mention alchemy to anyone,' she said. 'Join the club.'

'Anyway, I didn't think I'd hear from them again,'

he went on. 'But this morning, while you were sleeping, I had a call.'

'From them?'

'From their son, Pierre. We had an interesting talk. It turns out there were two brothers, André and Gaston. André was the successful one, and Gaston was the black sheep of the family. Gaston wanted to carry on his father's work, which André hated, saw it as witchcraft.'

'That figures.'

'And they basically disowned Gaston. Family embarrassment. They won't have anything to do with him any longer.'

'Gaston's still alive?'

'Apparently so. He lives a few kilometres away, on an old farm.'

She settled back in her seat. 'And that's where we're headed?'

'Don't get too excited. He's probably some kind of oddball . . . what did you call them?'

'Fruitcakes. Technical term.'

'I'll make a note of it.'

'So you think Gaston Clément might still have those papers, or whatever it was that Fulcanelli passed on to his father?'

'It's worth a try.'

'Anyway, I'm sure this is all very interesting,' she said. 'But I thought we were trying to find out what the fuck's going on and why someone's trying to kill us?'

He shot her a glance. 'I haven't finished yet.

There's one other thing Pierre Clément told me this morning. I wasn't the last person to make contact with his father asking questions about Fulcanelli. He said that three men turned up there a couple of days ago asking the same questions, and asking about me too. Somehow all this is connected – you, me, Michel, the people after us, and the manuscript.'

'But how?' She shook her head in confusion.

'I don't know how.'

The question was, he thought to himself, had the three men found out about Gaston Clément? He could be walking into another trap.

In another hour or so they'd reached the derelict farm where Pierre Clément had said his uncle lived. They pulled up in a wooded layby a few hundred metres up the road. 'This is the place,' Ben said, checking the rough map he'd written from the directions.

Grey clouds overhead were threatening rain as they walked towards the farm. Without letting her see, he quietly popped open the press-stud on his holster's retaining strap and kept his hand hovering near his chest as they reached the cobbled yard. There were deserted, decaying farm buildings on both sides. A tall, dilapidated wooden barn sat behind a wrecked cowshed. Broken windows were nailed over with planks. A slow curl of smoke was rising from a blackened metal chimney.

Ben looked around him cautiously, ready for trouble. There was nobody else about.

The barn seemed empty. Inside, the air was thick and smoky and laden with an unpleasant reek of dirt and strange smouldering substances. The building was one big room, dimly lit by milky rays of sunlight that shone through the cracks in the planking and the few dusty window-panes. Twittering birds were flying in and out of a hole high up in the gable end. At one side of the barn a raised platform on rough wooden poles supported a ragged armchair, a table with an old TV and a bed heaped with dirty blankets. At the other side was a huge sooty furnace whose black iron door hung open a few inches, exuding a stream of dark smoke and a pungent smell. The furnace was surrounded by makeshift tables covered in books, papers, metal and glass containers connected with rubber or Perspex tubing. Strange liquids simmered over Bunsen burners running from gas bottles and gave off foul vapours. Piled up in every shadowy corner were heaps of junk, old crates, broken containers, rows of empty bottles.

'What a shit-pit,' Roberta breathed.

'At least it's not full of flies.'

'Ha ha.' She smirked at him. '*Jerk,*' she added under her breath.

Ben went over to one of the tables, where something had caught his eye. It was a faded old manuscript weighted down at the corners by pieces of quartz crystal. He picked it up and it sprang into a roll, throwing up a cloud of dust particles that caught the ray of light from the boarded window nearby. He brought the manuscript into the path of the sunbeam, gently unfurling it to read the spidery script.

If the herb ch-sheng can make one live longer
Surely this elixir is worth taking into one's body?
Gold by its nature cannot decay or perish
And is of all things the most precious.
If the alchemist creates this elixir
The duration of his life will become everlasting
Hairs that were white now all return to black
Teeth that had fallen will regrow
The old dotard is once more a lusty youth
The crone is once more a maiden
He whose form has changed escapes the perils of life.

'Found something?' she asked, peering over his shoulder.

'I don't know. Could be interesting, maybe.'

'Let me see?' She ran her eyes down the scroll. Ben searched the table for more like it, but all he could find among the heaped rolls and dog-eared piles of dirty paper were abstruse diagrams, charts and lists of symbols. He sighed. 'Do *you* understand any of this stuff?'

'Um, Ben?'

He blew some dust off an old book. 'What?' he mumbled, only half-listening to her.

She nudged him. 'We've got company.'

CHAPTER 22

Ben's hand flew to his gun. But when he turned and saw the man approaching them, he let his arm drop to his side.

The old man's eyes flashed wildly behind long, straggly grey hair that hung down to merge with his bush of a beard. He hobbled rapidly towards them with a stick, boots dragging on the concrete floor.

'Put that down!' he shouted harshly, waving a bony finger at Roberta. 'Don't touch that!'

She gingerly replaced the scroll on the table, where it sprang back into a tight curl. The old man grabbed it, clutching it furiously to his chest. He was wearing an ancient, filthy greatcoat that hung from him in tatters. His breathing was laboured, wheezing. 'Who are you?' he demanded, baring blackened teeth. 'What are you doing in my home?'

Roberta stared at him. He looked as though he'd spent the last thirty years or so living rough under the bridges of Paris. *Jesus,* she thought. *These are the guys I'm trying to convince the world to take seriously?*

144

'We're looking for Monsieur Gaston Clément,' Ben said. 'I'm sorry, the door was open.'

'Who are you?' the old man repeated. 'Police? Leave me alone. Fuck off.' He retreated towards the shadows, clutching the rolled-up paper to him and waving his stick at them.

'We're not the police. We'd just like to ask you a few questions.'

'I'm Gaston Clément, what do you want from me?' the old man wheezed. Suddenly his knees seemed to give way under him, and he stumbled, dropping the scroll and his walking-stick. Ben picked him up and helped him to a chair. He knelt beside the old alchemist as he hacked and coughed into a handkerchief.

'My name's Benedict Hope, and I'm looking for something. A manuscript written by Fulcanelli . . . listen, should I call a doctor for you? You don't look well.'

Clément ended his coughing fit and sat panting for a minute, wiping his mouth. His hands were bony and arthritic, blue veins bulging through translucent pale skin. 'I'm all right,' he croaked. Slowly his grey head turned to look at Ben. 'You said Fulcanelli?'

'He was your father's teacher, isn't that right?'

'Yes, he gave great wisdom to my father,' Clément murmured. He sat back, as though thinking. For a minute he broke off into a rambling mutter, seeming confused and far away.

Ben picked up the fallen stick and propped it

up by the old man's chair. He unfurled the scroll that had dropped to the floor. 'I don't suppose . . .'

Clément seemed to come back to life when he saw the scroll in Ben's hands. A skinny arm shot out and snatched it away. 'Give that back to me.'

'What is that?'

'What do you care? It is *The Secret of Everlasting Life*. Chinese, second century. It is priceless.' Clément's old eyes focused more clearly on Ben. He staggered to his feet, pointing a trembling finger. 'What do you want from me?' he quavered. 'More fucking foreigners coming to steal!' He grabbed his stick.

'No, monsieur, we aren't thieves,' Ben assured him. 'We just want information.'

Clément spat. 'Information? *Information* – that's what that *salaud* Klaus Rheinfeld said to me.' He slammed the stick on the table, making papers fly. 'That filthy thieving little Kraut!' He turned to them. 'Now you get out of here,' he shouted at them, spit frothing from the corners of his mouth. He reached out to a rack of equipment and grabbed a test-tube filled with a steaming green liquid, waving it at them threateningly. But then his knees went again and he stumbled and fell. The test-tube smashed on the floor and the green liquid spattered everywhere.

They got old Clément back on his feet and helped him up the steps of the raised platform where he had his living-quarters. He sat down on the edge of the bed, looking frail and sick. Roberta brought him a drink of water. After a while he calmed down and seemed more willing to speak to them.

'You can trust me,' Ben told him earnestly. 'I don't want to steal from you. I'll pay you money if you help me. Agreed?'

Clément nodded, sipping his water.

'Good. Now, listen carefully. Fulcanelli gave your father, Jacques Clément, certain documents before his disappearance in 1926. I need to know whether your father might have had possession of some kind of alchemical manuscript given to him by his teacher.'

The old man shook his head. 'My father had many papers. He destroyed a lot of them before he died.' His face twisted in anger. 'Of the ones he left behind, most were stolen from me.'

'By the man Rheinfeld you mentioned?' Ben asked. 'Who was he?'

Clément's wrinkled cheeks flushed red. 'Klaus Rheinfeld,' he said in a voice full of hatred. 'My assistant. He came here to learn the secrets of alchemy. One day he arrives, that miserable scrawny shit, with nothing but the stinking shirt on his back. I helped him, taught him, fed him!' The alchemist's rage was making him breathless. 'I trusted him. But he betrayed me. I have not seen him for ten years.'

'You're saying that Klaus Rheinfeld stole your father's important documents?'

'And the gold cross too.'

'A gold cross?'

'Yes, very old and beautiful. Discovered by Fulcanelli, many years ago.' Clément broke off, coughing and spluttering. 'It was the key to great knowledge. Fulcanelli passed the cross to my father just before he disappeared.'

'Why did Fulcanelli disappear?' Ben asked.

Clément shot Ben a dark look. 'Like me, he was betrayed.'

'Who betrayed him?'

'Someone he trusted.' Clément's shrivelled lips twisted into a mysterious smile. He reached under his bed and, clutching it with reverential care, brought out an old book. Bound in scuffed blue leather, it looked as though mice had been nibbling at it for decades. 'It is all in here.'

'What's that?' Ben asked, peering at the book.

'My father's master tells his story in these pages,' Clément replied. 'This was his private Journal, the only thing Rheinfeld did not steal from me.'

Ben and Roberta exchanged glances. 'Can I see it?' he asked Clément.

The alchemist tentatively opened the cover for Ben to see, holding it close to him. Ben caught a glimpse of old-fashioned handwriting. 'This was definitely Fulcanelli's own writings?'

'Of course,' the old man muttered, and showed him the signature on the inner cover.

'Monsieur, I would like to buy this book from you.'

Clément snorted. 'Not for sale.'

Ben thought for a few moments. 'What about

Klaus Rheinfeld?' he asked. 'Do you know where he is now?'

The old man clenched his fist. 'Burning in hell where he belongs, I hope.'

'You mean he's dead?'

But Clément was off in one of his muttering fits again.

'Is he dead?' Ben repeated.

The alchemist's eyes were far away. Ben waved his hand in front of them.

'I don't think you're going to get much more out of him, Ben,' Roberta said.

Ben nodded. He put a hand on the old man's shoulder and softly shook him to his senses. 'Monsieur Clément, listen carefully and remember this. You have to leave here for a while.'

The old man's eyes slid back into focus. 'Why?' he croaked.

'Because there are some men who might come here. Not nice men, you don't want to meet them, you understand? They've been asking questions at your brother's house and they may know where to find you. I'm afraid they might want to hurt you. So I want you to take this.' Ben took out a thick wad of banknotes.

Clément's eyes opened wide when he saw how much there was. 'What is that for?' he quavered.

'It's to pay for you to leave here for a while,' Ben told him. 'Get yourself some new clothes, go to a doctor if you need one. Take a train as far away as possible and rent yourself a place somewhere for a month or two.' He reached back into his pocket and showed Clément another bundle of notes. 'And I'll give you this too, if you'll agree to sell me that book.'

CHAPTER 23

'Interesting reading?'

'Pretty interesting,' he replied absently, looking up from his desk. Roberta was sitting gazing out of the window, sipping on a coffee and looking bored. He returned to the Journal, carefully turning the age-yellowed pages and scanning through some of the entries composed in the alchemist's smooth and elegant hand.

'Worth thirty grand?'

Ben didn't reply. Maybe it was worth what he'd paid Clément, and maybe not. Many of the pages seemed to be missing, others damaged and unreadable. He'd been hoping the Journal might contain some clues about the fabled elixir, maybe even a recipe of some kind. As he leafed through it he realized that that was probably a naïve expectation. It seemed to be a diary like any other, a day-to-day account of the man's life. His eye settled on a lengthy entry and he began to read.

February 9th, 1924
The climb up the mountain was long and perilous. I am getting far too old for this kind

of thing. Many times I nearly fell to my death as I found myself inching my way numbly up near-vertical rock and the falling snow grew into a blizzard. Eventually, I dragged myself up onto the summit of the mountain and rested my weary body for a few moments, wheezing, muscles trembling from the exertion. I wiped the snow from my eyes and looked up to see the ruined castle in front of me.

The passing of the centuries has not been kind to what was once the proud stronghold of Amauri de Lévis. Wars and plagues have come and gone, warrior-dynasties have flourished and died out, the land has been passed from one ruler to another. It is over five centuries since the castle, by then already ancient and battered, was besieged, bombarded and finally wrecked in the course of some long-forgotten clan feud. Its strong round towers are mostly reduced to rubble, the battle-scarred walls covered with moss and lichen. At one time fire must have devastated the inside of the castle and collapsed the roof. Time, wind, rain, sun have done the rest.

Much of the ruin is overgrown with gorse and brambles, and I had to cut a way through the Gothic archway of the main entrance. The wooden gates have rotted away to nothing and only their blackened iron hinges remain, hanging by rusty rivets from the crumbling stone arch. As I entered the gate, the deathly silence of a graveyard hung over the empty grey shell. I despaired of ever finding what I had come for.

I wandered inside the snowy courtyard and looked around me at the remnants of the walls and ramparts. At the bottom of a winding, descending stairway I found the entrance to an old storeroom, where I sheltered from the wind and lit a small fire to warm myself by.

The blizzard trapped me inside the castle ruin for two days. The meagre rations of bread and cheese I had brought were sufficient to sustain me, and I had a blanket and a small saucepan for melting snow to drink. I spent my time exploring the ruin, fervently hoping that what my researches had revealed to me would prove true.

I knew that my prize, if it existed, would be found not above ground in what remained of the ramparts or the towers, but somewhere down below in the network of tunnels and chambers carved out in the rock beneath the castle. Many of the tunnels have collapsed over time, but others remain intact. At the lower levels I discovered dank dungeons, the bones of their miserable inhabitants long since reduced to dust. Wandering through the dripping black passageways and winding staircases by the light of my oil lamp, I searched and I prayed.

After many hours of cruel disappointment I crawled through a half-collapsed tunnel deep underground and found myself in a square chamber. I raised my lantern, recognizing the vaulted ceiling and crumbled coats-of-arms from the decayed old woodcut I had found back in Paris. At this moment I knew that my quest was fulfilled, and my heart leapt with joy.

I circled the chamber until I came to the spot. I scraped aside thick cobwebs and blew away clouds of dust, and the time-smoothed markings in the stone block appeared before me. As I had known they would, the markings directed me to a particular flagstone in the floor. I dug the damp earth away from its edges until I was able to get my fingers underneath, then with great effort I heaved it upright. When I saw the stone hollow it had concealed and realized what I had found, after a lifetime of searching, I sank to my knees with silent tears of relief and exultation.

My heart was pounding fearfully as I dragged the weighty object out of the hole and scraped away the dirt and the decayed remnants of its sheepskin wrapping. The steel casket is well preserved. There was a hiss of escaping air as I prised the box open with my knife. I reached inside with trembling fingers, and by the flickering glow of my lantern I drank in the sight of my incredible find.

Nobody in almost seven hundred years has laid eyes on these precious things. What joy!

I believe the artefacts to be the work of my ancestors, the Cathars. They are a work of great mastery, which has been hidden from ages and from generations. Together they may hold the key to the Secret of Secrets and the goal of all our work. It is a miracle so great that I fear to contemplate its power . . .

Ben flipped on a few pages, eager to find more.

3rd November, 1924

It is as I suspected. The ancient scroll has proved much harder to decipher than I had first anticipated. Many months I have laboured over the translation of its archaic languages, its deviously encrypted messages, its numerous deliberate deceptions. But today Clément and I have at last been rewarded for our long toil.

The substances were melted in a crucible over the furnace after being reduced to their salts and undergoing special preparations and distillation. There was a startling hiss and streams of vapour filled the laboratory. Clément and I were amazed by the scent of fresh earth and sweet-smelling flowers. The water turned a golden colour. To this we added a quantity of mercury and the solution was left to cool. When we opened the crucible . . .

The rest of the page was eaten away by damp and mice. 'Shit,' Ben breathed. Maybe there was nothing useful in this thing after all. He read on, staring closely at the faded writing. In some places it was barely visible through the damp stains.

December 8th, 1924

How does one test an Elixir of Life? We have prepared the mixture according to my ancestors' detailed instructions. Clément, that lovable fellow, was afraid to take it. I have now consumed approximately thirty drachms of the sweet-tasting liquid. I observe no adverse effect. Only time will tell of its life-preserving powers . . .

Time will tell, all right, Ben thought. Frustrated, he skipped a few pages and found himself looking at an entry from May 1926 that was undamaged and intact.

This morning I returned to Rue Lepic from my daily stroll to be greeted by the most putrid stench emanating from my laboratory. Even as I hastened down the stairway to the cellar

I knew what had happened, and much as I expected, when I threw open the laboratory door I discovered my young apprentice Nicholas Daquin standing surrounded by clouds of smoke and the wreckage of a foolish experiment.

I doused the flames, and coughing from the smoke I turned to him. 'I have warned you about this sort of thing, Nicholas,' I said.

'I'm sorry,' Nicholas replied with that defiant look of his. 'But master, I almost succeeded.'

'Experiments can be dangerous, Nicholas. You lost control of the elements. Balancing the elements requires a very fine touch.'

He looked at me. 'But you told me I had a good feel for this, master.'

'And so you do,' I replied. 'But intuition alone is not enough. Your talent is raw, my friend. You must learn to curb your youthful impulsiveness.'

'It all takes so long to learn. I want to know more. I want to know everything.'

My twenty-year-old novice is at times wilful and arrogant, but that he has a great talent I cannot deny. I have never before come across a young student so eager. 'You cannot expect me to condense into a few lessons three thousand years of philosophy and the efforts of my whole lifetime,' I told Nicholas patiently. 'The mightiest secrets of nature are things that you must learn slowly, step by step. This is the way of alchemy.'

'But master, I'm so full of questions,' Nicholas protested, fixing me with his dark, intense eyes. 'You know so much. I hate the feeling of being so ignorant.'

I nodded. 'You will learn. But you must learn to control your headstrong nature, young Nicholas. It is unwise to try to run when one has not yet learned to walk. You should confine yourself to theoretical studies for the moment.'

The youth sat down heavily on a chair, looking agitated. 'I'm tired of reading books, master. Learning the theory of our work is all very well, but I need something practical, something I can see and touch. I have to believe there's a purpose to what we're doing.'

I told him I understood. As I watched him, I worried that too much theoretical learning might, in the end, put off this extremely gifted student. I am all too well aware myself how arid and fruitless a life of study feels without the reward of a real breakthrough, a tangible prize.

I thought of my own prize. Perhaps if I could share a little of that incredible knowledge with Nicholas, it would surely satisfy his burning curiosity?

'All right,' I said after a long pause. 'I will

let you see more, something that is not in your books.'

The youth jumped to his feet, his eyes flashing with excitement. 'When, master? Now?'

'No, not now,' I replied. 'Do not be so impatient, my young apprentice. Soon, very soon.' Here I raised a warning finger. 'But remember this, Nicholas. No student of your age will ever have been taken so far or so quickly into alchemical knowledge. It is a heavy responsibility for you, and you must be ready to accept it. Once I have shared the greatest secrets with you, they must never be divulged to anybody. Not to anybody, do you understand? I will swear you to this oath.'

In his proud manner he raised his chin. 'I'll take the oath right now,' he declared.

'Reflect upon it, Nicholas. Do not rush into this. It is a door which, once opened, cannot be shut.'

As we spoke, Jacques Clément had come in and started quietly clearing up the mess from the explosion. When Nicholas had gone, Clément approached me with a look of apprehension. 'Forgive me, master,' he said hesitantly. 'As you know I have never questioned your decisions . . .'

'What are you thinking, Jacques?'

Jacques spoke cautiously. 'I know you have great esteem for young Nicholas. He is bright, and keen, of that there is no doubt. But this impetuous nature of his . . . he yearns for knowledge the way a greedy man lusts for wealth. There is too much fire in him.'

'He is young, that's all,' I replied. 'We were young ourselves once. What are you trying to say, Jacques? Speak freely, my old friend.'

He hesitated. 'Are you quite sure, master, that young Nicholas is ready for this knowledge? It is a great step for him. Can he handle it?'

'I believe so,' I replied. 'I trust him.'

Ben closed the Journal and reflected for a moment. It was clear that whatever this great knowledge was, Fulcanelli had learned it from the artefacts he'd recovered from the castle, and which were now, apparently, in the hands of Klaus Rheinfeld. At last, he had a proper lead.

Beside him at the desk, the laptop was humming quietly. Ben reached over to it and started clicking the keys. There was the familiar grinding screech of the internet connection, and the homepage for the Google search engine popped up. He entered the name *klaus rheinfeld* into the search box and hit GO.

'What are you looking for?' Roberta asked, pulling out a chair next to him.

The websearch results screen popped up, surprising him with 271 matches for the term 'klaus rheinfeld'. 'Christ,' he murmured. He started scrolling down the long list. 'Well, this looks promising.'

Klaus Rheinfeld directs 'Outcast', starring Brad Pitt and Reese Witherspoon . . .

'*A gripping suspense thriller . . . Rheinfeld is the new Quentin Tarantino,*' she read out.

Ben grunted and scrolled down further. Almost everything on the list was featuring reviews of the new movie *Outcast* or interviews with its director, a thirty-two-year-old Californian. Then there was Klaus Rheinfeld Exports, a wine merchant.

'And here's Klaus Rheinfeld the horse whisperer,' she pointed out.

Several pages into the search results they came to a regional news item. It was taken from a small newspaper in Limoux, a town in the Languedoc region of southern France. The headline read

LE FOU DE SAINT-JEAN

'*The madman of Saint-Jean,*' he translated. 'It's dated October 2001 . . . OK, listen to this . . .'

An injured man was discovered wandering semi-naked in the forest outside the village of Saint-Jean, Languedoc. According to Father Pascal Cambriel, the local village priest who found the man, he was babbling in a strange language and appeared to be

161

suffering from severe dementia. The man, identified from his papers as **Klaus Rheinfeld**, a former resident of Paris, is believed to have inflicted serious knife wounds on himself. An ambulance worker told our reporter: '*I have never seen anything like it. There were strange markings, triangles and crosses and things, all over him. It was sickening. How could someone do that to themselves?*' Rumours have suggested that these bizarre wounds are linked to Satanic rituals, though this was rigorously denied by local authorities. **Rheinfeld** was treated at the Hospital of the Sainte Vierge . . .

'Doesn't say where they took him after that. Damn. He could be anywhere.'

'He's alive, though,' she pointed out.

'Or *was* alive six years ago. If it's even the same Klaus Rheinfeld.'

'I bet you anything it's the same guy,' she said. 'Satanic markings? Read *alchemical markings*.'

'Why was he all cut up?' he wondered.

She shrugged. 'Maybe he was just crazy.'

'OK . . . so we've got one crazy German covered in knife wounds, who may or may not be carrying important secrets connected to Fulcanelli, and who could be anywhere in the world. That narrows things down nicely.' He sighed, cleared the screen and started a fresh search. 'While we're online we might as well check this out.' He typed in the name of Michel Zardi's email server, waited for the site to load up and entered the account name. He just needed the webmail password to access the messages, and he knew that most people use some word from their private life. 'What do you know about Michel's personal life? Girlfriend, anything like that?'

'Not much – no steady girlfriend that I know of.'

'Mother's name?'

'Um . . . hold on . . . I think her name is Claire.'

He typed the name in the password box.

claire

incorrect password

'Favourite football team?'

'Not a clue. I don't think he was the sporty type.'

'Make of car, bike?'

'Used the Métro.'

'Pets?'

'A cat.'

'That's right. The fish,' he said.

'That asshole with his fish . . . how could I forget? Anyway, the cat's name was Lutin. That's L – U – T – I – N.'

lutin

'Bingo.' Michel's messages scrolled down on the screen. They were mostly spam, selling Viagra pills and penis extensions. Nothing from any of his mysterious contacts. Roberta leaned forward and clicked on SENT ITEMS. All the messages containing Michel's reports to 'Saul' flashed up in a long column in order of date sent.

'Look at them all,' she said, running the cursor up the list. 'Here's the last one, with the attachment I told you about.' She clicked on the paper-clip logo again and showed him the JPEG photo files. He glanced through them before closing the box and clicking on COMPOSE NEW MESSAGE. A blank window flashed up.

'What're you doing?'

'Resurrecting our friend Michel Zardi.' He addressed the new message to Saul, like the others. Her eyes widened in alarm as he typed.

> Guess who this is? That's right, you got the wrong guy. You bastards killed my friend. Now, you want the Ryder woman, I have her. Follow my instructions and I'll give her to you.

'Not exactly Shakespeare, but it'll do the job.'

'What the hell are you writing?' She jumped to her feet, staring at him in horror.

He took her wrist. She struggled against his grip. He slackened it, and guided her gently back into her seat. 'You want to find out who these people are, don't you?' She sat down again, but he could see the mistrust in her eyes. He sighed and tossed a bunch of keys onto the desk. 'There. Like I told you, you're free to go any time you want. But you agreed to do this my way, remember?'

She didn't say anything.

'Trust me,' he said quietly.

She sighed. 'OK, I trust you.'

He turned back to the screen and finished writing his message. 'Bombs away,' he said as he hit SEND.

CHAPTER 24

Gaston Clément had been too slow to take Ben's advice. Counting his newfound wealth, he poured himself a glass of cheap wine and drank to the strange foreign visitor.

When three other visitors found him he was dozing in his tattered armchair, the half-empty bottle by his side. Godard, Berger and Naudon dragged the pleading Clément down off his platform and threw him bodily to the concrete floor. He was seized and held down in a chair. A heavy fist slammed into his face and broke his nose. Blood poured from his nostrils, soaking his grey beard.

'Who gave you this money?' roared a voice in his ear. 'Speak!' The cold steel of a pistol pressed against his temple. 'Who was here? What was his name?'

Clément racked his brain but couldn't remember, and so they beat him harder. They hit him again and again until his eyes were swollen shut and blood and vomit were all over the floor around him, his beard and hair slick with red. '*Il est Anglais!*' he let out in a garbled, bubbling scream, remembering.

'What'd he say?'

'The Englishman was here.'

Clément's face was down hard to the cold floor with a heavy boot across his neck that threatened to break it. He groaned, and then passed out.

'Go easy, boys,' said Berger, looking down at the pitiful unconscious form on the floor. 'We're to deliver him alive.'

As the Audi sped away through the derelict farm with Clément stuffed in the trunk, flames were already appearing at the barn windows and black smoke billowed into the sky.

Monique Banel was walking through the Parc Monceau with her five-year-old daughter Sophie. Monceau was a pleasant little park, with a peaceful atmosphere where the birds sang in the trees, swans paddled in the picturesque miniature lake and Monique liked to unwind for a few minutes after she finished her part-time secretarial work and went to pick Sophie up from her kindergarten. Monique said a cheerfully polite '*Bonjour, monsieur*' to the elegant old gent who was often sitting on the same bench around this time reading his paper.

The little girl, as always, was full of attention for all the sights and sounds of the park, her bright eyes sparkling with joy. As they walked down one of the paths that wound between the park's lawns, Sophie exclaimed in delight, '*Maman*! Look! A little dog's coming to see us!' Her mother smiled. 'Yes, isn't he pretty?'

The dog was a small neat spaniel, a King Charles Cavalier, white with brown patches and wearing a little red collar. Monique looked about. His owner must be somewhere nearby. Many Parisians brought their dogs here for a walk in the afternoon.

'Can I play with him, *Maman*?' Sophie was ecstatic as the little spaniel trotted up towards them. 'Hello, doggie,' the child called out to it. 'What's your name? *Maman*, what's that in his mouth?'

The little dog reached them and dropped the object it had been carrying on the ground at Sophie's feet. It looked up at her expectantly, tail wagging. Before her mother could stop her, the child had bent down and picked up the thing and was examining it curiously. She turned to Monique with a frown, holding the object up to show her.

Monique Banel screamed. Her little girl was clutching part of a severed, mutilated human hand.

CHAPTER 25

Montpellier, France

The electrician's apprentice couldn't get the cellar out of his mind. He kept thinking about the strange things he'd seen. What went on there? It wasn't a storage place. They *definitely* didn't keep dogs there. There were bars, like the bars of cages, and rings on the walls. He thought about what he'd been reading in his book about castles in olden days. The modern, glass-fronted building was no castle – but that cellar looked like some kind of weird dungeon to him.

He'd finished work at 6.30 and now he was free till Monday. Thank Christ. Uncle Richard was a nice enough guy – most of the time anyway – but the job was *boring*. Uncle Richard was *boring*. Marc wanted a more exciting life. His mother was always telling him he had an overactive imagination. It was all very well wanting to be a writer, but imagination was never going to bring in any money. A good trade – like an electrician – *that* was the way to go. He didn't want to end up like his father, did he? Always broke, a gambler, a lowlife who was in and out of prison all the time, who'd run out on his family because he couldn't bear any responsibility? To be like Uncle Richard – settled, respectable, with a new car every couple of years, a mortgage, membership at the local golf club, a devoted wife and two kids – that was the life his mother had in mind for him, and nothing less would do.

But Marc wasn't so sure he wanted to end up like either of the brothers. He had his own ideas. If he couldn't be a writer, maybe he could be a detective. He was fascinated by mysteries, and he was pretty sure he'd found one.

He kept going back to the drawer in his bedside table, where he'd hidden the thing he'd found in the cellar. He hadn't told anyone about it. It looked like it might be gold. Did that make him a thief, like his father? No, he'd found it, it was his. But what did it mean? What *was* that place?

He finished his evening meal, dutifully loaded his plate and cutlery in the dishwasher and headed for the door, grabbing his crash helmet and moped keys off the stand in the hallway. He threw a torch into a bag, slung it over his shoulder, then as an afterthought dropped a small bar of Poulain chocolate in there as well.

'Marc, where are you going?' his mother called after him.

'Out.'

'Out where?'

'Just out.'

'Well, don't be late.'

The place was pretty much within easy moped range, about fifteen kilometres away. After a few false starts and wrong turns, Marc found himself at the walled gateway to the building as night was beginning to fall. The tall black iron-barred gates were shut. Peering between them he could see the lit-up building in the distance among the dark, whispering trees. He killed the whirring moped engine and found a place across the other side of the road where he could tuck the lightweight bike away under some bushes.

The stone perimeter wall ran in a wide curve away from the roadside. He scrambled up an earth bank and followed its line, tramping through long grass, until he came to an old oak tree whose branches overhung the top of the wall. He slung his bag over his shoulder, shinned up the trunk and edged out along one of the thicker branches until he could get one foot on the top of the wall, then the other. He dangled his legs down the other side and dropped lightly into the bushes inside the grounds of the centre.

For a while he stood around under some trees, munching on his bar of chocolate and watching the building. The windows on the ground floor were lit up. He finished his chocolate, wiped his mouth and sneaked across the lawns, keeping to the shadowy bits. He reached the building. The ground-floor windows were too high to see in. A flight of steps led up to what looked like the front door, on the first floor. If he went halfway up them, he'd be able to see through those lit windows.

Just as he was starting up the steps, headlights appeared at the top of the drive. The iron gates whirred automatically open and two big black cars came purring down towards the building. They swept past him and turned a corner. Marc went after them, keeping in the shadows. He saw the cars go down a ramp, their engine noise suddenly amplified in an underground space. He crept around the corner, watching. He could hear doors slamming, and voices echoing. He tiptoed furtively down the ramp until, crouching low, he could see the men getting out of the cars and walking towards a lift.

But something was wrong. One of the men didn't seem to want to go with the others. In fact he seemed very unwilling indeed. He was being dragged by the arms, yelling and shouting in fear. To Marc's horror, another man took out a gun. He thought he was going to shoot the frightened man, but instead he hit him over the head with it. Marc saw blood splatter on the concrete. The man was half unconscious now, not protesting any more as his captors dragged him along and his feet trailed on the ground.

Marc had seen enough. He turned and ran.

Straight into the grasping hands of the tall man in black.

CHAPTER 26

Central Paris

Flann O'Brien's pub is an oasis of Irish music and Guinness just around the corner from the Louvre museum, not far from the Seine. At 11.27 that night, following the specific instructions they'd received from an email from the unexpectedly alive and kicking Michel Zardi, four men entered the pub. Glancing around them, they approached the bar, which was thronging with people. The pub was filled with raucous laughter, clinking glasses and the sound of fiddles and banjos.

The leader of the four men was stocky and muscular with a bald head, wearing a black leather jacket. He leaned across the bar and spoke to the large, bearded barman. The barman nodded, reached under the bar and took out a mobile phone. He handed it to the bald man, who signalled to his friends and led them back outside into the street.

At exactly 11.30 the phone rang. The bald man answered.

'*Don't speak,*' said the voice on the other end.

'*Listen to what I say, and follow my instructions exactly to the letter. I'm watching you.*'

The bald man looked up and down the street. '*Don't look for me,*' the voice in his ear said. '*Just listen. One false move and the deal's off. You lose the American and you'll be punished.*'

'OK, I'm listening,' the bald man replied.

'Use this phone to call a cab,' Ben said on the other end as he sat behind the wheel of the Peugeot 206 half a mile away across Paris. 'Go alone, repeat, go alone or the woman runs. When you're in the taxi, dial "Zardi" and I'll tell you where to go.'

The bald man sat in the Mercedes cab as his African taxi driver drove him along the quayside by the river Seine. Away from the brightly illuminated pleasure-boats and the parties of drinkers and tourists, the taxi turned off and took a route down a dark narrow road that led to the shadowy bank of the river. The bald man stepped out, still clutching the mobile phone. The taxi pulled away.

The bald man's footsteps echoed under the dark overhead bridge as he neared the rendezvous point he'd been given. He glanced around him.

'Ben, I've got a bad feeling about this,' she whispered in the darkness. 'You sure this was such a good idea?'

The moonlit river Seine rippled and gurgled beside them. Down below street level, the rumble of the city seemed muted and far away. In the distance, Notre Dame cathedral towered, gold-lit, over the water. He checked his watch. 'Relax.'

A door slammed on the street above them, a car pulling away, footsteps. She turned to see a figure approaching. 'Ben, there's . . .'

'Now listen,' he said softly in her ear. 'Just trust me here. It'll be all right.' He took her arm and led her out from under the shadows of the bridge as the bald man approached. A twisted smile appeared on the man's face. 'Zardi?' he asked, his voice echoing under the stone arch.

'*C'est moi,*' said Ben. '*Vous avez l'argent?*'

'The money's in here,' the bald man replied in French. He held up a briefcase.

'Set it down on the ground,' Ben commanded. The bald man gently laid the case down. He looked away from Ben for a second. Ben let go of Roberta's arm and moved towards him fast. He grabbed the man by the wrist, twisted him round and then the cold steel of the Browning's silencer was pressing against the man's crinkly neck. 'Down on your knees.'

Roberta stared in horror at the pistol in Ben's hand. She wanted to run, but her legs wouldn't move and she stood there frozen, unable to take her eyes off Ben as he shoved the gun against the back of the man's head and began to frisk him. Ben's gaze flicked momentarily to the expression on her face and he knew what she was thinking. He gave her a look that said *just let me deal with this.*

The bald man had come ready. There was a Glock 19 in his leather jacket. Ben kicked it across the ground and it slipped over the edge of the riverbank with a soft splash.

'You'll die for this, Zardi,' the bald man muttered.

'Are you Saul?' Ben asked.

The bald man wasn't talking. Ben brought the butt and trigger guard of the pistol down on his head. 'Are – you – Saul?' he repeated deliberately. The man whimpered and a trickle of blood ran down his shiny scalp.

Roberta looked away.

'No,' the bald man said. 'I'm not Saul.'

'Then who *is* Saul, and where can I find him?'

The man paused, and Ben hit him again. He fell to the ground and rolled over, staring up with frightened eyes. But not too frightened. Ben could see that this guy was used to a little punishment. 'OK, you're no use to me.' He thumbed off the safety and aimed the gun in his face.

It must have been the look in Ben's eye that persuaded the man that this was no bluff. 'I don't know who he is!' he protested, in the truthful way of a man with everything to lose. 'I just get orders over the phone!'

Ben lowered the pistol and took his finger out of the trigger guard. Clicked the safety back on. 'Who calls who? You call him? What's his number?'

The bald man knew the number well. He muttered it out.

Ben watched him, weighing up what to do with

176

him. The man's jacket was hanging open and under it he was wearing an open shirt with a gold chain nestling in his hairy chest. Ben saw something else and keeping the gun on his face he reached down and ripped the shirt open. By the dim light of the moon and the street above, reflected by the gently rippling water, he could see the tattoo.

It was a sword, of medieval type with a straight blade and flat crossguard, shaped to look like a crucifix. Wrapped around the blade was a banner with the words GLADIUS DOMINI.

'What's that?' Ben asked, motioning with the gun. The bald man glanced down at his chest. 'Nothing.'

'Gladius Domini. Sword of God,' Ben murmured to himself. He stepped on the bald man's testicles, and he let out a scream.

'For Christ's sake . . .' Roberta pleaded.

'I think you want to tell me,' Ben said to him quietly, ignoring her and keeping pressure on.

'OK, OK, take your foot off,' the bald man panted, sweat streaming down his contorted face. Ben took his foot away, the gun still pointed unwaveringly at his forehead. The man breathed a sigh of relief and lay back on the stone ground. 'I'm a soldier of Gladius Domini,' he muttered.

'What *is* Gladius Domini?'

'An organization. I work for them . . . I don't know . . .' His voice trailed off. He stared blankly. There was a vagueness, an empty look in his eyes that made Ben think back to the cathedral suicide. Someone was getting inside the heads of these guys.

'Soldier of God, are you?' Ben said. 'And when you kill innocent people, you do it for Him?' He raised the pistol and stepped back. Slipped his finger through the trigger guard. 'Now you're going to meet Him personally.'

Roberta ran out of the shadows towards them. 'What are you *doing*! Don't kill him! Let him go – please – you have to let him go!'

Ben saw the pleading earnestness in her eyes. He took his finger off the trigger and lowered the gun. It was against all his instincts.

'Go,' he said to the bald man. The man gathered himself up slowly, clutching his groin in agony. His shirt was wet with blood and sweat glistened on his face in the moonlight. He staggered to his feet.

Roberta stared at Ben. Her face was tight. She shoved him angrily. He didn't react. She thumped his chest. 'Who the fuck *are* you?'

He saw the bright red dot pass across her forehead a third of a second before he grabbed her collar and wrenched her violently to one side.

Then, all at once, the laser-sighted rifle across the river was tearing chunks of masonry out of the wall. Three-shot burst, fully automatic fire. One of the shots went straight through the bald man's head. His skull burst apart, spraying blood across Roberta. His falling body crashed against hers and took her down with him as it crumpled to the ground. Her legs kicked from under the corpse as she screamed in panic.

Ben had already seen the glint of the rifleman's scope lens fifty metres away and he was returning fire. The Browning flashed and kicked in his hand. The sniper let out a stifled cry, tumbled from his perch and splashed into the river. His AR-18 assault weapon clattered to the ground.

Two more men were running up the riverbank towards them. Pistols in their hands. A bullet went past Ben's ear and another sang off the wall next to him.

He raised the pistol. *Calm. Focus centre of target. The trigger breaks without conscious thought.* Two double-taps in rapid succession, bringing both men down in just over a second. Their bodies slumped to the ground and lay still, black shapes in the moonlight.

Ben hauled the dead man off Roberta and kicked the body to one side. Half of the bald crown was missing. Her clothes and hair were soaked in blood. 'Are you hurt?' he asked urgently.

She staggered to her feet. Her face was pale, and the next thing she was spewing her guts out against the wall. Ben heard police sirens in the distance, several of them, their high-pitched wails rising and falling in and out of phase with each other, approaching fast. 'Come on.'

She wasn't responding. There was no time to reason with her. He put his arm around her waist and half-carried her along the quayside to the flight of steps leading up to the street.

At the top of the steps she seemed to regain her senses. She struggled in his grip and tore away from him. He yelled her name. But she was running frantically the opposite way, straight towards the sound of the sirens. Any moment now the police would be on top of them. 'Get away from me!' she screamed at him. He chased her, tried to take her arm, reasoning with her. 'Don't *touch* me!' She staggered away from him.

Flashing blue lights were appearing at the end of the street among the scattered traffic. Ben had no choice. He had to let her go. At least she'd be safe in police hands, and within the hour he'd be out of the city and far away. With a last glance at her, he turned and started running back towards the Peugeot.

Roberta was staggering dazed up the middle of the road. A couple of cars honked, swerving to avoid her. Ben watched from a distance as the police car skidded to a halt beside her. Three cops got out, took one look at the shocked, bloody state of her and connected her right away with the reported shooting. More sirens were shrieking in the distance – three, maybe four more cars racing to the scene.

They were putting her into the back of the police car when the black Mitsubishi pulled up next to them.

Ben was a hundred metres away when he saw the Mitsubishi's doors fly open and the two men with sawn-off pump shotguns step out. They blasted the cops before either of them had a chance to draw a pistol. Roberta was crawling out of the back as they walked round the side of the police car, racking the slides on their shotguns.

The Peugeot slammed into the nearest one, sending him flying in a broken heap. Ben fired a shot through the open window at the other, who ducked for cover behind the police car and then ran for it. Ben threw open the door, hauled Roberta in and skidded off over the bridge and away, just in time to screech around the nearest bend down a sidestreet before the wailing fleet of police arrived on the scene.

CHAPTER 27

Two hours earlier

During the Nazi occupation of Paris the sprawling honeycomb of austere rooms and dark corridors had been used as a Gestapo prison and interrogation centre. Nowadays the enormous basement beneath the police HQ housed, among other things, the forensic lab and morgue. It was as though the place couldn't shake off its gruesome heritage.

Luc Simon was standing with the forensic pathologist, the tall thin white-haired Georges Rudel, in a stark neon-lit examination room. On the slab in front of them, a corpse lay covered in a white sheet. Only the feet were visible, protruding from underneath, pallid and cold. A label dangled from one toe. Simon wasn't a squeamish man but he fought the urge to look away as Rudel casually peeled back the sheet far enough to uncover the corpse's head, neck and chest.

They'd cleaned Michel up since the last time Simon had seen him, but he still wasn't a pretty sight. The bullet had entered under the chin, carved its wound channel up behind the face, taking most of it away before exiting through the top of the head. Just one eye remained, sitting in its socket like a hard-boiled egg with a pupil that seemed to stare right at them.

'What've you got for me?' Simon asked Rudel.

The pathologist pointed at the mess of Michel's face. 'Damage here is all consistent with the bullet found in the ceiling,' he said, speaking mechanically as though dictating a report. 'Entry wound here. Weapon was held against the upper chest with the muzzle in loose contact with the lower jaw. Edges of the entry wound are burned from combustion gases and blacked with soot. The weapon was a Smith and Wesson revolver, three inch barrel, .44 Remington Magnum. The powerful calibre accounts for the amount of bone and tissue damage.'

Simon tapped his foot impatiently. He hoped that this was leading somewhere.

'Typically that calibre uses much slower-burning powder than you get with semi-auto rounds like the nine millimetre,' Rudel went on matter-of-factly. 'That means you get a lot of unburnt residue, especially with a short barrel. Doesn't burn so clean.' He pointed. 'You can see it all here, embedded in the skin. Also here down the neck.'

Simon nodded. 'OK, so what are you telling me?'

Rudel turned to look at him with bleary eyes. 'The victim's prints are on the stocks and the trigger of the weapon. So we know he fired the shot without gloves.'

'He was found still clutching the gun. No gloves. We know that. Are you going to cut to the chase before one of us dies?'

Rudel ignored the sarcasm. 'Well, this is what I find perplexing. With all this mess of unburnt powder I'd expect to find a lot of it on the gun hand, as well as the normal chemical discharge that blows back when the weapon is fired. But this man's hands are clean.'

'You're sure about this?'

'Quite sure – it's a simple swab test for residue.' Rudel reached down and lifted a pale lifeless arm out from under the sheet. 'See for yourself.'

'You're saying he didn't fire the shot.'

Rudel shrugged, and let the dead hand flop back down by the corpse's side. 'Only thing on this man's hands, apart from the usual sweat and grease, are some traces of oily fish. Pilchard, to be precise.'

It struck Simon as absurd, and he laughed. 'You ran a test for pilchard?'

Rudel looked at him coldly. 'No, there was a half-opened tin of it on his kitchen table, next to a cat's feeding dish. Now, all I'm saying is, who would blow their brains out in the middle of feeding their cat?'

The boy was jerked semi-conscious as they dragged him off the hard bunk. He heard voices around him, the clang of metal doors and the jangling of keys. Sounds echoed in the empty space. A swirl of lights blinded him through his confusion. A sudden lancing pain in his arm made him wince.

It might have been minutes later, or it might have been hours – everything was hazy, unreal. He was vaguely aware of not being able to move, arms pinned behind him. The white light was burning into his head, making him blink and twist his head away as he sat tied in the chair.

He wasn't alone. Two men were in the cellar with him, watching him.

'Shall I dispose of him?' said one voice.

'No, keep him alive for the moment. He may be useful to us.'

CHAPTER 28

The warm water trickled over her head and tinkled against the side of the bath where she was bent over. The foam running into the plughole was tinged with red as he carefully washed the blood out of her hair.

'Ouch.'

'Sorry. You've got dried bits stuck in here.'

'I don't want to know, Ben.'

He hung the shower head up on its wall hook and squeezed more shampoo into his hand, lathering it into her hair.

Her nerves were steadier now – the nausea had left her and her hands weren't shaking any more. She relaxed against his touch, thinking how tender and gentle it was. She could feel the warmth of his body pressing up behind her as he rinsed the foam away from her hair and neck.

'I think it's all gone now.'

'Thanks,' she murmured, wrapping a towel around her head.

He gave her a spare shirt to wear, and then left her alone to clean the rest of herself up. While she showered, he quickly field-stripped, cleaned and

186

reassembled his Browning. As he went through these fluid, automatic motions, as deeply instilled in him as tying a shoelace or brushing his teeth, his mind was far away.

She emerged from the bathroom, wearing his oversize shirt knotted at the waist, her long dark red hair still damp and gleaming. He poured her a glass of wine. 'You OK?'

'Yeah, I'm OK.'

'Roberta . . . I haven't been totally straight with you. There are some things you should know.'

'This is about the gun?'

He nodded. 'And other things.'

She sat looking down at the floor and sipped her wine as he told her everything. He told her about Fairfax, about his quest, about the dying little girl. 'And that's basically all there is. Now you know everything.' He watched her for a reaction.

She was quiet for a while, her face still and thoughtful. 'So, is that what you do, Ben? Save kids?' she asked softly.

He looked at his watch. 'It's late. You need to get some sleep.'

That night he let her use the bed while he slept on the floor in the other room. She was woken at dawn by the sound of him moving about. She came sleepily out of the bedroom to see him packing up his green canvas bag. 'What's happening?'

'I'm leaving Paris.'

'*You're* leaving? What about me?'

'After last night, do you still want to come along with me?'

'Yes, I do. Where are we going?'

'South,' he said, slipping Fulcanelli's Journal carefully into the bag and wishing he had more time to read it. Then he opened a drawer of his desk and took out the passport he kept in there. He'd had it made for him in London, and it was indistinguishable from the real thing. The picture on it was his, but the name was Paul Harris. He slid it in the inside pocket of his jacket.

'But Ben, there's just one thing,' she remembered. 'I have to go back to my place first.'

He shook his head. 'Sorry. No chance.'

'I have to.'

'What for? If you need clothes and things, that's all right – we'll go and buy you whatever you want.'

'No, it's something else. These people who are after us – if they get into my apartment again they could find my address book. Everything's in that book, all my friends and family in the States. What if they did something to my family to try to get to me?'

When Luc Simon returned to his office, he found the whole police station in an uproar as news came in about the quayside shooting. Violent crime was a normal thing in Paris, part of life. But when there was a bloodbath like this, with two cops gunned down and five more bodies littering the banks of the Seine, guns and spent cartridges everywhere, the police force was coming out *en masse*.

Simon found a brown envelope on his desk. The report inside was from handwriting analysis. The writing on the Zardi suicide note was a mismatch with other samples of his handwriting found in his apartment, shopping lists, memos and a half-written letter to his mother. It was pretty close, but it was definitely a forgery. And fake suicide notes pointed in one direction only. Especially when you already knew the victim wasn't the shooter.

If it was a murder case after all, he'd really dropped the ball. He hadn't paid enough attention to the Ryder woman. Too much on his mind, maybe, with his and Hélène's relationship problems hanging over him on top of everything else. Trying to refloat a sunken marriage while trying to stop the whole of Paris from killing each other – the two just weren't compatible.

But no excuses. The fact was, he'd fucked up. Roberta Ryder wasn't just some crank. She *was* involved in something. What it was, and how she was connected, he'd have to find out.

But it was all questions, no answers. Who was the guy she'd turned up with on the night of Zardi's death? Something odd about the way they were acting together. It had been as though the man was trying to stop her saying too much. Hadn't he said she was his fiancée? They didn't look that close.

And hadn't Roberta Ryder told him, just hours earlier, that she was single?

The guy was important, somehow. What was his name? If Simon remembered rightly, he hadn't seemed too keen to give it and hadn't looked too pleased when Ryder gave it for him. He opened up the file on his desk. Ben Hope, that was it. British, despite his near-perfect French. He'd need to check him out. Then search the Ryder woman's apartment. He could easily get a warrant now.

Simon ran into his colleague Detective Bonnard and they walked down the busy corridor together. Bonnard looked serious, grey and haggard. 'Just got the latest on this multiple homicide and cop-killing,' he said.

'Fill me in.'

'We've got a witness. Motorist reported two people running from the scene of the incident, just around the time it was happening. Male and female Caucasian. Woman young, we *think* red hair, maybe early thirties. Male possibly a little older, taller, fair-haired. Looked as if the woman was struggling, trying to get away. Witness says she was covered in blood.'

'A blond man and a red-haired woman?' Simon repeated. 'Was the woman injured?'

'Doesn't look like it. We think she's the same woman our officers picked up just before they were killed. She left some blood traces on the back seat of the car, but it belonged to one of the bodies we found under the bridge, guy with his brains blown out by a rifle bullet. Pretty pictures all over the wall.'

'So where did she go?'

Bonnard made a helpless gesture. 'No idea. Looks like she just vanished. Either she got away on her own or someone took her away pretty damn quick before our boys got to the scene.'

'Great. What else do we have?'

Bonnard shook his head. 'It's a mess. We recovered the rifle. Military weapon, untraceable and not a print on it anywhere. Same with the pistols we found. A couple of the victims we know – stints for armed robbery and so on. Usual suspects, won't be missed. But we haven't much of a clue what the hell this is about. Drug-related, maybe.'

'I don't think so,' Simon said.

'One thing we do know is that we're missing at least one shooter. Nine-mil slugs were found in three of the bodies. Looks like they all came from the same gun, which the forensic guys tells us from the rifling pattern is a Browning type pistol. It's the only gun we haven't recovered.'

'Right,' Simon said, nodding, thinking hard.

'There is one more thing,' Bonnard went on. 'Based on what we can figure out, the mystery nine-mil shooter isn't your typical low-life crim. Whoever it is can hit high-speed one-inch groups on moving targets at twenty-five metres in the dark. Can you do that? I sure as hell can't do that . . . We're dealing with a serious pro.'

CHAPTER 29

'Y ou're sure it's on the bedside table?' Ben was saying as he parked the dented Peugeot a discreet distance from Roberta's building.

She was wearing the baseball cap he'd bought her at a market earlier that morning, her hair tucked into it. With that and the shades she was unrecognizable. 'Bedside table, little red book,' she repeated.

'You wait here,' he said. 'Key's in the ignition. Any sign of trouble, get out of here. Drive slowly, don't rush. Call me first chance you get, and I'll meet you.'

She nodded. He got out of the car and put on the sunglasses. She watched with trepidation as he walked briskly up the street and disappeared into the doorway of her building.

Luc Simon had had enough of hanging around Roberta Ryder's place. He'd been here half an hour now, waiting with his two agents for the forensic team to arrive. His impatient rage was giving him another one of his killer headaches. As usual, the forensic guys were keeping him hanging around waiting. Undisciplined bunch of bastards – he'd give them hell when they got here.

He thought about sending one of his uniforms out to get coffee. *Fuck it.* He'd do it himself – Christ knew what kind of shit they'd bring back. There was a bar across the street, *Le Chien Bleu*; stupid name but the coffee might not be too bad.

He thundered down the spiralling flights of stairs, trotted through the cool hallway and out into the sunshine, deep in thought. He was too preoccupied to notice the tall blond man in sunglasses and a black jacket coming the other way. The man didn't slacken his stride but recognized the police inspector immediately, and knew there'd be other cops waiting upstairs.

'That was quick,' the two officers thought when they heard the doorbell of Ryder's apartment. They opened the door, expecting Simon. If they were lucky, he'd have brought them a coffee and a bite to eat – though that was almost certainly wishing for too much considering that the chief was in an even fouler mood than usual.

But the man at the door was a tall blond stranger. He didn't seem surprised to find two policemen in the apartment. He leaned casually against the doorway, smiling at them. 'Hi,' he said, taking off his sunglasses. 'Wondered if you could help me . . .'

Simon returned to Ryder's apartment, sipping his paper cup of scalding espresso. Thank Christ, it was taking the headache away already. He hurried back up the stairs to the third floor, banged on the door and waited to be let in. After three minutes, he thumped harder and yelled through the door. What the hell were they doing in there? Another minute passed, and it was clear that something was wrong.

'Police,' he said to the neighbour, flashing his ID. The little old man craned his head on a shrivelled, tortoise-like neck and peered bemusedly at the ID, then up at Simon, then at the cup of coffee in Simon's hand.

'Police,' Simon repeated more loudly. 'I need to use your apartment.' The old man opened the door wider, stepping aside. Simon pushed past him. 'Hold this, please,' he said, handing the old man his empty cup. 'Where's your balcony?'

'This way.' The neighbour shuffled through the apartment ahead of him, down a little corridor lined with watercolour paintings, then into a neat salon with an upright piano and mock-antique armchairs. The television was blaring. Simon saw what he was looking for, the tall double windows leading out onto the narrow balcony.

There was a gap of only about a metre and a half between the old man's balcony and Ryder's. Keeping his eyes resolutely off the three-storey drop to the yard below, he climbed over the iron railing and jumped across from one balcony to the other.

Ryder's balcony window was unlocked. He drew

his service sidearm and thumbed back the hammer as he paced silently into the apartment. He could hear a muffled thumping coming from somewhere. It seemed to be coming from Ryder's makeshift laboratory. With the cocked .38 revolver pointed in front of him he moved stealthily towards the sound.

Inside the lab, he heard it again. It was coming from behind those doors where Ryder kept her revolting flies. *Thump, thump.*

Simon pulled open the doors, and the first thing he saw was the black, hairy insects swarming over the glass, their disturbed buzzing muted behind the thick walls of their tanks. Something moved against his leg. He looked down.

Crammed into the space beneath the tanks were his two officers, bound and gagged with tape, struggling. Their automatics were lying side by side on the desk, unloaded and stripped, their barrels missing.

The police squad found them later, one inside each of the fly tanks.

Ben tossed the little red book onto her lap. 'First chance you get,' he said, getting into the car, 'you destroy that, understood?'

She nodded. 'S-Sure.'

As the Peugeot speeded up and disappeared down the street, a man slouching in a doorway turned and watched it go. The man wasn't a cop, but he'd been watching the Ryder place since the night before. He nodded to himself and took up his phone. When someone answered after a couple of rings he said, 'A silver 206 coupe with a dented front wing just took off down Rue de Rome heading south. Man and a woman. You can pick them up at Boulevard des Batignolles but you'd better move fast.'

CHAPTER 30

Six months earlier, near Montségur, southern France

Anna Manzini was unhappy at having put herself in such a situation. Who would have thought that the author of two acclaimed books on medieval history and a respected lecturer at the University of Florence would have behaved in such an impulsive and idiotically romantic fashion? To give up a well-paid professional position to go off and rent a villa – a very expensive villa, at that – in the south of France to begin a whole new fiction-writing career from scratch wasn't the kind of measured and logical behaviour that Anna was known for amongst her former colleagues and students.

Worse, she'd deliberately chosen a secluded house, deep in the rugged mountains and valleys of the Languedoc, in the hope that the solitude would fire her imagination.

It hadn't. She'd been there for over two months, and had hardly written more than a sentence. To begin with she'd kept herself to herself, not seeing anyone. But more recently she'd started welcoming

197

the attentions of local intellectuals and academics who'd discovered that the author of the books *The Crusade that History Forgot* and *God's Heretics: Discovering the Real Cathars* was now living just a few kilometres away in the countryside. After months of boredom and loneliness she'd been relieved at the chance to befriend the vivacious Angélique Montel, a local artist. Angélique had introduced her to an interesting new circle of people, and Anna had eventually decided to have a dinner party at the villa.

While she waited for her guests, she remembered what Angélique had been saying on the phone two days before. 'You know what I think, Anna? You have writer's block because you need a man. So for your dinner party I'm bringing along a good friend of mine. He's Dr Edouard Legrand. He's brilliant, rich, and single.'

'If he's so wonderful,' Anna said smiling, 'then why are you so keen to pass him onto me?'

'Oh, you wicked girl, he's my *cousin.*' Angélique giggled. 'He's been divorced only a short while, and he's lost without a woman. He's six years older than you, forty-eight, but has the physique of an athlete. Tall, black hair, sexy, sophisticated . . .'

'Bring him along,' she'd said to Angélique. 'I look forward to meeting him.' *But the last thing I need in my life right now is a man*, she thought to herself.

There were eight for dinner. Angélique had strategically managed to ensure that Dr Legrand was seated beside Anna at the top of the table. She'd been right – he was very charming and handsome in a well-tailored suit, hair greying at the temples.

The conversation had dwelt for a while on a modern art exhibition that many of the guests had attended in Nice. Now they were all keen to know more about Anna's new book project.

'Please, I don't want to talk about it,' said Anna. 'It's so depressing. I have writer's block. I just don't seem to be able to do it. Maybe it's because I'm writing a book of fiction for the first time, a novel.'

The guests were surprised and intrigued. 'A novel? What about?'

Anna sighed. 'It's a mystery story about the Cathars. The trouble is that I have such difficulty imagining my characters.'

'Ah, but I have the right man here to help you,' Angélique said, seeing her opportunity. 'Dr Legrand is a famous psychiatrist and can help anyone with any kind of mental problem.'

Legrand laughed. 'Anna hasn't got a mental problem. Many of the most talented people have sometimes suffered from temporary loss of inspiration. Even Rachmaninov, the great composer, found his creativity blocked and had to be hypnotized in order to create his greatest works.'

'Thank you, Dr Legrand,' Anna said, smiling. 'But your analogy does me far too much credit. I'm no Rachmaninov.'

'Please, call me Edouard. But I'm sure you *are*

very talented.' He paused. 'However, if it's interesting characters you're looking for, with a taste of the mysterious and the gothic, there I may be able to help you.'

'Dr Legrand is director of the Institut Legrand,' said Madame Chabrol, a music teacher from Cannes.

'The Institut Legrand?' asked Anna.

'A psychiatric hospital,' Angélique filled in.

'Just a small private establishment,' Legrand said. 'Not far from here, outside Limoux.'

'Edouard, are you referring to that strange man you once told me about?' Angélique asked.

He nodded. 'One of our most curious and fascinating patients. He's been with us for about five years now. His name is Rheinfeld, Klaus Rheinfeld.'

'His name sounds like Renfield, from the Dracula story,' Anna commented.

'That's quite apt, although I haven't yet observed him eating flies,' Legrand replied, and everyone laughed. 'But certainly he's an interesting case. He's a religious maniac. He was found not far from here, in a village, by a priest. He self-mutilates – his body's covered in scars. He raves about demons and angels, convinced he's in Hell – or sometimes in Heaven. He continually recites Latin phrases, and is obsessed with meaningless series of numbers and letters. He scrawls them all over the walls of his ce– . . . his room.'

'Why do you allow him to have a pen, Dr Legrand?'

asked Madame Chabrol. 'Could that not be dangerous?'

'We don't, any longer,' he said. 'He writes them in his own blood, urine and faeces.'

Everyone around the table looked shocked and disgusted, except Anna. 'He sounds terribly unhappy,' she said.

Legrand nodded. 'Yes, I believe he probably is,' he agreed.

'But why would anyone want to . . . *mutilate* themselves, Edouard?' asked Angélique, wrinkling her nose. 'Such an awful thing to do.'

'Rheinfeld displays stereotypic behaviour,' Legrand replied. 'That is to say, he suffers from what we call an obsessive-compulsive disorder. It can be triggered by chronic stress and frustration. In his case, we think that the mental disorder was caused by his years of fruitless searching for something.'

'What was he searching for?' Anna asked.

Legrand shrugged. 'We don't really know for sure. He seems to believe he was on some form of quest for buried treasure, lost secrets, that sort of thing. It's a common mania among the mentally ill.' He smiled. 'We've had a number of other intrepid treasure hunters in our care over the years. As well as our share of Jesus Christs, Napoleon Buonapartes and Adolf Hitlers. I'm afraid they're often not very imaginative in their choice of delusions.'

'A lost treasure,' Anna said, half to herself.

'And you say he was found not far from here . . .' Her voice trailed off in reflection.

'Can nothing be done to help him, Edouard?' asked Angélique.

Legrand shook his head. 'We've tried. When he first came to us, he received psychoanalysis and occupational therapy. For the first few months he appeared to respond to treatment. He was given a notebook to record his dreams. But then we discovered that he was filling its pages with insane babble. Over a period of time, his mental state deteriorated and he began to self-mutilate again. We had to take away his writing implements and increase his medication. Since then, I'm afraid to say, he's descended deeper and deeper into what I can only describe as madness.'

'What a terrible pity,' Anna breathed.

Legrand turned to her with a charming smile. 'In any case you would be more than welcome to have a tour of our little establishment, Anna. And if it could help you gain inspiration for your book, I could arrange for you to meet Rheinfeld in person – under supervision of course. Nobody ever comes to see him. You never know, it might do him good to have a visitor.'

CHAPTER 31

Paris

The pieces of the puzzle were virtually flying together for Luc Simon. The description that the two seriously embarrassed officers had given of the man who'd bundled them into Roberta Ryder's cupboard exactly matched Ben Hope.

Then had come the report about the Mercedes limo involved in the recent railway incident. The car itself was hot as hell. No registered owner. False plates. Numbers filed off both engine and chassis. Its internal locking system had been altered like a kidnap car. It looked as though it had been used for that kind of purpose too, as someone had obviously been trying to shoot their way out of it with a 9mm handgun.

Whoever that someone was, judging by the analysis report on the spent 9mm case found in the back, they were the same person as the mystery shooter from the scene of the riverside killings. And who was he? It had seemed impossible to find out. But then the cops at the scene of the

203

railway incident had found a business card inside the Mercedes. The name on the card was Benedict Hope.

There was more. In the parking lot of a nearby bar-restaurant they'd found the Citroën 2CV that had been mixed up in the railway incident. The missing grille badge, traces of paint from the Mercedes, even the dirt on the wheels, all matched the railway scene. The 2CV was registered to Dr Roberta Ryder.

And it got even better. When the forensic team had gone through Ryder's apartment with a fine-tooth comb, they'd found something. Right in the spot where she'd claimed her attacker had been lying dead, a speck of blood that whoever had cleaned the place up had missed. Simon bullied forensics into the fastest DNA test they'd ever done, comparing it against samples from Ryder's hairbrush and other personal effects. The blood wasn't hers. It did, however, match DNA samples from a grisly find that had turned up in the Parc Monceau. A severed human hand.

The hand's previous owner had been one Gustave LePou, a criminal with a long history of sex offences, aggravated rape, assault with a deadly weapon, burglary and two suspected murders to his credit. It looked as though Ryder had been telling him the truth after all. But why had LePou been in her apartment? Was it just burglary? No chance. Something bigger was going on. Someone must have hired LePou to kill her, or to steal something from her – or maybe both. Simon felt like kicking himself that he hadn't taken her seriously at the time.

More questions. Who had covered up the traces of LePou's death, removed his corpse from Ryder's apartment, chopped it up and tried, rather unsuccessfully, to dispose of it? What was the connection with Zardi, the laboratory assistant, and had the same people killed him? Where did Ben Hope fit in – was he the Englishman who Roberta Ryder had told him was in danger? If the railway incident had been meant to kill Hope, when Simon had seen him later that evening he looked pretty cool for someone who'd just narrowly escaped a horrific death. Where were Hope and Ryder now? Was Hope predator or prey? The thing was a complete enigma.

Simon was sitting in his cramped office drinking a coffee with Rigault when the expected fax came through from England. He tore it out of the machine. 'Benedict Hope,' he muttered as he read. 'Thirty-seven years of age. Oxford educated. Parents deceased. No criminal record, not a parking-ticket. Squeaky clean, the bastard.' He slurped his coffee.

He passed the sheet to Rigault as the fax started churning out a second page. It spat the paper into his hand and he read it, his eyes darting along the lines. Across the top of the sheet was the British Ministry of Defence letterhead. There was a lot of text below. Official stamps and confidentiality warnings in large bold print everywhere. The second page was more of the same. So was the third. He whistled.

'What's that?' Rigault asked, looking up.

Simon showed him. 'Hope's military record.'

Rigault read it and his eyebrows rose. 'Fuck me,' he breathed. 'This is serious stuff.' He looked up at Simon.

'He's our mystery shooter, no doubt about it.'

'What's he doing? What's going on?'

'I don't know,' Simon said, 'but I'm going to bring him in and find out. I'm putting out an alert on him right now.' He picked up the phone.

Rigault shook his head and tapped the fax printout with his fingers. 'You're going to need half the French police force to catch *this* fucker.'

CHAPTER 32

The drive southwards down the autoroute from Paris was long and hot. At Nevers the motorway was interrupted for a while and they took the Nationale road as far as Clermont-Ferrand, then drove back onto Autoroute 75 heading towards Le Puy. Ben's destination was still a long way south, down in the Languedoc region where he could pick up the trail of Klaus Rheinfeld and, he hoped, make some progress on his search.

With only Fulcanelli's half-read Journal for guidance, he still had no clear idea of what he was even looking for. All he could do was follow the thin clues as best he could and hope that things got a bit more promising along the way.

Roberta was asleep next to him, her head rolling on her shoulder. She'd been sleeping for the last hour or so, which was about the same length of time he'd known for sure that they were being followed. The blue BMW that he was now watching with half an eye in the rearview mirror, keeping pace with them through the traffic, had been on their tail since sometime after Paris.

The pursuing car had first caught his attention

at a refuelling stop when the Peugeot had been ahead in the line. The four men in the BMW had been acting jittery. He could tell they didn't want to lose sight of him.

They headed back onto the road, and Ben tested them. Whenever he overtook a slower vehicle in front of him, the BMW would follow. When he slowed right down to a pace guaranteed to annoy other motorists, the BMW followed suit, ignoring the blaring horns of the indignant drivers until Ben accelerated and it accelerated with him. There was no doubt about it.

'Why're you driving so erratically?' Roberta complained sleepily from beside him.

'Just my erratic personality, I guess,' he replied. 'Actually, I hate to tell you this, but we've got a friend. The blue BMW,' he added as she twisted round in her seat, suddenly wide awake.

'You think it's them again?'

He nodded. 'Either that, or they want to ask directions.'

'Can we get out of it?'

He shrugged. 'Depends how sticky they are. If we can't shake them off, they're going to follow us until we get to a quiet road and then they're going to try something.'

'Try what? Don't answer that. See if you can shake them.'

'OK. Hang on tight.' He dropped down two gears and accelerated hard. The Peugeot surged forwards, weaving as he turned hard to overtake a truck. A horn sounded from behind. The roar of the engine filled the car. Ben glanced in the mirror and saw the BMW giving chase, dipping in and out between lanes. 'If that's the way you want it,' he breathed, and pushed the accelerator down harder.

Up ahead, a lorry was pulling out of its lane. The Peugeot darted into the gap and overtook it on the wrong side. The lorry gave a furious wobble as it shrank fast in his mirror, its airhorns blasting angrily.

'Are you suicidal?' she yelled over the engine noise.

'Only when I'm sober.'

'Are you sober?' She made a face. 'Don't answer that either.'

A clear stretch ahead. Ben floored the throttle, pushing the speedo needle past the 160 km/h mark. Roberta clutched the sides of her seat. The BMW emerged through the confusion of traffic they'd left in their wake, powering after them.

Ben wove the 206 at high speed in and out of the honking traffic. It was far more agile than the heavy BMW, and by the time they reached a turn-off their pursuers were lagging 100 metres behind. The Peugeot tore along a winding country road. Ben took two random junctions, left and then right. But what the BMW lacked in agility it gained in speed and with an obviously determined driver it was tough to shake off.

A sign flashed up for a village, and Ben skidded

into the turning. They were on a long straight. The bigger car edged up on them. His eye was on the dial and he was going as fast as he dared. Behind them, one of the passengers of the BMW stuck an arm out of the window and squeezed off several shots from a pistol. The Peugeot's rear window shattered.

They entered the village and sped through the main square, skidding to avoid a fountain and panicking some drinkers at a bistro terrace who roared and shook their fists only to dive for cover a second time as the BMW came roaring through and sent tables and chairs spinning across the pavement.

A junction flashed up and Ben skidded left with a screech of tyres. A truck swerved and narrowly missed them, crashing into a parked Fiat. The Fiat rolled into the path of the BMW as it veered around the bend in pursuit. The BMW hit the loose car a clanging blow from the side and spun it across the road into a wall. The BMW, with a crumpled wing and buckled bonnet, composed itself and came on again, picking up speed.

They were out of the village, blasting down a twisting road with trees zipping by on either side. A gap in the trees appeared on the right. Ben twisted the wheel and the Peugeot veered off the road, hitting the farm track with its tyres spinning on the loose surface. He controlled the skid and the car straightened up, then a severe rut hammered the suspension hard into its stops and their stomachs were in their mouths.

The BMW was doggedly hanging on behind. Dirt flew in their wake. Roberta twisted round again to see the BMW's crumpled nose disappear in a cloud of dust as it plunged through the rut.

The Peugeot raced into a sharp bend. Suddenly a tractor filled the road. Skidding wildly on the loose surface Ben managed to aim the car through a flimsy farm gate. It splintered like balsawood and the Peugeot crashed on through into the field. It went bucking across the ridged surface of the field and down a sharp incline. A sudden dip as the front of the car plunged into empty space. Then a crash as they smashed into the opposite bank of the deep trench. The Peugeot bounced and lay still.

They climbed out as the BMW came bounding down the hillside after them. Seeing the dust rising from the crashed Peugeot, the driver braked – too hard, sending the BMW into a sideways skid. It spun, hit another rut, went up sideways on two wheels and rolled, coming to a rest upside down in a great plume of dust.

Its four dazed occupants spilled out. A fat man with blood streaming down his temple fired a pistol at the Peugeot. The passenger window burst and showered Roberta with glass as she crawled for cover.

'Roberta!' Ben grabbed the Browning and returned fire, the gun bucking in his hand as his bullet went through the side of the BMW four inches from the fat man's head. She took cover next to him.

Three of their pursuers dived behind the BMW. The fourth scrambled behind a rock, clutching a short-barrelled shotgun. He fired. The shot blew a ragged hole in the roof of the Peugeot, and Roberta screamed. Ben brought the Browning up again and loosed off four rapid shots. Dust flew up around the prone shooter. Ben's fourth shot caught him in the upper arm. He rolled out from the cover of the rock, racking the shotgun. Ben fired at him again, and kept squeezing off round after round until he was down and the Browning was out of ammunition. He ejected the spent mag and reached into his pocket for a spare one.

His pocket was empty. He suddenly remembered that all the magazines and ammunition were in his bag inside the car.

Another man came out from behind the upside-down BMW. The gun in his hands was black and oblong, with a stubby silencer and a long pistol-grip magazine. He fired a chattering burst from the Ingram submachine gun which peppered the side of the Peugeot with holes and forced Ben to take cover as he tried to get into the car. The third and fourth shooters were stepping out from behind the BMW, pistols in their hands, cautiously advancing. The man with the Ingram let off another spray, whipping up dust and stones in a line to Ben's left. *Not good.*

Suddenly the Ingram had shot itself empty, and the man was struggling to reload it. Ben saw his chance. He reached inside the Peugeot and grabbed his bag. Fumbled with the catches and found what he was looking for. He slammed in a fresh magazine as the man with the Ingram came closer. Throwing his gun arm up over the top of the car, Ben shot him twice in the chest and saw him go down on his back with his legs kicking in the air. The gunman nearest the BMW ran back for cover, snapping a wild shot over his shoulder. His colleague, realizing he was too far from the car, went down on one knee and emptied his 9mm at Ben.

Ben ducked down as bullets whanged past him.

But one caught him. The blow to his right side jerked him round. He righted himself and returned fire. The man came down sprawling with his arms outflung and his pistol tumbling to the ground.

Ben staggered. There was blood everywhere. His vision clouded and suddenly he was gazing up at a circle of treetops and grey sky.

Roberta saw him go down, screaming *NO!!!* and catching his pistol as it fell. She'd never fired a gun before, but the Browning was easy – just point and squeeze. The last gunman stepped out again from behind the BMW and fired at her. She felt the crack as the bullet zipped past her. With the Browning in both hands she fired back and sent him under cover in a shower of glass. She grabbed her shoulder-bag out of the Peugeot's broken window.

'Can you run?' she yelled at him. Ben groaned, rolled and staggered to his feet. His knees were weak. Another shot rang out. Her wild answering bullet caught the man in the thigh, and with a scream and a spray of blood he fell back behind the car. Now the Browning was empty again and wouldn't work any more. The injured man came crawling back out with a double-barrelled shotgun. He fired and the Peugeot's wing-mirror exploded.

'Come on!' She grabbed Ben's arm and they ran down the steep slope. Below them, a rough earth bank led sharply down to a winding country lane. A farm truck carrying a load of hay was lumbering slowly by. In four running leaps they were ten feet right above it and then Roberta threw herself into the air, taking him with her. They sailed through space for a terrifying second. The back of the truck rushed up to meet them – and then they plummeted into the prickly bed of hay, all arms and legs and confusion.

The man with the shotgun hobbled swearing down the slope past his three dead companions. He roared with fury as he watched the truck, with Ben and Roberta in the back, disappear in the fading light.

CHAPTER 33

Paris

After the long, hot drive from Rome, Franco Bozza was in no mood for niceties. He filtered the black Porsche 911 Turbo through the traffic of the city outskirts and headed towards the suburb of Créteil. He soon found what he was looking for in a rundown industrial zone on the outer fringes. The disused packing plant stood back from the street, behind rusted iron gates that were locked with a chain. Weeds littered the forecourt. Bozza left the Porsche running and walked up to the gates. The padlock was shiny and new. He took the key from his pocket and unlocked it. Checked left and right that nobody was around, then pushed open the right-hand gate with a grating of rusty hinges. He drove the Porsche through, then locked the gates behind him. The street was empty. Bozza parked out of sight around the back of the neglected building, and walked in through the back entrance that he knew would be left open for him.

The appearance of the tall, broad and silent

figure in the long black coat created a chill in the air for the three men who'd been guarding the unconscious Gaston Clément. Naudon, Godard and Berger all knew the Inquisitor's reputation and stayed as far from him as possible, barely daring even to look at him as the man opened up the black bag he was carrying and laid out the shiny assortment of instruments on a trolley. Some of the implements were obviously surgical, like the scalpels and the saw. They could only guess at the grisly purpose of the bolt cutters, claw hammer and blowtorch.

In the centre of the wide empty space, the old alchemist was hanging naked and limp by his feet from a chain wrapped around a girder. The last item Bozza took out of his bag was the heavy plastic overall. He slipped it carefully over his head and smoothed it down over his body. Then he ran a gloved finger along the row of instruments, deciding where to start. His face was blank, impassive. He picked up a long, sharp probe and twirled it between his gloved fingers. He nodded to himself.

Then the whispering questions began, and the screaming.

A little over an hour later, the old man's screams had died to a constant babbling whimper. There was a spreading pool of blood under him, and Bozza's plastic overall and the tools on the trolley were thickly smeared with it.

But this had been a waste of time. The old man

was sick and frail, and Bozza could see from the bruises and blood-encrusted gashes on his face that his captors had beaten him into uselessness long before he'd even got there. Now his ravaged body had gone into total shock and the torturer knew there was no point in prolonging the agony. There was nothing to learn from him. Bozza walked to the trolley and unzipped a small pouch. The syringe inside contained a massive dose of the same substance vets used to euthanize dogs. He walked back to the hanging body and jabbed the needle into Clement's neck.

When it was all over, Bozza turned and looked coldly at the three men. Their anxiety at his presence had diminished, and they were standing in a distant corner of the factory, chattering and smoking cigarettes, laughing and joking about something.

He smiled. They wouldn't be laughing long. What they didn't know about his visit was that getting information out of Clément wasn't the only reason Usberti had sent him here. His orders to 'clean up the mess' went further. These three amateurs had bungled their jobs once too often. *Gladius Domini*'s days of hiring petty crooks to do its dirty work were coming to an end.

He motioned to them to come over. Godard, Naudon and Berger stamped out their cigarettes, shot serious looks at one another and approached. Their good humour had suddenly evaporated, quickly giving way back to nervousness. Naudon was wearing a weak grin, about to say something.

They were ten metres away when Bozza casually drew out a silenced .380 Beretta and dropped them in rapid succession without a word. The bodies slumped quietly to the floor. A spent case tinkled across the concrete. He looked down impassively at the dead men as he unscrewed his silencer and replaced the little pistol in its holster.

Four bodies to dispose of. This time there'd be no traces left.

CHAPTER 34

The van drove away in a haze of dust and diesel smoke. The delivery driver was more than happy with the bulge in his pocket, to the tune of 1,000 Euros, that his odd hitchhikers – the short-tempered American woman and her quiet, pale and sick-looking boyfriend – had given him to go the extra kilometres out of his way as far as the tiny hamlet of Saint-Jean. He wondered what *that* was all about . . . but then again, what did he care? The drinks would be on him that night.

Roberta was still picking bits of hay out of her hair after their uncomfortable night in the barn. The farmer whose truck they'd jumped on had never noticed his passengers. After the bumpy ride through the country lanes he'd backed the truck up into the barn and then disappeared. Roberta had sneaked down and hunted around until she'd found a rough old blanket to cover Ben with. He was shivering and in a lot of pain.

She'd spent most of the night sitting watching him and worrying that she should have got him to a hospital. Two farm cats had found them and snuggled up next to her in the deep bed of hay.

She'd fallen asleep sometime after three, and it seemed like only minutes had passed before the dawn cries of a rooster had woken them. They'd crept away before the farmer appeared.

It had taken hours to get to Saint-Jean, and the afternoon sun was beginning its downward curve. The village seemed deserted. 'This place looks like it hasn't changed much in the last few centuries,' Roberta said, looking about her.

Ben was slumped against a dry-stone wall, head hanging. He looked pretty bad, she thought anxiously. 'You wait here. I'll go see if I can find someone who can help us.'

He nodded weakly. She touched his brow. It was burning, but his hands were cold. The pain from his side was making it hard for him to breathe. She stroked his face. 'Maybe there's a doctor in the village,' she said.

'Don't want a doctor,' he muttered. 'Get the priest. Get Father Pascal Cambriel.'

For the first time in her life, Roberta found herself praying as she walked through the empty street. The road was bare earth, crumbly from lack of rain. The ancient houses, dirty in a way that would have looked squalid anywhere but the south of France, seemed to lean against each other for support. 'If you're up there at all, Lord,' she said to herself, 'then please let me find Father Pascal.' She was suddenly chilled at the thought of being told he was dead, or no longer there. She quickened her step.

The church was at the far end of the village. Beside it was a little graveyard and beyond that a stone cottage. She could hear the cosy sound of hens clucking from the shelter of an outbuilding. A dusty and well-used old Renault 14 was parked outside.

A man walked out from between two houses. He looked like a labourer, his deeply lined face like leather from years of working in the harsh sun. He slowed as he caught sight of her.

'Monsieur, excuse me,' she called out to him. He peered at her curiously, quickened his pace and disappeared into one of the houses, slamming the door in her face. Roberta was shocked – and then it dawned on her that a tousled and grimy foreign woman with a bloodstained shirt and ripped jeans might not be a typical sight in these parts. She hurried on, thinking of Ben.

'*Madame? Je peux vous aider?*' said a voice. Roberta turned and saw an elderly lady, dressed all in black with a shawl wrapped around her shoulders. A crucifix hung from a chain around her wrinkled neck.

'Please, yes, I hope you can help me,' Roberta answered in French. 'I'm looking for the village priest.'

The old lady raised her eyebrows. 'Yes? He is here.'

'Is Father Pascal Cambriel still the priest of this village?'

'Yes, he is still here,' she said, smiling a gap-toothed smile. 'I am Marie-Claire. I take care of his house.'

'Will you take me to him, please? It's important. We need help.'

Marie-Claire led her along to the cottage and they went in. 'Father,' she called. 'We have a visitor.'

The cottage was a humble abode, sparsely furnished yet giving off an air of immense warmth and security. The evening fire was ready for lighting, logs piled on twigs. At a plain pine table were two simple wooden chairs, and at the other end of the room was an old couch covered with a blanket. A large ebony crucifix hung on one whitewashed wall, and there was a picture of the Pope beside an image of the Crucifixion.

There were creaky, uneven footsteps on the stairs, and the priest appeared. Now seventy, Pascal Cambriel was having a little difficulty walking and he leaned heavily on his stick. 'What can I do for you, my child?' he asked, casting a curious eye over Roberta's unusual appearance. 'Are you hurt? Has there been an accident?'

'I'm not hurt, but I'm with a friend who's not well,' she said. 'You're Father Pascal Cambriel, aren't you?'

'I am.'

She closed her eyes. *Thank you, Lord.*

'Father, we were on our way especially to meet you when my friend was injured. He's sick.'

'This is serious.' Pascal frowned.

'I know what you're going to say, that he should see a doctor. I can't explain right now, but he doesn't want one. Will you help?'

'In any case, there is no doctor here any longer,' Pascal told her as they bumped back down the street in his Renault. 'Dr Bachelard passed away two years ago, and nobody has taken his place. No young people want to come to Saint-Jean. It is a dying place, I am sorry to say.'

Ben was semi-conscious when the priest's car ground to a halt on the village outskirts. 'My Lord, he is very sick.' Pascal limped over to Ben's slumped form and took him by the arm. 'Can you hear me, my son? Mademoiselle, you will have to help me get him into the car.'

Roberta, Pascal and old Marie-Claire nursed Ben up the stairs of the cottage, into the priest's spare bedroom. He was laid in the bed and Pascal unbuttoned his bloody shirt. He winced at the sight of the wound across Ben's ribs. He said nothing, but he could see that it was a gunshot wound. He'd seen them before, many years ago. He felt with his fingers. The bullet had passed straight through the muscle and out the other side.

'Marie-Claire, would you kindly fetch hot water, bandages and disinfectant? And do we still have any of that herbal preparation for cleansing wounds?'

Marie-Claire tiptoed dutifully off to attend to her task.

Pascal felt Ben's pulse. 'It is very fast.'

'Will he be OK?' Roberta was drained of all colour, her fists balled at her sides.

'We will need some of Arabelle's medicine.'

223

'Arabelle? Is she a local healer?'

'Arabelle is our goat. We have some antibiotics from when she suffered a hoof infection some time ago. I am afraid that is the limit of my medical prowess.' Pascal smiled. 'But Marie-Claire knows much about herbal remedies. Many a time has she helped me, and other members of our little community. I believe our young friend here is in good hands.'

'Father, I'm so grateful to you for your help.'

'It is my duty, but also my pleasure, to give service to the needy,' Pascal replied. 'It has been some time since this room was last used to tend to a sick man. I believe it must be five, even six years, since the last injured soul found his way to our village.'

'It was Klaus Rheinfeld, wasn't it?'

Pascal stopped what he was doing abruptly and turned to give Roberta a penetrating look.

'He is sleeping,' Pascal murmured as he came down the stairs. 'We will leave him for a while.'

Roberta was fresh from her bath and wearing the clothes Marie-Claire had given her. 'Thanks again for your help,' she said. 'I don't know what we'd have done . . .'

Pascal smiled. 'There is no need to thank me. You must be hungry, Roberta. Let us eat.'

Marie-Claire served a simple meal – some soup, bread and a glass of Pascal's own wine, pressed from his little vineyard. They ate in silence, the only sound the rasping of the crickets outside and a dog barking in the distance. From time to time the priest would reach out and take a split log from a basket and throw it into the fire.

After the meal was over Marie-Claire cleared the table, and then said goodnight before returning to her own cottage across the street. Pascal lit a long wooden pipe and moved to a rocking chair by the fireside. He turned out the main light so that they were bathed in the flickering orangey glow from the fire, and invited her to sit opposite him in an armchair. 'I think we have some things to discuss, you and I.'

'It's a long and strange story, Father, and I don't even know all there is to know. But I'll do my best to explain the situation to you.' She told him what she knew about Ben's assignment, the danger it had led him into, the things that had happened to her, her fears. Her account was rambling and disconnected. She was terribly weary and her body ached.

'I now understand your reluctance to see a doctor,' Pascal said. 'You are afraid of being reported and falsely accused of these crimes.' He looked at the clock on the wall. 'My child, it is getting late. You are exhausted and must rest. You shall sleep on the couch. It is actually very comfortable. I have brought you down some bedclothes.'

'Thanks, Father. I'm certainly exhausted but I think, if it's all right with you, that I should sit up with Ben.'

He touched her shoulder. 'You are a loyal companion to him. You care for him deeply.'

She was silent. The words struck her.

'But I will sit up with him while you take your rest,' Pascal continued. 'I have done little today except tend the chickens, milk Arabelle, God bless the dear creature, and hear two very routine confessions.' He smiled.

Pascal sat until late and read his Bible by the light of a candle, while Ben tossed and turned fitfully. Once, around four, he woke and said 'Where am I?'

'With friends, Benedict,' the priest replied. He stroked Ben's clammy forehead and settled him back to sleep. 'Rest now. You are safe. I will pray for you.'

CHAPTER 35

Ben tried to move his legs across the bed. He'd been lying here long enough.

It was tough going, an inch at a time. The pull on his injured muscles was agonizing. He clenched his teeth as he gently lowered his feet to the floor and slowly stood up. His shirt had been washed and neatly laid out for him on a chair. It took him a long time to dress.

Through the window he could see the village rooftops and the hills and mountains beyond rising up to the clear sky. He cursed himself furiously for letting this situation happen. He'd underestimated the dangers right from the start of this job. And here he was, stuck in this backwater, hardly able to move or do anything useful, while a dying child needed his help. He grabbed his flask and took a deep swig. *At least this is something I can do.* He wished he had a whole bottle, or maybe two.

Then he remembered Fulcanelli's Journal. He bent stiffly and fished it out of his bag. He lay on the bed with it, leafing through the pages, and resumed his reading.

3rd September, 1926

It has finally happened: the pupil has challenged the master. As I write, I can still hear Daquin's words ringing in my ears as he confronted me today in the laboratory. His eyes were blazing, and his fists were clenched at his sides.

'But master,' he protested. 'Aren't we being selfish? How can you possibly say it's right to keep such important knowledge a secret when it could benefit so many people? Don't you see the good that this could do? Think how it would change everything!'

'No, Nicholas,' I insisted. 'I am not being selfish. I am being cautious. These secrets are important, yes. But they are too dangerous to reveal to just anyone. Only the initiated, the adept, should ever be allowed to have this knowledge.'

Nicholas stared at me in fury. 'Then I can see no point in it,' he shouted. 'You are old, master. You've spent most of your life searching, but it's all for nothing if you don't use it. Use it to help the world.'

'And you are young, Nicholas,' I replied. 'Too young to understand the world you want so much to help. Not everyone is as pure of heart as you are. There are people who would use this knowledge to serve their own greed and their own purposes. Not to do good, but to do evil.'

On the table beside us was the ancient scroll

in its leather tube. I picked it up and shook it at him. 'I am a direct descendant of the authors of this wisdom,' I said. 'My Cathar ancestors knew the importance of preserving their secrets, at all costs. They knew who was seeking them, and they knew what would have happened if they had fallen into the wrong hands. They gave their lives trying to preserve this wisdom.'

'I know, master, but . . .'

I interrupted him. 'This knowledge we have been privileged with is power, and power is a dangerous thing. It corrupts men, and attracts evil. That is why I warned you about the responsibility I was giving you. And don't forget – you swore an oath of silence.' I hung my head in sadness. 'I fear I have revealed too much to you,' I added.

'Does that mean you're not going to tell me any more? What about the rest? The second great secret?'

I shook my head. 'I am sorry, Nicholas. It is too much knowledge for one so young and rash. I cannot undo what is already done, but I will not take you any further until you have proved greater wisdom and maturity.'

At these words, he stormed out of the laboratory. I could see he was on the edge of tears. I, too, felt a knife in my heart knowing what had come between us.

Ben heard a soft knock at the bedroom door. He looked up from the Journal as the door opened a crack and Roberta's face appeared.

'How are you feeling now?' she said. She looked concerned as she came in carrying a tray.

He closed the Journal. 'I'm OK.'

'Here, look, I prepared this for you.' She laid a bowl of steaming chicken soup on the table. 'Eat it while it's hot.'

'How long was I out of it?'

'Two days.'

'Two days!' He took a slurp of whisky, wincing at the movement.

'Should you be drinking, Ben? You've been on antibios.' She sighed. 'At least eat something. You need to get your strength back.'

'I will. Can you kick over my bag? My cigarettes are in it.'

'Smoking isn't good for you right now.'

'It's never good for me.'

'Fine. Have it your own way. I'll get them for you.'

'No, just–' He moved too abruptly and pain shot through him. He leaned back against the pillow, closing his eyes.

She reached down. As she rummaged around in the bag, a small object fell out and landed on the floor. She picked it up. It was a tiny photograph in a silver frame. She studied it, wondering what it was doing in there. The photo was old and faded, creased and worn at the edges as though it had been carried for years in a wallet. It was a picture of a child, a sweet little girl of about eight or nine with blond hair. She had sparkling, intelligent blue eyes and a freckly face, and she was smiling at the camera with an expression of open happiness.

'Who is she, Ben? She's lovely.' She looked at him and her smile faded.

He was staring at her with an expression of cold fury she'd never seen before.

'Put that down and get the *fuck* out of here,' he said.

Father Pascal saw the look of anger and hurt on Roberta's face as she came downstairs. He laid a hand on her arm. 'Sometimes when a man is in pain, he lashes out and says and does things he does not mean,' he said.

'Just because he's injured, that doesn't excuse him for behaving like a bas–' She caught herself. 'I was only trying to help him.'

'That was not the pain I was referring to,' Pascal said. 'The true pain is in his heart, his spirit, not in his wounds.' He smiled warmly. 'I will speak to him.'

He went into Ben's room and sat beside him on the edge of the bed. Ben was lying there staring into space, clutching his flask. The whisky was dulling his pain a little. He'd managed to retrieve his cigarettes, only to find the packet almost empty.

'You do not mind if I join you?' said Pascal.

Ben shook his head.

Pascal was quiet for a few moments, then he spoke gently and warmly to Ben. 'Benedict, Roberta has told me something of your occupation. You have a calling to help those in need – a noble and commendable thing indeed. I, too, have a calling, which I carry out as well as I can. I must say it is less dramatic, less heroic, than yours. But the purpose the Lord has for me is nonetheless an important duty to fulfil. I help men to release their suffering. To find God. For some, that simply is to find peace within themselves, in whichever form it may come.'

'This is my peace, Father,' muttered Ben. He held up his flask.

'You know it is not enough, that it will never be enough. It cannot help you, it can only hurt you. It drives your pain deeper in your heart. The pain is like a poisoned thorn. If it is not released, it will fester like a terrible wound. And not one that may be cured by the simple application of penicillin intended for a goat.'

Ben laughed bitterly. 'Yeah, you're probably right.'

'You have helped many people, it seems,' said Pascal. 'Yet you continue on your path of self-destruction, relying upon liquor, this false friend. When the joy of helping others has faded, does the pain not return soon after, and worse?'

Ben said nothing.

'I think you know the answer.'

'Look,' Ben said, 'I'm grateful for all you've done for me. But I'm not interested in sermons any longer. That part of me died a long time ago. So with the deepest respect to you, Father, if you've come up here to preach to me you're wasting your time.'

They sat in silence.

'Who is Ruth?' Pascal asked suddenly.

Ben threw him a sharp glance. 'Didn't Roberta tell you? The little girl who's dying, my client's granddaughter. The one I'm trying to save. If it's not too bloody late.'

'No, Benedict, that is not who I meant. Who is the other Ruth, the Ruth of your dreams?'

Ben felt his blood turn to ice and his heart quicken. With a tight throat he said, 'I don't know what you're talking about. There isn't any Ruth in my dreams.'

'When a man sits through two nights with a delirious patient,' Pascal said, 'he may discover things about him that might not be openly discussed. You have a secret, Ben. Who is Ruth – who *was* Ruth?'

Ben let out a deep sigh. He raised the flask again.

'Why don't you let me help you?' Pascal said gently. 'Come, share your burden with me.'

After a long silence Ben started talking quietly, almost mechanically. His eyes were staring into space as he played the familiar, painful images back in his mind for the millionth time.

'I was sixteen. She was my sister. She was only

nine. We were so close . . . we were soulmates. She was the only person I've ever loved with all my heart.' He gave a bitter smile. 'She was like the sunshine, Father. You should have seen her. For me, she was the reason to believe in a Creator. This might come as a surprise to you, but at one time I was going to become a clergyman.'

Pascal listened carefully. 'Go on, my son.'

'My parents took us on a holiday to north Africa, Morocco,' Ben continued. 'We were staying in a big hotel. One day my parents decided to go to visit a museum, and they left us behind. They told me to take care of Ruth and not to leave the hotel grounds under any circumstances.'

He paused to light his last cigarette. 'A Swiss family were staying in the hotel. They had a daughter about a year older than me. Her name was Martina.' Talking about it for the first time in years, he could remember it all perfectly. He saw Martina's face in his mind. 'She was great-looking. I really liked her, and she asked me out. She wanted to visit a souk without her parents being there. At first I said no, I had to stay in the hotel and look after my sister. But Martina was going back to Switzerland the next day. And she said that if I went with her to the souk, when we got back she'd . . . anyway, I was tempted. I decided it would be OK to bring Ruth along too. I figured that my parents would never know.'

'Go on,' Pascal said.

'We left the hotel. We wandered around the

market. It was crowded, full of stalls, snake-charmers, all those strange sights and music and smells.'

Pascal nodded. 'I was in Algeria, for the war, many years ago. A strange, alien world, for us Europeans.'

'It was a good time,' Ben said. 'I liked being around Martina, and she kept holding my hand as she was looking at all the stalls. But I kept a close watch on Ruth. She stayed right by my side. Then Martina saw a little silver casket she liked, to keep jewellery in. She didn't have enough money, so I said I'd buy it for her. I turned my back on Ruth while I was counting the money. It was only for a moment. I bought the present for Martina, and she hugged me.' He paused again. His throat was dry. He went to take another swig from his flask.

Pascal stopped his arm, gently but firmly. 'Let us leave deceitful friends out of this for the moment.'

Ben nodded, swallowed hard. 'I don't know how it could have happened so fast. I only took my eyes off her for a few seconds. But then she was . . . gone.' He shrugged. 'Just gone, just like that.'

His heart felt like a huge bubble ready to burst. He put his head in his hands, shaking it slowly from side to side. 'She just wasn't there any more. I never heard her cry out. I didn't see a thing. Everything around me was normal. It was as though I'd dreamed the whole thing. As though she'd never existed.'

'She had not simply wandered off.'

Ben took his head out of his hands and sat straighter. 'No,' he said. 'It's a lucrative trade, and the people who take them are expert professionals. Everything that could be done was done – police, consulate, months of searching. We never found a trace.'

The bubble burst. He'd held it back for so long. Something was pierced inside him, a sense of gushing. He hadn't cried since those days, except in his dreams. 'And it was all my fault, because I turned my back on her. I lost her.'

'You have never loved anyone since,' Pascal said. It wasn't a question.

'I don't know how to love,' Ben said, collecting himself. 'I can't remember the last time I was really happy. I don't know what it feels like.'

'God loves you, Benedict.'

'God's no more a friend to me than whisky is.'

'You lost faith.'

'I tried to keep faith then. At first I prayed every day that she'd be found. I prayed for forgiveness. I knew God wasn't listening to me, but I kept on believing and I kept on praying.'

'And what about your family?'

'My mother never forgave me. She couldn't stand the sight of me. I couldn't blame her. Then she went into a deep depression. One day her bedroom door was locked. My father and I shouted and beat on it, but she wasn't answering. She'd taken a massive overdose of sleeping-pills. I was eighteen, just starting my theology studies.'

Pascal nodded sadly. 'And your father?'

'He went downhill fast after we lost Ruth, and Mum's death made him worse. My only consolation was that I thought he'd forgiven me.' Ben sighed. 'I was home on vacation. I went into his study. I can't even remember why. I think I needed some paper. He wasn't around. I found his diary.'

'You read it?'

'And I found out what he really thought. The truth was, he hated me. He blamed me for everything, didn't think I deserved to live after what I'd brought on the family. I couldn't go back to university after that. I lost interest in everything. My father died soon after.'

'What did you do then, my son?'

'I can't remember much about the first year. I bummed around Europe a lot, tried to lose myself. After a while I came home, sold up the house. I moved to Ireland with Winnie, our housekeeper. Then I joined the army. I couldn't think of what else to do. I hated myself. I was full of rage, and put every bit of it into my training. I was the most disciplined and motivated recruit they'd ever seen. They had no idea what was behind it. Then, in time, I became a very good soldier. I had a certain attitude. A certain hardness. I was wild, and they made use of that. I ended up doing a lot of things that I don't like to talk about.'

He hesitated before going on, and his mind filled

briefly with memories, images, sounds, smells. He shook his head to clear them. 'In the end I realized the army wasn't what I wanted. I hated everything it stood for. I came home, tried to get my life back together. After a while I was contacted to find a missing teenager. It was in the south of Italy. When it was over and the kid was safe, I realized that I'd found what I wanted to do.' He looked up at Pascal. 'That was four years ago.'

'You found that by returning missing people to their loved ones, you were healing the wound caused by the loss of Ruth.'

Ben nodded. 'Every time I brought one home safe, it drove me on to the next job. It was like an addiction. It still is.'

Pascal smiled. 'You have been through much pain. I am glad you trusted me enough to speak of it, Benedict. Trust is a great healer. Trust and time.'

'Time hasn't healed me,' said Ben. 'The pain gets duller, but deeper.'

'You believe that finding the cure for this little girl Ruth will help you to cleanse out the demon of guilt.'

'I wouldn't have taken this assignment otherwise.'

'I hope you succeed, Ben, for the girl's sake and for yours. But I think that true redemption, true peace, must come from deeper within. You must learn to trust, to open your heart, and to find love within yourself. Only then will your wounds heal.'

'You make it sound easy,' Ben said.

Pascal smiled. 'You have already started out on

your path by confessing your secret to me. There is no salvation in burying your feelings. It may hurt to draw the poison from the wound – at such times we come face to face with the demon. But once it is brought to the surface and released, you may find freedom.'

Wax from the candle dripped onto Ben's hand as he crept into the church of Saint-Jean. The door was never locked, not even at two in the morning. His legs were still weak and shaky as he made his way up the aisle. Shadows flickered all around him in the empty, silent building. He fell to his knees in front of the altar and his candlelight shone on the gleaming white statue of Christ above him.

Ben bowed his head and prayed.

The trail was leading Luc Simon south. It was easy to follow – it was a trail of bullets and dead men.

A farmer in Le Puy in mid-France had reported shots heard and two cars involved in a chase on rural roads. When the police found the field where the gun battle had taken place they'd discovered three dead men, two wrecked cars shot to pieces, weapons and spent cartridge cases lying everywhere. Neither car was registered to anyone, and the BMW had been reported stolen a couple of days earlier in Lyon.

More interestingly, inside the other car, a silver Peugeot with Paris plates, they'd found prints that

239

matched Roberta Ryder's. Among the many spent cases found in the grass were eighteen 9mm empties that had come from the same Browning-type pistol as those found in the Mercedes limo and at the scene of the riverside killings.

Ben Hope might as well have carved his name on a tree.

CHAPTER 36

The Institut Legrand, near Limoux, southern France
Three months earlier

'Oh shit – look, Jules, he's done it *again!*' Klaus Rheinfeld's padded cell was covered in blood. As the two male psychiatric nurses entered the small, cube-shaped room, its occupant looked up from his handiwork like a child caught in the act of some forbidden game. His wizened face crinkled into a grin, and they saw that he'd knocked out two more teeth. He'd torn open his pyjama top and used the jagged teeth to reopen the strange wound pattern on his chest.

'Looks like time to increase your dose again,' muttered the male nurse in charge as Rheinfeld was led out of the cell. 'Better get the cleaners in here,' he said to his assistant. 'Take him to the clinic, give him a shot of diazepam and put him into some clean clothes. Make sure his nails are cut really short, too. He's got a visitor coming in a couple of hours.'

'That Italian woman again?'

Rheinfeld's ears pricked up at the mention of his visitor. 'Anna!' he sang. 'Anna . . . like Anna. Anna is my friend.' He spat at the nurses. 'Hate *you*.'

Two hours later a much more subdued Klaus Rheinfeld sat in the secure visiting room at the Institut Legrand. It was the room they used for more borderline-risk patients who were allowed to see outside guests from time to time but not trusted to be left alone with them. One plain table, two chairs, bolted to the floor, a male nurse either side of him and a third standing by with a loaded syringe, just in case. Through a two-way mirror on the wall, Dr Legrand, head of the Institut, was watching.

Rheinfeld was wearing a fresh pair of pyjamas and a clean gown to replace the ones he'd bloodied earlier. The new gap in his teeth had been cleaned up. His improved mood was due partly to the psychotropic drugs they'd pumped into him, and partly due to the strange calming effect that his new friend and regular visitor, Anna Manzini, had on him. Clasped in his hands was his prize possession, his notebook.

Anna Manzini was shown in by a male nurse, and the stark, sterile atmosphere of the visiting room became filled with her airy presence and perfume. Rheinfeld's face lit up with happiness at the sight of her.

'Hello, Klaus.' She smiled and sat opposite him at the bare table. 'And how are you today?'

The male nurses were always amazed at the way this normally difficult and agitated patient would settle down with the attractive, warm Italian woman. She had a way about her, so gentle and calm, never stressing or placing demands on him. For long periods he wouldn't say a word, just sitting there rocking gently in his chair with his eyes half shut in relaxation and one long, bony hand resting on her arm. At first the nurses had been unhappy about this physical contact, but Anna had asked them to allow it and they'd accepted that it did no harm.

When he did speak, for much of the time Rheinfeld kept muttering the same things over and over – phrases in garbled Latin and jumbled letters and numbers, obsessively counting his fingers in jerky movements as he did so.

Sometimes, with a little gentle prompting, Anna could get him to speak more coherently about his interests. In a low voice he would talk about things the nurses couldn't begin to understand. After a while his conversation would often fade back into an unintelligible mumble and then die away altogether. Anna would just smile and let him sit there quietly. These were his most peaceful times, and the nurses considered them a useful part of his treatment programme.

This fifth visit was no different from the others. Rheinfeld sat serenely clasping Anna's hand and his notebook and running through the same number sequence in his low, cracked voice, talking in his own weird language. 'N-6; E-4; I-26; A-11; E-15.'

'What are you trying to tell us, Klaus?' Anna asked patiently.

Dr Legrand stood watching the scene from behind the two-way mirror with a frown on his face. He checked his watch and then strode into the visiting-room through a connecting door. 'Anna, how wonderful to see you,' he said, beaming. He turned to the nurses. 'I think that will do for today. We don't want to tire the patient.'

At the sight of Legrand, Rheinfeld screamed and covered his head with his skinny arms. He fell off his chair, and as Anna was getting up to leave he clawed his emaciated body across the floor and clutched at her ankles, protesting loudly. The nurses dragged him away from her, and she watched sadly as they bundled him through a door back towards his room.

'Why is he so afraid of you, Edouard?' she asked Legrand when they were back out in the corridor.

'I don't know, Anna.' Legrand smiled. 'We have no idea about Klaus's past. His reaction to me may be the residue of some traumatic event. It's possible I remind him unconsciously of someone who has hurt him – perhaps an abusive father or some other relative. It's quite a common phenomenon.'

She shook her head sadly. 'I see. That would explain it.'

'Anna, I was thinking . . . if you're free tonight,

how about dinner? I know a little fish restaurant on the coast. The sea bass is just to *die* for. I could pick you up around seven?' He caressed her arm.

She pulled back from his touch. 'Please, Edouard. I told you I wasn't ready . . . Let's leave dinner for another time.'

'I'm sorry,' he said, withdrawing his hand. 'I understand. Please forgive me.'

Legrand watched from his window as Anna left the building and climbed into her Alfa Romeo. That was the third time she'd knocked him back, he thought. What was wrong with him? Other women didn't react this way. She didn't seem to want him to touch her. She continually gave him the cold shoulder, and yet she seemed to have no problem letting that Rheinfeld hold her hand for hours on end.

He turned away from the window and picked up the phone. 'Paulette, can you check and tell me if Dr Delavigne is scheduled for today's treatment assessment with one of the patients? . . . Klaus Rheinfeld . . . He is? . . . OK, can you call him and let him know that I'll take over from him . . . That's right . . . Thanks, Paulette.'

Rheinfeld was back in his padded cell, singing to himself contentedly and thinking of Anna, when he heard the rattle of keys from outside in the corridor and his door swung open.

'Leave me alone with him,' said a voice that he recognized. Rheinfeld cowered, his eyes bulging

245

with fear, as Dr Legrand walked into his cell and quietly shut the door behind him.

Legrand approached, and Rheinfeld backed away as far as he could into the corner. The psychiatrist towered over him, smiling. 'Hello, Klaus,' he said in a soft voice.

Then he drew back his foot and kicked Rheinfeld in the stomach. Rheinfeld doubled up helplessly in pain, winded and gasping.

Legrand kicked him again, and again. As the blows kept coming, Klaus Rheinfeld could do no more than weep and wish he was dead.

CHAPTER 37

On the third day Ben felt strong enough to come down and sit outside in the autumnal midday sun. He saw Roberta in the distance, feeding the hens and making a point of avoiding him. He felt bad, knowing he'd hurt her feelings. He sat and sipped the herbal tea that Marie-Claire had prepared for him, and carried on with Fulcanelli's Journal.

September 19th, 1926
I begin to truly regret the faith I had placed in Nicholas Daquin. It is with a heavy heart that I write these words, knowing now what a fool I have been. My one consolation is that I did not reveal to him the complete sum of the knowledge gained from the Cathar artefacts.

My worst fears were confirmed yesterday. Against all my principles and to my eternal shame, I have employed an investigator, a discreet and trustworthy man by the name of Corot, to follow Nicholas and report his movements to me. It appears that my young apprentice has for some time now been a member of a Parisian society called the Watchmen. Naturally I knew of the existence of this small circle of intellectuals, philosophers and initiates of esoteric knowledge. I also knew what had attracted Nicholas to them. The Watchmen's aim is to break away from the strictures of the secretive alchemical tradition. In their monthly meetings in a room above Chacornac's bookshop they discuss how the fruits of alchemical knowledge could be brought into modern science and used to benefit mankind. To a young man like Nicholas, they must represent the future, the foundation of a new era – and I well understand how torn he must feel between their progressive vision of a new alchemy and what he perceives as the antiquated, guarded, mistrustful approach that I represent.

Such youthful spirit and candour are not to be despised. But what Corot went on to report to me has given me great cause for concern. Through his association with the Watchmen, Nicholas has made a new friend. I know little of this man, save that his name is Rudolf, that he is a student of the occult and that they call him 'The Alexandrian' after his birthplace in Egypt.

Corot has observed Nicholas with this Rudolf on several occasions, watching them as they sit in cafés and have long discussions. Yesterday he followed them to an expensive restaurant and was able to eavesdrop on some of their conversation as they sat on the terrace.

Rudolf plied my young apprentice with glass after glass of champagne, and it is clear he was doing so to loosen his tongue.

'But it's the truth, you know,' Rudolf was saying as Corot secretively took notes from a nearby table. 'If Fulcanelli really believed in the power of this wisdom, he would not try to hinder one of its brightest stars.' Here he filled Nicholas's glass to the brim.

'I'm not used to such high living,' Corot heard Nicholas say.

'One day, you'll have all the high living you could ever desire,' said Rudolf.

Nicholas frowned. 'It's not fame and glory that I'm after. I just want to use my knowledge to help people, that's all. That's what I can't understand about the master, why he thinks that's such a bad thing.'

'Your selflessness is laudable, Nicholas,' Rudolf said. 'Perhaps I can help you. I do have some influential contacts.'

'Really?' replied Nicholas. 'Though it would mean breaking my oath of secrecy. You know that I've often thought about it – but I still can't make up my mind.'

'You should trust your feelings,' Rudolf

said. 'What right has your teacher to prevent you from fulfilling your destiny?'

'My destiny . . .' Nicholas echoed.

Rudolf smiled. 'Men of destiny are a rare and admirable breed,' he said. 'If I am right about you, that means I will have had the privilege of meeting two such men in my life.' He poured out the last of the champagne. 'There is a man I know, a visionary who shares the same ideals as you. I have told him about you, Nicholas, and he, like me, feels you could play a very important part in creating a wonderful future for mankind. You will meet him one day.'

Nicholas gulped his glass empty and set it down on the table. He took a deep breath. 'All right,' he said. 'I've decided. I'll share with you what I know. I want to make a difference.'

'I am honoured,' Rudolf replied, with a short bow of the head.

Nicholas leaned forward in his chair. 'If you only knew how much I've ached to talk about this with someone. There are two important secrets, both of which were revealed in an ancient encoded document. My master discovered it in the south, in the ruins of an old castle.'

'He has shown you these secrets, then?' Rudolf asked eagerly.

'He has shown me one of them. I have

witnessed its power. It is truly amazing. I have the knowledge. I know how to use it, and I can show it to you.'

'What about the second secret?'

'Its potential is even more incredible,' Nicholas said. 'But there's a problem. Fulcanelli now refuses to teach it to me.'

Rudolf placed a hand on the young man's shoulder. 'I'm sure you will learn it in time,' he said with a smile. 'But meanwhile, why don't you tell me more about this amazing knowledge of yours? Perhaps we should continue our discussion at my apartment.'

Ben laid the Journal down. Who was this 'Alexandrian'? What had Daquin told him? Who was the 'man of vision' Rudolf had promised to introduce him to?

It was probably some other weirdo like Gaston Clément, he thought. He flicked through the next few pages and found that the whole last section of the book had been severely damaged by rot. It was hard to tell how many pages were missing. He strained to read the last entry in the Journal, which he could only just make out. It had been written just before Fulcanelli's mysterious disappearance.

23rd December, 1926

All is lost. My beloved wife Christina is murdered. Daquin's betrayal has placed our precious knowledge in the hands of the

Alexandrian. May God forgive me for having allowed this to happen. I fear for much more than my own life. The evil that these men may do is unimaginable.

My plans are underway. I will be departing from Paris immediately with Yvette, my dear daughter who is all I have left now, and I leave everything in the hands of my faithful Jacques Clément. I have warned Jacques that he too must take all precautions. For my part, I shall not return.

So that was it. Somehow, Daquin's betrayal of Fulcanelli's trust had led to disaster. It all seemed to centre on this mysterious Rudolf, the 'Alexandrian.' Had he murdered Fulcanelli's wife? More to the point, where had the alchemist gone afterwards? He'd been in such a hurry to get out of Paris that he'd even left his Journal behind.

'What a beautiful day it is,' said a familiar voice, breaking in on Ben's reverie. 'May I join you?'

'Hello, Father.' Ben closed the Journal.

Pascal sat by him and poured a glass of water from an earthenware jug. 'You look better today, my friend.'

'Thanks, I feel better.'

'Good.' Pascal smiled. 'Yesterday you honoured me greatly with your trust in me, and by telling me your secret – which, naturally, will never go any further.' He paused. 'Now it is my turn, for I too have a little secret.'

'I'm sure I can't possibly offer you the kind of support that you've given me,' said Ben.

'Yet I think my secret will interest you. It concerns you, in a way.'

'How?'

'You have come looking for me, but in fact your goal was to trace Klaus Rheinfeld? Roberta told me.'

'Do you know where he is?'

Pascal nodded. 'Let me start from the beginning. If you knew to look for me, you must already know how I came across the poor wretch.'

'It was in an old news item.'

'He seemed to have completely lost his mind,' Pascal said sadly. 'When I first saw the terrible cuts he had made on his body, I thought it must be the work of the Devil.' He automatically made the sign of the cross, touching his forehead, chest and shoulders. 'And you probably know that I tended to the sick man, and then he was taken away and placed in the institution.'

'Where did they take him?'

'Patience, Benedict, is a great virtue. I am coming to that. Let me continue . . . What you do not know, what indeed nobody has *ever* known apart from myself and that poor lunatic, was the nature of the instrument Rheinfeld used to carve those dreadful cuts on himself . . . here is my secret.'

His eyes took on a faraway expression as he recalled the memory. 'It was a terrible night, the night Rheinfeld arrived here. So wild and violent a storm. When I followed him to the woods, just over there,' he pointed, 'I saw he had a knife, a dagger of a most peculiar sort. I thought to begin with that he was going to kill me. Instead I watched in horror as the poor fellow turned the blade on himself. I still cannot imagine the state of his mind. Anyhow, he soon collapsed and I carried him back to the house. We did what we could for him that night, though he was out of his wits. It was only after the authorities had come for him early the next morning that I remembered the dagger, lying fallen in the woods. I returned there, and found it among the leaves.'

He paused. 'The dagger is, I believe, of medieval origin, though perfectly preserved. It is a crucifix of clever construction, the blade concealed inside. It has many markings, strange symbols. The blade also bears an inscription. I was fascinated and shocked to learn that these symbols were the same as the marks Rheinfeld had cut into his body.'

Ben realized that this must be the gold cross that Clément had mentioned. Fulcanelli's cross. 'What happened to it?' he asked. 'Did you hand it over to the police?'

'To my shame, no,' Pascal said. 'There was no investigation. Nobody questioned that Rheinfeld had inflicted the wounds upon himself. The police did no more than note a few details. So I kept the dagger. I am afraid I have a weakness for old religious artefacts, and it has been one of the prizes of my collection.'

'Will you let me see it?'

'Why, of course.' Pascal smiled. 'But let me continue. About five months later, I had an unusual and illustrious visitor. A Vatican bishop, named Usberti, came to see me. He was asking many questions about Rheinfeld, about his madness, about things he might have said to me, about the markings on his body. But what he most wanted to know was whether Rheinfeld was carrying anything when I found him. From what he said, although he made no direct reference to it, I believe he was interested in the dagger. May the Lord forgive me, I told him nothing. It was so beautiful, and like a stupid greedy child I wished to keep it for myself. But I also sensed something that frightened me. Something about this bishop unnerved me. He hid it well, but I knew he was desperately seeking something. He also was most curious to know whether the madman was carrying any papers, documents. He kept mentioning a manuscript. *Manuscript* – he asked me this again and again.'

Ben started. 'Did he say any more about it?'

'The bishop was rather unclear. In fact I thought he seemed deliberately evasive when I asked him what kind of manuscript he was looking for. He would not say what his interest in it was. His manner seemed strange to me.'

255

'And *did* Rheinfeld have a manuscript?' Ben asked, trying hard to cover up his growing impatience.

'Yes,' Pascal said slowly. 'He did. But . . . I am afraid to say . . .'

Ben tensed up even more as he waited. Two seconds seemed like an eternity.

Pascal went on. 'After they took him away and I returned to the spot where the dagger lay, I found the soaked remnants of what seemed to be sheets of old scroll. They must have fallen out of his ragged clothes. They were crushed into the mud where he had collapsed. The rain had all but destroyed them – most of the ink was washed away. I could see some inscriptions and artwork still intact, and thinking the manu-script was precious and I might be able to return it to its owner I tried to pick it up. But it simply fell apart in my hands. I gathered up the pieces and brought them back here. But it was impossible to save them, and so I threw them away.'

Ben's heart fell. If Rheinfeld's papers had been the Fulcanelli manuscript, it was over.

'But I mentioned none of this to the bishop,' Pascal went on. 'I was afraid to, even though I could not understand why I felt this way. Something told me it would be wrong to tell him.' He shook his head. 'I have known since then that this was not the last I would hear of the Rheinfeld story. I always felt that others would come and find me, looking for him.'

'Where's Rheinfeld now?' Ben asked. 'I'd still like to talk to him.'

Pascal sighed. 'I am afraid that will be difficult.'

'Why?'

'Because he is dead. May he rest in peace.'

'Dead?'

'Yes, he died recently, about two months ago.'

'How do you know?'

'While you were ill I telephoned the Institut Legrand, the mental institution near Limoux where Rheinfeld spent his last years. But it was too late. They told me that the poor unfortunate had ended his own life in a gruesome manner.'

'Then that's that,' Ben muttered.

'Benedict, I have given you the bad news,' said Pascal, touching his shoulder. 'But I also have some good news for you. I told the people at the Institut who I was, and asked if it would be possible to talk to someone there who might have known Rheinfeld. Perhaps someone who had come to know him well during his time there. I was told that nobody at the Institut Legrand had managed to break through the madman's shell. He never allowed anyone to approach him or form any bond with him. His behaviour was disruptive and even violent. But there was a woman, a foreigner, who used to visit him occasionally during his final months. For some reason, her presence calmed Rheinfeld down, and she was able to speak quite normally to him. The hospital staff said that they used to talk together about things that none of the psychiatric nurses could understand. I am wondering, Benedict, if this woman might not have discovered some information that would be useful to you.'

'Where can I find her? Did you get her name?'

'I left my number and asked them to tell the lady that Father Cambriel would like to talk to her.'

'I bet she won't phone,' Ben said darkly.

'Trust is another virtue we discussed yesterday, Benedict, and one that you must learn to cultivate. In fact, Anna Manzini – that is her name – telephoned here early this morning, while you and Roberta were still sleeping. She is a writer, a historian if I gather correctly. She has taken a villa some kilometres from here. She is expecting to hear from you, and is free tomorrow afternoon if you would like to pay her a visit. You can use my car.'

So there was still a chance. Ben's spirits lifted. 'Father, you're a saint.'

Pascal smiled. 'Scarcely,' he said. 'A saint would not have stolen a gold crucifix and lied to his bishop.'

Ben grinned. 'Even saints have been tempted by the Devil.'

'True, but the idea is to resist him,' Pascal replied, chuckling. 'I am an old fool. Now – I will show you the dagger. Do you think Roberta would like to see it too?' He frowned. 'You will not tell her I stole it, will you?'

Ben laughed. 'Don't worry, Father. Your secret's safe with me.'

★ ★ ★

258

'It's beautiful,' Roberta breathed. Her mood was brighter now that Ben had apologized for his harsh words to her. She knew there was something about the picture that caused him pain, that she'd touched some raw nerve. But somehow, he seemed different since his talk with Pascal.

Ben turned the cruciform dagger over in his hands. So this was one of the precious artefacts that Fulcanelli had prized so highly. But its significance was beyond him. Nothing in the Journal gave any clue.

The cross was about eighteen inches in length. When the blade was sheathed inside the shaft-scabbard, it looked just like an exquisitely ornate gold crucifix. Curled around the scabbard, like the ancient symbol of the caduceus, was a golden snake with tiny rubies for eyes. Its head, which was placed at the top of the scabbard where it met the crosspiece, was a sprung catch. If you grasped the upper part of the cross like the hilt of a short sword and depressed the catch with your thumb, the glittering twelve-inch blade could be drawn out. It was narrow and sharp, and strange symbols had been engraved in fine lines into the steel.

He hefted the weapon. Nobody would be expecting a man of God suddenly to whip out a concealed dagger. It was a fiendishly cynical idea – or maybe just a very practical one. The dagger seemed to sum up medieval religion pretty well. On the winning side were the kind of churchmen who might stab you in the back. On the other side

259

were the priests who were always *watching* their back. From what Ben knew already about the history of the Church's relationship with alchemy, whoever had carried this cross might well have belonged to the latter.

Pascal pointed to the blade. 'This is the marking that Rheinfeld had made at the centre of his chest. It looked as though it had been re-cut again and again, a huge pattern of scar tissue that stood out from his skin.' He shuddered.

The symbol he was pointing to was a precise pattern of two intersected circles, one above the other. Within the upper circle was a six-pointed star, each of its points touching the circumference. Within the lower circle was a five-pointed star or pentagram. The circles intersected so that the two stars were locked together. Delicate criss-cross lines pinpointed the exact centre of the strange geometrical shape.

Ben stared at the design. Did it mean anything? It obviously had meant something to Klaus Rheinfeld. 'Any ideas, Roberta?'

She studied it carefully. 'Who can say? Alchemical symbolism is so cryptic sometimes, it's virtually impossible to figure out. It's like they're challenging you, teasing you with scanty information until you know where to go and look for more clues. It was all about protecting their secrets. They were fanatical about security.'

Ben grunted. *Let's just hope these 'secrets' are worth finding*, he thought. 'Perhaps this Anna Manzini will be able to shed more light on it,' he said out loud. 'Who knows, maybe Rheinfeld told her what the symbols meant.'

'If he knew.'

'You have any better ideas?'

He'd had to walk up the hill overlooking Saint-Jean before he'd been able to get any kind of reception on his mobile to contact Fairfax and give him a progress report. His side was aching as he looked out over the wooded valley.

Against the blue sky two eagles were swooping and curving around one another in an aerial dance of graceful majesty. He watched them riding the thermals, gliding and side-slipping as they called to one another, and he wondered fleetingly what that kind of freedom must feel like. He dialled Fairfax's number and shielded the phone from the crackling roar of the wind.

CHAPTER 38

It was late afternoon when they took Father Pascal's car and drove to Montségur, an hour or so away. The old Renault wheezed and rattled along the winding country roads, through landscapes that alternated between breathtaking rocky mountain passes and lush wine-growing valleys.

Just before the old town of Montségur they turned off the main road. At the end of a long lane, high on a hill and surrounded by trees was Anna Manzini's country villa. It was a fine-looking ochre stone house with shuttered windows, climbing wall-plants and a balcony running across its façade. The place was like an oasis in the middle of the arid landscape. Terracotta pots overflowed with flowers. Ornamental trees grew in neat rows along the walls, and water burbled brightly in a little fountain.

Anna came out of the house to greet them. She was wearing a silk dress and a coral necklace that showed off her honey-coloured skin. To Roberta she seemed the classic Italian beauty, as fine and delicate as porcelain. Amid the sweat and dust of the wilds of the Languedoc she seemed to come from another world.

They got out of the car and Anna welcomed them warmly, speaking English with a soft, velvety Italian accent. 'I'm Anna. I'm so pleased to meet you both. Mr Hope, this is your wife?'

'No!' Ben and Roberta said in unison, glancing at one another.

'This is Dr Roberta Ryder. She's working with me,' Ben said.

Anna gave Roberta an unexpected kiss on the cheek. Her delicate perfume was Chanel No. 5. Roberta suddenly realized that at close quarters she probably reeked of Arabelle the goat – she and Marie-Claire had milked her that morning. But if Anna noticed anything, she was too polite to wrinkle her nose. She flashed a perfect smile and led them inside.

The cool white rooms of the villa were filled with the scent of fresh flowers. 'Your English is excellent,' Ben commented as she poured them a glass of ice-chilled *fino* sherry. He drank it down in one, and noticed the hot glare Roberta threw at him. 'Don't gulp like that,' she whispered furiously.

'Sorry,' he said. '*Mea gulpa.*'

'Thank you,' said Anna. 'I've always loved your language. I worked in London for three years, at the start of my teaching career.' She laughed her musical laugh. 'That was a long time ago.'

She showed them into an airy living-room with french windows opening out onto a stone terrace

263

with the garden and the hills beyond. A pair of canaries sang and twittered in a large ornamental cage by the window.

Roberta noticed some copies of Anna's books on a shelf. '*God's Heretics – Discovering the Real Cathars*, by Professor Anna Manzini. I'd no idea we were coming to visit such an expert.'

'Oh, I'm no real expert,' Anna said. 'I just have an interest in certain under-researched subjects.'

'Such as alchemy?' Ben asked.

'Yes,' Anna said. 'Medieval history, Catharism, the esoteric, alchemy. That's how I got to know poor Klaus Rheinfeld.'

'I hope you won't mind if we ask you a few questions,' Ben said. 'We're interested in the Rheinfeld case.'

'May I ask what your interest is?'

'We're journalists,' he answered without missing a beat. 'We're doing research for an article on the mysteries of alchemy.'

Anna made them a black Italian coffee served in tiny little china cups, and told them about her visits to the Institut Legrand. 'I was so upset to hear of Klaus's suicide. But I must say it didn't come as a complete surprise. He was deeply disturbed.'

'I'm amazed they even allowed you access to him,' Ben said.

'They normally wouldn't have,' Anna replied. 'But the Director granted me these visits to help me research my book. I was well guarded, although poor Klaus was usually calm with me.' She shook her head. 'Poor man, he was so ill. You know about the marks he carved into his own flesh?'

'Did you see them?'

'Once, when he was very agitated and tore open his shirt. There was a particular symbol he was obsessed with. Dr Legrand told me that he had drawn it all over his room, in blood and . . . other things.'

'What symbol was that?' Ben asked.

'Two circles intersecting,' Anna said. 'Each circle contained a star, one a hexagram and the other a pentagram, their points touching.'

'Similar to this?' Ben reached into his bag and took out an object wrapped in a cloth. He laid it on the table and peeled back the edges of the cloth to reveal the glinting cruciform dagger. He drew out the blade and showed Anna the inscription on it. The two circles, just as she'd described.

She nodded, her eyes widening. 'Yes, exactly the same. May I?' He passed it to her. She carefully slid the blade back into the shaft and examined the cross from all angles. 'It's a magnificent piece. And extremely unusual. Do you see these alchemical markings on the shaft?' She looked up. 'What do you know about its history?'

'Very little,' Ben said. 'Only that it may once have belonged to the alchemist Fulcanelli, and we think it might date back to medieval times. Rheinfeld apparently stole it from its owner in Paris, and brought it with him down south.'

Anna nodded. 'I'm no antiquarian, but from these markings I would agree about its age. Perhaps tenth or eleventh century. It could easily be verified.' She paused. 'I wonder why Klaus was so interested in it. Not just because of its value. He was penniless, and he could have sold it for a lot of money. Yet he kept hold of it.' She raised one eyebrow. 'How did you come to find it?'

Ben had been ready for that one. He'd promised Pascal he wouldn't give away his secret. 'Rheinfeld dropped it,' he said. 'When he was found wandering and taken away.' He watched her reaction. She seemed to accept it. 'What about the twin-circle symbol on the blade?' he asked, changing the subject. 'Why was Rheinfeld so interested in it?'

Anna grasped the shaft of the cross and drew the blade back out with a quiet metallic *zing*. 'I don't know,' she said. 'But there must be a reason. He may have been deranged, but he wasn't stupid. He had areas of knowledge that were very deep.' She studied the blade thoughtfully. 'Do you mind if I make a copy of this symbol?' She laid the dagger down in front of her and took a piece of tracing paper and a soft-leaded pencil from a drawer. Laying the paper across the bare blade she did a careful rubbing of the markings on it. Roberta noticed her perfectly manicured hands. She glanced down at her own. Slipped them under the table.

Anna studied her finished rubbing, looking happy with it. 'There.' Then she frowned and looked at it more closely. 'It's not quite the same as the one in the notebook. There's a slight difference. I wonder . . .'

Ben looked at her sharply. 'Notebook?'

'I'm sorry, I should have mentioned it to you. The doctors gave Klaus a notebook in the hope that he would keep a record of his dreams. They believed this would help in his treatment, and perhaps help to shed light on what had caused his mental condition. But he didn't record his dreams. Instead he filled the pages with drawings and symbols, strange poetry and numbers. The doctors couldn't make any sense of it, but they allowed him to keep it as it seemed to comfort him.'

'What happened to it?' Ben said.

'When Klaus died, the director of the Institut, Edouard Legrand, offered it to me. He thought I might be interested in it. Klaus had no family, and in any case it wouldn't have been much of an heirloom. I have it upstairs.'

'Can we see it?' Roberta said eagerly.

Anna smiled. 'Of course.' She went to fetch it from her study. A minute later she returned, filling the room again with her fresh perfume, holding a small polythene bag. 'I put it in here because it was so filthy and smelly,' she said, laying the bag gently on the table.

Ben took the notebook out of the bag. It was frayed and crumpled and looked like it had been soaked in blood and urine a hundred times. It gave off a sharp musty smell. He flipped through it.

267

Most of the pages were blank, apart from the first thirty or so which were heavily stained with grubby fingerprints and reddish-brown smears of old dried blood that made it difficult in places to read the handwriting.

The bits he could make out were just about the strangest thing he'd ever seen. The pages were filled with snatches of bizarre verse. Obscure and apparently meaningless arrangements of letters and numbers. Scrawled notes in Latin, English and French. Rheinfeld had obviously been an educated man, as well as a competent artist. Here and there were drawings, some of them simple sketches and others drawn in painstaking detail. They looked to Ben like the kind of alchemical images he'd seen in ancient texts.

One of the most grubby and well-thumbed pages in the notebook had a drawing on it that was familiar. It was the diagram from the dagger blade, the twin intersecting star-circles that Rheinfeld had been so obsessed with.

He picked up the dagger and compared them. 'You're right,' he said. 'They're slightly different from one another.'

Rheinfeld's version was identical except for one small extra detail. It was hard to make out, but it looked like a tiny heraldic emblem of a bird with outstretched wings and a long beak. It was positioned at the dead centre of the twin-circle motif.

'It's a raven,' Ben said. 'And I think I've seen it

before.' It was the symbol he'd seen carved in the central porch at Notre Dame Cathedral in Paris.

But why had Rheinfeld altered the design from the blade?

'Does any of this mean anything to you?' he asked Anna.

She shrugged. 'Not really. Who knows what was in his mind?'

'Can I have a look?' Roberta asked. Ben passed the notebook to her. 'God, it's gross,' she said, turning the pages with revulsion.

Ben's heart was sinking again. 'Did you learn anything at all from Rheinfeld?' he asked Anna, hoping he might be able to salvage at least something of value.

'I wish I could say yes,' she replied. 'When Dr Legrand first mentioned this strange, intriguing character to me I thought he might help to inspire me for my new book. I was suffering from writer's block. I still am,' she added unhappily. 'But as I got to know him I felt so sorry for him. My visits were more for his comfort than for my own inspiration. I can't say I learned anything from him. All I have is this notebook. Oh, and there is one other thing . . .'

'What?' Ben asked.

Anna blushed. 'I did something a little . . . what's the word . . . *naughty*. On my last visit to the Institut I smuggled in with me the little gadget I use for dictating my book ideas. I recorded my conversation with Klaus.'

'Could I hear that?'

'I don't think it could be of any use,' Anna said. 'But you're welcome to listen to it.' She reached behind her and picked up a miniature digital recorder from a sideboard. She set it down in the middle of the table and pressed PLAY. Through the tinny speaker they could hear Rheinfeld's low, muttering voice.

It put a chill down Roberta's spine.

'Did he always speak in German?' asked Ben.

'Only when he was repeating these numbers,' Anna said.

Ben listened intently. Rheinfeld's mumbling tone started low, mantra-like. '*N-sechs; E-vier; I-sechs-und-zwanzig . . .*' As he went on his voice rose higher, beginning to sound frenzied: '*A-elf; E-funfzehn . . . N-sechs; E-vier . . .*' and the sequence repeated itself again as Ben scribbled it down in his pad. They heard Anna softly saying 'Klaus, calm down.'

Rheinfeld paused for a moment, and then his voice started again: '*Igne Natura Renovatur Integra – Igne Natura Renovatur Integra – Igne Natura Renovatur Integra . . .*' He chanted the phrase over and over, faster and louder until his voice rose into a scream that distorted the speaker. The recording ended with a flurry of other voices.

Anna turned the machine off with a sad look. She shook her head. 'They had to sedate him at that point. He was strangely agitated that day. Nothing seemed to calm him. It was just before he killed himself.'

'That was creepy,' said Roberta. 'What was that Latin phrase?'

Ben had already found it in the notebook. He was looking at a sketch of a cauldron, in which some mysterious liquid was bubbling. A bearded alchemist in a smock stood watching over it. The Latin words IGNE NATURA RENOVATUR INTEGRA were printed on the side of the cauldron. 'My Latin's rusty,' he said. 'Something about fire . . . nature . . .'

'By fire nature is renewed whole,' Anna translated for him. 'An old alchemical saying, relating to the processes they used to transform base matter. He was fixated on that phrase, and when he repeated it he would count his fingers, like this.' She imitated Rheinfeld's twitchy, urgent gestures. 'I have no idea why he did that.'

Roberta leaned across to see the picture in the notebook. Her hair brushed over Ben's hand as she moved up close. She pointed to the image. Beneath the cauldron, the alchemist had lit a raging fire. Under the flames was the label ANBO, printed clearly in capitals. '*Anbo* – what language is that?' she asked.

'None that I know,' Anna said.

'So the notebook and this recording are all you have?' Ben asked her.

'Yes,' she sighed. 'That is all.'

Then it was a waste of time coming here, he thought bitterly. *That was my last chance.*

Anna was gazing thoughtfully at the rubbing of

271

the dagger blade. An idea was forming in her mind. She couldn't be sure, but . . .

The phone rang. 'Excuse me,' she said, and went to answer it.

'So what do you think, Ben?' Roberta said quietly.

'I don't think this is leading anywhere.'

They could hear Anna on the phone in the next room, talking in a low voice. She sounded a little flustered. 'Edouard, I asked you not to call me any more . . . No, you can't come here tonight. I have guests . . . no, not tomorrow night either.'

'Me neither,' Roberta said. 'Shit.' She sighed and got up from her chair, started pacing aimlessly across the room. Then something caught her eye.

Anna finished her call and returned to join them. 'I'm sorry about that,' she said.

'Problems?' Ben said.

Anna shook her head and smiled. 'Nothing important.'

'Anna, what's this?' Roberta said. She was examining a magnificent medieval text hanging in a glass frame on the wall near the fireplace. The cracked, browned parchment depicted an early map of the Languedoc, scattered with old towns and castles. Around the edges of the map, blocks of old Latin and medieval French text had been highly coloured and ornamented by a skilled calligrapher. 'If this is an original scroll,' she said, 'it must be worth a packet.'

Anna laughed. 'The American man who gave it

to me thought it was priceless, too. Until he found out that the thirteenth-century Cathar script he'd paid twenty thousand dollars for was a fake.'

'A fake?'

'It's no older than this house,' Anna said with a chuckle. 'About eighteen-nineties. He was so *pissed off* – is that the right expression? – that he gave it to me for nothing. He should have known. As you say, a genuine item in that condition would have been worth a small fortune.'

Roberta smiled. 'We Yanks are suckers for anything more than three hundred years old.' She moved away from the framed scroll and looked across at the tall, wide bookcase, running her eyes along the hundreds of books in Anna's collection. There was so much here – history, archaeology, architecture, art, science. 'Some of this stuff is so interesting,' she murmured. 'One day when I get time . . .' She remembered she had a little book of Post-it notes in her bag, still out in the car. 'Excuse me for a moment, will you? I want to write down a few of these titles.' She trotted out of the room.

Anna moved close to Ben. 'Come, I'd like to show you something,' she said. He stood up, and she took his arm. Her hand was warm on his skin.

'What do you want to show me?' he said.

She smiled. 'This way.'

The two of them walked out of the french window and down the long garden. At the bottom, a rocky path led up to the open coun-tryside and after they had scrambled up a short

slope Ben found himself looking out at a magnificent sunset panorama. He could see for miles
across the mountains of the Languedoc, and
above it all the sky was a cathedral-rich canvas
of shimmering golds, reds and blues.

Anna pointed across the valley and showed him
two distant castle ruins, serrated black outlines
perched miles apart against the sky on high
mountain peaks. 'Cathar strongholds,' she said,
shielding her eyes against the falling sun.
'Destroyed by the Albigensian crusade in the
thirteenth century. The Cathars and their ancestors built castles, churches, monasteries, all across
the Languedoc. They were all crushed by the
Pope's army.' She paused. 'I'll tell you something,
Ben. Some specialist historians have believed that
these places have a deeper significance.'

He shook his head. 'What kind of deeper significance?'

She smiled. 'Nobody knows for sure. It was said
that somewhere in the Languedoc there lies an
ancient secret. That the relative positions of Cathar
sites give the clue to finding it, and that whoever
could solve the puzzle would discover great wisdom
and power.' Her dark hair was blowing in the gentle
evening breeze. She looked beautiful. 'Ben,' she said
tentatively. 'You haven't told me the whole truth. I
think you're looking for something. Am I right?
Something secret.'

He hesitated. 'Yes.'

Her almond eyes sparkled. 'I thought so. And it

has something to do with alchemy, with the legend of Fulcanelli?'

He nodded, and couldn't help but smile at her razor-sharp perceptiveness. 'I was looking for a manuscript,' he admitted. 'I think Klaus Rheinfeld knew about it, and I'd been hoping he could help me. But it looks like I was wrong.'

'Perhaps *I* can help you,' she said softly. 'We must meet again. I think we could work together on this.'

He said nothing for a moment. 'I'd like that,' he said.

Roberta had come back from the car to find the house empty. She heard their voices carrying on the wind, and looked out of the french window. She saw Ben and Anna climbing back down the slope towards the garden. She could hear Anna's chiming laugh. Her slim figure was silhouetted against the sunset. Ben offered her a hand. Was it her imagination? They seemed to be getting on very well.

What do you expect? Anna's gorgeous. She'd be hard for any man to resist.

'What kind of thoughts are these, Ryder,' she said to herself. 'What do you care, anyway?'

But then she realized. She did care. A terrible thing was happening to her. She was falling in love with Ben Hope.

CHAPTER 39

Ben was in a sombre mood the next day as he wandered aimlessly through the dusty streets of Saint-Jean. His search had slammed into a dead end.

When he'd phoned Fairfax two days earlier he'd held back from mentioning that the manuscript might have been destroyed. He'd been hoping that Anna Manzini would be able to tell him something positive. That had been a stupid false impression to give the old man. Now everything looked black, time was dragging by and he had no idea where to turn next.

In a square next to an ageing World War One memorial statue was the village bar, a one-roomed affair with a tiny terrace where leathery old men sat like reptiles in the sun, or played games of *pétanque* in the empty square. Ben walked in, and the clientele – all three of them, playing cards in a shady corner – turned to look as the tall, blond stranger appeared. He nodded them a sullen greeting, which was returned with grunts. At the bar, the proprietor was sitting reading the newspaper. The place smelled of stale beer and smoke.

He noticed a Missing Persons poster on the wall.

HAVE YOU SEEN THIS BOY?
MARC DUBOIS, AGE 15.

He sighed. Another one. *That's what I should be doing – helping kids like that. Not hanging around here wasting time.*

Leaning on the bar, he lit a cigarette and asked for his flask to be refilled. They only had one type of whisky in the place, an especially vile fluid the colour of horse urine. He didn't care. He ordered an extra double measure of the same and sat on a bar-stool, gazing into space and sipping the burning liquor.

Maybe it's time to give up this fiasco, he was thinking. This job had never been right for him, from the start. He should have stayed objective. His first impression had been right. Fairfax, like all desperate people who want to save someone they love, had fallen victim to his wishful thinking. So there was a good chance the Fulcanelli manuscript was lost – so what? It was probably all bullshit anyway. There wasn't any great secret. *Of course there wasn't.* It was all a fantasy, all myths and riddles and fodder for gullible dreamers.

But could he say that Anna Manzini was a gullible dreamer?

Who knows – maybe she is?

He slid his empty glass along the bar, tossed some coins on the pitted wooden surface and asked for another double. He'd already finished that one, and started on another, when the three old card players in the corner looked round at the sound of running footsteps.

Roberta burst in, looking flushed and excited.

'Thought I'd find you here,' she said. She was out of breath, as though she'd run all the way from Pascal's cottage. 'Listen, Ben, I've had an idea.'

He was in no mood for her enthusiasm. 'Tell me about it some other time,' he muttered. 'I'm thinking.' He was – thinking about picking up his phone and telling Fairfax it was over. He'd wire him back his money, give up and go home to his beach.

'Listen, this is important,' she insisted. 'Come on, let's go outside. No, don't finish that. You look like you've had enough already. I want you with a clear head.'

'Go away, Roberta. I'm busy.'

'Yeah, busy drinking yourself into a stupor with that gut-rot.'

'Gut-rot is what happens to you when you drink it,' he corrected her. He pointed at the glass. '*This* is *rot-gut*,' he said emphatically.

'Either way,' she grunted impatiently. 'Look at you. Call yourself a professional?'

He shot her a ferocious look, slammed the glass down on the bar and slid down off the stool.

'This had better be very, very good indeed,' he warned her as they stepped out into the late afternoon sunlight.

'I think it is,' she said, turning to face him with an earnest look as she got her thoughts in order. 'OK, listen. What if the manuscript Klaus Rheinfeld stole hadn't been destroyed?'

He shook his head, confused. 'What are you raving about? Pascal saw it in pieces. It was ruined in the storm.'

'Right. Now, remember the notebook, Rheinfeld's notebook?'

'What about it?' he grunted. 'This is what you drag me out here for?'

'Well, maybe it's more important than we thought.'

He furrowed his brow. 'What are you talking about?'

'Just listen, OK? Here's my idea. What if the notebook was the same thing as the manuscript?'

'Are you crazy? How could it be? They gave it to him at the hospital.'

'I don't mean the actual notebook, stupid. I mean what's written in it. Maybe Rheinfeld copied the secrets down into it.'

'Oh right. From inside a secure hospital, *after* he'd lost the original? What did he do, channel the information? I'm going back inside.' He turned impatiently to go.

'Shut up and listen to me for once!' she shouted, grabbing his arm. 'I'm trying to say something, you pigheaded bastard! I think Rheinfeld could have remembered it all and written it down later in his notebook.'

He stared at her. 'Roberta, there were over thirty fucking pages of riddles and drawings, geometric shapes, jumbled-up numbers and bits of Latin and French and all kinds of stuff in there. It's not possible to remember all that in perfect detail.'

'He walked around with it for years,' she protested. 'Probably living rough, with no money. It was all he had. He was fixated on it.'

'I still don't buy that anyone could have that kind of memory. Especially a fucked-up alchemy nut,' he added.

'Ben, I did a year of neurobiology at Yale. Granted, it's unusual – but it's *not* impossible. It's called eidectic memory, also known as photographic memory. It's usually lost by adolescence, but some people retain it all their lives. Rheinfeld had an OCD, from what I can gather –'

'OCD?'

'Obsessive Compulsive Disorder,' she said more patiently. 'He had all the symptoms, kept repeating actions and words for no apparent reason – or for no reason that anyone could understand except him. Now, it's been known for compulsive neurotics to have uncanny powers of memory. They can store huge amounts of detail that you and I would never be able to remember. Difficult mathematical equations, detailed pictures, enormous chunks of technical text. It's all on scientific record going back almost a century.'

Ben sat on a bench. His mind was quickly clearing of the whisky fog.

'Think about it, Ben,' she went on, sitting next to him. 'They gave Rheinfeld a notebook to write down his dreams – that's a standard part of psychotherapy. But instead, he used it to preserve the memories he was holding inside, keep a written record of the information that he'd stolen and then lost. The psychiatrists couldn't possibly have known what he was doing, where the stuff was coming from. They probably dismissed it as lunatic gibberish. But what if it was more than that?'

'But he was crazy. How can we trust the mind of a madman?'

'Sure, he was crazy,' she agreed. 'But mostly he was obsessive, and the thing about obsessives is, they're crazy about details. As long as the detail he wrote down was close enough to the original, what matters isn't his craziness but that the note-book might contain a perfect, or near-perfect, replica of the documents that Jacques Clément didn't burn because they'd been passed to him by Fulcanelli.'

He was silent for a few moments. 'You're sure about this?'

'Of course I'm not sure. But I still think we should go back and check it out. It's worth a shot, isn't it?' She looked at him searchingly. 'Well? What do you say?'

CHAPTER 40

Anna couldn't concentrate on her work. Still unable to come up with a satisfactory plot for her historical novel, she'd been reduced to sketching out a rough draft of the author's introduction. It should have been easy – she knew the subject so intimately. But the words just wouldn't flow. Now a new distraction had formed in her mind to add to the writer's block that had been troubling her for so long. Each time she tried to focus on the page in front of her, after a couple of minutes her mind began to stray and she found herself thinking about Ben Hope.

Something was niggling her. Something buried at the back of her mind. What was it? It was distant, hazy, like a half-forgotten word hovering teasingly on the tip of her tongue that she couldn't crystallize into clear thought. She glanced down at Rheinfeld's notebook, lying at her elbow on the desk, the dagger blade rubbing slipped between its pages. Maybe there was more to the notebook than she'd ever thought. The markings . . .

She reclined back in the swivel-chair, gazing out of the window. The stars were coming out,

282

beginning to twinkle in the darkening blue sky above the black-silhouetted line of mountaintops. Her eye followed the string of Orion's Belt. Rigel was a distant sun, over 900 light years away. The stars brought history alive to her. The light she was seeing now had started its journey through space almost 1,000 years ago; just to gaze up at it was to travel back in time, commune with the living past. What dark, terrible, beautiful secrets had the stars witnessed over medieval Languedoc?

She sighed and tried to get back to her work.

The mountaintop castle of Montségur, March 1244. Eight thousand crusaders, paid with Catholic gold, surrounded a defenceless band of three hundred Cathar heretics. After eight months of siege and bombardment the Cathars were starving. All but four of them were to die, burned alive by the Inquisitors after the final storming of the ramparts. Before the massacre, four priests fled the besieged castle bearing an unknown cargo, and disappeared. Their story remains a mystery. What was their mission? Were they carrying the fabled treasure of the Cathars, attempting to hide its secret from their persecutors? Did this treasure really exist, and if so, what was it? These questions have remained unanswered to this day.

She put down her pen. It was only just after nine, but she decided she'd have an early night. Her best ideas often came when she was relaxed in bed. She'd have a hot bath, make a drink and curl up with her thoughts. Maybe the morning would see her with a clearer mind, and she'd be able to call Ben Hope and arrange to see him again.

She wondered what trail he was following, what significance the gold cross and this Fulcanelli manuscript might have. Was it connected with her own research into the Cathar treasure? So little was known about it that most historians had all but given up on the old legend.

A curious feeling, one she hadn't felt for a long time . . . She smiled to herself. The excitement she felt at the prospect wasn't just out of intellectual curiosity. She was keenly looking forward to their next meeting.

She shut her study door and walked along the corridor to her bedroom. She went through to the ensuite bathroom beyond and turned on the bath taps, then undressed and slipped into a bathrobe, tying up her hair. She glanced at her face in the mirror, but it was already steaming up from the splashing hot water.

She stiffened. Was that a noise from downstairs? She turned off the taps and cocked her head, listening for it. Maybe the pipes. She turned the taps back on, clicking her tongue in irritation at her own jumpiness.

But as she was just slipping her robe off her shoulders to get into the bath, she heard it again.

She knotted the belt of her bathrobe as she

walked edgily back through the bedroom and out onto the landing. She stood listening, her head cocked to one side, a frown furrowing her brow.

Nothing. But she'd definitely heard something. She quietly lifted up the Egyptian bronze Anubis statue from the wooden pedestal on the landing. Weighing the jackal-headed god's effigy in her hand like a club, she padded silently down the stairs in her bare feet. Her breathing was quickening. Her knuckles were white as she gripped the statue. The dark downstairs hall rose up to meet her with every step. If she could get to the light switch . . .

There it was, that sound again.

'Who's there?' She wanted her voice to sound strong and confident, but it came out in a shaky treble.

The loud knock at the door made her jump. She gasped, her heart thumping. 'Who is it?'

'Anna?' said a man's voice from outside the door. 'It's me, Edouard.'

Her shoulders sagged with relief and her arm hung limp by her side, still clutching the Anubis. She ran to the door and opened it, letting him in.

Edouard Legrand hadn't been expecting such a warm welcome, after she had turned him down flat on the phone several times. He was pleasantly surprised as she ushered him inside the front hall.

'What are you doing with that thing?' he said with a smile, nodding at the statue in her hand.

She glanced down at it, feeling suddenly foolish.

She set the Anubis down on a table. 'I scared myself so much just now,' she said, placing her palm on her still-fluttering heart and closing her eyes. 'I heard noises.'

He laughed. 'Oh, these old houses are full of strange noises. Mine is just the same. You probably heard a mouse. It's amazing how much noise a tiny mouse can make.'

'No, it was you I heard,' she said. 'Sorry if I seemed flustered.'

'I didn't mean to alarm you, Anna. You were not asleep, I hope?' he added, noticing her robe.

She smiled, relaxing now. 'Actually I was just about to have a bath. Perhaps you could fix yourself a drink, and I will be down in five minutes.'

'Please, go ahead, don't let me rush you.'

Damn, she was thinking as she walked into the steamy bathroom. It looked like encouragement, the way she'd hurried him inside. Talk about giving out mixed signals.

She couldn't say she actually disliked Edouard Legrand. He wasn't completely without charm. He wasn't at all bad-looking either. But she could never in a million years return the feelings he obviously had for her. There was something about him, something she couldn't define, that made her feel uncomfortable around him. She'd have to get rid of him as gently as possible, but quickly and firmly before he started getting the wrong ideas. She couldn't help but feel a little pang of guilt. Poor Edouard.

Downstairs, Edouard was pacing up and down in the living-room, working over the lines he'd prepared. Then he remembered the champagne and flowers that he'd left in the car, not wanting to appear too boldly at the door like a serenading suitor brimming with expectations. But as she'd let him in without protest and was obviously eager for his company, now was the time to produce them. Where was the kitchen? Maybe he'd time to stick the bottle in the freezer to chill it down while she was having her bath. They could have such a perfect evening together. Who knew where it might lead? Jittery with excitement, he went back outside to the car.

Anna climbed out of the bath, towelled herself dry and pulled on a pair of jogging pants and a blouse. The Mozart symphony playing on her bedroom stereo system was entering its bright second movement, and she hummed along to it. As she came downstairs she still hadn't quite figured out how she should handle her unexpected visitor. Maybe she should let him stay a while, try to play it cool.

The front door was wide open. She tutted. Where had he gone? For a walk around the garden, in the dark? 'Edouard?' she called out through the doorway.

Then she saw him. He was leaning through the open window of his car, his head and shoulders inside as though he was reaching for something.

'What are you doing?' she said, half-smiling.

She trotted down the steps from the villa, breathing in the warm night scent of flowers.

His knees were bent and his body seemed to sag against the side of the car. He wasn't moving. 'Edouard, are you all right?' Was he drunk?

She reached out a hand and shook his shoulder.

Edouard's knees gave way and he flopped backwards. He crunched down on his back on the pebbles and lay staring up at her with sightless eyes. His throat was slashed open in a wound that gaped from ear to ear, cut to the spine. His body was soaked in blood.

Anna screamed. She turned and ran back towards the house. She slammed the door behind her and picked up the phone in the hallway with a shaking hand. It was dead.

She heard it again – the sound she'd heard before. This time it was clearer, louder. It was the metallic scraping of steel against steel. It was in the house. The living-room. A knife-blade dragging slowly, deliberately, down the bars of her birdcage.

She ran for the stairs. Her foot pressed against something soft, warm and wet. She looked down. It was one of her canaries, lying broken and bloody on the step. Her hands flew to her mouth.

Through the half-open door of the living-room she heard a laugh, the rasping chuckle of a man who was plainly enjoying his little game with her.

On the table by the foot of the stairs, the Anubis statue was standing where she'd left it. She snatched it up again in a trembling hand. She could hear footsteps coming towards her. She dashed back towards the stairs. Her mobile phone was in the bedroom. If she could get to it and lock herself in the bathroom . . .

Her head jerked back and she cried out in pain. The man coming up behind her was tall and muscular, with cropped steely hair and a face like granite. He yanked her hair again, twisted her around and punched her hard in the face with a gloved hand. Anna fell to the floor, her legs kicking. He bent down towards her. She lashed out with the Anubis and caught him across the cheekbone with a crunch.

Franco Bozza's head snapped sideways with the blow. He put his gloved fingers to his face and studied the blood with an impassive look. Then he smiled. All right, the game was over. Now to business. He grabbed her wrist and twisted it harshly. She screamed again, and the statue fell from her hand and bounced down the stairs. She crawled away, and he watched her go. She was almost at the top of the staircase when he grabbed her again. He slammed her head against the banister rail and her vision exploded into white light. She slumped on her back, tasting blood.

He knelt over her, taking his time. His eyes were shining as he slid a hand inside his jacket and drew out the blade from its sheath with a smooth hiss of steel on synthetic fibre. Her eyes opened wide as he playfully drew the blade from her throat to her abdomen. Her breath came in rapid tremors. He kept her head pinned back with a fistful of her hair.

'The information the Englishman was after,' he whispered. 'Give it to me. And I might let you live.' He calmly held the knife against her cheek.

She managed to speak. Her voice sounded tiny. 'What Englishman?'

She felt the coldness of the steel, and then she screamed in agony as he pressed the blade into her flesh. He took the knife away, looking at the three-inch gash. Blood streamed down her face. She shook her head from side to side, struggling against his grip. He held the knife against her throat. 'Tell me what he wanted from you,' he repeated in his rasping undertone. 'Or I will slice you into small pieces.'

Her mind raced. 'I gave him nothing,' she insisted, blood trickling between her lips.

Bozza smiled. 'Tell me the truth.'

'I am,' she protested. 'He was looking for a document – an ancient script.'

Bozza nodded. This was what he'd been told. 'Where is it?' he whispered.

She paused, thinking hard. He pointed the knife at her eye and looked at her enquiringly. 'Over the fireplace,' she whimpered. 'I–in the frame.'

His cold eyes looked into hers for a moment, as though assessing whether she was telling the truth. With deliberate movements he wiped the blade clean on the carpet and laid the knife down on the floor beside her head. Then he drew back his fist and smashed it into her face. Anna's head lolled to the side.

Bozza left her lying on the stairs, sheathing his knife as he went down to the living-room. He ripped the frame down from the wall, broke the glass against the corner of the mantelpiece and shook the fragments out. He pulled the medieval script away from its mounting, rolled it up into a tight cylinder and slipped it into the deep inside pocket of his jacket.

So Manzini hadn't given anything to the Englishman. Usberti would be pleased with him. He'd found the woman quickly and efficiently, and he had found what his boss had sent him to bring back.

Now he'd bring the woman round and enjoy her for a while. He loved the looks on their faces when they realized he wouldn't let them live after all. That terror in their eyes, that delicious moment when they were so powerless in his grasp. It was even better than the slow torture and the screaming climax that came afterwards.

He stepped back into the hallway and his eyes narrowed. The woman was gone.

Anna staggered into her study. She could hear the sound of breaking glass downstairs as the frame was torn apart. Blood was dripping down her throat from her gashed cheek, the front of her blouse sticky and warm with it. Her head was spinning but she managed to focus on the desk.

Her outstretched hand dripped spots of blood across her research notes. Her fingers closed around the notebook in its plastic wrapping. Clutching it tightly, half-blind with pain and nausea, she staggered back along the corridor towards the bedroom.

From the foot of the stairs Bozza saw the bedroom door close. He followed, climbing the stairs in his easy, unhurried walk. As he approached the bedroom door he was reaching for the plastic pouch on his belt.

The woman's bedroom was empty. On the far side of the room was another door. Bozza tried the handle. It was bolted from inside.

Locked in her bathroom, Anna jabbed panic-stricken at her phone, smearing the plastic with bloody fingerprints. With a sick lurch she remembered it was out of credits. She dropped the phone, giddy with horror. She knew this madman wasn't going to let her live. She was going to die horribly. Could she kill herself before he got to her? The window wasn't high enough. She would only be crippled and he'd soon catch her again.

The door flew open with a crackle of splintering wood. Bozza strode across the room and slapped her to the floor. Her head cracked against the tiles and she passed out.

Her outflung hand was clutching something. He uncurled her bloody fingers, took it away from her and studied it.

'Trying to hide this, were you?' he whispered at

her inert body. 'Brave girl.' He slipped the plastic-wrapped notebook into the pocket of his jacket, then took it off and hung it neatly over the back of a bathroom chair. Underneath he was wearing a double-sided shoulder holster, a small semi-automatic and spare clips under his left armpit and the sheathed knife under the right. First drawing out the knife and laying it down on the edge of the sink, he unzipped the pouch on his belt and took out the tightly folded overall. He pulled the rustling plastic garment over his head and smoothed it down carefully as he always did.

Then he picked up the knife up from the sink with a clink of steel against ceramic, and walked slowly over to Anna Manzini. He nudged her body with his foot. She groaned, stirring painfully. Her eyes half-opened. Then widened in horror as she saw him looming over her.

He smiled. The knife glittered, and so did his eyes.

'Now the pain will begin,' he whispered.

CHAPTER 41

Ben turned the Renault into Anna's driveway, its worn tyres crunching on the gravel and its headlights sweeping the front of the villa.

'Look, she's got visitors,' said Roberta, noticing the shiny black Lexus GS parked in front of the house. 'I told you we should have phoned first. It's awfully rude, you know, just landing on people like this.'

He was out of the car, not listening. He'd noticed something lying on the ground, sticking out from the shadow of the Lexus. He realized with shock that it was an arm. A man's dead arm, the hand clawed, bloody.

He ran round the side of the car, scenarios flashing through his mind. He crouched down beside the body and ran his eye over the gaping wound in the man's throat. He'd seen enough cut throats in his life to recognize the work of a professional. He touched the skin; it still had some warmth left in it.

'What is it, Ben?' she asked, coming up behind him.

He rose up quickly and took her by the shoulders, turning her away. 'Best not to look.' But Roberta had seen it. She pressed her hands to her mouth, trying not to gag.

'Stay close to me,' he whispered. He raced to the villa, leaping up the steps. The front door was locked. He ran around the side of the house, Roberta following, and found the french window open. He slipped into the house, drawing the Browning. Roberta caught up with him, ashen-faced, and he motioned to her to stay still and quiet.

He stepped over the twitching, broken body of a canary in its death throes, its yellow feathers stained red. A small statue lay on the floor at the foot of the stairs. He could see light from upstairs, music playing. His face hardened. He took the steps three at a time, flipping off the Browning's safety.

Anna's bedroom was empty, but the bathroom door was ajar. He burst in, bringing the gun up to aim, not knowing what he was going to find inside.

Franco Bozza had been enjoying himself. He had spent the last five minutes slowly slicing the buttons off her blouse one at a time, slapping her back down into the puddle of her blood when she struggled. A glistening crimson rivulet trickled down the valley between her breasts. He ran the flat of the blade down her skin to her quivering stomach, hooked the razor point behind the next button and was about to slice it off when the sudden sound of running footsteps startled him out of his trance.

He whipped round, saliva on his chin. He was a big, heavy man but his reactions were fast. He grabbed the woman by the hair and yanked her screaming to her feet as he leapt up, twisting her body round in front of him as the door swung open with a juddering crash.

Ben's horror at the scene in front of him slowed him down half a second too long. Anna's eyes met his, wide and white in a mask of blood. The powerful grey-haired man had his arm around her throat, using her as a shield.

Ben's finger was on the trigger. *You can't shoot.* His sights wavered, the target uncertain. He slackened the pressure on the trigger.

Bozza's arm jerked and the blade flashed across the room in a hissing blur. Ben ducked. The steel passed an inch from his face and embedded itself with a thud in the door behind him. Bozza's hand whipped across his chest and through the neck of his plastic overall, ripping the little Beretta .380 from his holster. Ben took a chance and fired off a shot, but his bullet went wide for fear of hitting Anna. At almost the same instant Bozza's pistol cracked and Ben felt the bullet turn on the hip-flask in his pocket. He staggered back a step, momentarily stunned, but recovering fast and bringing the Browning back up to aim as his rage exploded and his sights fell square on Bozza's forehead. *Got you now.*

But before Ben could fire, Bozza flung Anna across the room towards him like a limp doll. Ben caught her, saving her from crashing on her face on the bloody floor tiles. He lost his aim.

The big man flipped backwards out of the window like a diver. There was a ferocious ripping and rustling from outside as he scrabbled down the flimsy trellis. He dropped to the ground, torn and bedraggled. A shot rang out and a bullet went past his ear, tearing a furrow in the tree-trunk next to him.

Ben leaned out of the window and fired again, blind into the darkness. The attacker was gone. For a second he thought about giving chase, but decided against it. When he turned back to Anna, Roberta had arrived and was bending over her still body. 'Oh, my God.'

He felt her pulse. 'She's alive.'

'Thank Christ. Who the . . .' Roberta's face was white. 'This isn't just a coincidence, is it, Ben? This has something to do with us. Jesus, did *we* bring this on her?'

He didn't reply. He knelt down and checked Anna for injuries. Apart from an ugly gash on her face, its edges drying up and crusted with brown blood, she wasn't cut anywhere.

He took his phone out of his pocket and tossed it to Roberta. 'Call an ambulance,' he said. 'But not the police, and just say there's been an accident. Don't touch anything.'

Roberta nodded and ran into the other room.

He reached up to the chrome rail on the bath-room wall and brought down a fluffy white towel. He gently lifted Anna's head, then placed the towel underneath to cushion her. He covered her body with a bathrobe and another towel to keep her warm, and shut the window. Kneeling back down beside her, he gently caressed her hair. It was stiff and sticky with blood. 'You're going to be all right, Anna,' he murmured. 'The ambulance won't be long.'

She stirred, and her eyes opened. They slowly focused on him, and she mumbled something.

'Shh, don't try to speak.' He smiled, but his hands were shaking with fury and he silently vowed that he was going to kill the man who'd done this.

The attacker had dropped his pistol as he'd thrown himself at the window. Ben decocked it and stuffed it into his waistband. There were some empty cartridge cases lying on the floor. He picked them up and tucked them into his pocket. He could hear Roberta in the bedroom, talking urgently on the phone.

That was when he noticed the black jacket hanging on the back of the chair.

CHAPTER 42

The manor-house hotel was visible through the trees from the road, floodlit and inviting in the darkness. Ben swerved the Renault off the road and down its long, winding driveway into the wooded grounds. They pulled up in the front, next to some other cars and a touring coach.

'Bring your bag, we're staying here tonight.'

'Why a hotel, Ben?'

'Because two foreigners in a hotel is a normal thing, but two foreigners staying with a priest in a village gets talked about. We can't go back to Pascal's after tonight.'

Inside, Ben approached the reception desk and rang the bell. A moment later the receptionist appeared from an office.

'Have you got any rooms?' Ben asked.

'No, monsieur, we are full.'

'No rooms at all? It isn't even high season.'

'We have a group of English tourists here for the *Tour Cathare*. Almost everything is taken.'

'Almost?'

'The only accommodation left is our best suite.

But it is normally . . . that is to say . . . it is reserved for –'

'We'll take it,' he said without hesitation. 'Shall I pay you now?' He reached in his pocket. Took out the fake Paul Harris passport and his wallet. He laid the passport down on the desk and showed her the cash. There was enough in the wallet to rent the whole hotel for a month. The receptionist's eyes widened. 'N . . . no need to pay now,' she stammered.

She rang a bell on the reception desk. 'Joseph!' she called out in a bellowing voice, and a wizened old fellow in a bellboy's uniform instantly appeared at her side. 'Show Madame and Monsieur 'Arris to the honeymoon suite.'

Old Joseph led them up the stairs, opened up a door and shambled into their room carrying their bags. 'Just leave them on the bed,' Ben told him, and tipped him with a large note, which was all he had by way of change.

Roberta looked around her at their accommodation. The ante-room, with sofa, armchairs and coffee-table, opened out into a huge square space dominated by a four-poster bed adorned with a giant red love-heart. On a large walnut table were flowers, chocolates tied up with ribbons, and statuettes of little brides in white dresses and grooms in tuxedos.

Ben sat on the bed and kicked off his shoes, leaving them where they fell on the Cupid rug. *What an absurd room*, he thought. If it hadn't been for Roberta, he'd be sleeping in the car, hidden in some secluded forest somewhere. He took off his jacket and holster and tossed them on the bed, then lay back, stretching his tired muscles. As an afterthought he reached into his pocket and took out the flask. It was dented where it had deflected the bullet earlier. If the .380 round had hit it square on, it would have gone straight through.

He gazed at it for a few seconds. *That's another life gone*, he thought, took a swig and put the flask away.

'Will Anna be OK?' Roberta asked in a faint voice.

He bit his lip. 'Yeah, I think so. She might need a few stitches and treatment for shock. I'll phone around in the morning and find out what hospital she's at.' At least he could rest easy knowing she was safe. The minute the ambulance had got there, the cops would have been alerted and she'd be under protection in hospital.

'How did they get to her, Ben? What did they want with her?'

'I've been wondering that myself,' he muttered.

'And the dead man outside her house? Who was he?'

He shrugged. 'I don't know. Maybe a friend of hers who was just in the wrong place at the wrong time.'

She sighed loudly. 'I can't stand thinking about it. I'm going to take a shower.'

He sat and thought as he listened vaguely to the

301

splashing water in the background. He was disgusted at himself. It was pure luck that they'd got to Anna in time. He'd seen an awful lot of death and suffering in his life, but he didn't even want to imagine the way she would have died if they'd arrived five minutes later.

Long ago, he'd promised himself that he'd never again allow his mistakes to harm the innocent. But it was happening, somehow. These people were getting close again, and the stakes were rising much too high.

He made a decision. Tomorrow he was taking Roberta to the nearby town of Montpellier and putting her on a flight to the States. And he was staying at the airport until he saw the plane leaving the ground with her in it. He should have done it days ago.

He sank his head into his hands, trying to shut out the gnawing feelings of guilt. Sometimes it seemed that no matter how hard he tried to do the right thing, everything he did in his life – every move, every decision – was somehow inexorably, magnetically impelled to return to haunt him. How much regret and self-reproach could one man carry?

A knock at the door disrupted his thoughts. As he walked into the ante-room to answer it, he slipped the Browning into his belt, against the flat of his lower back. He untucked his shirt to cover it. 'Who is it?' he asked suspiciously.

'The food you ordered, Monsieur 'Arris,' came Joseph's muffled voice. 'And your champagne.'

'I didn't order any champagne.' Ben unlocked the door, his hand hovering near where the pistol nestled coldly against his skin. When he saw the shrivelled old man standing alone outside with the service trolley he relaxed and pulled the door open.

'Monsieur, the champagne is complimentary,' Joseph said as he wheeled the trolley into the room. 'It comes with the suite.'

'Thanks, just leave it there.'

With his large tip from earlier on still nestling in his pocket, and the promise of more to come, the old man's step seemed more sprightly as he wheeled in the trolley. There was *charcuterie* and a selection of cheese, fresh baguette and champagne on ice. Ben gave Joseph some more cash, showed him out and locked the door behind him.

The champagne took the edge off their mood. They ate in silence. In the background the radio was playing soft jazz. By the time the bottle was empty it was nearly midnight. Ben grabbed a pillow from the four-poster and tossed it on the leather couch near the window at the opposite end of the room. He took some spare blankets from the wardrobe and threw down a rough bed for himself.

The radio had moved on to playing an old Edith Piaf song. Roberta moved close to him. 'Ben, will you dance with me?'

'Dance?' He looked at her. 'You want to dance?'

'Please. I love this song.' She took his hands, smiling uncertainly, and could feel him tensing up.

'I don't know how to dance,' he said.

'Oh yeah, that's what they all say.'

'No, really, I don't know how. I've never done it.'

'Never?'

'Never once in my life.'

From his wooden, awkward movements she could see he was telling the truth. She looked up at him. 'It's OK, I'll show you. Just take my hands and relax.' She moved towards him gently and rested one hand on his shoulder, taking his hand with the other.

'Put your free hand here on my waist,' she prompted him. His hand was rigid. She moved with him, and he tried to follow her motion, shuffling stiffly with her steps.

'See? Feel the rhythm.'

'OK,' he said hesitantly.

The song ended and another followed straight on: '*La Vie en Rose*'.

'Oh, this is a good one too. OK, here we go again . . . that's it . . . enjoying it?'

'I don't know . . . maybe.'

'I think you could be good at this, if you could relax a bit more. Ouch, my foot.'

'Sorry. I did warn you.'

'You're thinking about it too much.'

From a simple dance he could feel a million conflicting emotions. It was the strangest sensation, and he couldn't decide whether it was pleasant or not. A warm and inviting world seemed to beckon to him. He wanted to embrace the warmth, let it into his heart again after so many years alone in the cold. Yet the moment he began to feel himself giving in to it, he stiffened, and a barrier seemed to come crashing down somewhere inside him.

'Thought you had it for a moment there.'

He pulled away. It was too much for him. It was as though his space had been invaded, his comfort zone breached after years of being alone. He threw a sidelong glance at the mini-bar.

She saw his eye. 'Don't, Ben, please.' She laid a warm hand on his.

He looked at his watch. 'Hey,' he laughed nervously. 'It's getting late. We've got an early start in the morning.'

'Don't stop. It's nice,' she murmured. 'Come on, we've had such a rotten day of it. We both need this.'

They danced a little longer. He felt her body close to his. He ran his hand up her arm to her shoulder and caressed it. His heart was beating faster. Their heads began to move closer to one another.

The song came to an end, and the voice of the radio presenter spoilt their moment. They stepped apart, feeling suddenly self-conscious.

There was silence between them for a few minutes. They both knew what had come close to happening and they both, in their different ways, felt a sadness descending on them.

Ben went over to his makeshift bed on the couch and, too tired to undress, he got into it. Roberta climbed into the vast nuptial bed and lay looking up at the canopy above. 'I've never slept in one of these before,' she said after a while.

Silence again as they lay there on opposite sides of the dark room.

'How's the couch?' she said.

'Fine.'

'Comfortable?'

'I've slept in worse places.'

'There's room in this bed for about six people.'

'So?'

'I just thought.'

He raised his head off the pillow and gazed at where she lay in the dark. 'You're asking me to get in the bed with you?'

'O . . .*On* the bed, then,' she stammered, embarrassed. 'It wasn't a come-on, if that's what you think. I'm just a bit nervous. I could use a little company.'

He hesitated for a few moments. Then he got up and pulled the blankets off the couch. He felt his way over to the bed, groping blindly about in the unfamiliar room. He moved to the far side of the bed and lay down beside her. He pulled the spare blankets over him.

They lay there in the darkness, a wide space between them. She turned towards him, wanting to reach out to him, feeling awkward. She could hear his breathing next to her.

'Ben?' she whispered.

'Yeah?'

She hesitated before saying it. 'Who's the little girl in the picture?'

He raised himself up on one elbow and looked at her. Her face was a pale blur in the moonlight.

She yearned to put her hand out and touch him, hold him tight.

'Let's get some sleep,' he said quietly, lying back down.

Around two, he woke up to find her slender arm draped over his chest. She was asleep. He lay there for a time, staring upwards at the dim play of the moonlight on the canopy of the bed, feeling the gentle rise and fall of her warm body as she slept.

The touch of her arm was a curious feeling. It was strangely electrifying, unnerving and yet deeply comforting. He let himself relax into the feel of it, closed his eyes and dozed off with a smile curling at the corners of his mouth.

CHAPTER 43

Ben slept less than an hour before his dreaming thoughts jerked him guiltily awake and he kicked his legs from the bed. He carefully lifted Roberta's sleeping arm off his chest and rolled out from under it. He got up, lifted the Browning from the table and grabbed his bag.

Finding his way by moonlight he padded quietly into the ante-room. He clicked the door softly shut behind him and flicked on a side-lamp.

The rules of the game had changed. Suddenly it was clearer that these people, whoever they were, were after the manuscript too. He had work to do.

The plain black jacket he'd taken from Anna's house was still in his bag. He pulled it out and went through the pockets again. Apart from Rheinfeld's notebook and the fake scroll that her attacker had torn out of its frame, they were empty. There wasn't a scrap of a clue as to its owner's identity. Who was he? A contract killer, maybe. He'd come across those people before, but never one like this, never a sick maniac who tortured women.

He wondered about the fake scroll. Why had the

man taken it down from Anna's wall? Just like its previous owner who had passed it on to Anna, he must have been fooled by its carefully forged antiquated style and appearance. That could only mean that whoever else was looking for the manuscript had no better idea than he did exactly what it was or looked like. But certainly it was important to them. Important enough to kill for.

He took out Rheinfeld's notebook, pulled it from its plastic wrapping and sat down with it on a couch near the lamp. Until now, he hadn't had a good chance to study it up close. Was Roberta right about it? Was it possible that Rheinfeld had transcribed from memory the secrets that he'd stolen from Gaston Clément? He hoped so. There was nothing else to go on.

He turned the filthy pages slowly, scrutinizing the text and drawings. So much of it seemed like nonsense. Scattered apparently at random throughout, appearing on the corners and margins of some of the pages, were scribbled alternating combinations of letters and numbers. Some of the combinations were long, some short. He flipped back and forth and counted nine of these scribbles. They reminded him a little of Klaus Rheinfeld's ravings on Anna's dictaphone recording.

N 18   N 26 O 12 I 17 R 15   22 R   20 R 15
U 11 R   9 E 11 E   22 V 18 A 22 V 18 A
13 A 18 E 23 A 22 R 15 O

What to make of them? To his eye they looked like a code of some kind. Perhaps a set of alchemical formulae. None of them seemed to relate to anything else on whatever page they appeared. Whatever significance they had, it was impenetrable.

He ignored them and moved on. He came across an ink sketch of what looked like a fountain. Its base was marked with strange symbols similar to ones on the gold crucifix. Below the drawing was an inscription in Latin.

Dum fluit e Christ benedicto Vulnere Sanguis,
Et dum Virgineum lac pai Virgo permit,
Lac fuit et Sanguis, Sanguis conjungitur et lac
Et sit Fons Vitae, Fons et Origo boni

Back in his student days he'd had to wade through a lot of old religious texts written in Latin. But that had been a long time ago. It took him a while to scratch about with the words and come up with a translation. It read *While the blood flows from the blessed wound of Christ and the holy Virgin presses her virginal breast, the milk and the blood spurt out and are mixed and become the fountain of life and the spring of Wellbeing.*

The fountain of life . . . the spring of wellbeing. These sounded like references to some elixir of life. But they were so vague. He read doggedly on. He came to a page with just one line of text, and beneath it a circular symbol. The writing was French, the curly script barely visible through splotches of old blood and Rheinfeld's finger-marks. Again he translated.

> Let us consider the symbol of the raven, because it conceals an important point of our science

The symbol beneath it, he recognized right away. He flipped back a few pages. Yes, it was that same raven emblem again. It seemed to appear again and again. So the text was telling him that it concealed an important point. But what?

A bloodstain was covering something written under the raven image. Ben carefully scratched away the dried blood with his fingernail until he could make it out. The hidden word was DOMUS. Latin for house. What to make of that – *House of the Raven*?

The only other reference he could find to the raven was an equally puzzling rhyming stanza. This time, it was written in English.

> These temple walls cannot be broken
> Satan's armies pass through unaware
> The raven guards there a secret unspoken
> Known only to the seeker faithful and fair

He wasn't even going to try to figure that one out. Moving on, he came to the last three pages in the notebook. They were identical except for three different arrangements of apparently meaningless jumbled letters, one on each page. He read them over and over again. At the top of each of the three pages were the cryptic words 'The Seeker Shall Find'. They read to Ben almost like a taunt. 'The seeker shall get totally lost, more like,' he muttered.

Below these three inscriptions, a line of Latin read *Cum Luce Salutem*. *With the light comes salvation.*

Below that, each page had an even more perplexing arrangement of baffling text. The first of the three pages read:

FIN

A   TI

L   L   D S

M.L.R

The second page read:

FIN

'E   U   E

AC   A

M.L.R

And on the third page the text was arranged:

FIN

L   RO

E   ' NG

M.L.R

The last three letters in each arrangement, M.L.R, looked like initials. Did the R stand for Rheinfeld? But his first name was Klaus. What about the ML? It didn't seem to make any sense.

What about the broken words above the MLR? Ben sat back on the couch. He'd always hated puzzles. He gazed into space. A moth flew past his nose and he watched it flit towards the lamp on the table next to him. It darted here and there and then flew inside the thin cloth lampshade. He could see it walking up the other side of the material, transparent with the light from the bulb.

Then it hit him. *With the light comes salvation.*

He gripped the three pages together on their own, folding the rest of the notebook away from them, and held them up to the lamp. The light shone through the flimsy paper, and suddenly the jumbled letters formed themselves into recognizable words. Taken together, the three blocks of text now read:

FIN
L'EAU ROTIE
LE LAC D'SANG
M.L.R

THE END
THE ROASTED WATER
THE LAKE OF BLOOD
M.L.R

Maybe we're getting somewhere now, he thought.

Then again, maybe not.

OK, break it down into bite-size pieces. 'The End' – what was that, just saying it was the end of the book? That was all he could make of it. But at least that was more than he could understand of roasted water and lakes of blood. He rubbed his eyes, bit his lip. For a moment, his frustration gave way to fury and he had to control a powerful urge to tear the notebook to shreds. He gulped, tried to calm down, stared sullenly at the phrases for a long minute. Willed them to reveal some kind of meaning to him.

FIN
L'EAU ROTIE
LE LAC D'SANG
M.L.R

But if it really didn't mean anything, why go to the trouble of setting up the phrases over three consecutive pages like that?

Like most self-taught linguists, Ben's spoken French was far more fluent than his grasp of the written language. As far as he could make out, though, the line 'the lake of blood' should have read in French '*LE LAC DE SANG*'. Instead it had been written as '*LE LAC D'SANG*', with an important letter missed out. Was it just a mistake? It didn't seem to be. The spelling looked deliberately done that way. But why?

314

He struggled to think clearly. It was almost as if . . . as if the writer was playing with the form, toying with the letters . . . compensating for a lack of letters? Now why would he *do* that?

An *anagram*?

He snatched a piece of hotel notepaper from the table and started scribbling. He began eliminating one letter at a time by circling them, trying to create new words out of the strange phrases. He got as far as *'L'UILE ROTIE N'A MAL* . . . 'the roasted oil has not wrong' . . . when he realized it was a blind alley and lost patience with it.

Scrunch. He threw the paper ball furiously across the room and started again on a fresh sheet.

Five more attempts, and he was beginning to think he'd end up buried alive in crumpled paper. But now it was beginning to look like something coherent.

In another fifteen minutes he had it. He looked down at his sheet. The new words weren't in French, but in the real author's native Italian.

IL GRANDE MAESTRO FULCANELLI.
The great master Fulcanelli.

It was his *signature.* Ben breathed deeply. It looked as though this was what he'd been searching for all along.

There was only one small problem. Even if what he had here *was* a word-for-word transcription of the elusive Fulcanelli manuscript, he still didn't have anything worth taking back to Fairfax. If the old man had thought the manuscript was going to offer up some kind of medical prescription, or a simple home recipe for making life-saving potions with easy step-by-step diagrams, he couldn't have been more mistaken. A cryptic mass of arcane riddles and gibberish wasn't ever going to help little Ruth. This search wasn't over yet. It was only just beginning.

It was after 6.30 am. Light-headed with fatigue, Ben rested back on the couch and closed his burning eyes.

CHAPTER 44

The night breeze rustled the treetops above him. He sat on his haunches, perfectly still and unseen in the bushes, waiting and watching, as silent and patient as any of the wild predatory creatures that lived in the dark forest around him. His mind was shut off from the pain of his cuts and bruises, the graze on his cheekbone and the rawness of his palms after sliding down through the branches of the trellis. He hardly felt anything any longer. But his rage felt like a bubble of molten steel in his throat.

There was nothing Franco Bozza hated worse than failure, than being thwarted, especially when success had seemed so assured. His prizes had been taken from him, and he was powerless to do anything about it. He'd lost.

For the moment.

He waited a while longer, his breathing slowing down as his fury diminished to a simmering rage. His head cocked as he heard the siren in the distance. The wail of the ambulance grew louder on the empty country road, and then it sped by

Bozza's hiding-place, turning the trees and bushes momentarily blue with its flashing lights.

He watched it approaching the entrance to the villa further up the road, slowing for the turn. Before it got there, car headlights appeared, coming the opposite way. Seconds later a battered Renault passed the ambulance in the narrow road. It seemed to slow as the ambulance turned into the villa's drive, then it picked up speed and Bozza could hear the rattle of its engine approaching. As it came by, he was already moving through the trees to the hidden Porsche.

He caught up with it easily and quickly. As he drew nearer, he waited for a bend in the road where a junction turned off. He switched off the lights. If the Renault driver was paying attention, it would look as though the car behind had turned off in another direction.

Now he sat focused with all his concentration in the darkened, invisible Porsche, with only the dim tail-lights of the Renault to lead the way down the twisting lanes. After a few miles his quarry slowed and turned into the drive of a small country hotel. He pulled the Porsche over to the side of the road, got out and slipped into the grounds.

Hope and the American woman didn't see him as they walked inside the hotel, but he was only fifty metres away in the shadows. He was under the trees looking up at the building when he saw lights come on. Middle window, first floor.

Time passed. Around midnight he saw two figures

in the window. They were dancing. *Dancing*. Then they disappeared and the windows went dark.

Bozza waited a while longer, methodically calculating the layout of the hotel. Then he circled the building until he found a kitchen entrance that wasn't locked. He stalked along the quiet corridors until he came to the door he wanted. His spare knife was tucked through his belt.

Bozza was inserting his wire pick into the lock when the strip of yellow light appeared at the bottom of the door to the honeymoon suite. He cursed silently, withdrew the lock-pick and retreated into the dark corridor. Hope was too dangerous to confront without the element of surprise. He'd have to wait longer for his chance.

But it would come, it would come.

CHAPTER 45

Ben awoke with a jolt. He could hear the sound of footsteps and movement from the room above. Voices in the corridor outside.

He looked at his watch and swore. It was almost nine. All around him were his notes and scribbles from last night. He suddenly remembered his discovery of the encrypted Fulcanelli signature. He wanted to tell the news to Roberta.

He went into the bedroom and saw that the four-poster was empty. He called her name at the bathroom door, then went in when there was no answer. She wasn't there either. Where the hell had she gone?

He didn't like it. He grabbed the pistol, tucked it away out of sight. Left the suite and made his way downstairs. Down in the dining-room, the British tourist group were eating breakfast and all talking loudly. There was no sign of Roberta. He walked into the empty lobby. Through a door, a group of staff were huddled in a circle jabbering in loud, urgent whispers.

He went outside. Maybe she'd gone for a walk.

She should have told him. Why hadn't she woken him?

He walked out of the entrance and across the car-park. The sun was already hot, and he shielded his eyes against the glare from the white gravel. People were milling about. A car-load of new guests were arriving, hauling luggage out of the back of their Renault Espace. There was no trace of her.

As he turned back towards the hotel his pressing thoughts were broken by the sudden shriek of a siren behind him. He spun round. Two police cars were crunching across the gravel in a hurry, throwing up clouds of dust. They pulled up either side of him. Each one had a driver and two passengers. The doors opened, and two cops climbed out of each car and started walking. They were looking at him.

He turned and walked fast away from them.

'Monsieur?' All four were coming after him. A radio crackled.

Ben walked faster, ignoring them.

'Monsieur, one moment,' the officer called louder.

Ben stopped, his back to them, frozen. The cops caught up with him and circled him. One had the insignia of a sergeant. He was solid and stocky, square shoulders, big chest, somewhere in his mid-fifties. He looked confident, as if he could handle himself. The youngest one was a kid in his early twenties. He had nervous eyes and a shine of sweat on his brow. One hand on his pistol-butt.

Ben knew that if they made a move against him, all four would be disarmed and on the ground before they could get a shot off. The hefty sergeant would be the first to go for. Then the nervy kid. He would be scared enough to shoot. Numbers three and four wouldn't be a problem. But the two other cops in the cars were out of reach and would have time to get their pistols ready. That was a bigger problem. Ben didn't want to have to kill anybody.

The sergeant spoke first. 'Are you the man who called the police?' he asked Ben.

'Officer! I'm the one who called you!' A guest was coming out of the hotel, a little fat man with grey hair.

'Pardon me, sir,' the sergeant said to Ben.

'What's going on?' Ben asked.

The fat guy joined them. He was agitated, breathless. 'I called you,' he said again. 'I saw a woman being abducted.' He pointed and spilled out the details.

Ben stood back, listening with mounting alarm. 'It was just over there,' the fat guy was saying. His words came out all in a stream. 'He was a big fella. I think he had a weapon . . . Walked her to a car . . . Black Porsche . . . Foreign registration, maybe Italian . . . She was struggling. A young woman, reddish hair.'

'Did you see which way the car went?' the cop asked.

'Turned left at the bottom of the drive – no, right . . . no, left, definitely left.'

'How long ago was this?'

The fat guy sighed and looked at his watch. 'Twenty minutes, twenty-five.'

The sergeant talked into his radio. Three of the cops stayed to take a statement from the witness and question the staff. The fourth climbed back into his car and it took off up the road.

'I saw her arrive last night, with her husband,' the fat man was saying. 'Wait a minute – now I remember it, he was the man who was standing here just now.'

'The blond man?'

'Yes – it was him, I'm sure of it.'

'Where did he go?'

'He disappeared a few moments ago.'

'Anyone see where he went?'

There was a shout. 'Sergeant!' It was the young rookie. He was waving a sheet of paper. The sergeant snatched it from him and his eyes opened wider. The picture was probably about ten years old, crew-cut hair, military look. But it was the writing underneath that drew most of his attention.

RECHERCHÉ
ARMÉ ET DANGEREUX

CHAPTER 46

Sixteen minutes later, police tactical response units were massing outside the Hotel Royal. Breaking up into groups, black-clad paramilitary officers heavily armed with submachine guns, short-barrelled shotguns and tear gas grenade launchers surrounded the building. The bewildered guests and staff were herded out and made to assemble at a safe distance in the grounds. Word spread, and soon everyone knew about the dangerous armed criminal the police were looking for. Was he a terrorist? A psychopath? Everyone had their own version of the story.

The man's trail was soon found at the back of the hotel. Behind the staff car-park was an unmown field of grass leading off in the direction of neighbouring farms. A sharp-eyed police officer found the track where the long grass had been bent over. Someone had recently run through it. The police German Shepherd dogs picked up the scent immediately. Barking furiously and straining on their leashes they led their handlers across the field as armed officers followed close behind. The trail cut across the field and into a clump of woodland. The fugitive couldn't have got far.

But the trail led nowhere. It stopped at the edge of the woods. The officers looked up the trees but there was no sign of him. It was as though he'd vanished into thin air.

It took a few minutes for the pursuers to realize that their quarry had tricked them. He'd doubled back on himself to leave a false trail.

Muzzles to the ground, the German Shepherds led them back to the hotel. The scent led them round the back, through an entrance into the kitchens. The officers drew their pistols. More joined them with shotguns.

Suddenly the dogs stopped, disorientated, sneezing, pawing at their noses. Someone had spilled a catering-sized container of ground pepper all over the floor.

On the signal, the helmeted, black-clad tactical squad swept through every room of the hotel. Exchanging hand signals, covering one another with their weapons, they moved slickly from corridor to stairway and took one floor at a time, one room at a time, checking every possible corner for the fugitive.

They found a man in the honeymoon suite, but not the one they'd expected to find. He was a fifty-two-year-old Frenchman in his underwear, fastened with his own cuffs to one of the bedposts. His face was red and eyes bulged as the police shooters burst in and pointed their guns at him.

Someone had stuffed a hotel hand-towel in his mouth. His name was Sergeant Emile Dupont.

The tactical police uniform was a little baggy for Ben, and the trousers were a couple of inches too short. But nobody noticed as he strode confidently out of the hotel, shouting stern orders at some junior officers. Nobody noticed the non-issue green military bag he was carrying.

And nobody noticed when he made his way through the crowds of chattering guests, slipped into one of the police cars parked out front and quietly drove away.

The witness had said the black Porsche had turned left. He'd been hesitant. Ben took a right. Once clear of the hotel he nailed the throttle, glancing in the rear-view mirror to check he'd got away clean. Messages were coming over his radio. He couldn't stay with this car for long.

She'd only come downstairs to look at the little clothes boutique off the hotel lobby. Ben had been fast asleep over a bunch of notes and papers in the ante-room. She hadn't wanted to disturb him. She'd be back in five minutes anyway, with something clean and fresh to wear at last.

The boutique didn't open until 8.45. She gazed in the window, decided on a jumper she liked the look of, and a pair of black jeans. A few minutes to kill, and the morning air was cool and fresh. She took a walk out front, admiring some of the plants, still trying not to think about yesterday.

She hadn't noticed the man come up behind her. His approach was silent and fast. Next thing, a black-gloved hand was over her mouth and a prickly cold knife point was pressing against her throat. 'Start walking, bitch,' said a hoarse whispering voice in her ear. The accent was thickly foreign.

Across the car-park, half hidden behind a broad ornamental shrub, sat a black Porsche with the doors open. The man was big and powerful. She couldn't struggle free from his grip on her arm, or scream out with that strong hand clamped over her face. He bundled her into the car and punched her in the face, hard. She tasted blood before she passed out.

There was no telling how far they'd come down the road before she came to her senses. Her mind cleared quickly as the adrenaline pumped through her. Beside her in the cramped cockpit of the sports car, her kidnapper's face looked like granite. He held the blade against her stomach, driving with one hand. The Porsche was racing down the country road with 150 on the clock, open countryside and the occasional tree flashing by.

It would be madness to do anything. *Kill us both. Or else he'll put the knife in me.*

But she did it anyway.

The car was coming into a series of tight S bends, slowing down to 85. For an instant he was distracted.

She punched out with all her strength and caught him on the ear. The knife clattered to the floor. He roared. The Porsche swerved. Roberta sprang up in her seat and grabbed the wheel, wrenching it towards her. The car veered crazily to the right, skidded onto the rocky bank and smashed into a tree sideways. Roberta was cannoned against the passenger door, and the force of the impact threw her kidnapper on top of her. His heavy body knocked the wind out of her momentarily.

The Porsche sat still in a haze of dust. Inside, he was pressing hard down on top of her. He picked the knife up and pressed the blade against her neck. He could imagine how, with just a little more pressure, the razor edge of the carefully whetted steel would break through the layers of skin and begin its slow, deliberate journey inwards through the flesh, deeper and deeper as the blood began to spill out. It would come slowly at first. Then in pulsing jets as he held her down and felt her body wriggling against his grip.

But through the red haze of his lust he remembered his phone call to the archbishop the night before. 'The Englishman has got the manuscript,' he'd told Usberti, without giving away how he'd let it slip through his fingers.

'*I want them kept alive, Franco,*' Usberti's voice had ordered him. '*If you cannot retrieve the manuscript, we will have to think of a way to force Hope to give it to us.*'

Bozza loved his work for *Gladius Domini*, but

politics and intrigue held no interest for him. He looked angrily down at Roberta Ryder's struggling form, pinning her to the car seat as she squirmed and spat in his face. It was frustrating to be denied the pleasure of killing her. He put down his knife, punched her again and drove on.

The stolen police car threw up clouds of dust as Ben pushed it hard down the empty roads. He was beginning to wonder if he should have gone the other way when he came to the S-bends and saw the fresh black skidmarks leading off to the right, up the rocky bank. At the top of the bank, an old tree had been damaged, bark ripped away from the trunk and a branch left dangling like a broken arm.

He stopped the car and crouched by the side of the road. On the ground and embedded in the torn bark of the damaged tree, he found flakes of black paint.

Something dark and glistening on the roadside caught his eye. He dabbed it with his finger. A blob of motor-oil, still warm to the touch. Judging by their width the skidmarks were made by fat, grippy sports tyres. A black performance car, going somewhere in a hurry. It had to be the Porsche.

He found more oil a little way further down the road, regular spots and dribbles leading away in the direction he was going. The driver must have hit a rock and damaged the sump. Why had the car crashed? How badly damaged was it?

There might be a chance of finding it broken down further along the road, if it continued losing a lot of oil. But even though the police car was fast and powerful, it was highly conspicuous and he was a sitting duck in it.

He followed the oil trail for a few more kilometres, keeping an ear open for the crackling messages on the police radio. As he'd expected, it wasn't long before they noticed that the car was missing and were sending more out to find it. He was going to have to switch vehicles, and lose his chance of catching up with the damaged Porsche.

On the edge of a sleepy rural hamlet was a small garage with a single petrol pump and a sign that flapped creaking in the breeze. Just beyond it was a rutted mud track leading off to the side. He swung the car over into it, sighing with frustration. He followed the track for about half a kilometre before it ended in a rock-strewn field of yellowed brush and thorn-bushes. He took off the police uniform and changed back into his own clothes, wiped down everything he'd touched inside the car, then tossed the keys down a ditch and started running back up towards the garage.

The mechanic looked up as the tall blond man walked through the opening in the metal shutter and into the workshop. He rubbed his bristled chin with coarse, blackened fingers, came away from the battered van he was fixing and lit a smoke. Yes, he'd seen a black Porsche come by. It had been a bit less than an hour ago. Nice car, shame about the damage. Seemed like it'd been in a crash, rear wheel-arch all dented in. Something rubbing on the wheel, sounded like.

'Yeah, Italian plates? Crazy bastard smacked into me,' Ben said. 'Ran me off the road some way back. I've had to walk miles.'

'Need a tow?' The mechanic jerked his chin in the direction of the rusty tow-truck sitting on the forecourt.

Ben shook his head. 'I've got a special deal through my insurance. I'll give them a call. Thanks anyway.' As they talked, he cast his eye around the place. There was a little showroom attached to the garage, selling mostly used small cars and pick-ups. His eye lit on something. 'Tell you what, though. Is *that* for sale?'

He hadn't been on a motorcycle for over ten years. The last one he'd ridden was an ancient military despatch bike that vibrated like a pneumatic drill and leaked oil and petrol. The sleek Triumph Daytona 900 triple he was riding now was a different order of machine, brutally powerful and faster than most things on four wheels. He followed the road, keeping a sharp watch for more oil spots. If he was lucky, those small round splashes would be the trail of breadcrumbs that could lead him all the way to wherever the Porsche had gone.

A few kilometres up the road, his heart sank as the oil trail suddenly petered out. He rode on a mile or so, peering down carefully as he backed off the throttle and the Triumph rumbled along at walking-pace. Nothing. He cursed. Either the leak had magically repaired itself, or else the driver had been trailered away somewhere. Roadside service, with a kidnap victim sitting in the car? It seemed unlikely. He must have called a local contact to come and tow him away. And now he was gone.

Ben stopped the bike and sat staring up the empty road.

He'd lost her.

CHAPTER 47

Among the trees at the edge of Saint-Jean he eased the big Triumph down onto its sidestand and slung the full-face helmet over the handlebar. The village streets were as quiet and deserted as always. He found Father Pascal at home.

'Benedict, I was so worried about you.' Pascal clasped him by the shoulders. 'But . . . where is Roberta?'

Ben explained the situation and the priest's face fell further and further. He slumped despairingly onto a stool. He suddenly looked all of his seventy years.

'I can't stay here long,' Ben said. 'The police won't waste any time tracing the Renault at the hotel to you. They'll come here to question you about me.'

Pascal stood up. There was a fierce glint in his eye that Ben hadn't seen before. He took Ben's arm. 'Follow me. There is a better place we can talk.'

Inside the church, Ben knelt in the confessional. Pascal's face was half-visible through the mesh window between them.

'Do not worry about the police, Benedict,' Pascal said. 'I will tell them nothing. But what are you going to do? I am terribly afraid for Roberta.'

Ben looked grim. 'I don't know what's best,' he said. He couldn't put a dying child on hold. Every minute he delayed was time lost for her. He could walk away and finish his job – but it was signing Roberta's death warrant. He could go after her, but if she was dead already or he couldn't find her, he risked sacrificing the child for nothing. He sighed. 'I can't save them both.'

Pascal sat in thoughtful silence for a minute or two. 'It is a difficult choice that lies before you, Ben. But you must choose. And once the decision is made, you must not regret it. There has been too much regret in your life already. Even if your choice leads to suffering, you must not look back. God will know your heart was pure.'

'Father, do you know what *Gladius Domini* is?' Ben asked.

Pascal sounded taken aback. 'The Latin means "sword of God". A curious expression. Why are you asking me this?'

'You've never heard of a group, or organization, by that name?'

'Never.'

'Do you remember, you told me about a bishop–'

'Sssh.' Pascal interrupted him with an urgent look. 'Someone is here,' he whispered.

The priest walked down the central aisle and

greeted the police detectives under the arch of the doorway.

'Father Pascal Cambriel?'

'Yes.'

'My name is Inspector Luc Simon.'

'Let us speak outside,' Pascal said, leading him away from the church and shutting the door behind him.

Simon was tired. He'd just flown down by police helicopter from Le Puy. The trail there had gone dead, but he'd known that Ben Hope would resurface somewhere soon. He'd been right. But why Hope's footsteps were leading him to this dusty little village in the middle of nowhere was beyond him. His head was hurting and he was missing his coffee.

'I believe you've lost a car,' he said to Pascal. 'A Renault 14?'

'Have I?' Pascal looked surprised. 'What do you mean, lost? I have not used it for weeks, but as far as I know it is still . . .'

'Your car has been found at the Hotel Royal near Montségur.'

'What was it doing there?' Pascal asked incredulously.

'That's what I thought you could tell me,' Simon replied in a suspicious voice. 'Father, your car is implicated in a manhunt for an extremely dangerous criminal.'

Pascal shook his head blankly. 'This is all very shocking.'

'Who were you talking to in there?' Simon demanded, pointing into the church. He started opening the heavy arched door.

Pascal blocked his way. The priest suddenly seemed twice his normal size. His eyes were hard. 'I was hearing a confession from one of my parishioners,' he growled. 'And a confession is sacred. My parishioners are not criminals. I will not let you desecrate God's house.'

'I don't give a damn *whose* house it is,' Simon replied.

'Then you will have to use force against me,' Pascal said. 'I will not let you in until you come back with a proper warrant.'

Simon glared hard at Pascal for a few seconds. 'I'll be seeing you again,' he said as he turned and walked away.

Simon was fuming as he got back to his car. 'That old bastard knows something,' he said to his driver. 'Let's go.'

They were passing through the village square when he ordered the driver to stop. He got out and strode briskly to the bar.

He ordered a coffee. At the back of the room, the three old card-players turned to look at him. Simon laid his police ID flat on the counter. The barman glanced at it dispassionately. 'Has anyone here seen any strangers in the village recently?' Simon asked, addressing the room. 'Looking for a man and a woman, foreigners.'

*　　*　　*

The police were back sooner than Pascal had expected. Less than five minutes later, Simon was striding down the aisle, his quick footsteps echoing in the empty church.

'Did you forget something, Inspector?'

Simon smiled coldly. 'You're a pretty good liar,' he said. 'For a priest. Now, are you going to tell me the truth, or would you like me to arrest you for obstructing the course of justice? This is a murder investigation.'

'I –'

'Don't try to bullshit me. I know that Ben Hope was here. He was staying with you. Why are you protecting him?'

Pascal sighed. He sat in a pew, resting his bad leg.

'If it turns out you've been harbouring a criminal,' Simon went on, 'I'll bury you so deep in shit you'll never get out again. Where's Hope, and where's he taken Dr Ryder? I know you know, so you'd better start talking.' He drew his gun and jerked open the door of each confessional box.

'He is not here,' Pascal said, looking furiously at the drawn revolver. 'I will request you to put that gun away, officer. Remember where you are.'

'In the presence of a liar and possibly an accessory to crime,' Simon retorted. 'That's where I am.' He slammed the door of the last confessional box with a bang that echoed through the church. 'Now – I suggest you start talking.'

Pascal glowered at him. 'I will tell you nothing.

What Benedict Hope has confided in me is between him, myself and God.'

Simon snorted. 'We'll see what the judge says about that.'

'You can take me to your prison if you want,' Pascal said evenly. 'I have been in worse jails, in the Algerian war. But I will not speak. I will tell you just one thing. The man you are chasing is innocent. He is not a criminal. This man does only good. Few men I have known are so heroic and virtuous.'

Simon laughed out loud. 'Oh, really – is that a fact? So perhaps, *Father*, you'd like to tell me more about this saint and his charitable works.'

CHAPTER 48

The Daytona took him far and fast away from Saint-Jean, slicing through the rugged landscape, crouched low across the tank with the wind screaming around his helmet and the road zipping past under his feet. Ben's face was hard as he rode, thinking what his next move should be. He knew in his heart that there was only one thing he could do, to find Roberta. But she could be anywhere. She could well be dead already.

He backed off the throttle on the approach to a bend, a wall of sandy rock on one side of the road and a plunging drop to the forest below on the other. The motorcycle leaned sharply into the turn, his outstretched knee almost grazing the road. On the apex of the bend he gunned the throttle and the machine straightened up as it accelerated powerfully and the engine note rose to a howl between his knees.

Sunlight glinted off metal in the distance ahead. He swore behind the black visor. Three hundred metres away at the end of a long straight, a road-block was stopping vehicles. An army of police must have mobilized across the Languedoc by now. Murder at the Manzini villa, kidnapping, and a fugitive on the run. They would have circulated pictures of him to every cop in the region.

He slowed. Four police cars, cops with machine-pistols slung low, but ready. They'd stopped a Volvo estate. The driver was out of the car, and they were checking his paperwork. Ben didn't have any, and as soon as they made him take off his helmet he'd be caught.

Being caught wasn't so much the problem. It was the kind of trouble he'd bring down on himself if he resisted arrest, as he knew he'd be forced to do. He didn't want to have to hurt them, and he could ill afford to have a thousand cops and military tearing all of southern France to pieces to find him when he needed every minute to find Roberta and finish what he'd started.

He braked and the bike halted in the road a hundred metres from the roadblock. He sat blipping the throttle for a moment. If he ran the roadblock they might shoot. It was too dangerous. He twisted the handlebar and brought the Triumph round in a tight U-turn. Opened the throttle hard and felt his arms stretch and the back wheel spin and wobble with the brutal power of the engine.

As the bike reached high speed and the road snaked towards him as fast as he could think and react, a snatched glance in the fairing-mounted mirror told him that they'd seen him and were following – headlights and flashing blue, followed by a siren. He opened the throttle harder, daring to release a little more of the Triumph's power. The high mountain pass plunged downward in a long sweeping set of curves and the rocky landscape flashed out of sight as he plummeted into a wooded valley. The police car in his mirrors, already far in the distance, was fast shrinking to a tiny speck.

A straight opened up ahead, carrying him up a long slope between thick banks of green and gold forest. By the time he had passed through the woods and the road was climbing steeply back up towards the next mountain pass, the police car was gone.

He turned off the road at the next junction, knowing more cars would come looking for him. He rode the winding paths higher and higher until the sweep of the whole Aude river valley was laid out below him like a miniature model. The twisty lane became an unrideable rutted track. He stopped the motorcycle near the lip of a precipice, propped it on its stand, and dismounted, unbuckling his helmet and walking a little stiffly from the saddle.

Here and there in the distance he could make out the ruins of ancient forts and castles, specks of jagged grey rock against the forest and the sky. He walked close to the edge of the precipice, so that his toes overhung the brink. He looked down, a dizzying drop of thousands of feet.

What was he going to do?

He stood there for what seemed an eternity, the chilly mountain wind whistling around him. Darkness seemed to be closing in on him. He took out his flask. It was still half full. He closed his eyes and brought it to his lips.

He stopped. His phone was ringing.

'*Benedict Hope?*' said the metallic voice in his ear.

'Who are you?'

'*We have Ryder.*' The voice waited for his response, but Ben didn't offer one.

The man went on. '*If you want to see her alive again, you will listen to me carefully and follow my instructions.*'

'What do you want?' Ben asked.

'*We want you, Mr Hope. You, and the manuscript.*'

'What makes you think I have it?'

'*We know what you got from the Manzini woman,*' the voice went on. '*You will deliver it to us person-ally. You will meet us tonight at the Place du Peyrou in Montpellier. By the statue of Louis the Fourteenth. Eleven o'clock. You will come alone. We will be watching you. If we see any police, you will get Ryder back one piece at a time.*'

'I want proof of life,' Ben demanded. As he listened, he heard a rustling sound of the phone being passed to someone. Roberta's voice was suddenly in his ear. She sounded afraid. '. . . you, Ben? I . . .' Then her voice was cut off abruptly as the phone was snatched away from her.

Ben was thinking fast. She was alive, and they

wouldn't kill her until they had what they wanted. That meant he could buy time.

'I need forty-eight hours,' he said.

There was a long pause. '*Why?*' the voice demanded.

'Because I don't have the manuscript any more,' Ben lied. 'It's hidden in the hotel.'

'*You will go there and retrieve it,*' the voice said. '*You have twenty-four hours, or the woman dies.*'

Twenty-four hours. Ben thought about it for a moment. Whatever plan he might be able to come up with to get her out of there, he was going to need longer than that to put it into place. He'd negotiated many times with kidnappers and he knew how their minds worked. Sometimes they were inflexible in their demands and would execute a victim at the drop of a hat. But that was mostly when they knew they didn't have much to gain, when the bargaining was breaking down or when it looked as though nobody was going to pay. If these guys wanted the manuscript badly enough and thought he was going to deliver it to them, it was a card he could play for all it was worth. He'd already got the guy backing down. He could push him a little more.

'Hold on,' he said calmly. 'Let's be reasonable. We have a problem. Thanks to you people, the hotel is crawling with armed police right now. I'm confident I can get the manuscript back, but I'll need that extra time.'

Another long pause, muffled conversation in the

background. Then the man's voice was back. '*You have thirty-six hours. Until eleven o'clock tomorrow night.*'

'I'll be there.'

'*You had better be there, Mr Hope.*'

CHAPTER 49

Police HQ, Montpellier

The vending-machine swallowed Luc Simon's coins and spurted a jet of thin brown liquid into a plastic cup. The cup was so flimsy he could hardly pick the damn thing up without squeezing all the coffee out of it. He took a sip as he walked back down the corridor towards Cellier's office, and screwed up his face.

On the wall of the corridor was another one of those Missing Person posters he'd been seeing everywhere, about the teenager who had disappeared a few days before. There'd even been one pinned up in the dingy bar in the village where that old priest lived.

He looked at his watch. Cellier was more than ten minutes late now. He needed to share notes with him about the Ben Hope case, and show him the new information he'd just got through from Interpol. Why was everyone always so fucking *slow*? As he paced up and down, he kept looking at the poster.

He took another slurp from his plastic cup and

decided he just couldn't drink this stuff. He stuck his head around the dimpled glass door of Cellier's office. The secretary looked up from her typing.

'Where can I get a decent cup of coffee around here?' he said. 'Someone filled your vending-machine with diarrhoea.'

The secretary grinned. 'There's a good place up the road, sir. I always go there.'

'Thanks. When your boss comes in, if he ever does, tell him I'll be back in a few minutes, OK? Oh, where can I pour this shit out?'

'Give it to me, sir,' she said, laughing, and he leaned across the desk to pass it to her. There was a file open on her desk, with a photo of Marc Dubois, the missing kid. Sitting on top of the file was a small transparent plastic bag with some items in it.

'OK, see you in a bit. Coffee place this way or that way?' he said, pointing up and down the street through the window.

'That way.'

Simon was heading out of the door when he suddenly stopped. He turned back towards her desk, and bent down to look at that file again. 'Where did this come from?' he asked.

'What, sir?'

'This in the bag.' He jabbed his finger through the plastic bag at the object that had caught his eye. 'Where did they find this?'

'That's all stuff from the Dubois missing persons

346

case,' she said. 'Just a jotter and a couple of other things belonging to the boy.'

'What about this thing here?' He pointed.

She frowned at it. 'Think they found it in the boy's bedroom. They don't think it's important, though. I'm just typing up the case notes. Why d'you ask?'

In too much of a hurry to walk the three blocks to the café and back, he jumped into the unmarked car he'd been allocated and drove up. He came out three minutes later with a brioche and a cup of something that smelled and looked a hell of a lot more like the real thing. He climbed back into the car and sat sipping the coffee. Ah, yes, much better. The coffee helped him get his thoughts in order.

He was so lost in thought, he didn't notice the figure approach the car until Ben Hope was opening the door, getting in beside him and holding a pistol at his head.

'I'll have that .38,' Ben said. 'Carefully, now.'

Simon hesitated for a second, then sighed and drew the revolver slowly from his holster, keeping his fingers well clear of the trigger and handing it to Ben butt-first. 'You've got a nerve, Hope.'

'Let's go for a drive.'

They drove out of the town in silence, north-westwards towards the Bois de Valène and down wooded lanes by the banks of the river Mosson. After a few kilometres Ben pointed to an opening in the trees and said, 'Pull in here.' The police car bumped down a dirt road and arrived at a shady forest glade. Ben walked Simon from the car at gunpoint to where the trees opened up onto the riverbank and the sparkling blue water sloshed and burbled against the rocks.

'Are you going to shoot me,' asked Simon, '*Major Hope*?'

'Been checking up on me.' Ben smiled. 'I wouldn't do a thing like that. You and I are going to have a little talk in this pretty spot.'

Simon was wondering if Ben would get close enough to give him a chance to grab the pistol off him. Didn't seem likely.

They walked down to the river. Ben motioned the gun at him to sit on a flat rock. He sat a couple of metres away from the detective.

'What's there to talk about?' Simon asked.

'For a start, we *could* talk about how you're going to call your dogs off me.'

Simon laughed. 'And why should I do that?'

'Because I'm not your killer.'

'No? It seems that everywhere you go, there are dead bodies in your wake,' Simon said. 'And hijacking a police officer at gunpoint isn't the behaviour of an innocent man.'

'I won't come in.'

'You realize that this points to your guilt.'

'I know,' Ben replied. 'But I have a job to do, and I can't do it if your people are on me every step of the way.'

'That's what we do, Hope. Where's Roberta Ryder?'

'You already know that. She's been kidnapped.'

'I'm losing track of all the times she's been kidnapped,' Simon replied.

'This is only the first time. She and I have been working together.'

'On what?'

'Sorry, can't tell you that.'

'I take it you've brought me out here to tell me *something*?'

'I have. Does the term *Gladius Domini* mean anything to you?'

Simon paused. 'Yes, as a matter of fact it does. One of your victims had it tattooed on him.'

'He wasn't my victim. One of his own people shot him. With a bullet meant for Roberta Ryder – or for me.'

'What the fuck are you involved in, Hope?'

'I think they're a Christian fundamentalist cult. Maybe a bit more than a cult. They're well-organized, well-financed and they mean business. They've got Roberta.'

'Why? What would they want with her?'

'They've been trying to kill her, and me, for the last week. I'm not sure why. But I can rescue her.'

'That's a police matter,' Simon protested.

'No, this is my territory. I know what happens when the police get involved in kidnap cases. I've seen it often enough. The victim usually winds up in a bodybag. You have to back off and let me handle this. I'll give you something in return.'

'You're in no position to negotiate with me.'

Ben smiled. 'I'm the one holding the gun.'

'What makes you think you'll get away from me, Major Hope?'

'And what makes you think you'll get away from me, *Inspector* Simon?' Ben replied. 'I could have killed you. And I can get to you any time I want.'

'Huh. Covert assassination. That's what they train you to do, isn't it?'

'I'm not threatening you. I want us to help each other.'

Simon raised his eyebrows. 'What's in it for me?'

'I'll give you your cop-killers. The people who killed Michel Zardi, and who also tried to kill Roberta Ryder – when you thought she was just crazy.'

Simon looked down at his feet, feeling uncomfortable at the reminder.

'That's just for starters,' Ben went on. 'I think you'll be surprised where the trail leads.'

'OK, so what is it you want?'

'There's something I need you to do.' Ben tossed him a card with the phone number he'd got from the bald man under the bridge.

'What's this?' Simon asked, reading it and looking puzzled.

'Just listen. Get your most efficient people in Paris to call this man. He goes by the name "Saul". Your guy should pretend to be Michel Zardi.'

'But Zardi's dead.'

Ben nodded. 'Yes, but Saul thinks he's alive. And he probably thinks he's working with me somehow. Don't worry about the details. Tell Saul that Ben Hope ran back to Paris, and that you've double-crossed him and are holding him. Say he can have Hope for a price. Make it a high one. Arrange a rendezvous.'

Simon bit his lip, trying to fit the pieces together in his mind.

'Get your men to take Saul into custody,' Ben continued. 'Press him hard. Tell him the cops know all about *Gladius Domini*, that the bald man sold him out before he died, and he'd better tell you everything.'

'You've lost me,' Simon muttered, frowning.

'You'll understand, if you do as I say. But you have to move fast.'

Simon was quiet for a few minutes, turning over what Ben had told him. Ben relaxed the gun a little, letting it rest on his lap. He picked up a pebble and tossed it into the river with a splash.

'So, tell me more about you and Roberta Ryder,' Simon said. 'Are you an item, as they say?'

'. . . No,' Ben answered after a pause.

'Men like us are bad news for women,' Simon said pensively, copying Ben and throwing in another stone. They watched it arc against the sunlight and drop into the water, ripples radiating outward. 'We're lone wolves. We want to love them, but we only hurt them. And so they walk away . . .'

'Talking from experience?'

Simon looked at him, smiled sadly. 'She said life with me was like death. All I can think about,

351

talk about, is death. It's my job, the only thing I know.'

'You do it pretty well,' Ben said.

'Pretty well,' Simon conceded. 'But not well enough. As you were quick to point out, you're the one holding the gun.'

Ben tossed him back the .38. 'Sign of good faith.'

Simon looked surprised, and slipped the gun back in its holster. Ben offered him a cigarette, and they sat smoking in silence as they both gazed at the flowing water and listened to the birds. Then Simon turned to Ben. 'All right. Supposing I go along with you on this. There's something else I want you to do in return.'

'What?'

'I want you to help find a missing teenager. That's what you do, isn't it?'

'You really have been doing your homework.'

'Your priest friend told me. I didn't believe him at first, so I checked it out with Interpol. You wouldn't happen to know anything about the Julián Sanchez kidnap case, would you? Spanish police are still wondering about the mystery rescuer who did such a . . . *rigorous* job.'

Ben shrugged. 'Off the record, I might know something about it. But I can't help you with this one. There's no time. I've got to find Roberta.'

'What if I told you that I think this missing persons case is connected?'

Ben looked at him sharply. 'What the hell do you mean?'

Simon smiled. 'A gold medallion was found in the boy's bedroom. You'd recognize the symbol on it, I'm sure. A sword with a banner and the words *Gladius Domini* engraved on it?'

CHAPTER 50

Montpellier

'**M**ore questions? Why aren't you people out looking for my son, instead of coming around here all the time?' Natalie Dubois showed Ben inside the simple, modest house and led him into a living-room. She was a small blonde woman in her thirties, pale and tense-looking with large black circles under her eyes. 'It won't take long,' he promised her. 'I just need a few details.'

'I already told the other officers everything,' she retorted. 'He's been gone for days – what more do you need to know?'

'Madame, I'm a specialist. Please, if you co-operate with me I believe we have a much better chance of finding Marc quickly. May I sit down?' He took out his pad and pen.

'I just know that something awful has happened to him. I feel it. I think I'm never going to see him again.' Madame Dubois' face was drawn and haggard. She sobbed quietly into a handkerchief.

'So, the last time you saw him, he was riding off on his moped. He didn't say where he was going?'

'Of course not, I would have mentioned it,' she replied impatiently.

'Maybe you could write me down the registration number of the bike. Has he ever done anything like this before? Disappeared for a few days, gone off somewhere?'

'Never. He's come home late a few times, but nothing like this.'

'What about friends? Is there anyone he might have gone off with, or gone to see – like a music event, maybe, or a party somewhere?'

She shook her head, sniffing. 'Marc isn't that kind of boy. He's shy, introverted. He likes reading and writing stories. He has friends, but he doesn't go off with them.'

'He's still at school?'

'No, he left earlier this year. He works with my brother-in-law Richard, as an apprentice electrician.'

'Does Marc's father live with you?' He'd noticed she wasn't wearing a ring.

'Marc's father walked out of here four years ago,' she said coldly. 'We haven't seen him since.'

Ben noted down on his pad: *Father involved in abduction?*

She gave a bitter laugh. 'If you're thinking his father's got him, you're wrong. That man isn't the least bit interested in anyone but himself.'

'I'm sorry to hear that,' he said. 'Is Marc religious?

Did he ever talk about joining a Christian organization, anything like that?'

'No. Are you asking because of that thing they found in his room?'

'The medallion.'

'I don't know where that came from, I'd never seen it before. The cops – I mean, the other officers – think he stole it. But my Marc's no thief.' Madame Dubois rose defensively in her chair.

'No, I don't think he's a thief either. Listen, do you think it's possible I could talk to Marc's uncle, Richard?'

'He lives not far away, just up the road. But he won't be able to tell you anything I couldn't.'

'I'd still like to pay him a visit. Will he be at home now?'

As he was getting up to leave, she gripped his wrist and looked into his eyes. 'Monsieur, will you find my boy?'

He patted her hand. 'I'll try.'

'The kid hasn't been *kidnapped*, for Christ's sake. He's run off somewhere, probably got a girlfriend. Or a boyfriend. Who fucking knows, these days?' Richard offered Ben a beer. 'First cop I've ever known who takes a drink on duty,' he laughed as Ben cracked open the can and pulled up a chair at the kitchen table.

'I'm what you might call an outside consultant,' Ben said. 'What makes you so sure he's just run off?'

'Look, between you and me, he takes after his father, my brother Thierry. Total waster. Guy never held down a job in his life, in and out of jail for all kinds of petty crimes. The kid's going down the same road, I reckon, and his mother can't see it. Thinks the sun shines out of his arse. Me, I rue the day I ever let her talk me into taking the little bastard on. He's a complete waste of time and money, and if I don't fire him pretty soon he'll probably fry himself on a live wire and I'll get the blame . . .'

'I understand, but I still have to treat this as suspicious until we know better. You're his uncle, and he's got no father. Did he ever confide in you, maybe mention anything out of the ordinary?'

'You kidding? Everything's out of the ordinary with Marc. Talk about head in the clouds.'

'Like what, for instance?'

Richard made an exasperated gesture. 'You fucking name it. The kid lives in a dream world – if you believed half of what he told you, you'd think . . . I dunno . . . Dracula was your neighbour and aliens run the world.' He slurped his beer, and drew the can away with a ring of foam on his upper lip. He wiped it away with his sleeve. 'Like the job we did just before he ran away . . .'

'Or disappeared.'

'Yeah. Whatever.' Richard told Ben about the cellar. 'And then he wouldn't stop going on about it. Convinced it was something weird.'

Ben leaned forward in his chair, setting down

the beer can and taking out his pad. 'This was a private residence?'

'Nah, it's some kind of place for Holy Joes.' Richard grinned. 'You know, a centre for Christian something or other. Like a school. Nice folks, friendly, decent. Paid cash, too.'

'Have you got the address there?'

'Yeah, sure.' Richard went into the hall and came back leafing through a thick business diary. 'Here it is. Centre for Christian Education, about fifteen kilometres from here, out in the sticks. But you're wasting your time if you think that godless little turd went there.' Richard sighed. 'Look, maybe I'm sounding rough on the kid. If something's happened to him, I'm sorry and I'll eat my words. But I don't believe it. Three or four days, he'll have run out of whatever cash he lifted from Natalie's purse, and he'll be home again with a hangover and his tail between his legs. And this is what you guys spend our tax money on, instead of catching crooks?'

Roberta didn't know how long she'd been lying there on the hard, narrow bunk. Her mind cleared slowly as she blinked and tried to remember where she was. Frightening memories came back. A big, strong guy dragging her out of a car. She'd been held down. Injected with something, screaming. Then she must have passed out.

Her head was throbbing and her mouth tasted bad. She was in a dim, cold, windowless cellar. The room was long and wide, but the cell she was locked in was tiny and cramped. On three sides she was surrounded by steel bars. The wall behind her was cold stone. A single naked bulb hung from a strand of wire in the middle of the cellar, its pale yellow light shining weakly off thick stone pillars.

In another cell a few metres away, a teenage boy was lying comatose on the concrete floor. He seemed heavily sedated, or dead. She tried calling out to him. He didn't stir.

Her guard was a scrawny-looking man of about thirty. He had bulbous, shifting eyes and a straggly yellow beard. A submachine gun hung from a sling around his neck. He paced nervously up and down all the time. She watched him, measuring the cellar by the number of his steps. Every so often he shot a look at her, the bulging eyes scanning her from head to toe.

After a while the scrawny guard was replaced by a stocky man with a shaven head, older, more confident. He brought her a mug of thin coffee and some beans and rice in a tin dish. After that he ignored her.

The teenager in the next cell came to. He lifted himself groggily up on his hands and knees, and turned to look at her with bloodshot eyes.

'I'm Roberta,' she whispered across the gap. 'What's your name?'

The boy was too out of it to respond. He just stared at her. But the stocky guard obviously didn't want them talking. He took a syringe out of a zipper bag, grabbed the boy's arm through the bars of his cage and gave him a shot. After a minute the kid was slumped flat again.

'What the fuck are you giving him?' Roberta hissed at him.

'Shut up, bitch, or you'll get it too.' Then he went back to ignoring her.

It seemed like hours and hours later when the stocky guard eventually swapped places with the scrawny, bearded man again. Soon after he'd resumed his watch over her, he gave her a tentative smile and she returned it. 'Hey, you couldn't get me a glass of water, could you?' she called over to him. He hesitated, then went to a table where the guards had a jug and a few dusty glasses.

After she drank the water, he seemed to want to hang around closer to her cage. She smiled again. 'What's your name?'

'A-André,' he replied nervously.

'André, c'mere a minute. I need your help.'

The scrawny guard glanced over his shoulder, even though there was nobody else around. 'What d'you want?' he muttered suspiciously.

'I lost an earring,' she said. That much was true. It must have fallen out somewhere between here and the hotel. She pointed down at the shadows of the floor. 'It fell down there, your side. I can't reach through the bars.'

'Fuck you, find it yourself.' He turned away with a sour look.

'Please? It's antique, twenty-four carat gold. Worth a lot of money.'

That got his interest. He hesitated, then slung the submachine gun behind his back and approached her. He dropped to his knees, searching in the dust. 'Where abouts?'

Roberta crouched down facing him through the bars. 'Just around there, I think . . . maybe this way a bit . . . yeah, round there . . .'

'I can't see it.' He was scraping around with his fingers, a look of avid concentration on his face. He moved closer to her and she caught the scent of rancid sweat mixed with cheap deodorant, a kind of cold baked-beans smell. She waited until his head was almost touching the bars of the cage. She passed her hands through the bars either side, her heart beginning to race as she thought about what she was going to do. His attention was fixed on the floor. She took a deep breath and then went for it.

In a sudden movement she grabbed hold of his beard with both hands. He wrenched his head back with a stifled shout, but she held him fast. She used her knees against the bars to brace herself. Yanked with all her strength and his bony forehead crashed against the steel cage. He cried out in pain and grabbed at her wrists. Tightening her grip on his beard, she threw herself violently backwards and smashed his head against the bars a second time. He sagged to the floor, stunned but still struggling. She dug her fingers into his

361

greasy hair, bunching up a tight fistful of it, and with the unthinking brutality that comes with desperation she dashed his head repeatedly against the concrete floor until he stopped yelling and struggling. He lay limply with blood oozing from his broken nose.

She let go of him and fell back into the cage, breathing hard and wiping the sweat out of her eyes. She saw the ring of keys on his belt and crawled forward in the dust. She stretched her arm out for it. It was just within reach of her straining fingers and she unclipped it, fumbling clumsily with the fear that someone would come in and catch her. As she tried the different keys on the ring she glanced nervously up at the steel door at the top of the steps.

The fourth key she tried turned the lock. She pushed hard at the steel door to shove the slumped body out of the way, picked up the fallen sub-machinegun and slung it around her neck.

'Hey, wake up.' She banged on the bars of the teenager's cage, but he wasn't responding. She thought about opening up his cell and carrying him out – but he'd be too heavy for her. If she could get out of here alone, she'd come back later with the police.

She ran across the cellar to the stone steps. Just as she reached the third step, the steel door at the top swung open, and she froze.

The tall man in black appeared in the doorway above her. Their eyes met.

She knew this guy. Her kidnapper. Without hesitating she pointed the SMG at his head and squeezed the trigger.

But he just kept walking down the steps, grinning broadly at her. She squeezed harder on the trigger, but it was stuck or something – the gun wouldn't work. Three more guards filed through the doorway, all pointing similar weapons at her.

And they'd all remembered to cock theirs.

Bozza snatched the gun away from her. He caught the fist she swung at him, and twisted her arm up tight behind her back. A stab of pain. Another quarter inch and he'd break it. He marched her back to her cell and flung her into it. The barred door clanged shut behind her.

Bozza was filled with desire to cut this woman up, slowly and deliberately. He took out his knife and scraped the blade down the steel bars. 'When your friend Hope gives himself up to us,' he whispered in that hoarse, strangled voice, 'we are all going to have some fun.'

She spat in his face, and he wiped it away with a harsh laugh.

Then she watched as Bozza slit the scrawny guard's throat and bled him squealing like a pig into the drain in the middle of the cellar.

CHAPTER 51

France's long hot summers, easy pace of life, good food and wine were qualities that attracted a great many retired British folks to leave behind the decaying island empire and resettle in mainland Europe. But not all of the ex-pats who settled there were the usual former solicitors, academics or businesspeople. It had been years since Ben's old forces friend Jack had left the rain-drenched city of Blackpool and found himself a nice beach house near Marseille. Jack was semi-retired now, but he still had a few clients. His business was electronic surveillance . . . and a few related things on the side.

The Triumph Daytona blasted down the French coastal road like a missile. It was a two-hour drive to Marseille. Ben aimed to do it in one.

Five hours later he was riding back the other way with a large black hold-all strapped to the pillion.

The broad paved driveway cut between lush lawns to the sparkling glass and white stone façade of the modern building nestling in the trees. On one of the tall stone pillars at the gateway was a shining brass plaque with a cross and the inscription CENTRE FOR CHRISTIAN EDUCATION. Parked outside the building were rows of cars. From where Ben was standing at the gateway he could make out the discreet security cameras that swivelled and scanned the grounds from the foliage. The wrought-iron gates were shut. There was another camera on the wall, with a buzzer for visitors.

The kid would have climbed the wall to get in, which meant that his moped should be outside the grounds somewhere. Ben parked the Triumph a few metres down the road, and walked up and down peering under the bushes and trees. Where the rough grassy bank met the tarmac on the opposite side of the road, he found a light tyre-track in the dirt. The bank led gently up to a clump of thorny bushes and the trees beyond. He followed the flattened grass and found part of a footprint in the earth. Through the greenery he made out something bright yellow. He lifted a leafy branch and found the tail-end of the 50cc Yamaha protruding from the bushes. The registration number bolted to the rear mudguard was the same one Natalie Dubois had given him.

Ben walked quietly back to the Daytona. He'd already figured out his plan. He unstrapped the black hold-all from the pillion seat and laid it gently on the grass. He opened the side panniers of the motorcycle and reached inside for the blue overall and electrical equipment.

★　　★　　★

The receptionist was just about to take her coffee break when the electrician walked into the plush lobby of the Centre for Christian Education and came up to her desk. He was wearing work overalls and a cap, carrying a hold-all and a small toolbox.

'I thought all the rewiring work was finished,' she said. She noticed that he had nice blue eyes.

'I'm just here to inspect it all, mademoiselle,' the electrician replied. 'Won't take long. I just need to check a few things, take a few notes. Health and safety, all that red tape – building regs, you know how it is.' He flashed her a laminated card, which she supposed was OK although he didn't quite give her time to read it.

'What's in there?' she asked, nodding at the hold-all.

'Oh, just rolls of wire and stuff. Electrical meter, bits and bobs, tools of the trade. Want to have a look?' He dumped the bag on the desk and partly unzipped it to show coloured wires poking out from inside.

She smiled. 'No, that's OK, I'll take your word for it. See you later.'

CHAPTER 52

Place du Peyrou, Montpellier

The unmarked van pulled up in the square at one minute to eleven. As arranged, Ben was waiting for it by the Louis XIV statue. The rear doors burst open and four large men spilled out. He raised his arms in surrender as they encircled him. A pistol was shoved in his back and he was frisked. He was unarmed. They bundled him roughly into the van, and made him sit between two of his captors on a hard bench. The rear windows were painted over, and a wooden partition sealed the cab off from the back and hid any view of the outside world. The van lurched away and the clattering diesel engine reverberated in the metal shell.

'I don't suppose anyone would care to tell me where we're going?' he asked, wedging his feet on the wheel-arch opposite him to keep from sliding across the bench. He wasn't expecting a reply. As they sat in silence, four cold pairs of eyes, a Glock 9mm, a Kel-Tech .40 calibre and two Skorpion machine pistols were all trained steadily on him.

The bumping, rattling journey lasted about half an hour. Judging by the way the van was bouncing around, they must have left main roads behind and headed out into the country. That was what he'd expected. Eventually the van slowed to a crawl, turned sharply to the right, and crunched over gravel. Then onto concrete. A lurch, and down a steep ramp. Then it stopped and the rear doors opened.

More armed men. A torch shone in Ben's face. Harsh orders were spoken and he was dragged out of the van and landed heavily on his feet. They were in an underground car-park.

With gun barrels in his back, he was prodded and pushed up a short flight of stone steps. They walked into the darkened building, through dim corridors. Torchlight darted from behind him. At the end of a narrow corridor was a low doorway. One of the guards, the bearded one with the Skorpion, rattled keys and unfastened padlocks. The heavy door swung open and in the flashing light he saw it was iron, riveted, armoured.

A flight of stone steps led down to a cellar. The echoing voices of his guards told him that it was a big space. Torchlight reflected off stone pillars. And something else, a glint of steel bars. At the far end of the room he thought he saw a face peering blinking at the bright lights.

It was Roberta.

Before he could call to her, he was shoved towards another doorway. An iron bolt ground open. A door creaked and he was pushed into the cell. The door slammed shut behind him and the bolt ground home.

In the darkness he explored his surroundings. He was alone in the cell. The walls were solid, probably double-bricked. No windows. He sat on a hard bed and waited. The only light was the dim green glow of his watch.

After some twenty minutes, around midnight, they came for him, and he was led at gunpoint back through the cavernous cellar.

'Ben?' It was Roberta's voice, edged with fear, calling him from far away. She was silenced by a harsh word from a guard standing near her cage.

Up through the dim corridors. A flight of stairs. More light as they approached the first floor of the building. Through a doorway, and he blinked in the sudden glare of white-painted walls and strong neons. They steered him up another flight of steps, along a corridor and through a door into an office.

At the far end of the office, a large grave-looking man in a suit rose from behind a glass-topped desk. Ben was nudged in the back by a machine-gun barrel, shoving him across the room.

'It's a pleasure to meet you at last, Bishop Usberti.'

Usberti's broad, tanned face broke into a smile. He spoke with a heavy Italian accent. 'I am impressed. But it is Archbishop now.' He motioned to Ben to sit in one of the leather chairs by the desk, opened a cabinet and took out two cut-crystal brandy glasses and a bottle of Rémy Martin. 'Would you like a drink?'

'How civilized of you, Archbishop.'

'I would not like you to think we treat our guests badly,' Usberti replied graciously as he poured them each a generous measure and dismissed the guards with an authoritative gesture of his free hand. He caught Ben's eye as he watched the guards leave the room. 'I hope I can trust you not to try any of your tricks while we speak in private,' he said, handing Ben his glass. 'Please remember that there is a gun pointed at Dr Ryder's head at this very moment.'

Ben didn't show any glimmer of response. 'Congratulations on your promotion,' he said instead. 'I see you left your garb at home.'

'I should be the one to congratulate you,' Usberti replied. 'You have the Fulcanelli manuscript, do you not?'

'Yes, I do,' Ben said. He swirled the cognac around in the glass. 'Now why don't you let Dr Ryder go free?'

Usberti laughed, a deep rumble. 'Go free? My plan was to have her killed once I had the manuscript.'

'You kill her, I'll kill you,' Ben said quietly.

'I said my plan *was* to kill her,' Usberti replied. 'I have changed my mind about that.' He swivelled his glass on the desktop, watching Ben curiously. 'I have also decided not to have *you* killed, Mr Hope. Subject to certain conditions, I should add.'

370

'That's very magnanimous.'

'Not at all. A man like you can be useful to me.' Usberti smiled coldly. 'Though I will confess it took me a while to see it. At first I watched in rage as, one by one, you threw off my men and all my attempts to dispose of you and Ryder. You have proved hard to kill. So hard, that I began to think that such a man is too valuable not to turn to one's own advantage. I want you to come and work for me.'

'You mean work for *Gladius Domini*?'

Usberti nodded. 'I have great plans for *Gladius Domini*. You can be a part of those plans. I will make you a rich man. Come with me, Mr Hope. Let us take a walk.'

Ben followed him out of the office into the corridor. The armed guards were flanking the door, and walked a few paces behind them, their weapons trained on Ben. They stopped at a lift. Usberti pressed the button and from somewhere below them there was a whoosh of hydraulics.

'Tell me, Usberti. What does all this have to do with the Fulcanelli manuscript? Why are you so interested in it?' The lift doors opened with a whirr and they stepped in, the guards still following.

'Oh, I have been interested in alchemy for many, many years,' Usberti replied. He reached out with a blunt finger and prodded the button for the ground floor.

'Why?' Ben asked. 'To suppress it because it was heresy?'

Usberti chuckled to himself. 'Is that what you think? On the contrary, I wish to make use of it.'

The lift came to a smooth halt and they stepped out. Ben looked around him. They were in a large brightly lit science lab operated by some fifteen or so technicians who were busily attending to scientific equipment, writing up charts and sitting at computer terminals, all wearing white labcoats and the same serious expression.

'Welcome to the *Gladius Domini* alchemical research facility,' Usberti said, with a wide gesture. 'As you see, it is a little more sophisticated than Dr Ryder's establishment. My teams of scientists work in shifts, all around the clock.' He took Ben's elbow and led him around the edge of the lab. The muzzles of the machine guns were still carefully trained on him.

'Let me tell you a little about alchemy, Mr Hope,' Usberti continued. 'I do not suppose you have ever heard of an organization called the Watchmen?'

'Actually I have.'

Usberti raised his eyebrows. 'You are remarkably well-informed, Mr Hope. Then you will know that the Watchmen were an élite group in Paris, formed after the First World War. One of their members was a certain Nicholas Daquin.'

'Fulcanelli's apprentice.'

'Indeed. As you may know, then, this brilliant

young man learned that his teacher had discovered something of enormous importance.' Usberti paused. 'There was another member of the Watchmen who was interested in Fulcanelli's discovery,' he went on. 'His name was Rudolf Hess.'

CHAPTER 53

At that moment the man known to certain people only as Saul parked his Mazda two-seater convertible outside an old empty warehouse on the outer edge of Paris. The night was cool. The stars twinkled above the city lights. He checked the time and kicked his feet, waiting.

The briefcase in his hand was filled with banknotes amounting to a quarter million US dollars, the sum the caller had demanded in exchange for what he claimed to possess: the Englishman Ben Hope, captured, bound and gagged. Usberti would be pleased when he found out what Saul had got for him.

Naturally, the money was counterfeit, obtained from one of Saul's *Gladius Domini* sub-agents. The cash was only a diversion anyway. Even though it was fake, Saul had no intention of handing it over to anyone. In a concealed holster under his jacket was a compact .45 auto. He intended to make use of it once he'd picked up the goods. Or if it should turn out that there weren't any.

Saul still couldn't figure out this business with Michel Zardi. They seemed to have underestimated him. First he'd managed to evade assassination, then he'd somehow contrived to lure several of Saul's best men to their deaths, and now he was claiming to be holding the Englishman Ben Hope? He never would have imagined that a little nerd like Zardi had that much guts and talent.

But if this was some kind of trick, he wouldn't get away this time. And in case Zardi had friends with him, Saul had already taken care of it. A sniper armed with a night-scoped Parker-Hale 7.62mm rifle had been posted on the roof of the warehouse immediately after he'd got the call.

A minute or two went by, and then Saul heard the sound of an engine. He watched as the headlights wound up through the industrial estate and approached the warehouse. The rusty Nissan van pulled up beside his Mazda. The driver wasn't Michel Zardi. It was a little fat man with a moustache and flat cap. Perhaps he was one of Zardi's cronies, Saul thought.

'You Saul?' the man asked, getting out of the van.

'Where's Hope?'

The man grunted. 'You got the money?' At Saul's nod he motioned to the back of the van. Saul smiled to himself as he imagined his rifleman watching this chubby fool in his sights.

The man threw open the back doors of the Nissan, and Saul approached. Lying on the rough wooden floor inside was a body. Bound and gagged.

And staring at Saul in horrified recognition. It wasn't Ben Hope.

It was his sniper.

Before Saul could react, Lieutenant Rigault had his gun against his temple and armed officers were flooding out of the building. The red beads of laser sights that were floating all over the back of Saul's head and jacket belonged to élite police marksmen, trained fingers on hair triggers.

Rigault threw Saul down onto the floor of the van next to the *Gladius Domini* sniper and cuffed his hands behind his back as he read him his rights. As Saul was led away to a waiting police van, Rigault called Simon. 'The fish has taken the bait,' he said.

CHAPTER 54

The lift rose smoothly upwards. The guns were still pointing straight at Ben's head as Usberti led him back to the office. He followed the Archbishop inside, the guards taking up their position outside the door. Usberti motioned to him to sit down, and poured another drink.

'There's only one Rudolf Hess I've ever heard of,' Ben said. 'The Nazi.'

Usberti nodded, smiling. 'Adolf Hitler's long-time acolyte and deputy Führer. All his life Hess had a strong interest in the esoteric, which may have been inspired by his early years growing up in Alexandria, Egypt. In his teens his family returned to Europe. Hess pursued his interests, and in the 1920s he learned important alchemical secrets from Fulcanelli's student Nicholas Daquin. Of course, by that time Hess was also deeply involved in the rising National Socialist Party. Knowing its importance, he immediately passed his new knowledge on to his leader and mentor, Adolf Hitler.'

Ben's head was spinning. The Alexandrian – Daquin's mysterious friend Rudolf – could it really have been the arch-Nazi Hess?

Usberti went on, pleased at Ben's reaction. 'Long before the war, the Nazi Party was very interested in alchemy's potential to help them build the Third Reich. Company 164 was a secret Nazi research facility whose purpose was to research the alchemical transmutation of matter by altering its vibration frequency.'

'But how could alchemy have helped the Third Reich?'

Usberti grinned. He opened a drawer, and something glinted in his hands. He laid the heavy object down on the desk in front of Ben. 'Mr Hope, I give you the secret knowledge of Fulcanelli, as revealed to his student Nicholas Daquin.'

The gold bar shone dully in the lamplight. Stamped on its side was a small Imperial eagle perched over a Swastika.

'You're joking.'

'Not at all, Mr Hope. The primary aim of Company 164 was the creation and manufacture of alchemical gold.'

'Out of base metals?'

'Iron oxide and quartz, mainly,' Usberti replied. 'These were highly processed according to strict methods that Daquin confided to Hess. You see, it was all thanks to our unwitting friend Fulcanelli that the Nazis were able to gain this incredible knowledge.'

'And they succeeded?' Ben asked, narrowing his eyes sceptically.

'The evidence is before you.' Usberti smiled.

'Suppressed Nazi documents tell that Party members witnessed the making of alchemical gold at Company 164's plant outside Berlin in 1928. The factory was destroyed in World War Two, under the pretext of blowing up industrial facilities. How much gold they were able to produce during those years, nobody knows for sure. But I believe it was a very considerable quantity indeed.'

'You're suggesting that the Nazis were funded by alchemical gold.'

'No, Mr Hope, I am stating it as fact.' He laid his hand on the gold bar. 'The millions of these recovered by the Allies at the end of the war – and there are many more yet to be found – did not come from the gold fillings and melted-down trinkets taken from Jews in the concentration camps, as the history books tell us. Even six million Jewish prisoners could not possibly have provided that much gold. The whole story was fabricated by Allied governments to conceal the fact that Hitler was really producing *alchemical* gold. They feared that if the truth were to be revealed, it would threaten to destabilize the entire global economy.'

Ben laughed. 'I've heard some wild conspiracy theories in my time, but this one's got to be the best.'

'Laugh all you like, Mr Hope. It will not be long before we can create alchemical gold. Unlimited wealth. Think of it.'

'You don't seem short of funds as it is. Your operation must cost you a packet.'

'You would be surprised at some of our investors,' Usberti replied. 'They come from all denominations, all over the world. They include several of the world's most powerful corporate players. But my plans require a great deal of funding.'

'Just like Hitler's plans?'

Usberti shrugged. 'Hitler had his grand design, I have mine.'

There was silence for a minute as Ben pondered the enormity of what Usberti was telling him.

'So now you understand why I want the Fulcanelli manuscript,' the archbishop went on, strolling up and down by the dark window. 'Thanks to the destruction of the Nazi gold plant, we are lacking certain details we need to complete the process. I believe that the manuscript holds the key. And this was not the only secret of alchemy that Fulcanelli possessed.' He paused, looking hard at Ben, then continued. 'But when the old fool discovered that the secret of gold-making had fallen into the hands of Hess and his colleagues, he panicked. He disappeared. And took with him the second great secret, which he never passed on to his student Daquin and which I believe is to be revealed within his manuscript.'

'Go on.'

'You see, Mr Hope, the two things I most need to build up *Gladius Domini* are wealth, and time. I am fifty-nine years old. I will not live for ever. I do not wish to see all my hard work pass into the hands of a successor who may ruin everything. I want to stay in control for at least another fifty years, or even longer, to see my goals accomplished.'

Ben held out his glass as Usberti poured another brandy. 'And so you're looking for the elixir of life?'

Usberti nodded. 'To make use of it for myself, as well as to protect its secret. When my spies told me how close Dr Ryder was getting to discovering it, I decided to have her killed.'

'Bit extreme, considering she didn't have all the answers. She was only at the start of her research.'

'True. But she was blabbing about it to anyone who would listen.'

'Couldn't you have just employed her to work for you?'

That cold smile again. 'All my scientists are *Gladius Domini* members. They fervently believe in our cause. Dr Ryder is an individualist – her behaviour shows that clearly. She is ambitious, and full of resentment against her fellow scientists. She wants to prove them wrong as much as she wants to develop her discovery. She would never have worked for me.'

'Why keep her alive now?'

'She is alive at the moment,' Usberti said. 'But whether she stays alive much longer depends entirely on you, Mr Hope.'

'On me?'

'Indeed.' Usberti nodded gravely. 'I mentioned before that I want you to work for me. Have you considered my offer?'

'You didn't say what you wanted me to do for you.'

'I am building an army. Armies need soldiers, men like you. My sources have told me about your impressive background.' Usberti paused. 'I want you to be *Gladius Domini*'s military commander.'

Ben laughed out loud.

'You will have wealth, power, women, luxury, anything you like,' Usberti said earnestly.

'I thought you only recruited believers, not individualists.'

'When I meet a man with exceptional talents, I make exceptions.'

'I'm flattered. But if I turn down your offer?'

Usberti shrugged. 'Roberta Ryder dies. And you too, naturally.'

'That's quite a deal,' Ben said, smiling. 'But tell me. Why would a Catholic archbishop want to build a private army? You're already high up in a powerful organization. Why don't you just do it the orthodox way? With your ambition you could become Pope one day. You'll have all the power you want then to make reforms, from the inside.'

Now it was Usberti's turn to laugh out loud. '*Reforms?*' he spat contemptuously. 'You think I am interested in their Church? What is a Pope? A mere puppet to be wheeled out to please the crowds. A decaying figurehead, like your English Queen. No, that is not for me. I want much more power than that.'

'All in the name of God? Your organization doesn't seem very pious to me. Espionage, brainwashing, murder, kidnap . . .'

Usberti interrupted him with a chuckle. 'You know little about the history of the Church, Mr Hope. It has always done those things. In fact, the problem is that it has *stopped* doing them. That parcel of flabby old men in Rome has let everything become weak. The faith of the West is failing. The people have been abandoned. They are like soldiers without a leader. Like a motherless child.'

'And you want to be their mother, is that right?'

Usberti stared at him. 'They must have a strong leader, a hand to guide them. What have they got otherwise? Science? Filthy. Corrupt. Only interested in profits, human cloning, colonizing other planets because they are destroying this one. Technology? Toys to tempt them. Computer games. Television that lets the media control their minds. They need a leader. I am it. I will give them something to believe in and fight for.'

Ben frowned. 'Fight? Against whom?'

'We live in unstable times,' Usberti replied. 'While the faith of the Christian world is failing, a new power is rising. The dark forces in the Middle East.' The archbishop brought his fist down on the desktop. He had fire in his eyes. 'The enemy that the Church crushed centuries ago is massing its forces. We are weak, they are strong. They have faith, we have only fear. This time they will win. It is already happening. The West has no idea what they are up against. Why? Because we have forgotten what it means to believe in something. Only *Gladius Domini* can prevent this rot from destroying the whole fabric of our Western world.'

'And you think that a tin-pot fundamentalist terror organization like the Sword of God can change the world?'

Usberti flushed. 'This tin-pot organization, as you call it, is a growing force. *Gladius Domini* is not restricted to a few agents in France. What you have seen of our strength is like one drop in a whole ocean. We are an international agency. We have agents across the whole of Europe, America, Asia. We have friends at the highest levels of politics and the armed forces. In China, the fastest growing economic power in the world, two million new recruits are joining the fundamentalist Christian movement each year. You have no idea what is happening, Mr Hope. In a few years' time we will have a fully equipped army of devotees that will make the Third Reich look like the Boy Scouts.'

'And then? An independent strike against the Islamics?'

Usberti smiled. 'If we are unable to exert sufficient influence on US foreign policy-makers, our contacts in Intelligence and the military, then yes. Just as the Church once sent its armies to crush the pernicious forces of Saladin and other Muslim kings, we will launch a new era of holy war.'

Ben thought for a moment. 'If I understand you,' he said slowly, 'you're talking about starting World War Three. Provoking a jihad between a new

Christendom and the united forces of the Muslim world is only going to spell destruction for everyone, Usberti.'

The Italian made a dismissive gesture. 'If it is God's will, then let the blood be spilt. *Neca eos omnes. Deus suos agnoscet.*'

'*Kill them all. God will recognize his own,*' Ben translated. 'Spoken like a true murderous tyrant, Archbishop.'

'Enough talk,' Usberti hissed. 'Give me the manuscript.'

'I don't have it,' Ben replied calmly. 'You think I'd have brought it here, just like that? Come on, Usberti, you should know better.'

Usberti's cheeks darkened to a furious purple. 'Where is it?' he demanded. 'Do not play games with me, I warn you.'

Ben checked his watch. 'Right now it's in the hands of an associate of mine. I told him I'd call around one-thirty. If he doesn't hear from me, he'll assume something's happened to me and he'll burn it.'

Usberti glanced at the clock on his desk.

'Time's running out, Archbishop. If the manuscript burns, you'll lose everything.'

'And you will lose your life.'

'True. But my death is worth less to you than your own immortality.'

Usberti snatched up the phone from his desk. 'Use it,' he commanded. 'Or you will hear Ryder's screams before you die. The Inquisitor is a man who knows how to prolong agony.'

Ben could do that too. He waited a long moment, letting Usberti feel every second of it.

'Quickly,' the archbishop said. His tanned face was turning to white as he held out the phone.

Eventually Ben shrugged. He took the phone. 'OK. And you'll have my answer to your offer.'

He punched a number on the tiny silver keys. The number appeared on the screen. *Dial?* prompted the phone.

Ben's finger hovered over the last button in the sequence. There was a quizzical look on Usberti's face.

'And here's my answer,' Ben said.

Usberti stared at him in sudden horror as he realized that something had just gone very, *very* wrong.

CHAPTER 55

Ben didn't take his eyes off Usberti's as he pressed the button and heard the fast bleeps of the speed-dial sequence.

Six remote receivers scattered around the *Gladius Domini* building responded instantly to the phone signal. They were wired to six miniature Instantaneous Electrical Detonators, which in turn electronically activated their six fist-sized packages of PBX plastic-bonded explosive.

Less than half a second later, the massive combined blast rocked the building. Masonry ruptured into pieces, walls burst outwards. Fire tore through the underground car park, turning every vehicle into an incendiary device in its own right. The plush reception area was ripped to pieces as a huge fireball unfolded itself and poured down corridors like a sea of blazing liquid. Men staggered screaming, ablaze. On the first floor, every window exploded in a lethal burst of flying shards as the blast destroyed the laboratory, hammering science equipment and computers into scattered debris.

Upstairs in his office, Usberti was transfixed with

terror as the floor under their feet lurched with the deafening explosion. The shockwave knocked the air out of the room. Ben was up on his feet and rushing at the panicked Italian. But then the guards burst into the room from the smoky corridor, waving their machine pistols. Ben grabbed one of the tubular steel chairs and killed the nearest one with a thrust that drove a leg through his soft palate and into his brain. His Skorpion clattered to the floor. A burst of fire from the second guard shattered the glass top of Usberti's desk. Ben rolled and threw out his arm for the fallen machine pistol. He fired, slashing 9mm holes across the wall and the guard's body. The man crumpled, his face contorted.

Usberti was gone. Behind a curtain, a glass fire door was still swinging. Heavy footsteps rattled down the steel fire escape outside.

Ben tore himself away. Roberta was what mattered. He ran out into the corridor and headed for the lift, punching a second number into the phone as he went. As the lift glided downwards to the basement he jumped up and hooked his hands around the steel frame of the hatch in the middle of the ceiling. He hung there for a moment, then flipped up the hatch cover. The small kit-bag he'd left was still there. He dropped down to the floor, opening the bag as the lift juddered to a halt. He stepped out and pressed the call button on the phone. At the other end of the building a smaller charge of PBX took out the main fuse. The whole building blacked out.

Ben took the Browning out of the bag, cocked it and switched on the underbarrel LED torch. He headed for the cellar, sweeping the light this way and that in the darkened corridors.

It had all happened exactly as Ben Hope had said it would. The simultaneous explosions had been over in an instant. Suddenly they heard a smaller blast, no more than a muffled thump, and the building went dark. Only the orange flicker of flames could be seen from the ground below.

At Simon's signal the police tactical units emerged from the cover of the wooded grounds and stormed the building. In their black entry vests, hoods and goggles the armed units swarmed through the chaos. A few scattered men fired blindly at them in their panic. The police shooters were much faster, much cooler and much more accurate. They only shot the ones who were an immediate threat. Those who tried to run or threw down their weapons were quickly trussed up on the floor with their wrists and ankles bound together and MP-5 machine carbines pointing at the backs of their heads. Down in the science lab, technicians crawling dazed, blackened and bleeding among the smoky wreckage were jerked to their feet and marched out at gunpoint. In less than five minutes the police had secured the whole place.

Usberti thought his heart was going to give out. Explosions rattled the building and he could hear yelling and the crackle of small-arms fire from inside as he ran around the side of the wall. His chest heaving, breath rasping, he staggered into the grounds. He leaned against a tree, bent double with wheezing, trembling with shock and rage.

Ben Hope had pulled the rug out from under him. For all his appreciation of the man's skills, and for all his own cunning, he'd managed to underestimate him disastrously. He still couldn't understand what the hell had just happened.

'You there,' said a voice. 'Put your hands behind your head.' Usberti rolled his eyes up to see two men in black uniforms standing a few metres away in the darkness pointing guns at him. A radio fizzed. Slowly, he moved away from the tree and lifted his arms. *To be caught, like this . . .*

One of the men reached back to his belt for a set of cuffs.

But then the two officers were lifted off their feet like straw men. They flew into one another and their heads smashed together with a dull, meaty crunch. They dropped to the ground without a noise.

Usberti's face split into a wide grin of relief as he recognized the tall figure standing over the slumped bodies. 'Franco! Thank the Lord!'

Bozza drew out his knife and quickly, efficiently, cut the throats of the two men. He picked up one of their radios and a fallen MP-5. With a glance over his shoulder he calmly took his archbishop by the arm and guided him through the trees into darkness.

It was a half a kilometre across the woods to the road. Bozza helped Usberti down the leafy bank to the tarmac. He saw the approaching lights of a car in the distance. Letting go of Usberti's arm, Bozza stepped out and stood in the middle of the road, bathed in the headlights as the car came closer. As it came near, he pointed the MP-5 at the windscreen. The car squealed to a halt diagonally across the road.

There was a young couple inside. Bozza ripped open the driver's door and dragged the man out by the hair. He sent him sprawling across to the edge of the road and casually fired a fully automatic burst into his chest. The man crumpled bloodily into the leaves.

Inside the car, the girl was screaming hysterically. Bozza pulled her bodily out through the open window, looked coldly into her face and snapped her neck in a single twisting movement. The Inquisitor dragged their bodies into the ditch and covered them with pieces of shrubbery.

'Good work, Franco,' Usberti said. 'Take me away from here.'

Bozza helped him into the back seat and then they were gone, heading for the airfield.

The last item Ben had packed in his kit-bag earlier that day was a small armour-piercing shape charge. He pressed the connected blobs of plastic explosive against the steel cellar door, stuck in the two electrodes and quickly retreated back down the corridor before thumbing the button on the phone. The percussive detonation ripped the air, and when the smoke cleared the door looked as though a giant mouth had taken a perfectly oval bite out of it. The edges around the hole glowed faintly red. Ben stepped through into the smoky cellar, gun first.

The one cellar guard must have been standing near the door when the charge went off. Ben shone the pistol light on him. He was on his back, blood running from his ears and nostrils. A triangular shard of steel protruded eight inches from his chest. Ben grabbed the ring of keys from his belt and ran down the cellar steps into the huge smoky room. He called her name.

'Ben!' Roberta shouted, recognizing his voice through the high ringing in her ears that the sharp explosion had set off. 'There's a boy over there.' She pointed to the next cell along. Ben flashed the light and saw Marc's drugged, slumped figure. He opened both cage doors. 'Come on, let's go,' he said quietly, gently avoiding her embrace. He stooped and lifted the stirring boy over his shoulder.

The puzzled officers found Marc Dubois lying in the back of one of the police cars ten minutes later. 'Where the hell did *he* come from?' asked one. 'Beats me,' said his companion. It was a while before it dawned on them that he was the kid on the Missing Person posters.

Simon watched, deeply satisfied, as his men brought more than thirty coughing, spluttering, smoke-blackened personnel out of the shattered building. Six bodies had been recovered so far, and enough weapons and ammunition to lay serious criminal and terrorism charges against the whole organization.

Speed, Aggression, Surprise. He'd heard that that was the unofficial motto of a certain British Army regiment. He grinned and shook his head.

CHAPTER 56

Roberta was swinging between wild elation and trembling exhaustion as Ben led her away in the darkness. With one arm around her waist he steered her through the shadowy woods. Back towards the little lane outside the police cordon where he'd hidden the rental car. He was evasive and silent, ignoring the questions she fired at him.

They arrived at the car. He turned sharply at the sound of the foliage rustling behind them. But it was just an owl, disturbed by their passage.

He kept to the backroads, and they sat in silence for a while as he drove. Roberta closed her eyes. Already the details of her imprisonment were beginning to seem hazy and distant in her mind.

After two kilometres of cutting across rough country lanes they came out onto a narrow road.

'Where are we going?' she asked.

'I rented a place.'

They passed through a couple of small villages and twenty minutes later they arrived at a country cottage tucked away behind a clump of trees up its own private track. Ben led Roberta up the path, opened the door and flipped on the light. The cottage was bare and functional, but it was safe.

She flopped down in an old armchair, leaning her head back and shutting her eyes. He came and handed her a glass of red wine. She drank it down quickly, and could feel the immediate relaxing effect of it. She watched him as he piled kindling wood and logs and lit a crackling fire in the stone inglenook fireplace. He was strangely quiet, distant.

'Are you OK, Ben? What's wrong?'

He said nothing, kneeling in front of the fire with his back to her, stirring up the flames with a poker.

'Why won't you talk to me?'

He dropped the iron poker with a clang, got to his feet and turned round to face her. 'What the hell were you playing at?' he demanded furiously.

'What do you mean?'

'Have you any *idea* how worried I was? I thought you were dead. What possessed you to go wandering off like that?'

'I–'

'Of all the stupid, idiotic . . .'

She stood up. Her lip was quivering and her hands were shaking.

He softened when he saw her face. 'Look, don't cry. I'm sor–'

He didn't get to finish the sentence. Her fist flew up and connected with his jaw. He saw lights, and staggered back two steps.

'Don't you talk to me like that, Ben Hope!'

They stood facing each other. He rubbed his

jaw. Then she threw her arms around him and buried her face in his shoulder. She felt him tense up and she backed off, looking at him uncertainly with hot tears in her eyes.

But then his tension broke and something welled powerfully up inside him. He wanted it now, that warmth he'd rejected for so long. He wanted to plunge into it like a diver into a warm ocean lagoon, and never come out again. As he stood looking into her sad, wet, blinking, searching eyes he knew that he loved her more than he'd ever realized.

He reached out for her, grasped her arms and drew her to him. They held one another tight, caressing, gasping, running their fingers through each other's hair.

'I was so scared,' he whispered. 'I thought I'd lost you.' He ran his fingers up to her face and wiped away the tears from her laughing cheeks. Their lips drew together and he kissed her, long and longingly, as he'd never kissed anyone in his life before.

She was woken up the next morning by a crowing cockerel in the distance. Her eyelashes fluttered open and after a couple of seconds she remembered where she was. Sunlight was streaming through the bedroom window. A little smile spread across her lips as the memory of last night came back to her. It wasn't a dream. When she'd told him how much she loved him, he'd said he felt the same way. He'd been so tender with her, a whole new side to him opening up as their passion had mounted.

She rolled on her back and stretched her body out under the sheet, luxuriating in the crisp cotton. Brushing the tousled hair out of her eyes, she stretched out an arm to touch him. Her hand felt an empty pillow. He must have gone downstairs.

For a while she swam in that nebulous, drifting haze between sleep and wakefulness. The horror of her kidnap and imprisonment seemed a faraway memory, as though they belonged in a different life, or a half-forgotten nightmare from long ago. She wondered what it would be like to live in Ireland, by the sea. She'd never lived by the sea . . .

More awake now, she wondered what he was doing. She couldn't smell coffee, and couldn't hear any sounds apart from the singing of the birds in the trees outside. She swung her legs out of the bed, and walked naked across the bedroom to gather up the trail of discarded clothes she'd left from the top of the stairs to the bed. More fresh memories, and she smiled to herself again.

He wasn't downstairs making breakfast. She searched around the little cottage, calling his name. Where was he?

It was when she saw that the car and his things were gone that she began to worry. She found his note on the kitchen table, and knew what it was going to say even before she unfolded and read it.

Tears gathered in her eyes and spilled down her cheeks. She sat at the kitchen table, sank her head into her arms and wept for a long time.

CHAPTER 57

Palavas-les-Flots, Southern France, three days later

Autumn was setting in now. The busy season was coming to an end for the seaside resort, and the only tourists still out there bathing in the sea were Brits and Germans. Ben sat on the beach and gazed out at the blue horizon. He was thinking of Roberta. By now she should be heading back home to safety.

He'd left early after their night of love. *You shouldn't have let that happen,* he thought. It wasn't fair on her. He felt terrible that he'd admitted his feelings to her, all the while planning to slip away at first light while she was asleep.

At dawn he'd sat at the kitchen table and written to her. It wasn't much of a letter and he wished he could have said more, but it would only have made his leaving more painful for both of them. Beside the note, he'd left her enough money to get her safely and quickly back home to America. He'd grabbed his things and been about to head straight out of the door.

But he couldn't just walk away. He wanted to see

her one last time, and he tiptoed back up the creaking stairs, careful not to wake her. He'd stood for a moment or two, watching her sleeping soundly. Her body was rising and falling slowly under the sheet, her hair spread out across the pillow. Very gently, he pulled a curl away from her eye. He'd smiled fondly at the look of complete childlike relaxation on her sleeping face. He'd wanted so badly to take her in his arms, kiss her, make a fuss of her, bring her breakfast in bed. Stay together, live happily.

But none of that was possible. It was like a dream that hovered out of reach. His destiny lay another way. He remembered what Luc Simon had said. *Men like us are like lone wolves. We want to love our women, but we only hurt them.*

He'd blown her a last kiss, and then forced himself to leave.

And now he had to turn his mind back to his quest. Fairfax was waiting for him. Ruth was waiting for him.

He walked back to the boarding-house by the beach. In his room, he sat on the bed, picked up the phone and dialled a number.

'So I'm officially off the hook?'

Simon laughed. 'You were never really officially on it, Ben. I only wanted you in for questioning.'

'You had a funny way of showing it, Luc.'

'But the unofficial answer is yes, you're free to go,' said Simon. 'You kept your side of the bargain, and I'll keep mine. Marc Dubois is back with his family. *Gladius Domini* is being investigated and half their people are in custody under murder, abduction and a whole shitload of other charges. So I'm willing to forget certain matters as far as you're concerned, if you understand me.'

'I understand you. Thanks, Luc.'

'Don't thank me, just don't cause any more trouble for me. Make me happy and tell me you're leaving France today.'

'Soon, soon,' Ben assured him.

'Seriously, Ben. Enjoy what's left of the weather, go to a movie, see the sights. Be a tourist for a change. If I hear you've been up to anything, I'll be on you like a ton of bricks, my friend.'

Simon put the phone down, smiling to himself. Despite everything, he couldn't help feeling a certain liking for Ben Hope.

The office door swung open behind him, and he turned to see a balding, ginger-haired detective walk in. 'Hello, Sergeant Moran.'

'Good morning, sir. I'm sorry, I didn't know you were still here.'

'Just leaving,' Simon said, looking at his watch. 'Was there something you wanted, Sergeant?'

'Just wanted to pull a file, sir.' Moran went over to the filing cabinet and slid out a drawer, thumbing through the cardboard dividers.

'Well, anyway, I'm off.' Simon picked up his brief-case, gave Moran a friendly slap on the shoulder, and headed for the lobby.

Moran watched him disappear down the corridor.

He pushed the filing drawer shut, quietly closed the door and picked up the phone. Dialled a number. A female voice answered from Reception.

'Can you tell me the last call made to this phone?' he asked. He scribbled down the number. Then he hung up. He dialled the number he'd scribbled.

A different woman's voice answered. 'Sorry, I must have the wrong number,' he said after a pause, and hung up.

He dialled a third time. The voice that replied this time was a rasping whisper.

'This is Moran,' the detective said. 'I have that information for you. The target is at the Auberge Marina in Palavas-les-Flots.'

Sitting at his desk in the boarding-house, Ben sipped his coffee, rubbed his eyes, and started combing through all his notes. 'Right, Hope', he muttered to himself. 'Let's get on. What do we have so far?'

The unavoidable answer was, he didn't have an awful lot. A few disconnected scraps of information, a whole load of unanswered questions, and he was out of leads. He just didn't know enough. He was worn out from lack of sleep, mentally drained from endless days of running, planning, and trying to balance all the elements of the equation in his head. And now, whenever he tried to focus, all he could see was Roberta's face in front of him. Her hair, her eyes. The way she moved. The way she laughed, the way she cried. He couldn't shut her out, couldn't fill the void he was feeling now that she wasn't there any more.

He was almost out of cigarettes again. He took out his flask and gave it a shake. Still some left. He started unscrewing the top. *No.* He put the unopened flask down on the table and pushed it away from him.

He was still bothered by those seemingly random and meaningless clusters of alternating numbers and letters that appeared on nine of the notebook's pages. Wearily grabbing up a pen, he combed through the notebook and wrote the strange numbers and letters down in the order in which they appeared.

   i.   N 18
   ii. U 11 R
  iii. 9 E 11 E
  iv. 22 V 18 A 22 V 18 A
   v. 22 R 15 O
  vi. 22 R
 vii. 13 A 18 E 23 A
viii. 20 R 15
  ix. N 26 O 12 I 17 R 15

Written in normal script, they looked even more like a code than they did in the notebook. What did they mean? He knew enough about cryptography to know that a code like this required a key to crack it. The key often used by spies and intelligence agents was a line chosen at random out of a book. The first twenty-six letters of the line could be matched up to the letters of the alphabet, or to numbers, or both. These could run forwards or backwards against the key line, giving different variants on the code and throwing up completely different readings. If you knew what book, what page and what line to use, it was a simple matter to decipher the coded message.

But if you didn't know, it was completely unbreakable. And Ben had no way of knowing. Fulcanelli could have chosen absolutely anything, from any book or text, as the key line for these sequences. He could have used any of the languages he knew, French, Italian, English, Latin, or a translation from or into any of them.

He sat for a while, desperately thinking over the possibilities. The proverbial needle in the haystack was an easy challenge by comparison. He cast his mind back and suddenly remembered the recording that Anna had played them of her session with Klaus Rheinfeld. Rheinfeld had been muttering similar sequences of alternating numbers and letters. Ben had written them down.

He searched through his pockets and found the little pad. Rheinfeld had been repeating the same sequence of letters and numbers over and over. N-6; E-4; I-26; A-11; E-15. But these didn't appear anywhere in the notebook. Did that mean Rheinfeld had been working the code out for himself? Ben remembered Anna describing how he'd obsessively counted on his fingers while he repeated the figures. He'd also counted on his fingers while repeating that other phrase . . . what was it again? Something in Latin, some alchemical saying. Ben screwed his tired eyes shut, trying to recall.

The phrase was somewhere in Rheinfeld's notebook. He flicked through the grimy pages and found the ink drawing of the alchemist standing watching his bubbling preparation. There it was inscribed on the side of the cauldron. IGNE NATURA RENOVATUR INTEGRA. By fire nature is renewed whole.

If Rheinfeld was counting on his fingers while chanting the phrase . . . did that mean . . . Ben counted the letters of the Latin phrase. Twenty-six. Twenty-six letters of the alphabet. Was this the key line for the code?

He wrote the phrase out on a piece of paper. Above and beneath the words he ran the letters of the alphabet and the numbers 1-26. It looked too simple, but he'd try it anyway. He quickly discovered that while the numbers in the code could only equate to one letter, because of the repeated letters in the phrase the coded letters could have a variety of meanings. Using this key he decoded the first two words of the hidden message, N 18 / U 11 R:

C	R		H	K	I
E			R		K
M					S
U					Y

The horizontal letters should have been able to form into some kind of recognizable word, drawing on the vertical columns of alternatives thrown up by the code. But it was nonsensical. *Try again, it was too obvious anyway.* He reversed the numbers 1-26 so that they ran backwards against the key line, and decoded the first two words again.

C	I		H	P	I
E			R		K
M					S
U					Y

Now it was looking as though he'd got this all wrong. The key line was probably something completely different.

'God, I hate puzzles,' he muttered to himself. Chewing on his pen, he gazed back at the notebook for inspiration. His eye settled on the picture of the alchemist with his cauldron. Beneath the cauldron was the fire. Beneath the fire was the inscription ANBO.

Then it hit him. *Of course, stupid.* ANBO was the coded form of IGNE, Latin for fire. If ANBO was IGNE, then it meant that the alphabet had been lined up against *alternating* letters of the key line. When it reached the end it simply started again at the beginning, filling in the gaps.

26 25 24 23   22 21 20 19 18 17   16 15 14 13 12 11 10 9 8   7 6 5 4 3 2 1

I G N E   N A T U R A   R E N O V A T U R   I N T E G R A

A N B O   C P D Q E R   F S G T H U I V J   W K X L Y M Z

Set against the numbers running backwards from 1-26, this gave a totally different key to work with. 'OK,' he muttered, 'here we go, one more time.' N18 U11R, the code read. Based on his new key, N could be B or C or G or K; 18 could only be E. Moving on to the second word, U could be Q or V; 11 could only be U; and R could be any of E, F, J or M.

He stared fixedly at his scribbles, starting to feel a little snow-blind. But then his heart gave a jump. *Wait a minute.* A shape was forming. Out of the available letters he could spell out two distinct words. CE QUE. *THAT WHICH.* He wrote the key out more neatly.

A: I/26	G: N/14	M: R/2	S: E/15	Y: G/3
B: N/24	H: V/12	N: G/25	T: O/13	Z: A/1
C: N/22	I: T/10	O: E/23	U: A/11	
D: T/20	J: R/8	P: A/21	V: U/9	
E: R/18	K: N/8	Q: U/19	W: I/7	
F: R/16	L: E/4	R: A/17	X: T/5	

And now the hidden message began to reveal itself quickly as he used the key to unlock the code, picking out the words from the available letters.

i.	N 18:	CE
ii.	U 11 R	QUE
iii.	9 E 11 E	VOUS
iv.	22 V 18 A 22 V 18 A	CHERCHEZ
v.	22 R 15 O	CEST
vi.	22 R	LE
vii.	13 A 18 E 23 A	TRESOR
viii.	20 R 15	DES
ix.	N 26 O 12 I 17 R 15	CATHARES

WHAT YOU ARE SEARCHING FOR IS THE TREASURE OF THE CATHARS

The excitement of his discovery gave Ben a new surge of energy. He flipped through the notebook pages, looking for more messages that could cast further light on what he'd found. At the bottom of the page where he'd found the coded word TRESOR was a block of three more encrypted words.

22E 18T 22 E 18I   26   T12 U20 A18

22E 18T 22E 18 I – 26 – T12 U20 A18. The pattern was looking familiar now – but when he applied his key to crack the message, his heart sank.

C	L	E	D	C	L	E	A		A		D	H	Q	D	P	E
O		I		O	W				I						R	
S		X		S					X						U	
														V	Z	

There was no way to create meaning out of it. COEICSEW A IHVDRE?

All right, you old bastard, you can't throw me off that easily. Beginning to understand the mischievous tricks Fulcanelli seemed to enjoy playing, he reversed the key, now running the numbers forwards along the key line and the alternating alphabet backwards. This threw up a very different reading.

C	H	E	C	C	H	E	D		A		C	H	E	D	A	E
O		R		L		Z					R		J		F	
S		W		O							W				I	
															K	

Running across the line and scavenging odd letters from the vertical columns, he was suddenly able to form intelligible words in French.

CHERCHEZ A . . .
SEARCH AT . . .

Only the last word baffled him. It could have been any of RHEDIE, WHEDIE, WHEDAE, RHEDAE, or a number of weirder alternatives such as CHJKE which obviously made no sense at all.

He scratched his head. *Search at . . .* Judging by the context, the mysterious third word had to be a place name: search at *somewhere*. He looked up all the possible alternatives on his map, but he couldn't find any. Suddenly remembering that there was a selection of local guide books for sale downstairs in the hallway of the boarding house, he raced down the stairs, bought one from the landlady which covered the whole of the Languedoc, and ran back to his room already flipping through the index. But none of the names existed there either.

'Fuck!' He hurled the book across the room. It burst open in mid-air with a flap of pages, crashed into the wall and bounced back into a vase of flowers on the mantelpiece. The vase toppled and smashed. '*Fuck!*' he shouted more loudly.

Then a thought came to him that made his anger drop away, instantly forgotten. What about the codes that Rheinfeld had been repeating to himself in the recording? Would those give him an answer? He tore open the pad again and worked out the five letters. He almost laughed when he saw the result.

KLAUS

So Rheinfeld had cracked it, the poor bastard. Ben wondered whether the German had been driven over the edge of madness by the frustration of not knowing the rest. He was beginning to understand exactly how the man had felt.

As he mopped up the spilt water and picked up the limp flowers and broken pieces of porcelain, cursing under his breath, something else suddenly occurred to him. *What an idiot – of course.* He dropped everything and ran over to rummage in his bag. Inside it he found the fake medieval map, depicting the old Languedoc, which had been hanging on Anna's wall. He unrolled the ornately drawn script and spread it across the table.

When he found the place, he checked its location against the modern map. There was no doubt about it. The ancient name for the medieval village of Rennes-le-Château, not twenty miles from St-Jean, was Rhédae. He banged his fist on the table. CHERCHEZ A RHEDAE suddenly had a new and very real meaning: *SEARCH AT RENNES-LE-CHÂTEAU.*

And, according to his guidebook, Rennes-le-Château was the site that legend associated most strongly with the lost treasure of the Cathars.

CHAPTER 58

As he drove through the rugged countryside along the D118 heading towards Rennes-le-Château, Ben was thinking about what he'd read about the place in his new guidebook. It was a name he'd vaguely recalled from some half-watched television documentary, but he hadn't realized that the once sleepy medieval hamlet was now one of southern France's most sensational tourist attractions. His guidebook read: '*an important centre for seekers of holy treasure and magical phenomena. Whether or not you believe in the occult, kabbalistic ideas, UFOs or crop circles, there is no denying the strange mystery of Rennes-le-Château.*'

The enigma of Rennes-le-Château rested on the story of a man called Bérenger Saunière. He'd been the humble village priest who, in 1891 during a renovation of the old church, was said to have discovered four parchments sealed inside wooden tubes. The parchments were dated between 1244 and the 1780s, and, so the story went, had led Father Saunière to find a great secret.

Nobody knew what Saunière had found, but immediately after this discovery the priest had

411

seemingly been transformed from a pauper to a millionaire overnight. Where the money had come from remained a mystery. Some sources said that he'd found the fabled treasure of the Cathars – a fortune of gold that the heretics had hidden from their oppressors in the thirteenth century. Others claimed that the treasure wasn't money or gold, but a great secret, some kind of ancient knowledge, that the Church had bribed Saunière to keep quiet.

Unsurprisingly, rumours of treasure and the obscurity of the facts had combined to provoke a hysterical flurry of interest when the story had hit the media in the early 1980s. It had sparked a feverish cult following for anything to do with the mystery of Rennes-le-Château. Mystics, hippies and treasure-seekers flocked there in droves every summer. The Languedoc tourist industry had been Cathar-crazy ever since.

Ben turned off the main road at Couiza and the car wound up a tortuous mountain path. After four kilometres of increasingly wild scenery he arrived at the little village of Rennes-le-Château.

The church was set back a few metres from the street behind an iron gate. Beside it was a tourist centre which marked a strange contrast to the ancient, crumbling medieval village. There was a tour in progress, a crowd of camera-snapping travellers following a guide. Ben joined them, and from the buzz of conversation he realized that they were British.

'And now, ladies and gentlemen,' droned the

412

languid tour guide, 'if you would all like to come this way, we will enter the mysterious church itself. Now, like all medieval churches the building faces east-west and the floor plan is shaped like a cross. The altar is . . .'

Ben followed as the group filtered in through the narrow doorway and milled around inside, gazing about them at the florid décor. Immediately inside the entrance was a vivid statue of a staring horned demon. Above him stood four angels, looking out across the church in the direction of the altar.

The guide motioned towards the demonic figure. His voice echoed in the church. 'This frightening fellow here is believed to represent the demon Asmodeus, custodian of secrets and guardian of . . . *hidden treasures*.' This seemed to delight the crowd but Ben could already see it wasn't going to enlighten him. He broke away from the group and walked back into the sunshine, kicking a stone across the dusty street in frustration.

Rennes-le-Château was perched high on a rocky hillside overlooking a sweeping panoramic landscape. At the western edge of the village the ground fell away in a sheer drop of escarpment. Ben stood on the edge of the cliff and looked out across the hills and valleys, shielding his lighter from the wind as he lit a cigarette. He sighed. He wondered where Roberta was now. It had been years since he'd felt so painfully alone.

Here and there in the distance he could see quite a number of old towers and ruined buildings, as

413

well as a couple of ancient ochre stone villages. Far below him in the arid valley was the village that his map told him was Esperaza. He smiled at the name. *Hope.* His eye followed the horizon to some faraway ruins, which the map identified as Coustaussa.

A memory stirred him. It had been a scene just like this one. They'd been standing high on the hillside near her villa, looking across the valleys. He remembered what she'd told him. In some special place, the relative positions of ancient sites gave a clue to a secret that would bring great wisdom and power to the one who solved the mystery.

'What were you trying to tell me, Anna?' he muttered as he looked out to the horizon. Fulcanelli. The Cathars. Lost treasures. It was all linked, had to be. Had the alchemist discovered the ancient scroll and cross around here somewhere? Was that why Usberti had chosen this part of France for his *Gladius Domini* headquarters?

He wandered around the village a while, dragging his feet. Not far from the church he found a little tourist café that sold postcards and souvenirs. The place was almost empty, and the coffee smelled good. He took a table in the far corner and sat sipping on a cup while he tried to get his thoughts in order. What the hell was it all about? He pulled Rheinfeld's notebook from its plastic covering and flicked it open. His eye landed once more on that odd rhyming stanza.

These Temple walls cannot be broken
The armies of Satan pass through unaware
The Raven guards there a secret unspoken
Known only to the seeker faithful and fair

Maybe it was the wild thinking of a burned-out, sleep-deprived brain, or perhaps it was a ray of clarity piercing through all the fog of alchemical riddles. But a sudden thought hit him like a thunderbolt.

He flipped back through the notebook until he found the twin-circle design from the dagger blade. As he'd remembered, what distinguished the notebook's version of the diagram from the blade inscription was the raven symbol that marked out its centre. If Rheinfeld had copied this accurately from the original, it meant that Fulcanelli had deliberately added the new feature to the motif. It had to be significant – but how?

The raven guards there a secret unspoken.

He looked again at the other page, where the same raven symbol appeared together with the word DOMUS. The House of the Raven.

He sat and pondered. A hypothesis: if the House of the Raven – leaving aside for the moment what it actually *was* – stood at the centre of the geometric twin-circle shape, was it possible that the twin-circle shape represented an actual *place*? A place, as Anna had hinted, marked out by lines superimposed on the physical landscape and using ancient sites as reference points?

415

It seemed crazy, but in its own way it made the most perfect sense.

He went back to the rhyming stanza. *These temple walls cannot be broken.*

What kind of temple walls couldn't be broken? Not the stone kind, that was for sure, judging by the number of old ruins around here. The crusading armies had been ruthlessly thorough in destroying the strongholds and churches of their heretic enemies.

But then another idea hit him. What if the temple walls had never been built in stone at all – had never intended to be? What if they were the lines of an invisible geometric ground-plan that lay across the land, known only to the *faithful and fair* who were in on the secret? The marauding armies wouldn't even have known such a temple was there. Because its walls were invisible. It was a *virtual* temple.

In effect, it was a map. Whatever the House of the Raven was, it was at the centre of the layout and it seemed to be a marker for something. Maybe something that could get you into a lot of trouble. Secret alchemical treasure? Usberti was obsessed with finding it. The Nazis had lusted after it. Perhaps those who had launched the holocaust against the Cathars had been looking for it too.

Ben's mind was racing now. He ripped his road map out of his bag, unfolded the flapping square of paper and spread it across the plastic table.

His finger landed on Rennes-le-Château. This was the place Fulcanelli had guided him to. This was where the search would begin, at the very nucleus of Cathar country and the hub of the mystery of their lost treasure.

Using the edge of the laminated café table menu as a ruler, he started tracing out tentative lines in pencil on the map. He soon began to notice patterns emerging.

St Sermin – Antugnac – La Pique – Bugarach.

Couiza – Le Bezu.

Esperaza – Rennes-les-Bains.

And at least a dozen more. All were straight lines that perfectly connected the nearby churches, villages and castle ruins directly through the spot where he was sitting, the heart of Rennes-le-Château. This bizarre find seemed to confirm that he was looking in the right place. More lines, and soon he was building up an extensive grid that stretched bewilderingly across the entire area.

Visitors to the café came and went, and he didn't notice them. His coffee cooled at his elbow. He was transfixed by the dizzying maze of controlled complexity that began to unfold under his pencil. After the first hour, he had established a perfect circle whose circumference connected four ancient churches in the area, Les Sauzils, St Ferriol, Granès and Coustaussa. To his astonishment, his projected lines generated a six-pointed star whose points fitted perfectly within the circle and touched exactly on the first two churches.

The first circle centred precisely on Esperaza, the village in the valley below Rennes-le-Château.

After another hour the café staff were beginning to wonder how long the strange customer was going to sit there scribbling on his map. Ben was oblivious of them. Now a second circle was generated, and he traced it out with a steady hand. It centred on a place called Lavaldieu – *Valley of God*. The circles were identical in size and lay diagonally NW / SE across the map. He traced out more lines and shook his head in amazement as the complex alchemical symbol slowly revealed itself.

The hexagram in the Esperaza circle had one of its southern points at Les Sauzils and another at St Ferriol. The pentagram in the Lavaldieu circle had its two western points at Granès and Coustaussa. A perfect straight line connecting Peyrolles to Blanchefort to Lavaldieu provided the southern point of the pentagram where it touched the edge of the Lavaldieu circle. Lastly, another perfect straight line connecting Lavaldieu at the centre with the more distant castle of Arques, gave the position for the easternmost point of the star.

He sat back and contemplated the heavily lined and scored map. He could hardly believe what he was seeing. The twin star-circles were complete. The diagram was perfect in its geometry – the virtual temple, right there on a cheap filling-station road map.

Whatever civilization had created the phenomenon, long, long before Fulcanelli had stumbled upon it, must have been awesomely skilled in surveying, geometry, and mathematics. The logistics of just spinning this elaborate web of design across a harsh, mountainous landscape were mind-boggling enough, let alone the extreme lengths they must have gone to in deliberately building churches and entire settlements on the exact locations marked out by the invisible sweep of a circle or the intersection of two imaginary lines. And all this just to set up a concealed location for some cryptic piece of knowledge? What knowledge was worth that kind of trouble?

Maybe he was going to find out. He was walking in Fulcanelli's historical footprints. Now all he had to do was to find the centre point, and that should give him the exact location of whatever it was the alchemist had discovered. He drew out two extra lines that cut diagonally and symmetrically through the motif in an elongated X, marking out the dead centre.

'X marks the spot,' he murmured. The centre point was close to Rennes-le-Château. It couldn't be much more than a couple of kilometres, approximately north-west.

But what would be waiting for him when he got there? There was only one way to find out. He was getting close now.

CHAPTER 59

Ben set off across country. Starting out from the western edge of the village he discovered a winding route down the hillside. With stones and loose dirt sliding under his feet he scrambled downwards. Sometimes the bone-dry ground gave way under him and he slipped a few metres, struggling to keep his balance. By the time he reached the tree line a hundred metres below, the going was firmer and branches offered a hand-hold down the last of the slope. The trees were sparse at first, but as the ground levelled out they became a dense forest.

He picked a leafy path between the tightly clustered conifers, oaks and beeches. The birds were singing in the trees above him and the milky rays of the autumn sun flickered through the green and gold foliage. For the first time in days he was almost able to clear his mind of troubled thoughts. Though he missed her badly, it was a relief to know that Roberta was safely out of the way. Whatever happened, she'd be all right.

Beyond the wooded valley the ground began to rise again. A kilometre away across a rocky plateau, an escarpment sloped dramatically upwards to a high ridge. He saw that his route was going to take him straight over the top of it. He walked on steadily through the rocks, ignoring the thorny shrubs that caught at his ankles. The jagged ridge loomed closer.

Far away, Franco Bozza was watching the tiny figure of his quarry through powerful binoculars. He'd followed Ben Hope all the way from Palavas, staying carefully out of sight. He'd watched him scramble down the hillside away from Rennes-le-Château and cut a straight path across country. He obviously knew where he was heading. Whatever the Englishman was looking for, he would find it too. This time, he wasn't going to let him get away.

Bozza had stalked in a semicircle around Ben's flank. A goat path through a copse of trees shielded him from sight. Keeping low through the increasingly rocky terrain, stopping from time to time to check the progress of the small faraway figure, he'd worked his way right round and now he was high above Ben, near the escarpment's summit. Behind him, where the ground sloped away far below into a green valley, was a house in the distance.

The rock face soared up to a flat ledge, like a shallow plateau, and then rose up again to the summit. To the right, the hillside plunged dramatically away down some 300 metres into a deep valley thick with trees. Ben began the long climb. After half an hour or so he reached the first level, some ten metres across. A jutting shelf of grey rock overhung the cliff face to create a shallow cave. He stopped and rested for a few minutes, squinting up at the slope that he still had to climb.

Above him, Bozza crawled out a little further across the big rock. From this vantage point he had a good view of the Englishman through his binoculars. The wide, flat rock hung out over the edge of a steep slope. It felt stable enough under his weight, and it was secure enough to have stayed where it was for a thousand years. But Bozza was a heavy man and the further he moved towards the edge, the more strain he was putting on the rock's balance.

By the time he knew it was beginning to slide, it was already too late to do anything about it.

Bozza rode the falling rock flat on his belly for the first few metres of the drop. It plunged over the edge and smashed into a cluster of smaller boulders and sent them spinning down with it. Bozza was thrown clear and went rolling and tumbling down thirty metres. He clawed frantic-ally for a handhold but everything was sliding with him. The landslide gathered momentum, carrying away a slice of the hillside.

Ben could see the dust from a hundred tumbling rocks from where he was standing looking up at the rest of his climb. His blood froze. It was coming straight towards him. He dived under the shelf just as the spinning rocks reached the ledge. They hammered down all around and tore most of the ground away. He shielded his face from the loose earth and dust that poured down in a choking curtain. Suddenly the ground was giving way under his feet. He reached out in desperation and grasped the edge of the shelf above him. He hung there, praying it wouldn't break away and crush him. A large jagged stone bounced off the cliff face and struck him on the shoulder, tearing his grasp away from the hanging rock. He slid and rolled a long way down the slope, boulders and dirt crashing all around him. A white flash of pain jolted through him as his body hit a protruding tree root. Somehow he managed to get a hold on it as the landslide battered him on its way past. The root held. The violence of the slide diminished, and then it was over.

The air was thick with dust. He spluttered and coughed, his mouth and throat full of it. He managed to find a secure footing, and slowly he let his weight onto his feet, testing the fragile slope. He gave the tree root a grateful pat and made his way cautiously back up the escarpment, heading for solid ground.

Bozza had come to a stunned, bloody stop among the rocks. His fingertips were raw from where he'd been scrabbling for a hold. He picked himself shakily up off the ground and looked around him at the debris from the landslide. He'd slid and tumbled a long way. Another couple of metres and he would have plunged straight over the edge of a sheer drop down the face of the escarpment and into the steeply sloping wooded valley below.

He heard a noise and spun around to see Ben Hope standing ten metres away.

Bozza didn't have time to reach for his gun. Ben's sights descended squarely, deliberately on the man's chest and the Browning barked twice in rapid succession.

The flat reports hammered through the silence of the mountain air. Bozza's body jerked back like a shaken doll. For a moment he teetered on the edge of the precipice, his arms outflung as he struggled to keep his balance. Ben watched him coldly and then fired again. Bozza clutched at his chest, and with a last wild look of hatred he disappeared over the edge and was gone.

It was another hour before Ben found his way down to the tree-dotted valley beyond the hill. He sat down on a mossy fallen trunk and caught his breath. He could have done with a pair of decent army boots. His lightweight shoes were just about wrecked. His feet were painfully raw inside.

This can't be the place, he thought to himself, looking across the valley. And yet, according to the map and the compass, it had to be. There was nothing else anywhere, just more of the same wild landscape.

What he was looking at was a white house that nestled in the trees a few hundred metres away on the other side of the valley. It was tucked in close to the foot of a high, looming mountain. He sighed. He hadn't known what he was going to find – maybe a ruin, even a stone circle or something. But this trim, white modern villa was the last thing he'd been expecting to come across at the site of the 'House of the Raven'.

It was a radical design, boxy, flat-roofed and very unlike the usual stone houses of rural Languedoc. It looked as though it had been built sometime in the last few years. Yet it seemed to blend into its wild natural surroundings with almost magical ease, as though it had been there for centuries.

He approached the walled gateway and was gazing up at the house when a voice called out, 'Hello? Is there anyone there?' A woman was walking towards him across a pretty, well-kept garden. She was tall, thin, upright, maybe in her mid-to-late fifties. But the main things Ben noticed about her were the dark glasses and the white stick she used to probe the way ahead. She stepped carefully down the path to the gate. She smiled, looking somewhere over Ben's shoulder.

'I was just admiring your beautiful house,' Ben said to the blind woman.

Her smile broadened. 'Ah, so you're interested in architecture?'

'Yes, I am,' Ben replied. 'But I also wondered if I could trouble you for a glass of water? I've just come over the mountain and I'm pretty thirsty . . . would you mind?'

'Of course not. You must come inside,' the woman said, and turned towards the house. 'Follow me – watch the latch on the gate, it's stiff.'

He followed the blind woman up the flagstone path to the villa. She led him through a large hallway into a modern kitchen, and tapped her way to the fridge. She took out a bottle of mineral water. 'There are glasses in the cupboard. Please, help yourself.' She sat with him at the table, a benign expression on her face as she listened to him drink two tall glasses of water.

'You're very kind,' he said. 'I've walked all the way from Rennes-le-Château. I was looking for the House of the Raven.'

'You've found it,' she said simply, shrugging. 'This *is* the House of the Raven.'

'This?' But it couldn't be. This place was modern. How could it crop up on an eighty-year-old alchemical manuscript? 'Perhaps I'm in the wrong place,' he said. 'The house I was looking for is old.' A thought occurred to him. 'Was this house built on the site of an earlier building?'

She laughed. 'No, this is the original house. It's much older than it looks. It was built in 1925. It gets its name from its architect.'

'Who was the architect?'

'His real name was Charles Jeanneret, but he was better known as Le Corbusier. His nickname was *Corbu.*'

'House of the Raven,' Ben repeated, nodding. Corbu – the French *corbeau* meaning a raven. So despite its ultramodern, almost futuristic appearance, the place dated from more or less the period of Fulcanelli's manuscript.

426

'Why were you looking for the house?' she asked curiously.

He instinctively fell back on his well-tested ploy. 'I was doing some historical research. It's mentioned in some old documents, and as I was in the area I thought I'd come and visit.'

'Would you like to see round the place?' she asked. 'My eyes failed me some years ago, but in my mind I can see it as clearly as ever.'

She showed him around from room to room, tapping her stick and pointing out this feature and that. In the main sitting-room was a tall and elaborately carved oak fireplace. Its ornate style was completely at odds with the sparse, straight-lined, almost ascetic design of the rest of the house. Ben stared at it. It wasn't its craftsmanship and beauty that drew his eye, impressive as they were. He was staring at the carving above the mantelpiece, which dominated the whole fireplace.

It was a raven carved on a circular emblem, just like the one in Fulcanelli's manuscript and Notre Dame cathedral. He ran his eye along the carving, its bladelike feathers, curved talons and cruel beak. Its eye was a glittering ruby-red glass inset that seemed to stare back at him.

'Is this an original feature?' he asked. 'The fireplace, I mean,' he added, remembering she was blind.

'Oh yes. It was carved by Corbu personally. In fact he began his career studying carving and jewellery-making before he became an architect.'

427

Below the raven, the Latin words HIC DOMUS were carved in gold-lettered gothic script. '*Hic* . . . here,' Ben translated under his breath. 'Here the house . . . this is the house . . . *This is the House of the Raven* . . .'

But where was this leading? Why had Fulcanelli put the house on the map? There had to be a reason. There must be something here. What?

As he searched his mind for some kind of connection, he gazed around the room. His eye lit on a painting hanging on the opposite wall. It showed an old man dressed in what looked like medieval garb. In one hand the man clutched a large key. In the other he held up a circular shield, or perhaps a plate, that was oddly blank as though the artist had never completed the painting. The old man was smiling mysteriously.

'You never told me your name, monsieur,' said the blind woman.

He told her.

'You are English? It was nice to meet you, Ben. My name is Antonia.' She paused. 'I'm afraid I will have to ask you to leave now. I am going to visit my son in Nice for a couple of days. The taxi will be arriving soon.'

'Thanks for the tour.' He bit his lip, trying to hide the frustration in his voice.

Antonia smiled up at him. 'I'm glad you found the place. And I hope you will find what you are seeking, Ben.'

CHAPTER 60

He sat amongst the trees overlooking the valley with the Le Corbusier house below him, and tried to get his thoughts in order. Evening was falling fast, and the wind was picking up. It was close and sticky. He could see black clouds scudding beyond the treetops. A storm was coming.

Antonia's last comment struck him as a little odd, a little out of place. *I hope you find what you are seeking.* He'd told her he was looking for the house, that was all. As far as she was concerned, he'd already *found* what he was seeking. And *seeking* seemed too strong, too evocative a word for someone who was just checking out an old house they found on a map.

Maybe he was reading too much into it. Or did the blind woman know something she wasn't letting on? Did the house have something to yield up to him? If it didn't, that was it. There was nowhere to go from here.

There was a rumble of distant thunder. He put his hand out and felt a large, heavy raindrop splatter against his palm. It was soon joined by another, then another. The rain was lashing down by the time car headlights appeared, winding slowly up the private road to the house. Lights went off in the windows. Antonia came out, and the driver helped her to the taxi under an umbrella. Ben watched from under the dripping canopy of an old oak tree as the car drove off.

When the taillights had vanished to red pinpricks in the falling darkness, he turned up his collar and headed across the valley.

He moved quietly and cautiously around the outside of the house. Rain was cascading from the guttering, churning neat flowerbeds into mud. There was a sharp flash of lightning, and thunder rumbled angrily overhead a second later. He brushed the water out of his eyes.

Darkness had fallen fast as the black thunder-clouds rolled in. He used the LED pistol torch to find his way around the side wall until he came to a back door. The lock was flimsy and easy to pick, and in less than a minute he was in the house. The thin white beam of the torch led him from room to room, throwing long shadows. The storm was right overhead now and building in intensity. There was another flash, two seconds of flickering strobe lightning, and the crash of thunder that followed instantly afterwards rocked the house.

Remembering his way around, he quickly found the room with the ornate fireplace. He shone his light on the carved raven, which looked even more alive in the shadows than it had in daylight. Its beady red eye glinted in the light beam.

He stood back, thinking. What was he looking for? He didn't really know. The raven symbol had led him this far, and his instinct told him he should keep following it. He stared at the fireplace, his mind working furiously as rain beat against the windows. Something occurred to him. He went back outside into the downpour and saw he was right.

From inside the house, the fireplace seemed to be set into the outer wall – yet as he stood in the garden, wiping the rain out of his eyes and sweeping the torch beam along the line of the roof, he saw that the squat chimney stack protruded from the roof inboard of the gable end by about three metres. He'd noticed that the window in the wall adjacent to the fireplace was about a metre from the corner, but looking from the outside it was about four metres from the end of the house.

As he hurried back inside, dripping and shivering, he realized that unless it was some quirk of the ultramodern design, it meant there was a hidden cavity behind the fireplace. An insulation space? Too big, surely. It had to be about three metres deep. Maybe it was a corridor, or even a cupboard, that could be accessed from some other room.

But where was the way in? He tried all the doors, but nothing led in the right direction. The room above was a bedroom with solid floorboards and no way down. There was no cellar beneath the house, from where the hidden room might have been accessible through a stairway or trapdoor. He returned to the living-room and scrutinized the fireplace again. If there was a way through, it must be here.

He turned on the lights and tapped around the wall, listening to the sound. All around the fireplace, the wall was solid. Moving to the left of the fireplace, his tapping made a different note. Another metre to the left and the wall sounded quite hollow. There were no cracks or joins anywhere, nothing that could have been a hidden doorway. He tried levering away the wooden panels on the walls, in the hope that one of them might reveal something. Nothing.

He reached his arm up behind the fireplace surround, groping up into the sooty chimney. Maybe there was a lever or some mechanism to open a way through. There wasn't. He wiped the black dusty soot off his hands. 'Must be something,' he muttered. He ran his hands all over the fireplace, down the sides, his fingertips running over the intricate carvings, feeling for something that would press in, or give or turn. It seemed hopeless. The rain hit the windows with a crackling like flames.

He stood back from the fireplace, thinking desperately. There was nothing for it. He *was* going through that wall, and if there wasn't a ready-made doorway he'd make one himself. *Fuck it.*

He found a wood-axe in a tool-shed outside, buried in a chopping block surrounded by a pile of split logs. He grasped the long axe-handle and wrenched it out of the block. Back in the house, he swung the axe up over his shoulder and aimed it at the hollow part of the wall. If his guess was right, he could smash a hole through to the other side.

What if I'm wrong, though? He lowered the axe, suddenly filled with doubt. He shot a guilty glance at the raven, and its glittery red eye seemed to meet his knowingly.

He looked thoughtfully into its impassive face. The bird was so lifelike that he almost expected it to fly at him. He put down the axe and ran his hand along the smooth lines of its wing and neck, up to the glassy red eye. Suddenly seized by a crazy idea, he pressed the eye, hard.

Nothing happened. He supposed that would have been too obvious. He took out the LED pistol-torch again and shone it all around the contours of the carving, carefully examining it. He passed the beam over the raven's eye and a sudden glare of powerful reflected light dazzled him. There seemed to be a complex system of tiny internal mirrors in the eye that were concentrating his torch-beam and firing it back at him.

Another idea came to him. He walked to the light-switch on the wall and turned it off, plunging the room back into darkness. He shone the LED into the raven's eye again, standing a little to one side to avoid being dazzled.

The reflected light from the raven's eye hit the wall across the room and cast a circular red spot, about three inches wide, on the painting he'd noticed earlier. It landed exactly on the oddly blank round shield that the old man in the painting was holding up.

Ben kept the light on the eye. He moved a little closer to the painting and saw with astonishment that the red dot contained the twin-star-circle motif from the dagger blade and the notebook.

He remembered that Antonia had said the architect had been a jewellery maker in his time. *You clever bastard.* It was a work of almost unbelievable intricacy to have engraved the reflecting mirror with a minute yet perfect replica of the geometric design. But what did it mean?

He pulled the picture away from the wall and his heart leapt. There was a concealed safe behind it. He switched the lights back on and hurried back to examine it more closely. What might be inside?

The safe was from the same period as the house, its steel door adorned with enamelled designs in art nouveau style. In the middle of the door was a knurled rotary combination lock with two unusual concentric dials, one with numbers and the other with letters of the alphabet.

'Oh, Christ, please – not more *codes*!' he groaned. He pulled the notebook out of his bag. Folded between its pages was the sheet on which he'd written out the keys to crack the code. The combination to open the safe might be something from the note-book. But what? He flipped through the book. It could be anything.

He sat down with the notebook on his knee, guessing wildly at a few possibilities and quickly working out the coded versions in combined letters and numbers. First he tried the French for 'House of the Raven'. It was a long shot, but he was desperate.

LA MAISON DU CORBEAU

He twisted the dials this way and that, entering the complex sequence. E/4, I/26; R/2, I/26 . . . It took him a minute or two to dial up the entire phrase. He sat back and waited for something to happen.

Nothing did. He sighed impatiently and tried another combination. *The Cathar treasure.*

LE TRESOR DES CATHARES

No good either. This could take for ever. He glanced at the axe lying on the floor and wondered fleetingly whether he should just hack the damn thing out of the wall and try to shoot his way into it from behind. He smiled to himself as he recalled what a grizzled Glaswegian sergeant-major had once said to him: *'If in doubt, lad – resort tae violence'.* Maybe it wasn't a bad maxim, in the right circumstances.

Then his eye fell on the painting that he'd taken down from the wall, and he stooped to look at it more closely.

What an idiot I am. The key!

The large silvery key that the old man was clutching had something written in tiny letters up its shaft. He dropped down on his knees to read it.

LE CHERCHEUR TROUVERA

The seeker shall find. Ben grabbed his pen and feverishly scribbled the phrase out in code.

E/4, R/18; N/22, V/12, R/18, A/17, N/22, V/12, R/18, A/11, A/17;
O/13, A/17, E/23, A/11, U/9, R/18, A/17, I/26

His heart was thumping as he dialled in the last number. From deep within the safe's mechanism he heard a metallic clunk. Then there was silence. He grasped the handle of the safe door and yanked it. It held firm. He swore. The combination must have been the wrong one, or else something had gone wrong with the safe's mechanism after all these years. The door was stuck fast.

A sound from behind startled him, and he twisted around as his hand went for the Browning.

The fireplace was opening. A gentle shower of dirt fell from the chimney as soot-encrusted panels swung slowly open to reveal a space just large enough for him to walk through.

Ben took a deep breath and stepped through the fireplace into the darkness. He flashed his torch around him and blinked at what he saw.

He was in a narrow room, some six metres long and three deep. At one end sat a large old oak table, covered in a thin layer of dust. On it rested a heavy metal chalice, like a huge wine goblet studded around the edge with iron rivets. Lying in the goblet, staring up with empty eyes, was a human skull. On either side of this grim ornament sat two iron candlesticks, two feet high with broad round bases and each holding a thick church candle.

His torch was dimming; he reached into his pocket for his lighter and lit the candles. He picked up one of the heavy candlesticks, and the flickering light threw shadow around the room. The toothless skull leered at him. Around the walls were dusty shelves lined with books. He picked one up and blew the dust and cobwebs off it. Holding the candle close he read the old gilt script on the leather cover – *Necronomicon*. The Book of the Dead. He replaced it and picked up another leather-clad book. *De Occulta Philosophia*. Secrets of Occult Philosophy.

It looked as though he was in someone's private study, long since abandoned. He put the books back carefully on the dusty shelf and swept the heavy candlestick around him. The walls of the room were painted with murals depicting alchemical processes. He walked up close and studied one that showed a hand emerging from a cloud. The Hand of God? From the hand, water was dripping into a strange vessel that was being held up by little winged nymphs. From an opening at the bottom of the vessel there flowed an ethereal, misty substance scattered with alchemical symbols and the label *Elixir Vitae*.

He turned away and raised the candle to illuminate other corners of the room. Above the entrance he'd come through, a face looked down on him. It was an oil portrait in a broad gilt frame. The face belonged to a heavily built man with a grizzled beard and a thick mane of silvery hair. Looking out from under the bushy grey eyebrows, his eyes seemed to twinkle with a sense of humour that belied his stern expression. A gold plaque below the portrait read in stark gothic letters:

FULCANELLI

'So we meet at last,' Ben murmured. He moved away from the portrait and walked around the edges of the room, looking down at the floor. The stone tiles were partly covered by a dusty old rug. Beyond the edges of the rug he could see the outer parts of a mosaic pattern on the floor. He knelt and set the candlestick down with a metallic clunk. Clouds of dust floated up in the wavering light. He lifted the edge of the rug, and a large spider scuttled out and disappeared into the shadows. He rolled the rug up into a long tube and pushed it against the wall. He blew the dust away, revealing the coloured stone mosaic set into the flagstones. After a minute or two of brushing and blowing he stepped back to look at it.

The pattern was about fifteen feet long and took up the whole width of the study. Here they were again, the twin star-circles. At the exact centre of the design was a circular flagstone with an iron ring inset flush with the floor. He grasped the ring with both hands and pulled hard. There was a rush of escaping cold air from below.

He shone his torch down into the hole. The fading beam lit up a spiral stairway carved into solid rock, descending into blackness.

CHAPTER 61

The long descending stone spiral carried him down into solid rock. As he corkscrewed deeper and deeper into the vertical tunnel, the sound of the storm outside faded away to nothing.

After a while, the staircase ended and met a level passageway that snaked off into the dark. There was only one way to go, and the only sound was his echoing footsteps and the drip of water. The smooth rounded walls of the tunnel were high enough for him to walk upright. It must have taken centuries to dig this out of the mountain terrain. A rough tunnel would have done just as well, yet whoever had created this had been interested in far more than utility. They were chasing perfection. But why? Where was the tunnel leading? He walked on.

Without warning, the tunnel snaked around a sharp bend and for a moment he thought he'd come to a dead end. But then he felt something stirring his hair. A cool breeze, coming from above. He raised the torch. There was a passage to the left, more steps leading upwards. He climbed on and on. It seemed to him that he was going up much further than he'd come down. That could mean only one thing – that he was now climbing up above ground level. He remembered the cliff next to the house, and realized that he must be *inside* the mountain. Deep inside it, surrounded on all sides by thousands of tons of solid rock.

His torch was getting dimmer. When it faded away to yellow and then to nothing, he stuffed it in his pocket and used his Zippo lighter to see by. It was getting colder, and wind was whistling around him even though the walls of the stairwell were close and tight. His fingers were burning as the metal of the lighter heated up, and he was worried about the flammable fuel inside igniting if it overheated too much. Suddenly his foot missed a step in the darkness, and he slipped and almost fell. He paused for a moment, his heart pounding. He let the scalding hot lighter cool down for a while, then relit it and climbed on.

The stairway soon ended and Ben found himself in a chamber. He clambered to his feet. Holding up his lighter, he blinked in amazement. The chamber seemed to stretch out far and wide on all sides. He came to a stone pillar that seemed to grow out of the floor, all the way to the vaulted archways of the ceiling some six feet above his head. The pillar had been laboriously smoothed and carved, covered in intricate designs depicting religious scenes and icons. A few feet away from it was another similar pillar, and then another.

He swept the lighter-flame around him. Rows of golden crucifixes glinted in the flickering light. A huge altar stood in front of him, sculpted from solid stone and heavily adorned with gold.

He was in a church. A medieval Gothic church carved out inside a mountain.

Ben lit the altar candles. There were scores of them, all held by massive solid gold candlesticks. One candle at a time, the church gradually filled with amber light. He gasped at the size of the carved-out space. The wealth of it was staggering.

Then he saw the stone chests that lined the walls. There were dozens of them, knee high and a metre square. He moved closer. They were filled to the brim with gold. He sifted through one, his fingers raking through solid gold coins and nuggets, rings and amulets. There was enough gold in the church to make its finder the richest man in the world.

Carrying a heavy candlestick to see by, he went over to the towering altar. Carved in smooth stone, two white lions converging into a single head supported a circular stone basin that was some eight feet in diameter. Candlelight glimmered off the dark water inside. Around its smooth edge, carved in flowing letters, were the words:

Omnis qui bibit hanc aquam, Si fidem addit, Salvus erit
He who drinks this water shall find salvation, if he believes

At the feet of an angelic statue was a gold pedestal, and on it rested a long leather tube. Inside it he found a scroll. He delicately unfurled the cracked, archaic document on the floor and knelt down to study it. It was obviously medieval, though fabulously well-preserved. The writings on it were in a strange form of Latin that he couldn't understand, mixed with what looked like Egyptian hieroglyphics.

He blinked as the truth dawned. So was *this* the legendary manuscript that everyone had been looking for? It was clear now that the papers Rheinfeld had stolen from Clément, the copy he'd made in the notebook, had never been more than Fulcanelli's own notes. They were the alchemist's record of the clues that had led him to find the manuscript itself. The same clues that would guide the next seeker who followed in his steps.

Now, faced with it at last, he understood the power of this mysterious document and the terrible hold it had had over so many people. There was no telling how much blood had been spilled on its account through the ages, either to protect it or to acquire it. It had the power to inspire evil. Did it also have the power to do good?

Something else had fallen out of the leather tube. It was a folded sheet of paper. Ben opened it. It was a letter, and he'd seen that handwriting before.

To the Seeker:
My Dear Friend,
If you have come so far as to read these words,
I applaud you. This secret, which has eluded the
great and the wise since the dawn of civiliza-
tion, is now in your brave and resolute hands.

It remains to me only to pass on this warning:
When success has at last crowned his long toil,
the Wise man must not be tempted by the vani-
ties of the world. He must remain faithful and
humble, and forever be mindful of the fate of
those who were seduced by the powers of evil.

In Science, in Goodness, the Adept must ever-
more KEEP SILENT.
    Fulcanelli

Ben looked up at the stone basin at the foot of the altar. The *elixir vitae* was right there in front of him. His search was over. There was no time to lose.

He jumped to his feet, looking around him for some vessel he could use to take the elixir back to Ruth. He remembered his flask, and without a second thought he unscrewed the top and poured out his whisky, the liquor spattering on the stone floor. His heart thumped as he dipped the flask into the water and filled it. *Did he believe?* Could this special substance really cure?

Drops of the precious liquid splashed from the mouth of the filled flask as he raised it up from the stone basin. His curiosity was overwhelming. He put the flask to his lips.

The foul taste of it almost made him vomit. He spat and gagged, wiping his mouth in disgust. Holding the candle closer he poured more of the water back into the basin. It was full of greenish scum.

Ben fell to his knees, his head hanging. It was over. He was at the end of the road. He'd failed.

The sudden crashing explosion in the chamber was like a knife through his eardrums. One of the white stone lions split apart and collapsed. The basin cracked and fell in two. The stagnant water gushed down over the base of the altar and spilled in a slimy greenish slick across the floor.

He scrabbled to his feet in a panic. Before he could have the Browning out of its holster he was staring down the barrel of a heavy Colt automatic that was advancing towards him out of the shadows.

'Surprised to see me, English?' Franco Bozza rasped in his hoarse whisper as he stepped into the flickering light. His face was wild, bloody, a mask of pure hatred. 'Drop your gun.'

Beneath his bullet-proof vest Bozza's upper torso was still aching badly from the slamming impact of the three 9mm bullets. The long, twisting fall down the cliff had been broken by a tree. Its branches had ripped his flesh and almost impaled him. Blood seeped from a hundred cuts and his right cheek was torn open from mouth to ear. But he'd hardly felt the pain as he'd scrambled back up the cliff and made his way over the hillside in the raging storm. His mind had been focused on one thing alone – what he was going to do when he caught up again with Ben Hope. Things that even his most wretched victims hadn't experienced.

And now he had him.

Ben stared at him for a second, then moved his hand across and slid the Browning from its holster. He dropped it on the floor and kicked it away from him, not taking his eyes off Bozza's.

'And the Beretta,' Bozza said. 'The one you took from me.'

Ben had hoped he'd forgotten that one. He slowly drew the concealed .380 from his waistband and tossed it.

Bozza's pale, thin lips creased into a twisted grin. 'Good,' he whispered. 'And now here we are together alone at last.'

'It's a real pleasure.'

'The pleasure will be all mine, I assure you,' Bozza croaked. 'And when you are dead I will find your little friend Ryder and will have some fun with her.'

Ben shook his head. 'You'll never find her.'

'Oh no?' Bozza said, with what was almost a laugh in his voice. A black-gloved hand reached into his pocket and waved Roberta's red address-book. 'After this I am going on vacation.' He smiled. 'To the USA.'

A sickening wave of horror washed over Ben when he saw the book. He'd told her to destroy it. It must have been in her bag when Bozza kidnapped her.

'She will be the last to die,' Bozza continued, grinning to himself. Ben could see he was relishing every word. 'First she will watch as her family are cut slowly to pieces in front of her. Then, before I kill her, I will show her the little trophy I have brought her. Your head. And finally, I will turn my attentions to Dr Ryder. *For strong is the Lord God who judgeth her.*' Bozza smiled sadistically and lowered the Colt, aiming down at Ben's left knee. His finger tightened on the trigger. First he'd blow out one kneecap, then the other. Then one arm, then the other. Then, when his victim was wriggling helpless on the floor, the knife was coming out.

Ben had been trained years before in the techniques of disarming a hostile gunman at close range. It was all a question of distance, though it was a desperate manoeuvre at the best of times. If the opponent was close enough it was relatively less insane to try to take the weapon away from them. If they were standing just one step too far away, it was virtually impossible to move fast enough. All it took was a flick of the finger and you were dead.

As Bozza was talking, Ben had been assessing the distance between them. It was just on the cusp between extreme high risk and recklessly suicidal. He knew he had only a slight reflex advantage, half a second at best. It was crazy, but he had only one life – he had to fight for it.

It took a tenth of a second to make his decision. He was about to fly at Bozza when the gunshot ripped the air.

447

Bozza's craggy face froze in a look of surprise, his mouth opening in a soundless 'O' as he dropped the gun with a clatter and clawed desperately at the spurting exit hole in his throat.

The figure in the shadows raised the pistol again and fired a second deafening shot that crashed around the chamber. The top of Bozza's head was blown away in a spray of blood and brains. For a moment he stood there as though hanging in space, his eyes searching Ben's as the light faded in them.

Then he collapsed abruptly to the floor. His body gave a couple of arching, twitching spasms as the life left it, and then it lay flat and inert.

Ben stared incredulously at the dark figure, an almost ghostlike apparition, that was slowly advancing towards him from between the shadowy pillars. It was a woman. In the gloom he couldn't make out her face.

'Roberta, is that you?'

But as the woman came closer into the light, he saw that it wasn't. The antiquated C96 Mauser pistol was still trained on Bozza's corpse, a thin wisp of smoke curling from its long, tapered barrel. The precaution wasn't needed. Franco Bozza wouldn't be getting up again this time.

The golden candlelight bathed the woman's face as she approached. He recognized her with a shock. It was the blind woman.

And she wasn't blind any more. The dark glasses were gone and she was looking straight at him with hawk-like intensity. An enigmatic little smile curled the corners of her mouth.

'Who *are* you?' Ben asked, stupefied.

She was silent. He looked down and saw that she was pointing the Mauser automatic straight at his heart.

CHAPTER 62

'Put your hands on your head and get down on your knees,' she ordered. He saw from the look in her eye and the unwavering muzzle of the gun that she meant it. She was much too far away to risk anything. He obeyed. She produced a bright torch and shone the beam in his face.

'You told me you were interested in old houses,' she said as he knelt there helplessly, blinking in the strong white light. 'But it seems that you were also interested in other things.'

'I'm not here to rob you,' he said firmly.

'You break into my house, you bring a gun, you sneak into my private chapel, yet you tell me you're not here to rob me?' She motioned the torch beam at Bozza's body. 'Who is he? A friend of yours?'

'Does it look like it?'

She shrugged. 'Thieves may quarrel. What's in there?' She pointed the light at Ben's bag, which was lying by the altar. 'Empty it out on the floor. Move slowly so I can see your hands.'

He carefully up-ended the bag and she directed the torch to look at the contents as they spilled out onto the stone floor. The pool of white light rested on Rheinfeld's notebook and Fulcanelli's Journal. 'Throw those over to me,' she commanded, tucking the torch under her arm. He picked them up and tossed them to her. Keeping the gun on him, she leafed through them, nodding thoughtfully to herself. After a pause she placed them gently on the floor and lowered the gun to her side. 'I'm sorry,' she said in a softer tone. 'But I had to be sure.'

'Who are you?' he repeated.

'My name is Antonia Branzanti,' she said. 'I am the granddaughter of Fulcanelli.' She cut off his reply with a gesture. 'We can talk later. First we must dispose of this filth.' She pointed at Bozza's corpse, where the pool of blood was merging with the slick of stagnant green water from the broken altar.

Shining the way ahead, Antonia led him through the columns to a passageway where a huge circular rock, like a six-foot millstone, stood on its edge against the wall. 'This doorway leads out to the mountainside. Open it.'

Grunting with effort, he rolled it back through a groove cut in the stone floor. As it turned backwards on itself with a grating sound, the cold night air rushed into the chamber. The rock covered the entrance to a short tunnel, some five metres deep, and through the mouth of the cave he could see a craggy-edged semicircle of night sky. The storm was over, and the full moon was shining over the rocky landscape. Below them was a dizzy drop into a deep ravine.

'Nobody will ever find him down there,' Antonia said, pointing down. Ben returned to where Bozza's body lay. He grasped the heavy corpse under the arms and dragged it to the hole, leaving a trail of watery blood across the stone floor. He dropped the body in the windy tunnel, and rolled it with his foot until it slid off the edge. He watched as it tumbled down the sheer cliff, a cartwheeling black shape against the moonlit rock, and disappeared in the dark tree-studded ravine hundreds of metres below.

'Now we go,' Antonia said.

Defeat was weighing heavily on him as he followed her back through the tunnel to the house. So the elixir had turned out to be worthless. It was just a legend after all. Now he'd have to return to Fairfax empty-handed, look the old man in the eye and tell him that the child would have to die.

They reached the house. She shut the fireplace behind them and led him to the kitchen, where he washed some of the blood off his hands and face. 'I'll be leaving now,' he said grimly, putting down the towel.

'You don't want to ask me anything?'

He sighed. 'What's the point? It's over.'

'You are the seeker my grandfather said would come here one day. You have followed the hidden path. You have found the treasure.'

'I didn't come here for gold,' he replied, tears burning in his eyes. 'It's not about that.'

'Gold is not the only treasure,' she said, cocking her head with a curious smile. She walked over to a cupboard. On a shelf inside were bottles of olive oil and vinegar, jars of dried herbs and preserves, peppercorns and spices. She parted them and took out from behind a small, plain earthenware container which she carefully brought over and set on the table. She lifted the lid. Inside the container was a little glass bottle. She gave it a gentle shake and the clear liquid inside caught the light and shimmered. She turned to Ben. 'Is this what you were looking for?'

He reached out for it. 'Is it . . .?'

'Careful. It is the only sample my grandfather prepared.'

He slumped in a chair, feeling suddenly as drained and spent as he was relieved. Antonia sat opposite him, rested her hands flat on the table and looked at him keenly. '*Now* would you like to stay a while and hear my story?'

They talked. Ben told her about his mission and the events that had led him to the House of the Raven. Then it was his turn to listen as she continued the story told in Fulcanelli's Journal.

'After Daquin betrayed my grandfather's trust, things happened quickly. The Nazis raided the house and ransacked the laboratory to find the secrets. My grandmother surprised them, and they shot her.' Antonia sighed. 'After that, my grandfather fled from Paris and came here with my mother.'

'What happened to Daquin?'

'That boy did so much damage.' Antonia shook her head sadly. 'I suppose he thought he was doing good. But when he began to see what kind of people he had given away my grandfather's teachings to, he couldn't live with himself. Just like Judas, he put a rope around his neck.'

'What was the connection between Fulcanelli and the architect?' Ben asked. 'The House of the Raven?'

'Corbu and my grandfather had a special bond between them,' she explained. 'They were both direct descendants of the Cathars. When Fulcanelli discovered the lost Cathar artefacts, this led him to locate the site of the hidden temple where their treasures were stored. The house was built the year after his discovery, to pay homage to the temple and to guard the treasures inside. Who would have guessed that a house like this marked the entrance to a sacred shrine?'

'Fulcanelli lived here with you and your mother?'

'My mother was sent to Switzerland to study. My grandfather remained here until 1930, when my mother returned with her new husband. By that time, my grandfather knew that his enemies had lost his trail. My mother then took over the role of guardian of the house and its secret. Fulcanelli went away. He disappeared.' Antonia smiled wistfully. 'That's why I never met him. He was a restless soul, who believed there was always more to learn. I think he may have gone to Egypt, to explore the birthplace of alchemy.'

'He must have been ancient by then.'

'He was in his mid-eighties, but people took him for a man in his sixties. The portrait you saw was painted soon before he went away. Some time later, in 1940, I was born.'

Ben raised his eyebrows. She looked a good deal younger than her age.

Antonia noticed his look and gave an enigmatic smile. 'When I grew up I became the guardian of the house,' she went on. 'My mother moved to Nice. She is in her late nineties now, and still going strong.' She paused. 'As for my grandfather, we never heard from him again. I think he was always afraid that his enemies might catch up with him, and that's why he never contacted us or revealed his identity to anyone.'

'So you don't know when he died?'

Another mysterious little smile lifted the corners of her mouth. 'What makes you so sure he's dead? Perhaps he's still out there, somewhere.'

'You believe the elixir of life could have kept him alive all these years?'

'Modern science doesn't have all the answers, Ben. They still understand only the tiniest fraction of the universe.' Antonia fixed him with her penetrating gaze. 'You've taken so many risks to find the elixir. Don't you believe in its power?'

Ben hesitated. 'I don't know. I want to believe in it. Perhaps I need to.' He took Fulcanelli's Journal, Rheinfeld's notebook and the dagger-blade-rubbing out of his bag and laid them on the

455

table. 'Anyway, these are yours now. This is their rightful place.' He sighed. 'And so, what happens now?'

Antonia frowned. 'What do you mean?'

'Am I free to take the elixir with me? Does the guardian let the seeker take the bottle away? Or is the next round in that Mauser reserved for me?'

Her eyes twinkled with mirth and Ben could see the family resemblance to Fulcanelli's portrait. She laid her hand on the elegant old pistol in front of her. 'It was my grandfather's gun. He left it to my mother, in case our enemies ever found us here. But it's not meant for you, Ben. My grandfather believed that one day a true initiate would decipher the clues he left behind, and would come and find the secret. Someone pure of heart who would respect its power, never abuse it or publicize it.'

'That's a big chance to take on me,' he said. 'How can you be certain I'm so pure of heart?'

Antonia looked tenderly at Ben. 'You are thinking only of the child. I can see that in your eyes.'

Rome

A procession of unmarked police cars wound their way between the lavish gardens of the Renaissance villa and pulled up in an orderly semicircle in the courtyard at the foot of the grand white columns.

From his window, high up in the magnificent dome, Archbishop Massimiliano Usberti watched them get out of their cars, brush by his servants and climb the steps to the house. Their faces were dour and official. He'd been expecting them.

Thanks to one man, Benedict Hope, *Gladius Domini* had been badly damaged. For all his seething hatred, Usberti had to admire the man. He hadn't believed he could be so easily outdone, but somehow Hope had done it. Usberti had been bettered, and he was impressed.

The attack had been swift and decisive. First the simultaneous arrest of his top French agent Saul and the disaster in Montpellier. Then the highly co-ordinated Interpol swoop on his people across Europe. Many of his agents were under questioning. Some, like Fabrizio Severini, had gone into hiding. Others had folded under police interrogation. Like a row of falling dominoes, like a blazing powder-trail of information, the investigation had led with alarming speed all the way to the top, all the way to him.

He could hear voices on the stairs leading up to the dome. They'd be here any minute. They probably thought they had him.

Fools. They had no idea who they were dealing with. A man like Massimiliano Usberti, with the contacts and influence they could never even begin to imagine, wasn't going to go down easily. He'd find a way out of this mess, and then he'd come back and take his revenge.

The door burst open at the far end of the room, and Usberti calmly turned from the window to meet them.

CHAPTER 63

Ben had called Fairfax to say the mission was completed and he was coming in. There were a few spare hours before the private jet was due to pick him up at the airport near Montpellier.

Father Pascal was tending to his little vineyard when he heard the gate creak and he looked up to see Ben coming towards him with a broad smile. The priest embraced him warmly. 'Benedict, I knew you would come back to see me again.'

'I haven't got much time, Father. I just wanted to thank you again for all your help.'

Pascal's eyes widened with concern. 'And Roberta? Is she . . .'

'Safely back home in the USA.'

The priest let out a sigh. 'Thank the Lord she is all right,' he breathed. 'And so, your work is done here?'

'Yes, I'm going back this afternoon.'

'Well, then it is goodbye, my dear friend. Look after yourself, Benedict. May the Lord be with you and watch over you. I will miss you . . . Oh, how foolish of me, I nearly forgot. I have a message for you.'

★   ★   ★

Ben was feeling self-conscious as the nurse showed him into the private room. The police guard had been lifted after his call to Luc Simon earlier.

Anna was sitting up in her bed, reading a book. Behind her, sunlight streamed through her window. She was surrounded by vases of yellow, white and red roses that filled the room with sweet perfume. She looked up as Ben came in, and her face spread into a smile. Her right cheek was covered with a large gauze dressing.

'It's good to see you again,' he said. He was hoping she wouldn't notice the nervous edge in his voice.

'I woke up this morning to find all these beautiful flowers. Thank you so much.'

'It's the least I could do,' he said. He looked uncomfortably at the mottled bruises around her eye and forehead. 'Anna, I'm so sorry for what happened to you. And your friend . . .'

She laid her hand on his arm, and he bowed his head. 'It wasn't your fault, Ben,' she said softly. 'If you hadn't come, he was going to murder me. You saved my life.'

'If it's any consolation, that man is dead now.'

She didn't reply.

'What are your plans, Anna?'

She sighed. 'I think I've seen enough of France. It's time I went back to Florence. Perhaps I can get my old job back at the university.' She chuckled. 'And perhaps one day – who knows? – I'll finish my book.'

'I'll look out for it,' he said. He checked his watch. 'I have to go. There's a plane waiting for me.'

'You're going back home? Did you find the thing you were looking for?'

'I don't know *what* I found.'

She reached out and grasped his hand. 'It was a map, wasn't it?' she breathed. 'The diagram? It came to me, as I was lying here. So stupid not to have thought of it . . .'

He sat on the edge of the bed and squeezed her hand. 'Yes, it was a map,' he said. 'But take my advice and just forget everything you know about this stuff. It attracts the wrong kind of people.'

Anna smiled. 'I noticed.'

They sat quietly together in the stillness of the flower-filled room for a while longer, then she looked at him searchingly with her almond eyes. 'Do you ever go to Italy, Ben?'

'From time to time.'

Gently, insistently, she pulled his hand towards her, and he leaned down. She sat up straighter in the bed and pressed her lips to his cheek. They were warm and soft, and her touch lingered for a few seconds. 'If you should ever find yourself in Florence,' she murmured in his ear, 'you must give me a call.'

CHAPTER 64

Three hours later Ben was sitting in the back of the Bentley Arnage for the second time on his way to the Fairfax residence. Dusk was beginning to fall as they swept down the leaf-strewn lanes between rows of golden beeches and sycamores, and pulled in through the gates of the Fairfax estate. The Bentley passed the neat little red-brick estate cottages that Ben remembered from his first visit.

A short way further down the private road, the car began to pull to the right and Ben could feel a faint bumping from the front end. The driver swore quietly to himself, stopped the car and climbed out to see what the matter was. He poked his head back in through the open door. 'I'm sorry, sir. Puncture.'

Ben got out as the driver fetched the tools from the back of the car and unhitched the spare wheel. 'Need any help?' he asked.

'No, sir, it'll only take a few minutes,' the driver said.

As he started unbolting the wheel, the door of a nearby estate cottage opened and an elderly man in a flat cap walked grinning across the verge. 'Must've picked up a nail or somethin',' he said, plucking a pipe out of his mouth. He turned to Ben. 'Would you like to come in for a moment while Jim changes the wheel? Evenings're getting chilly now.'

'Thanks, but I thought I'd just have a smoke and look at the horses.'

The old man walked with him towards the paddocks. 'Like horses, do you, sir?' He put out his hand. 'Herbie Greenwood, head of stables for Mr Fairfax.'

'Good to meet you, Herbie.' Ben leaned over the paddock fence and lit a cigarette.

Herbie chewed on his pipe stem as two horses, a chestnut and a dark bay, came thundering across the pocked surface. They curved round in a parallel arc towards the fence, slowed and approached the old man, shaking their heads and blowing through their nostrils. Herbie patted them as they nuzzled him affectionately. 'See this one 'ere?' He pointed at the bay. 'Three times Derby winner, Black Prince. Out to grass now, like I will be soon. Ain't ya, boy?' He stroked the horse's neck as it snuffled his shoulder.

'He's a beauty,' Ben said, running his eye down the horse's rippling muscles. He held his palm out flat and Black Prince pressed his soft, velvety nose against it.

'Twenty-seven and still gallops about like a young colt,' Herbie chuckled. 'I remember the day 'e was born. They thought 'e wouldn't thrive, but he's done well for 'imself, the old boy.'

463

In the next paddock Ben could see a small grey pony grazing contentedly on a clump of grass, and it made him think of the picture Fairfax had shown him of little Ruth. 'I wonder if Ruth will ever be able to ride again?' he thought out loud.

The Bentley crunched to a halt on the gravel in front of the mansion a few minutes later, and an assistant met Ben on the steps. 'Mr Fairfax will see you in the library in half an hour, sir. I am to show you to your rooms.' They walked through the marbled hall, their footsteps echoing up to the high ceiling. The assistant led him up the staircase to the upper floor of the west wing. After freshening up, Ben came down half an hour later and was shown to the galleried library.

Fairfax rushed across the room, extending his hand. 'Mr Hope, this is a wonderful moment for me.'

'How's Ruth?'

'You couldn't have come at a better time,' Fairfax replied. 'Her condition's been declining steadily, even since we last spoke. You have the manuscript?' He held out his hand expectantly.

'The Fulcanelli manuscript is worthless to you, Mr Fairfax,' Ben said.

A ripple of fury shot through Fairfax's reddening face. 'What?'

Ben smiled, and reached inside his jacket. 'What I've brought you instead is this.' He took it out and gave it to him.

Fairfax stared at the dented drinking flask in his hand.

'I put it in there for safekeeping,' Ben explained.

Understanding dawned on Fairfax's face. '*The elixir?*'

'Prepared by Fulcanelli himself. This is it, Mr Fairfax. This *is* what you were looking for, I assume?'

There were tears in Fairfax's eyes as he grasped the precious object. 'I cannot thank you enough for this. I will take it up to Ruth's quarters immediately. My daughter Caroline is nursing her night and day.' He paused sadly. 'And then, Mr Hope, I trust you will join me for dinner?'

'So you had a difficult time of it,' Fairfax was saying.

The two of them were seated at the long burnished walnut table in Fairfax's dining-room. Fairfax sat at the head of the table, and behind him a log blaze crackled in the hearth. To one side of the fireplace stood a tall knight in armour, holding a glittering broadsword.

'I knew it would be a hard task,' Fairfax continued. 'But you've more than fulfilled my expectations. I raise my glass to you, Mr Hope.' The old man looked triumphant. 'You have *no* idea what you've done for me.'

'For Ruth,' Ben said, raising his glass.

'For Ruth.'

Ben watched him. 'You never told me: how *did* you get to hear about Fulcanelli in the first place?'

'The search for the elixir has long been my pre-occupation,' Fairfax replied. 'I've been a student of the esoteric for many years. I've read every book on the subject, tried to follow every clue. But my investigations led me nowhere. I'd almost given up hope when a chance encounter with an old bookseller in Prague led me to discover the name Fulcanelli. I came to understand that this elusive master alchemist was one of the very few men to have uncovered the secret of the *elixir vitae*.'

Ben listened, sipping his wine.

Fairfax went on. 'At first I thought Fulcanelli's secret would be simple enough to find. But it proved much harder than I anticipated. Men I hired to bring it back to me either ran off with my money, or they ended up dead. It became clear to me that there were dangerous forces bent on deterring me from my quest. I understood that ordinary private investigators or researchers were of no use to me. I needed a man of far greater skills. Then my investigations led me to you, Mr Hope, and I knew I had found the best man for the job.'

Ben smiled. 'You flatter me.'

The *hors d'oeuvre* plates were taken away and servants brought in an array of antique silver dishes. The lid of the main dish was lifted to reveal a glistening saddle of roast beef. The head servant carved delicate slices with a long carving-knife. More wine was served.

'Don't be modest, Benedict – may I call you

Benedict?' Fairfax paused, chewing on a piece of the tender beef. 'To return to what I was saying, I've examined your life story in meticulous detail. The more I found out about you, the more I realized that you were ideal for my purposes. Your activities in the Middle East. Special counter-terrorist operations in Afghanistan. Your reputation for cold efficiency and unflinching application to tasks that would be considerably too challenging for most men. Later on, your complete dedication to your new role rescuing lost or kidnapped children, and your ruthless punishment of evil men who harmed the innocent. An incorruptible man, of independent wealth. You wouldn't try to rob me, and you wouldn't be deterred by the dangers of the mission. You were definitely the man I needed. Should you have refused my offer, there was little I could have done to change your mind.'

'You know why I took the job,' Ben said. 'It was only for your granddaughter Ruth's sake.' He paused. 'But I wish you'd told me more about the risk factor. That information might have saved a lot of trouble, if I'd known.'

'I had faith in your abilities.' Fairfax smiled. 'I also felt that, if I told you the complete truth, you might turn me down. It was important to me to find a way to persuade you.'

'The complete truth? Persuade me? What are you getting at, Fairfax?'

'Let me explain,' replied Fairfax, leaning back

in his chair. 'A man in my position learns early in his career that men can be – shall we say – influenced. Every man has a weakness, Benedict. We all have something in our lives, or in our past. A skeleton in the cupboard, a secret. Once you know what these secrets are, you can exploit them. A man with a shameful past or a hidden vice is easy to bend to one's will. A man who has committed a crime is even easier to influence. But you, Benedict . . . you were different.' Fairfax poured himself more wine. 'I couldn't find anything in your background that I could use to persuade you to accept my offer, should you initially refuse. I was unhappy with this situation.' Fairfax smiled coldly. 'But then my investigators turned up an interesting detail of your life. I recognized its importance immediately.'

'Go on.'

'You're a very driven man, Benedict,' Fairfax continued. 'And I know why. I came to understand what motivates you in your work . . . It's also the reason you're a drinker. You're plagued by demons of guilt. I knew you'd never refuse to help me in my quest if you thought you were saving Ruth. Because Ruth is very dear to your heart, isn't she?'

Ben frowned. 'If I *thought* I was saving Ruth?'

Fairfax finished his glass and poured another, a look of amusement crossing his face. 'Benedict,' he said thoughtfully. 'That's a name with strong religious connotations. Your family were devout Christians, I take it?'

Ben was silent.

'I only thought . . . for parents to name their two children Benedict and Ruth. A rather Biblically-orientated choice, wouldn't you say? Ruth Hope . . . a sadly ironic name. Because there *was* no hope for her, was there, Benedict?'

'How did you find out about my sister? It's not part of my professional résumé.'

'Oh, when you have money, you can find out anything, my dear young friend. I thought it was interesting that you chose the work you did, Benedict,' Fairfax went on. 'Not a detective, not a finder of information or stolen property – but a finder of lost people, especially lost *children*. It's obvious that what you were truly seeking was to expiate your guilt over losing your sister. You've never got over the fact that your negligence caused her death . . . and perhaps suffering that was worse than death. Slave-traders aren't known for their kind ways. Rape, torture, who knows what they may have done to her?'

'You've been busy, haven't you, Fairfax?'

Fairfax smiled. 'I'm always busy. I realized you could never refuse a mission to save the poor, sick little child of the same name and same age as your lost sister. And I was right. It was the story of my granddaughter that persuaded you to help me.'

'Interesting choice of words, Fairfax. *Story*?'

Fairfax chuckled. 'However you prefer to put it. A fabrication. A deception, if you want me to be completely honest. There is no Ruth. No dying

469

little girl. And, I'm afraid, no redemption for you, Benedict.'

Fairfax got to his feet and walked to a sideboard. He lifted the lid of a large casket and brought out a small gold chalice. 'No, no dying girl,' he repeated. 'Only an old man who lusts after one thing above all else.' He gazed in dreamy fascination at the chalice. 'You've no idea what it feels like, Benedict, to approach the end of a life like mine. I've achieved so many great things and created such wealth and power. I couldn't bear the thought of leaving my empire in the hands of lesser men – men who would squander and spoil it. I would have gone to my grave a most unhappy and frustrated man.' He held up the chalice as though proposing a toast. 'But now my worries are over, thanks to you. I will become the richest and most powerful man in history, with all the time in the world to fulfil my ambitions.'

The door opened and Alexander Villiers came into the room. Fairfax glanced knowingly at his assistant as he approached them. Villiers' lips spread into a broad grin as he drew a snub-nosed Taurus .357 revolver from his pocket and aimed it at Ben.

Fairfax laughed. He raised the chalice to his lips. 'I wish I could drink to your good health, Benedict. But I'm afraid it's the end of the road for you. Villiers, shoot him.'

CHAPTER 65

Villiers pointed the revolver at Ben's head. Fairfax closed his eyes and drank greedily from the gold chalice.

'Before you shoot me, there's something you should know,' Ben said. 'What you've just drunk isn't the elixir of life. It's tapwater from your own bathroom.'

Fairfax lowered the chalice. A dribble of the water ran down his chin. The look of rapture on his face drained away. 'What did you say?' he said slowly.

'You heard me,' Ben said. 'I must admit, you had me fooled. You were right about me – I *was* blind to your lies. It was brilliant, Fairfax. And it almost worked. If it hadn't been for a punctured tyre and meeting your head of stables, you'd be standing there with the real elixir.'

'What are you talking about?' demanded Fairfax in a strangled voice.

Villiers had lowered the gun. His face was twisted in thought.

'Herbie Greenwood's been working on your estate for thirty-five years,' Ben went on. 'But he'd never heard of any Ruth. You never even had children, Fairfax, let alone grandchildren. Your wife died childless. There was never any little girl here.'

'What have you done with the real elixir?' Fairfax shouted. He threw down the gold chalice. It clanged dully and rolled across the floor.

Ben reached into his pocket and took out the small glass bottle that Antonia Branzanti had given him. 'Here it is,' he said. And before they could stop him, he whipped back his hand and hurled the bottle into the fireplace. It smashed into a thousand tiny shards against the iron grate, and the flames flared high for an instant as the alcohol preservative in the mixture burned up.

'How does *that* grab you, Fairfax?' Ben asked, looking him in the eye.

Fairfax turned, white-faced, to Villiers. 'Take him and lock him up,' he ordered in an icy voice, barely containing his fury. 'By God, Hope, you will talk.'

Villiers hesitated.

'Villiers, did you hear me?' Fairfax thundered, his face turning from white to red.

Then Villiers raised the revolver again. He turned towards his employer and trained the gun on him.

'Villiers, what are you doing? Have you gone mad?' Fairfax backed away, cowering.

'He hasn't gone mad, Fairfax,' Ben said. 'He's a spy. He works for *Gladius Domini*. Don't you, Villiers? You're the mole. You've been reporting back every move I've made to your boss Usberti.'

Fairfax had backed away as far as the fireplace, the flames roaring and crackling behind him. His eyes were pleading, and his trousers were wet with urine. 'I'll pay you anything,' he bleated. '*Anything.* Come on, Villiers – let's work together. Don't shoot.'

'I don't work for you any more, Fairfax,' Villiers sneered. 'I work for God.' He pulled the trigger. The high bark of the .357 Magnum drowned out Fairfax's scream. The old man tore at his clothes as a dark-crimson stain began to spread rapidly across his white shirt. He staggered, clutched at a curtain and brought it down.

Villiers shot him again. Fairfax's head snapped back, a small round hole between his eyes. Blood spattered up the wall. His knees crumpled and he slid lifelessly down to the floor, still clutching the curtain. It fell with him, one end in the fire. The curling flames ate greedily along its length.

Before Ben could leap across the dining-table, Villiers had spun round and was aiming the gun at him from across the room. 'Stop right there.'

Ben walked around the table and moved steadily towards Villiers, watching his reactions. He could see the man was nervous, sweating and breathing a little harder and faster than usual. He'd probably never shot anyone before, and he was all alone in a tough situation. He hadn't reckoned on this turn of events, and his organization was in tatters with no back-up to offer him. But a nervous man could be as deadly as a confident one. Perhaps even deadlier.

He tensed the gun and aimed it at Ben's face. 'Stay back,' he hissed. 'I'll shoot.'

'Go ahead and kill me,' Ben said calmly. He walked on. 'But then you'd better start running. Because when your boss gets out of jail he'll track you down and have you tortured in ways you can't imagine for losing him his prize. Shoot me, you might as well shoot yourself.'

Flames had spread from the curtain across the rug. Fairfax's trousers were on fire. A sickly smell of smoke and burned flesh filled the room. Fire trickled up the side of a sofa, quickly gaining a hold on the upholstery, licking and crackling.

Villiers had edged backwards close to the spreading flames. The hand clutching the gun was shaking.

'There's only one problem,' Ben went on. He could feel his rage building up inside him like a cold, white light. He glared hard at Villiers as he advanced steadily towards him. 'You can't take me alive, not on your own. You're going to have to pull that trigger, because if you don't I'm going to kill you myself, right now. Either way, you're a dead man.'

Villiers tightened his grip on the trigger, sweat pouring down his face. The revolver's hammer moved back. Ben could see the jacketed hollow-point round in the chamber rotating into place, ready to align with the breech just as the hammer came down to punch the primer and ignite the cartridge that would blow a hole through his skull.

But by now he had Villiers right where he wanted him, up close and unable to back away any further. He threw a sudden slicing blow that caught the man's wrist. Villiers cried out in pain and the .357 sailed into the fire. Ben followed up the blow with a kick to the stomach that sent Villiers sprawling into the suit of armour. It collapsed in a crash of steel plates, and its broadsword fell with a clatter. Villiers scrabbled desperately for the fallen sword and lunged at him, the heavy blade humming through the air. Ben ducked and the wild swing of the blade smashed into an antique cabinet, spilling crystal decanters of brandy and whisky. A lake of fire whooshed up and spread across the floor.

Villiers came at him again, hacking the sword from side to side. Ben backed away, but his foot came down on the gold chalice that Fairfax had thrown to the floor. It rolled, and he slipped and fell, hitting his head against the leg of the dining-table.

The sword came down again, hissing towards him. Stunned from the fall, he moved to the side just in time and the blade crashed into the table next to him. Dishes and cutlery fell to the floor around him. Something glinted at him out of the corner of his eye and he reached for it with groping fingers.

The black smoke was thickening as the blaze spread across the room, uncontrollable now as everything in its path burst alight. Fairfax's body was burning from head to toe, his clothes little more than curling tatters of carbon, the flesh inside roasting.

Villiers' figure loomed against the flames as he raised the heavy sword for the final strike. Fire glittered down the blade. His eyes were filled with a kind of animal triumph.

Ben twisted himself half-upright. His arm flicked in an arc. Something blurred through the smoke between them.

Villiers stopped. His fingers slackened their grip on the sword. The heavy blade clattered to the floor. He teetered, one step backwards, then another. His eyes rolled upwards in his head and then his body fell backwards into the flames. Three inches of steel and the ebony handle of the carving knife protruded from the centre of his forehead.

Ben staggered to his feet. The whole room was on fire around him. He could feel his skin shrivelling from the heat. He grabbed a dining chair and hurled it at one of the tall windows. The eight-foot pane shattered. Air rushed into the room and the fire became an inferno. He saw a gap through the flames and dashed at it for all he was worth. Threw himself wildly through the splintered hole in the window and felt a sliver of glass slice his forearm. He hit the grass and rolled to his feet.

Half blinded from the smoke and clutching his bleeding arm, he staggered away from the house and down the garden towards the acres of parkland. He leaned against a tree, coughing and spluttering.

Flames were pouring from the windows of the Fairfax residence and a huge column of smoke rose upwards into the sky like a black tower. He watched for a few minutes as the unstoppable blaze ripped through the whole house. Then, as the distant sirens drew nearer, he turned and disappeared into the trees.

CHAPTER 66

Ottawa, December 2007

The plane touched down at Ottawa's small airport with a squeal of tyres. Some time later, Ben walked out into the cold, crisp air. A flurry of snow swept over him as he climbed into a waiting taxicab. The Sinatra version of *I'll Be Home for Christmas* was playing on the radio, and a silvery length of tinsel dangled from the rear-view mirror.

'Where to, buddy?' the driver asked, turning his head round to look at him.

'Carleton University campus,' Ben said.

'Here for Christmas?' the driver asked as the car glided smoothly round the city's broad, snowy-banked circular road.

'Just passing through.'

The lecture theatre at Carleton's science block was full when Ben arrived. He found a seat in the back row of the sloping auditorium, near the central exit. He and the 300 or so students had come to hear a biology lecture by Drs D. Wright and R. Kaminski. Its subject was *Effects of Weak Electromagnetic Fields on Cell Respiration*.

There was a low murmur of conversation in the theatre. The students all had pads and pens at the ready to make notes. Down below the auditorium was a small stage with a podium and two chairs, a couple of microphone stands, a slide projector and screen. The lecturers hadn't yet appeared on the stage.

Ben hadn't the least bit of interest in the subject of the lecture. But he did have an interest in Dr R. Kaminski.

The theatre went quiet and there was a discreet round of applause as the two lecturers, a man and a woman, walked on to the stage. They took their positions on either side of the podium. They introduced themselves to the audience, their voices coming through the PA system, and the lecture began.

Roberta was blonde now, her hair pulled back in a pony-tail. She looked every bit the serious scientist, just as she had when he'd first met her. Ben was pleased that she'd taken his advice and changed her name. She'd taken quite a bit of finding – that was a good sign.

Around him, the attentive students were deep in concentration and scribbling notes. He sank a little in his seat, trying to make himself as inconspicuous as possible. He couldn't understand the words she was saying, but over the speakers the tone of her voice, the warm soft sound of her breath, felt so close that he could almost feel her touching him.

It wasn't until that moment that he fully realized how much he'd longed to see her again, and how badly he was going to miss her.

He'd known, even as he was setting out for Canada, that this was going to be the last time he would see her. He didn't plan to hang around long. He'd just wanted to check that she was safe and well, and to say a private goodbye. Before coming into the lecture, he'd left an envelope for her at the main reception desk. In it was her red address book, and a brief note from him to let her know he'd got back all right from France.

He watched her co-lecturer Dan Wright. He could see from the man's body language – the way he seemed to want to stay close to her on the stage, the way he nodded and smiled when she was talking, the way his eyes followed her as she moved between the lecture podium and the screen – that he liked her. Maybe he liked her a lot. He seemed like a decent kind of guy, Ben thought. The kind that Roberta really deserved. Steady, dependable, a scientist like her, a family kind of man who would make a good husband, and a good father one day.

Ben sighed. He'd done what he planned to do, finished what he came for. Now he waited for his cue to leave. As soon as she turned her back for a few seconds, he would slip away.

It wasn't easy. He'd run through this moment a

million times in his mind over the last couple of days. But now, being in her presence with the sound of her voice washing over him through the PA system, it seemed unthinkable to him that he was about to walk out of here, take the next flight back home and never see her again.

But does it have to be like this? he thought. What if he didn't leave? What if he stayed? Could they make a go of it, have a life together? Did it really have to end this way?

Yes, this is the best way. Think of her. If you love her, you have to walk away.

'. . . And the biological effect of this EM wave-form can be illustrated by this diagram here,' Roberta was saying. With a smile at Dr Wright she picked up a laser pointer from the lecture podium and turned round to aim the red beam at the image that flashed up on the big screen behind her.

Her back was turned for a few seconds. *This is it*, Ben thought. He took a deep breath, made his decision, tore himself out of his seat and made his way quickly towards the centre aisle.

Just as he'd started up the aisle, a ginger-haired girl in the back row put her hand up to ask a question. 'Dr Kaminski?'

Roberta spun round from the screen. 'Yes?' she said, scanning the audience for a raised hand.

'I wondered if you could please explain the connection between rising endorphin levels and shifting T-lymphocyte cell cycles?'

Ben disappeared through the door and made for the outer exit. The cold hit him as he stepped outside.

'Dr Kaminski . . .?' the ginger-haired girl repeated quizzically.

But Dr Kaminski hadn't heard the question. She was staring up at the exit where she'd just seen someone walk out.

'I – I'm sorry,' she murmured absently into the microphone, and cupped her hand over it with a thump that jolted the PA speakers. 'Dan, you take over from here,' she whispered urgently to an astonished Dr Wright.

Then, as the lecture theatre erupted into a frantic buzz of chatter and confusion, Roberta jumped off the stage and ran up the centre aisle. Students twisted in their seats and craned their necks to watch her as she sprinted past. On the stage, Dan Wright's mouth was hanging open.

Ben hurried down the steps of the glass-fronted science building and walked briskly away across the snow-covered university campus with a heavy heart. Drifting flakes spiralled down around him from the steely grey sky. He pulled his coat collar up around his neck. Through a gap in the squat buildings that formed a wide square around the edges of the campus he could see the road in the distance, and the university parking lot and taxi-rank. A couple of taxis were standing by, their roofs and windows dusted with snow.

He breathed a deep sigh and headed that way.

A plane roared deafeningly overhead, taking off from the nearby airport. He'd be there in ten minutes, killing time before his flight out of here.

She burst out of the double doors and into the falling snow, and looked across the campus from the top of the steps. Her eyes settled on a figure in the distance, and she instantly knew it was him. He was almost at the taxi-rank. The driver was out of the car, opening the rear door for him. She knew that if he got into that car, she'd never see him again.

She yelled his name, but her voice was drowned out by the sudden thunder of a 747 flying low over Carleton, the red maple-leaf Air Canada symbol on its tailplane.

He hadn't heard her.

She ran, slipping in the snow in her indoor shoes. She felt the icy wind cooling the hot tears on her face. She yelled his name again, and in the distance the tiny figure tensed and froze.

'*Ben! Don't go!*' He heard her shout, far away behind him, and shut his eyes. There was a note of something like desperation, almost a scream of pain, in her voice that made his throat tighten. He slowly turned to see her running towards him across the empty square, her arms open wide, footprints tracing a weaving line behind her in the snow.

'You coming, mister?' asked the taxi driver.

Ben didn't reply. His hand was resting on the edge of the car door. He sighed and pushed the door shut. 'Looks like I'm staying a while longer.'

The taxi driver grinned, following Ben's gaze. 'Looks like you are, mister.'

With a flood of emotions, Ben turned and walked towards the approaching figure. His walk quickened into a trot and then a run. He had tears in his eyes as he called her name.

They came together at the edge of the square, and she flew into his arms.

He spun her round and round.

There were snowflakes in her hair.

THE END

AUTHOR'S NOTE

R eferences to alchemy, alchemical science and history in this book are based upon fact. The mysterious Fulcanelli is a real-life figure, believed to have been one of the greatest alchemists of all time and the guardian of important knowledge. Various theories over the years have speculated as to his real identity, but this remains as mysterious now as it ever was. The enigma of Fulcanelli has captivated the imagination of artists as diverse as the Italian horror film maestro Dario Argento – who featured a Fulcanelli-based alchemist character in his 1980 movie *Inferno* – and Frank Zappa, who wrote a song titled *But Who Was Fulcanelli?* More recently, a character who may or may not have been Fulcanelli appeared in the BBC television series *Sea of Souls*.

The scientific community of the last three centuries or so has refused to take seriously any of the teachings of alchemy. However, this may be set to change. In 2004 a collection of alchemical research papers by Isaac Newton, the father of classical physics, was rediscovered after being lost for eighty years. Scientists at Imperial College,

London, believe that Newton's alchemical work may have inspired some of his later pioneering discoveries in physics and cosmology. As modern science continues to push back the boundaries of human ignorance, it is becoming increasingly clearer that the ancient alchemists may really have been, in the words of Dr Roberta Ryder, the original quantum physicists.

The historical details of the acts of genocide committed by the Catholic Church and Inquisition are accurate and, if anything, understated. The Albigensian Crusade of the 13th century is undoubtedly one of the darkest chapters in the history of the Catholic Church, a period of brutal bloodshed and cruelty that spread all through southern France and whose aim was ostensibly to exterminate the peaceful and widespread Christian movement known as Catharism on the express orders of Pope Innocent III. The Pope's real motives may, of course, have had less to do with religious zeal than with the acquisition of land and, especially, the fabled lost treasure of the Cathars. As historian Anna Manzini writes in *The Alchemist's Secret*, to this day nobody knows what treasure the Cathars were guarding or, for that matter, what might have become of it.

Charles-Edouard Jeanneret, more famously known as Le Corbusier or simply Corbu, was one of the most inventive and pioneering architects of the twentieth century. While the 'House of the Raven' and its hidden treasure were created for the purposes of the novel, it is a fact that Le Corbusier was believed to have been one of the last descendants of the Cathars. Fascinated all his life by esoteric philosophy, he made active use in his architectural designs of the geometric phenomenon known throughout history as 'the Golden Ratio' and to mathematicians as Phi. This fascinating principle of nature, believed by some scientists to govern the structure of all things, was also precious to the alchemists of ancient times. Le Corbusier's death by drowning in 1963 is somewhat shrouded in mystery.

The incredible geometric designs carved on the landscape around Rennes-le-Château in southern France really exist, and can be traced on a map to create the same bizarre twin-circle and star design featured in this novel. Nobody knows who created it, or when. This novel draws speculatively on the amazing true-life phenomenon to suggest that it could have been used as a secret marker to pinpoint the location of a hidden treasure. To this day, Rennes-le-Château remains an important centre for treasure-hunters!

Rudolf Hess, the infamous Nazi and deputy to Adolf Hitler, really was a member of the secretive esoteric society known as The Watchmen (Les Veilleurs), which used to congregate in 1920s Paris – at just the same time that the alchemist Fulcanelli himself is said to have lived there. Born in Alexandria, Hess was indeed fascinated by the occult, and by alchemy. This may have been partly responsible for Adolf Hitler's own interest in the subject, and the historical possibility that the Nazis were really experimenting with ways of creating alchemical gold to fund their war effort and the Thousand-year Reich they were planning to establish.

Gladius Domini is fictitious. However, the last fifteen years have seen a sudden worldwide rise of militant fundamentalist religious organizations, primarily Christian, preaching intolerance and hard-line dogma. The world stage is set for a new era of holy wars that could far eclipse the horror of the medieval crusades.

I hope you enjoyed reading *The Alchemist's Secret* as much as I enjoyed researching and writing it. Ben Hope will be back.

Scott Mariani